The Key *and* The Case of Congressman Coyd

TWO CLASSIC ADVENTURES OF

by Walter B. Gibson
writing as Maxwell Grant

plus a new historical essay
by Will Murray

SANCTUM BOOKS

This Sanctum Books edition is an unabridged republication of the text and illustrations of two stories from *The Shadow Magazine,* as originally published by Street & Smith Publications, Inc., N.Y.: *The Key* from the June 1, 1934 issue and *The Case of Congressman Coyd* from the December 15, 1935 issue. These stories are works of their time. Consequently, the text is reprinted intact in its original historical form, including occasional out-of-date ethnic and cultural stereotyping. Typographical errors have been tacitly corrected in this edition.

International Standard Book Number:
978-1-60877-037-3

First printing: November 2010

Series editor: Anthony Tollin
anthonytollin@shadowsanctum.com

Consulting editor: Will Murray

Copy editor: Joseph Wrzos

Cover and photo restoration: Michael Piper

Published by Sanctum Books
P.O. Box 761474, San Antonio, TX 78245-1474

Visit The Shadow at www.shadowsanctum.com.

Volume 43

CONTENTS

Thrilling Tales and Features

THE KEY by Walter B. Gibson
(writing as "Maxwell Grant") 4

INTERLUDE by Will Murray 65

THE CASE OF CONGRESSMAN COYD
by Walter B. Gibson
(writing as "Maxwell Grant") 67

THE MAN WHO CAST THE SHADOW 126

Cover art by George Rozen
Interior illustrations by Tom Lovell

Murder—Treachery—Intrigue all follow in the wake of the hunt for

THE KEY

From the Private Annals of The Shadow, as told to

Maxwell Grant

Book-length novel complete in this issue.

CHAPTER I
HALF A MILLION

"HALF a million dollars!"

The speaker, a bluff-faced man with angry eyes, brought his fist upon the table with an emphatic stroke. The action brought solemn looks from the others gathered in the conference room. Silence followed.

"A paltry half million!" With this surprising modification of his first statement, the bluff-faced man arose to tower above his companions at the table. "Upon that sum depends the success of our entire enterprise. Mind you, gentlemen, investments of more than fifty millions are at stake unless we can acquire that money!"

New silence. Perplexed, troubled looks appeared upon the faces of the executives who were gathered at the table. The bluff-faced man studied his companions. He noted that certain latecomers to the conference were looking for an explanation. He gave it.

"Let me repeat the situation," declared the speaker. "I, Charles Curshing, am president of the Dilgin Refining Corporation. Our company and its subsidiaries are engaged in destructive competition with the Crux Oil Company. If this fight keeps on, one concern is bound to fail; and the finish of the conflict will inevitably draw the other into bankruptcy with it.

"There is only one hope of avoiding this catastrophe. That is for us, the directors of the Dilgin Corporation, to acquire a controlling interest in the Crux Company within the next sixty days. Such action will preserve both concerns; but we must not sacrifice any of our present holdings.

"We require a total of ten million dollars to swing the deal. By pressing every available spring, I have arranged to obtain to within a half million dollars of that sum. The limit has been reached. Unless we can manipulate the half million, my efforts will be to no avail. We will be unable to negotiate for Crux control before the deadline has been reached."

"How about Torrence Dilgin?"

The inquiry came from a man near the foot of the conference table. It brought a grim smile from Charles Curshing. Leaning forward on the table, the president spoke in a confidential tone.

"Torrence Dilgin," he stated, "is a wealthy man. He was the founder of our corporation. Retired, he is living in Rio de Janeiro. It would be logical to suppose that Torrence Dilgin would aid us in this crisis. It is also natural that I would have looked to him for such assistance.

"I communicated with Torrence Dilgin. I did not over-emphasize the present situation, because I did not choose to alarm him. Torrence Dilgin is past eighty, gentlemen. He is enjoying the twilight of his career. This grand old man responded to my cautious inquiry. His letter told me that his estate is in the keeping of a New York attorney, who is with us here tonight. Let me introduce him: Lester Dorrington."

DIRECTORS shifted in their chairs as a tall, cadaverous man arose at the side of the table. Lester Dorrington was a prominent New York attorney; one noted for his skill in handling criminal cases. It was something of a surprise to learn that Dorrington, who specialized in defending men charged with heavy crimes, was the attorney whom old Torrence Dilgin had chosen as manager of his estate.

There was magnetism in Dorrington's personality. Keen eyes gave light to a face that was almost expressionless. A man of fifty odd years, Dorrington had gained the steady persuasion that characterizes the successful criminal lawyer. Though his manner was quiet, it brought a dominating effect. The conference room was hushed as this pallid, cold-lipped attorney bowed in response to the chairman's introduction.

"Upon his retirement from active business," announced Dorrington, "Torrence Dilgin conferred upon me the honor and trust of handling his affairs. I have followed his instructions to the full. His will is in my keeping.

"This crisis in the affairs of the Dilgin Corporation has brought an inquiry regarding the total amount of Torrence Dilgin's holdings. Despite the fact that your president, Charles Curshing, has summoned me here at Torrence Dilgin's order, there are certain privileges which I must exert as custodian of Torrence Dilgin's private possessions.

"I cannot, for instance, announce the size of Torrence Dilgin's estate. That would be unfair to my client. I can, however, state the nature of his assets. Gentlemen, Torrence Dilgin's estate consists entirely of stock in Dilgin Corporation and associated enterprises, with the exception of certain trust funds that cannot be touched.

"Mr. Curshing has stated that it would be unwise to utilize any Dilgin Corporation securities in the acquisition of the needed half million. His point is well chosen: any use of such stocks would injure the standing of your enterprises. Mr. Curshing's own decision automatically makes it impossible for Torrence Dilgin to aid you with half a million dollars."

Pained hush resumed sway when Dorrington ceased speaking. The tall lawyer sat down, his face expressionless as before. The last ray of hope had flickered. It was Curshing, however, who revived it.

"One possibility remains," stated the corporation president. "Mr. Dorrington has given us a clear statement of Torrence Dilgin's holdings. We know that Torrence Dilgin is living upon the interest from his investments in Dilgin Corporation.

"Torrence Dilgin, therefore, has as much to lose as any of us—more in fact—should Dilgin Corporation fail. If he is properly informed of this crisis, he will certainly rally to our aid, if possible."

"But his holdings are frozen," came an objection. "According to Mr. Dorrington—"

"Mr. Dorrington," interposed Curshing, "has spoken only of Torrence Dilgin's known assets. Why should we presume that the grand old man now in Rio de Janeiro has placed all of his holdings in Mr. Dorrington's keeping? Torrence

Dilgin was a financial genius. It was never his policy to carry eggs in a single basket—"

Curshing paused. A buzz of acknowledgment was coming from the directors. The corporation president had hit home. All could visualize the possibility. Torrence Dilgin—multimillionaire—might well have some large amount of money tucked aside for old-age emergency.

The buzz subsided as Curshing raised his hands for silence. Dorrington, his own statement ended, was sitting like a statue. On the opposite side of the table, however, was a keen-faced, middle-aged man whose dark eyes were staring toward Curshing from beneath close-knit brows. It was to this individual that Curshing turned.

"Gentlemen," suggested the president, "let us hear from our own attorney, Edwin Berlett."

THE heavy-browed man arose. Stocky, of middle height, his face square and dark-skinned, Edwin Berlett was a man of action. As a lawyer, he formed a marked contrast to Lester Dorrington, whom he faced. There was a tinge of irony in his voice.

"Gentlemen," said Berlett, firmly, "I represent the Dilgin Corporation. I owe much to Torrence Dilgin. He and I were close friends. Mr. Curshing is right. Torrence Dilgin did not carry his eggs in one basket.

"For instance: he raised me to the position of attorney for the Dilgin Corporation. But when he came to arrange his private affairs, he chose a man whose selection came as a surprise to me, namely: Lester Dorrington.

"Such was always Torrence Dilgin's way, so far as people were concerned. But Torrence Dilgin has another peculiarity. When he trusts any person, he does so to the full extent. Having chosen Dorrington as his own attorney, he would give him entire capacity to act. Therefore, I feel positive that Dorrington has given us a statement of all the assets which Torrence Dilgin possesses. In my opinion, it would be useless to approach Torrence Dilgin for aid."

"You're wrong, Berlett!" The challenge came from Curshing. "The very fact that Dorrington was chosen out of a clear sky to handle Torrence Dilgin's estate shows that there may be more to this matter.

"You, Berlett, are going to Rio. You are to see Torrence Dilgin. You are to state our case. As president of the Dilgin Corporation, I impose this duty upon you."

"The trip will be useless."

"Not in my opinion."

"It will mean a large fee if I go."

"We shall pay it."

Berlett shrugged his shoulders as he resumed his chair. He seemed to take Curshing's words at discount. The president, however had won the support of the directors.

"I have cabled Torrence Dilgin," declared Curshing, in a decisive tone. "In my message, I told him that you are on your way to Rio. You will leave today, Berlett, by plane."

"At what time?" questioned the lawyer, indignantly.

"Two o'clock this afternoon," returned Curshing. "I sent the cable two days ago. Remember, Berlett, this corporation holds the privilege of calling upon your entire services at any time. We are exerting that privilege right now."

Approval came from the directors. Hearing their audible expression of unanimous agreement with Curshing, Berlett submitted. He smiled sourly as he arose from his chair.

"Very well, gentlemen," he declared. "I must leave you and return to my office. I shall have to hurry to arrange my own affairs and prepare for my trip—"

"You will meet me here at half past twelve," ordered Charles Curshing, as the lawyer started for the door. "It is ten o'clock now, Mr. Berlett."

As Berlett passed out through the door, Curshing waved his arms as a signal for adjournment. Approaching Lester Dorrington, Curshing shook hands with the cadaverous lawyer and thanked him for his statement. He ushered Dorrington out through the offices of the Dilgin Refining Corporation.

AS soon as he had left Curshing, Dorrington permitted himself to smile. The twist that appeared upon his pale lips was a knowing one. It still existed, half an hour later, when Dorrington appeared in his own offices.

Standing in a private room, amid heavy, expensive furnishings of mahogany, Lester Dorrington stared from the window as he surveyed the steplike skyline of Manhattan. He was thinking of the events that had taken place at the directors' meeting.

Moving to a corner of his office, Dorrington brought a telephone from a little cabinet. This was a private line—one that was not connected with the switchboard in Dorrington's suite. The lawyer dialed. He heard a whiny voice across the wire.

"Hello, Squeezer," began the cadaverous man, in a cautious tone. "This is Mr. Dorrington... Yes. From my office in the Bylend Building... Yes, a job for you... Go to 918 Hopewell Building. Trail Edwin Berlett, the lawyer... He's going out from Newark airport at two o'clock... Right..."

Dorrington hung up the receiver. He paused thoughtfully, smiled in dry fashion, then decided to call another number. It was plain that Lester

The Shadow!

A dark shape of the night; a weird creature that goes by unheard and unseen. Garbed in black cloak, wide-brimmed hat turned low to cover his features, nothing but the burning eyes peer forth to haunt those who do evil. The taunting, mirthless laugh of The Shadow, which throws fear into the hearts of gangsters, comes from this muffled figure of the night.

As mysterious as the night is The Shadow. No one knows from whence he comes, or where he goes. Even his closest agents are as unknowing of the real Shadow as is the worst crook in the land. For The Shadow is one lone individual who chooses to fight crime in his own manner, paving the way for others to bring justice to trapped criminals, letting others take credit which rightly belongs to The Shadow.

Weird, strange creature of darkness, crooks gasp out the name of The Shadow with their last breath, for when The Shadow comes, Justice is avenged, and crime is conquered. Beware, men of evil—beware The Shadow! No one lives who has attempted to thwart this master of crime, this avenger who strikes unknown and unseen!

As far different as possible from the weird creature known as The Shadow is this figure of a man of wealth, of travel, of great leisure. Lamont Cranston, from his palatious home in New Jersey, plays an important part in the conquests of The Shadow.

Is Lamont Cranston The Shadow?

Only when the master chooses the role of Lamont Cranston is this true. Knowing every movement of the real Lamont Cranston, who is away on his travels most of the time, The Shadow takes his role to make contacts necessary. As a man of wealth and position, he gains access to information and places necessary to carry on his campaigns.

How does he accomplish this perfect impersonation? Because The Shadow is master of disguise, not only in make-up, but in all personal characteristics and manners. Also, The Shadow's knowledge and contacts keep him so well informed of people's activities that he can talk intelligently with even the closest friends of the real Lamont Cranston. Impersonation, disguise, disappearance and strange reappearance—these are part of The Shadow's skilled activities.

Dorrington was deeply interested in the affairs of Edwin Berlett.

THE situation, however, was mutual. While Dorrington was telephoning from his office in the Bylend Building, Edwin Berlett, seated at his desk in room 918, Hopewell Building, was also busy on the wire. Berlett had arrived at his office fifteen minutes earlier.

"Hello..." Berlett's tone was keen. "Yes... You'll take care of everything... That's right... Through the proper parties. Be sure that the messages are sent. Very good, Morgan.

"When everything is done, keep an eye on Lester Dorrington, 2416 Bylend Building... That's right... No... Nothing more. I'm all finished. Ready to leave..."

Berlett's lips wore a hard smile as the receiver clattered on the hook. The stocky attorney was ready to leave for Rio. He had placed his affairs in order. He was starting upon a mission that Charles Curshing believed would involve half a million dollars.

Why did Lester Dorrington mistrust Edwin Berlett? Why, in turn, did the corporation attorney decide that the criminal lawyer would bear watching? What sinister factors were involved in the affairs of Torrence Dilgin?

LESTER DORRINGTON

Why did Lester Dorrington, an attorney whose professional dealings did not tend toward the handling of estates, become the personal administrator of Torrence Dilgin, wealthy magnate? Why, strangely, was he the lawyer of trust for other men, all wealthy, who died suddenly and mysteriously?

No one could have gained an inkling of the actual suspicions from either of those poker faces. Dorrington and Berlett were cagey men, of long experience. Each had preserved complete composure during the directors' meeting. Only when alone and apart, outside the conference room, had they shown their individual craftiness.

Half a million dollars seemed the sum at stake. It had loomed as probably the issue of Edwin Berlett's coming trip to Rio. But the actions of the two crafty lawyers indicated that more lay in the balance.

Hidden schemes; vast sums; the lives of unsuspecting men—such were the factors in the coming game. Charles Curshing, honest president of Dilgin Corporation, had unwittingly touched the spark that was to loose a blast of evil!

CHAPTER II
THE SHADOW ENTERS

NIGHT in Manhattan. The glare of the metropolis cast a flickering glow upon the walls of massive buildings. Light, reflected from the sullen sky, gave artificial dusk to silent offices that would otherwise have been filled with inky blackness.

A blackened figure was moving through the gloom of a long corridor. Like a phantom of darkness, the mysterious shape approached a door and paused, crouching. Dully, words showed upon the glass panel of the barrier:

INTERNATIONAL IMPORT COMPANY

A soft laugh shuddered in the corridor. The phantom shade came close to the door. Soft clicks sounded as a blackened hand worked upon the lock. The barrier gave. Entering the office of the International Import Company, the gliding figure straightened as it neared the window. Momentarily, it was revealed as a form clad in flowing cloak, with head topped by a dark slouch hat.

The Shadow!

Weird prowler of the night, strange adventurer whose paths were those of danger, this sinister visitor had come with some known purpose to the office of the International Import Company. He had picked the lock of the door; his next design would soon be evident.

For The Shadow was a master who battled crime. A lone wolf amid the towers of Manhattan, a traveling, living phantom who could fade into unseen hiding places, a fierce, ready warrior who could spring into view with the same startling rapidity, The Shadow had chosen a career that meant death to crooks.

His presence in this office could mean but one thing. The Shadow had come to forestall crime. A master investigator, aided by capable agents who did his bidding, The Shadow had a remarkable ability for ferreting out the truth in evil schemes. Crookery was afoot tonight. The Shadow was ahead of it.

Gliding from the window, The Shadow reached a corner where the heavy door of a vault showed dimly in the gloom. While distant electric signs brought dull flickers to the office, The Shadow's flashlight directed a steady beam upon the combination. His right hand held the torch; his left, ungloved, was working with a knob. A sparkling gem—The Shadow's girasol—glittered changing hues amid the light.

THE SHADOW'S touch was uncanny. A soft laugh came from above the flashlight. The left hand slipped into its thin black glove. The same hand drew open the door of the vault. In the space of half a dozen minutes, The Shadow had solved the combination.

A locked gate showed within. The Shadow made short work of it. He found the combination of this second barrier. He stepped into the vault. The flashlight glimmered upon metal drawers set in the wall. Suddenly, the light clicked out.

Swishing toward the front of the vault, The Shadow drew the outer door shut. This done, he softly closed the metal gate. Dropping to the rear of the vault, he crouched in Stygian darkness. His keen ears had told him of approaching footsteps in the outer corridor.

The Shadow had acted with swift precision. Less than five seconds after the big door of the vault had closed, a key clicked in the office door. Two men entered. One crossed the room and drew the shades. The other then turned on the office light.

"Open the vault, Hurnor," ordered the man who had gone to the windows.

"All right, Frenchy," replied the other, in a cautious tone. He strode across the room, turned the combination and drew back the heavy door. He paused, with hand upon the inner gate.

"Ready?" he asked.

"No," returned "Frenchy." "Just wanted to make sure your vault was locked. We'll wait for Lapone."

The interior of the vault was blackened; hence The Shadow was invisible to the men in the office. They, however, were plainly in view to The Shadow. Keen eyes that stared from beneath the hat brim were studying the waiting men.

One, a bald-headed man of portly build, was Cyrus Hurnor, who owned the International Import Company. The other was Frenchy Duprez, a crook known in Europe as well as America; a man who had cunningly evaded the law by scampering from one continent to the other when places became too hot for him.

"Worried, Hurnor?" Frenchy laughed in grating tone. "You don't need to be. Lapone and I have been behaving. We're supposed to be has-beens so far as crooked work is concerned."

"But both of you were in wrong—"

"A year ago. They thought we had a lot of stolen rocks on us. That's when we unloaded the swag to you for safe keeping. Don't worry about Lapone and me. We're ace high right now. I've got a clean bill of health in Europe; he has the same in South America. We're going back where we belong. You'll get your cut when we fence the stuff. It's cold now—those jewels have been forgotten in a year."

Hurnor nodded. His doubts were fading. His face, however, showed one last qualm.

"But you come here at night," he protested. "That means that you think someone may know—"

"I'm taking no chances," interposed Frenchy, "and neither is Lapone. I don't think anyone is on my trail; neither does Lapone. I called him at noon today."

"Was that necessary? I thought you arranged this meeting last night."

"We did. I called Lapone on another matter—"

A soft tap was sounding at the outer door. Hurnor shivered. Frenchy smiled and nodded.

"It's Lapone," he stated. "Let him in."

HURNOR went to the door to admit a tall, dark-faced fellow who looked like a Spaniard. Lapone waved a greeting to Frenchy. With Hurnor, he approached the vault.

"I'll open the gate," said Hurnor, nervously. "Are you ready?"

"Wait a minute," interrupted Frenchy. Then, to Lapone: "Did you send that cable?"

"Sure," grinned the dark-skinned man. "Here's the copy of it."

Frenchy took the paper. He nodded as he read the message; then tore the sheet in quarters and threw the pieces in the wastebasket.

"You're sure your friend in Rio will understand it?" questioned Frenchy.

"Positive," replied Lapone.

"He'll be sure to find Warren Sigler?" came the next inquiry.

"Why not?" demanded Lapone. "You said Sigler's at the Hotel Nacional. That's the first place my friend will pick."

"All right."

"What's this about?" The question came nervously from Hurnor. The fake importer wanted an explanation from Duprez. "I thought you fellows were keeping clear of complications. You weren't to unload the swag yet—"

"Easy, Hurnor," interposed Frenchy. "This has nothing to do with the jewels."

"What is it then?"

"Lapone has contacts in South American cities. Friends, like I have in Europe. What's more, we've both got friends in New York. This morning, I received a call from a man whom I know. He wanted a job done—an important one—down in Rio. It was something that he had anticipated. I had already told Lapone to notify his contact in Rio, should a message be going through. Well—the message came to me—I called Lapone and he sent it. That's all."

"But why didn't this man send the message himself?"

"You were never cut out for real work, Hurnor," returned Frenchy, sadly. "My friend did handle his own communications until this one was necessary. Then he wanted something that couldn't be traced. He had a job, I tell you. A job to be done. That's why the word was to be passed by Lapone.

"It's got nothing to do with jewels. So keep your shirt on. Let's get busy. Open that gate. Lapone and I will each take half of what's inside."

"We'll let Hurnor make the division," suggested Lapone.

"No need," decided Frenchy. "We'll get it fifty-fifty, in a rough way. In a hurry, too; there'll be no time for argument."

The gate had swung open under Hurnor's pull. The portly man had pressed a light switch. His bulky form obscured the view of the others. Suddenly, Hurnor emitted a gasping cry. He came staggering backward from the lighted vault.

"Get him!" he screamed. "Get him! Quick!"

Frenchy and Lapone had thrust hands to pockets even before Hurnor shouted. As the stout man cleared the opening by his backward motion, both crooks aimed for the vault, knowing that an enemy must be within. As Hurnor's words rang in their ears, they saw their rising foeman.

THE SHADOW was in the center of the vault. A blackened outline, his shape made a perfect silhouette target for the upcoming guns. Snarling vicious oaths, Frenchy and Lapone sought to fire.

One revolver spoke. It was Frenchy's. The crook loosed his first shot too quickly. A bullet winged the side of the vault. Lapone, determined upon perfect aim, pressed finger to trigger a half second after Frenchy's futile shot.

To The Shadow, half seconds were long intervals. Between Frenchy's shot and Lapone's attempt, The Shadow acted.

Long tongues of flame spat from his extended hands. The roars of twin automatics came cannon-like from the echoing hollow of the vault.

Lapone's finger wavered. Frenchy lost his hold upon his gun. Side by side, these crooked pals went slumping to the floor. They had shared the spoils of crime in life. They had gained their reward—death—together.

Frenchy and Lapone had found the contents of the vault. They had split fifty-fifty, in a hurry, and in a rough way that they had not expected. Each, instead of stolen jewels, had received a hot bullet from an automatic.

It was Hurnor, roused by the shots, who provided the most startling opposition. Wildly, the false importer leaped forward as his companions fell. Lunging through the door of the vault he hurled his huge bulk upon The Shadow.

As Hurnor grappled for an automatic, his adversary whirled in his grip. Together, The Shadow asnd his bulky antagonist came spinning from the vault. Gloved fists opened. Automatics clattered to the floor. Hurnor screamed in triumph as The Shadow's form sank beneath him.

Then came a wild gasp from the big man's lips as the black-garbed form shot upward like a massive spring of steel. The Shadow's hands gained their grip. Hurnor rose struggling toward the ceiling. His body did a cartwheel as snapping shoulders acted beneath the black cloak.

Landing flat on his back, Cyrus Hurnor lay stunned. He did not hear the ring of a distant alarm; the response of a whistle from the streets. But The Shadow heard. He knew that a watchman in the building had caught the sounds of the fray.

Whirling toward the wastebasket, The Shadow stooped and gained the pieces of the cable message. Yellowed paper disappeared beneath the black cloak. Swiftly, the black-clad figure, clearly outlined in the lighted office, moved toward the outer door.

THREE minutes passed. Cyrus Hurnor moved. He came up to a seated position and rubbed the back of his neck. He stared at the prone forms of Frenchy and Lapone. Footsteps were pounding along the corridor. Wildly, Hurnor looked about him. He saw that The Shadow was gone. These were human enemies who were arriving!

Gaining his feet, Hurnor grabbed Frenchy's revolver. Hurnor knew that the police investigation would uncover the wealth in stolen gems that lay within the opened vault. Caught with the goods,

Hurnor swung to the door just as a policeman hurled the barrier open.

Hurnor fired. The excited shot went wide. The policeman responded. Hurnor fired again, but he was slumping. The bluecoat, pumping lead into the big target before him, had gained the edge in the fight. Hurnor's spasmodic, dying shots were useless.

The Shadow had broken the jewel ring. He had dropped two enemies who had sought his life. He had left the third to meet the law. His hand remained unseen. By the cards, tonight should have ended The Shadow's work.

CROSSING trails, however, had changed the story. While the police were studying the scene of death in the import office, The Shadow was studying the clue to other crime. A bluish light was burning in a black-walled room. Its rays, focused upon a table, showed hands that held torn sheets of paper.

The Shadow was in his sanctum—a hidden abode which he alone could enter. Before him, on the table, his hands placed the fragments of Lapone's cable to Rio de Janeiro. The message read as follows:

GUYON, RIO:
DISCHARGE EXECUTIVE BEFORE REPRESENTATIVE ARRIVES.
LAPONE.

To The Shadow, this cable, apparently addressed to a concern in Rio de Janeiro, was the tip to crime. "Executive" meant someone to be eliminated; "representative" signified a person en route to Brazil.

The Shadow recalled words uttered by Duprez, in questioning Lapone. Frenchy had made it plain that the instructions were not for the man to whom the message had been sent—Guyon—but for another whom Frenchy had named.

Upon a blank sheet of paper, The Shadow inscribed the name that he had heard Frenchy mention; with that name, the address:

Warren Sigler
Hotel Nacional
Rio de Janeiro

A soft laugh whispered through the sanctum. The writing faded from the paper—a peculiar phenomenon due to the special ink that The Shadow used in transcribing written thoughts.

Hands stretched forward and gained earphones. A little light glowed on the wall. A quiet voice came over the wire:

"Burbank speaking."

In a weird, clear whisper, The Shadow began to speak. To Burbank, his contact agent, he was announcing his intended plans. Danger—joined with crime—lured The Shadow. He was responding to the beck.

The Shadow was setting out for Rio de Janeiro. On the morrow, a swift plane would be carrying him en voyage to the Brazilian capital. The master who hounded men of crime was ready to take the course that Edwin Berlett had already begun.

Twenty-four hours behind the corporation lawyer, The Shadow would be on the trail of crime! The Shadow had entered the field where insidious evil lurked.

CHAPTER III
THE LAST GASP

"I DID not expect you so soon, Mr. Berlett."

The speaker was a crafty-faced man who was seated in an armchair in the corner of a small but luxurious living room. He was looking toward Edwin Berlett who was standing by the curtained window.

The lawyer did not reply. He was staring from the window, out into the night. From this suite in the Hotel Nacional, he could view the brilliant lights of Rio de Janeiro. Beyond a balcony outside the window, he spied the long, curving twinkle of the crescent waterfront that seemed to dwindle endlessly in each direction.

"I supposed," said the man in the chair, "that you were coming by boat. Mr. Curshing, when he sent his cable, announced that you were on your way. I did not expect you, Mr. Berlett, for a few days to come."

"Quite right." Berlett was terse as he swung from the window to face the man who was hunched in the chair. "I would have come by steamship, Sigler. It was Curshing who insisted that I come by plane. I thought that he would send a second cable. Evidently he decided it was unnecessary."

There was a tinge of annoyance in Berlett's tone. It brought a response from a third man who was seated in another corner. This man was a gray-haired Brazilian. He spoke in English, with barely a trace of Portuguese accent.

"It is well, *Senhor* Berlett," he announced, "that you did come by air. The doctor does not think that *Senhor* Dilgin will live past midnight. His sudden illness is most unfortunate."

"It is," agreed Berlett. Then, swinging to Sigler, he ordered, brusquely: "Give me the exact circumstances."

"The cable came from Curshing," explained Sigler. "Mr. Dilgin had not been well; nevertheless, I showed him the message. I have been his secretary for seven years; I did not expect that so simple a cable could produce a shock.

"Mr. Dilgin began to worry. He said, sir, that the message meant trouble with the corporation. He wanted me to cable to New York. I restrained him, assuring him that you were on the way."

"I see."

"Mr. Dilgin called in the physician. The doctor seemed worried. Mr. Dilgin then insisted upon an attorney. That is why I summoned this gentleman"—he indicated the gray-haired Brazilian—"*Senhor* Dario."

Berlett nodded. He again returned to the window. Staring out toward the crescent beach, he inquired:

"So you sent no cable to New York?"

"None, sir," responded Sigler, with emphasis. "I went to the cable office; but merely to learn if other cables had come."

"And you received no message outside of Curshing's cable?"

"None, sir."

"All right." Berlett swung to Dario. "I have heard Sigler's statement. Tell me your connection with the case, *Senhor*."

BERLETT was looking squarely at Dario. The Brazilian was facing the American attorney. Warren Sigler relaxed. A slight smile showed on the secretary's crafty face.

"*Senho*r Dilgin was very ill," declared Dario, seriously. "I thought he wanted to make a will. He said no. He wanted to speak to you, he said, so that you could help his company."

"Exactly," returned Berlett. "That is why I have come here, *Senhor*. But since he wanted to talk to me, why did he send for you?"

"To have a witness," explained Dario. "I handled some legal matters—of a slight sort—for *Senhor* Dilgin. He placed reliance in me."

"I understand. Then you have, as yet, learned nothing?"

"Nothing. Up to last night, it was not alarming. But this morning, *Senhor* Dilgin became very bad. He has not been able to speak all day. We were sure that he would die."

As Dario concluded, a door opened. A tall Brazilian, obviously the physician, came into view and looked toward Berlett. The lawyer returned a bushy gaze as he saw a smile upon the doctor's lips.

"The patient has awakened!" exclaimed the physician, in English. "He has come from his coma. He can talk, *Senhor*. He has asked for you!"

The doctor held his hand upon the door knob, expecting Berlett to respond. The bushy-browed lawyer shook his head.

"Not yet, doctor," he declared. "Let him recover his strength. He may have much to say."

"No, no!" exclaimed the physician. "You do not understand, *Senhor*. The patient is not improved. He may die at any time. There is no chance for him"—the speaker paused with a sad shake of his head—"but it is possible that he will talk to you if you come quickly."

"What do you think of it, Sigler?" inquired Berlett, turning to the secretary.

"I agree with you, Mr. Berlett," returned Sigler. "Mr. Dilgin is apt to weaken when he sees you."

"It will strengthen him!" protested the physician, in an excited tone. "Every minute counts, *Senhor*. Every minute! Come! At once!"

"Sigler tells me that Mr. Dilgin experienced his first shock when he read a cablegram," retorted Berlett. "If that is true, he may experience another through the excitement of seeing me. I rely upon you, doctor, but remember: Sigler has been with Mr. Dilgin for years."

The doctor waved his hands excitedly. He swung to Dario and loosed a flow of voluble Portuguese at which the gray-haired lawyer nodded. Firmly, Dario turned to Berlett.

"*Senhor*," he said, "you must be guided by what the physician has said."

"I do not want to be responsible for Dilgin's death," returned Berlett, coldly.

"Remember!" Dario wagged a finger in Berlett's face. "I am here to represent *Senhor* Dilgin. We are in Brazil, not in the United States. I can protest to the law!"

Berlett stood indignant at the challenge. For a moment, conflict seemed impending. Then came an interruption. The door of the bedroom opened. A Brazilian nurse appeared. The woman shook her head as she spoke in Portuguese to the physician.

"You see!" exclaimed the doctor. "It is too late, *Senhor*. The nurse thinks that *Senhor* Dilgin has died. Come! You have delayed too long."

SOBERLY, the four men filed into the sickroom. Stretched in a bed lay the withered form of Torrence Dilgin. Illness had played havoc with a frame that Edwin Berlett had remembered as robust. Scrawny hands; cheekbones in a dried face; these were the motionless impressions of Torrence Dilgin that showed above the sheets.

Life had apparently ended. The physician approached the near side of the bed to make an examination. Dario was beside him. Berlett crossed the room and stood at the other side of the bed.

"I think," announced the physician, "that he is dead. If you had come sooner, *Senhor*—"

"This is no time to discuss the matter," interposed Berlett. "The fact that he subsided quickly proves that he could not have talked."

The sound of Berlett's voice produced a magical

effect. Like a corpse from its coffin, Torrence Dilgin came to life. Scrawny hands twitched while blued eyelids opened. Torrence Dilgin was staring straight toward Edwin Berlett!

"You are here!" gasped Dilgin. With an amazing effort, the old man clawed his body half upright. "Here! Berlett! With witnesses! Listen!

"The key! Get it, Berlett. For—for the company. The key! One—one million—dollars—"

Berlett caught Dilgin's shoulders. The withered frame was sagging. Leaning along as Dilgin sank, Berlett spoke these words.

"What key? Who has it?"

An incoherent gasp came from Torrence Dilgin's lips. Dried lips twitched, trying to repeat a name. The gasp, however, made the word inaudible. Slipping from Berlett's grasp, Torrence Dilgin rolled sidewise in the bed and spoke no more.

It was the physician who took charge. No question remained. That gasp had been Torrence Dilgin's last. When the doctor announced that the old man was dead, the three visitors filed from the room. They assembled beyond the door which the nurse closed behind them.

EDWIN BERLETT strolled to the window. He stood staring toward the lights. It was impossible to determine the emotion that the death scene had inspired in his mind. When Berlett swung from the window, his face had all its firmness.

"Sigler," he ordered, "get your notebook. Take down the death statement as I heard it."

"Yes, sir," replied the secretary.

Word for word, Berlett repeated the dying words. Finished, he turned to Dario. The Brazilian lawyer nodded.

"It is exactly as I heard it," he announced. "But there was one thing, *Senhor*. There was a name which *Senhor* Dilgin tried to speak—"

"Did you hear it?" questioned Berlett, keenly.

"No, *Senhor*," returned the Brazilian, "but you were close—"

"I could not catch the name," interposed Berlett simply. "In accordance with Torrence Dilgin's apparent wishes, I shall require affidavits from you, *Senhor* Dario, and from the physician. Did you hear the last words, Sigler?"

"No, sir. Only a few of them."

"Your statement will not be needed. Perhaps, after I have made my report in New York, I may be able to trace this reference to a key and the sum of one million dollars.

"However"—Berlett paused to eye Dario steadily—"that will be my concern. You, *Senhor*, are but a witness. Your affidavit will end your connection with the case. It will be a matter for the United States, not for Brazil."

"Very well, *Senhor*," bowed Dario, in acknowledgment. "I understand."

Edwin Berlett returned to his window. His meditative gaze again sought the sparkling lights of the city. Beyond the glow of lights in the *Parque da Acclamacao*, he stared toward that inevitable stretch of landlocked bay.

Dying words! Edwin Berlett had heard them. They were the beginning of a revelation; Torrence Dilgin's statement of a strange secret which involved a key and the sum of one million dollars.

Yet more important than the words themselves had been the final gasp. A name—lost amid the dying breath—was the answer upon which Torrence Dilgin's secret hinged. To Edwin Berlett, the old millionaire had tried to give the all important words.

Who was the person whom Torrence Dilgin had tried to name? What could that person reveal regarding the old man's statements of a key and one million dollars? Had the secret died with Torrence Dilgin?

From the solemn look upon Edwin Berlett's steady face, one would have supposed the secret gone. *Senhor* Dario, viewing Berlett's profile from one side, was clucking sadly. Warren Sigler, seeing that same profile from the opposite angle, was repressing a triumphant smile.

Brazilian and American had watched by Torrence Dilgin's bedside while awaiting Edwin Berlett's arrival. Yet the effect of Dilgin's apparent failure to convey a final clue to Berlett had produced an opposite effect.

Where *Senhor* Dario felt that misfortune had been the reward of a long vigil, Warren Sigler was satisfied that his own hopes had been fulfilled.

CHAPTER IV
FROM THE DARK

TWENTY-FOUR hours had elapsed since the death of Torrence Dilgin. The piazza of the splendid Hotel Nacional was thronged with evening visitors. The glittering lobby buzzed with gaiety. A death in an obscure suite high above was no disturbance in the life of this huge hotel.

A tall stranger entered the lobby. American in appearance, he was evidently an arriving guest. Stopping at the desk, he received a registration card and signed his name as Lamont Cranston. The clerk affixed a room number and asked if any special service was required.

"Yes," came the statement, in a quiet tone. "I believe that I may have friends stopping here. Do you have a list of Americans registered at this hotel?"

"Certainly, *Senhor*." The clerk turned and

obtained a card that bore a list of names. "We have occasional inquiries like yours. We keep this list in readiness."

The clerk watched the new guest as he studied the list. The man behind the desk at the Hotel Nacional had observed many unusual travelers, but never one who had impressed him more distinctly. Lamont Cranston's countenance might well have been hewn from living rock. Molded with the firmness of a statue, it was almost masklike.

Though Cranston's head was slightly inclined, the clerk could catch the flash of burning eyes. Involuntarily, the man behind the desk followed the direction of Cranston's gaze—toward the list that the new guest was studying.

Beside one name was a check mark in red ink. Cranston's eyes were focused upon that name. Almost involuntarily, the clerk found himself leaning forward to deliver a low-toned explanation.

"The red mark, sir," said the clerk. "It is most unfortunate. *Senhor* Torrence Dilgin died last night. He was a very old man. He had been ill—"

"I understand." Cranston's quiet interruption came as the guest returned the list to the clerk. "I suppose you naturally keep such matters quiet. I see no persons whom I know upon this list. Thank you."

The blaze of Cranston's eyes had faded when the guest faced the clerk. Stepping from the desk, the firm-faced arrival followed the waiting attendant to the elevators. He was conducted to his room.

LAMONT CRANSTON'S lodging was at the front of the hotel, a floor below the suite in which Torrence Dilgin had died. As soon as the bell boy had gone, Cranston extinguished the light and walked through darkness to the window.

Across the outer balcony, he commanded the brilliant view of the *Parque da Acclamacao* and the crescent of lights that indicated the shore line of Rio's bay. These lights, however, were not the ones that had attracted him.

Leaning from the window, Cranston gazed upward, at an angle. He located two lights on the floor above; they were situated in adjoining windows. One was bright; the other dull. These marked the rooms of Torrence Dilgin's suite.

A soft laugh came from Cranston's lips. That tone was a weird echo of The Shadow's sinister mirth. Death at the Hotel Nacional was in itself significant. On the list, however, Lamont Cranston had noted a name directly below that of Torrence Dilgin. It was the name of the man whom The Shadow sought: Warren Sigler.

The list was not alphabetical. Guests had been marked according to the date of their arrival. The fact that Sigler's name was with Dilgin's, coupled with the location of Sigler's room—on the same floor, near Dilgin's—was proof sufficient of a connection between the two.

Dead man and living! This new guest who used the name of Lamont Cranston was determined to gain an insight into their affairs. Motion occurred within the darkened room. A bag clicked open. The folds of a dark cloak swished in the blackness. Shortly afterward, a figure emerged upon the balcony.

Each window, on every floor, had its own railed projection. These had been designed for appearance rather than occupancy. No persons were visible along the front of the dull-surfaced hotel. Lamont Cranston had become The Shadow. His form, garbed in black, was no more than a moving splotch of darkness as it rose upon the rail.

A swinging spring carried The Shadow to the adjoining balcony. He repeated his maneuver and gained the next projection in the line. Continuing, he came directly beneath the balcony outside of Dilgin's living room. Grasping the projection above, The Shadow swung himself clear of the wall. A few moments later, his form swung over the upper rail.

THE night was mild; the window was open. Yet The Shadow's arrival, accomplished with the utmost stealth, was unnoticed by those within the room. Three men were engaged in conversation. They were Warren Sigler, Edwin Berlett and *Senhor* Dario. Tonight, Berlett was seated in an armchair. He was not near the window.

"We have arranged everything, *Senhor*," Berlett was saying to Dario. "The *Southern Sta*r sails tomorrow; Sigler and I have engaged passage. We shall have the body transported aboard the ship."

"Very well, *Senhor* Berlett," returned Dario, with a bow. "I shall aid you by making the proper reports to the authorities. The death certificate has been prepared."

"You saw the physician?"

"One hour ago. He will be here shortly."

Berlett paced across the room. The Shadow, watching from the balcony, eyed him closely. He had noted Berlett's name upon the clerk's list. It had been at the bottom, signifying that Berlett was the most recent arrival at the Hotel Nacional.

"Here are the affidavits, *Senhor*." Berlett ceased pacing as Dario spoke. The lawyer was drawing folded papers from his pocket. "One is mine. The other is Doctor Antone's. They correspond exactly with yours."

Berlett nodded as he received the affidavits. Sigler arose and approached the lawyer. He put forth a natural question regarding the papers.

"Shall I file these, sir?"

"Certainly," decided Berlett, handing the affidavits to the secretary. "Keep them with my own statement. I can repeat mine verbatim—from your notes—when we arrive in New York."

"Very singular, *Senhor*," mused Dario. "We all heard the same—a key—a million dollars—then a name which none of us could catch. I have been thinking about it, *Senhor*. I have wondered—"

"Wondered what?"

"If *Senhor* Dilgin tried to say a name. Perhaps, *Senhor*, he thought that you would know the person who had the key. Could that be? You have known *Senhor* Dilgin for many years."

Edwin Berlett stood stock-still. He rubbed his chin and furrowed his heavy brows. Sigler, placing the papers in the drawer of a trunk, paused, listening. His face was away from the other men. The Shadow, however, could spy the secretary's profile.

"No." Berlett shook his head. "I can think of no one. Lester Dorrington—the attorney who will handle Dilgin's estate—said nothing about a key when we had our last conference. I know of none."

"Another lawyer? A friend, perhaps?"

"I do not know of any. Frankly, *Senhor* Dario, I believe that Torrence Dilgin was delirious when he died. I am preserving his death statement purely as a matter of procedure."

A smile showed on Warren Sigler's face. Again, The Shadow detected the secretary's expression. Edwin Berlett had turned. He was moving toward the window. The Shadow crouched into the darkness below the level of the sill. His action was unnecessary. Berlett turned as someone knocked at the door. Sigler answered the rap.

It was the physician. The man bowed politely; then spoke to Dario in Portuguese. The Brazilian attorney nodded. He turned to Berlett, who had swung back to the center of the room.

"We must observe a formality," explained Dario, "to comply with the law. As *Senhor* Dilgin's legal representative in Rio de Janeiro, I have made out papers turning the body over to you. Doctor Antone has prepared the death certificate.

"You and I must identify the body in his presence. Suppose we step into the other room and go through the procedure. No other witness is necessary. You have the papers, doctor? Good. We can sign them in there."

THE three men stepped into the inner room. Doctor Antone closed the door behind them. Immediately, Warren Sigler sidled over to the barrier to listen.

The Shadow saw the action; but he did not linger. Moving to the edge of the balcony, he mounted the rail and swung headforemost to the adjoining projection. Like a trapeze artist, he caught the further rail with silent skill. He brought his tall form up to the next balcony.

Peering through the opened window of the dimly lighted room, The Shadow saw the three men—Berlett and the two Brazilians—gathered at the foot of Dilgin's bed. The withered form of the dead millionaire was lying in full view while the trio spoke in whispers that one might have expected in a death room.

But The Shadow's keen ears detected a different reason for their soft tones. *Senhor* Dario was explaining to Edwin Berlett that this formal view of Dilgin's body was unnecessary. The old Brazilian attorney had a different purpose. He wanted to speak to Berlett, without the presence of Warren Sigler.

"Doctor Antone," Dario was saying, "has made a very serious discovery. He believes that arsenic was administered to *Senhor* Dilgin; that the poison caused the old man's death."

Berlett's raised brows demanded further explanation. It came.

"The doses," interposed Antone, "could have been given in the medicine that *Senhor* Dilgin took before I came on the case. They would account for the sudden illness."

"But after that?"

"A few heavy doses, given with my prescriptions, would have finished the work."

"You are sure of this poisoning?"

"No, *Senhor*; but I suspect it."

"Whom do you suspect?"

Doctor Antone pointed toward the door, to indicate the man beyond—Warren Sigler. *Senhor* Dario nodded his belief. Edwin Berlett, however, shook his head.

"Warren Sigler was with Torrence Dilgin for many years," declared Berlett. "I cannot believe him guilty of such crime. Never—with mere suspicion as the only basis."

"That is the reason we have brought you here," whispered Dario, gripping Berlett's arm. "There is only one way to gain the proof. An autopsy."

"Which would mean?"

"That the body would have to be turned over to the local authorities. It would be a matter for the Brazilian courts. You, *Senhor*, would be detained for weeks."

"Impossible! I must go back to New York."

"Exactly," whispered Dario. "That is what I told Doctor Antone. That is why we wished to speak to you. If you wish, Doctor Antone will not mention his suspicions to anyone."

"Good. Very good."

"But when you reach New York, you can have

an autopsy performed upon the body. Then you will learn the truth. However, *Senhor*, you must protect Doctor Antone."

"In what way?"

"By stating that the suspicions were your own; that you wondered about *Senhor* Dilgin's death after you were on the high seas. You, yourself, must cast suspicion upon Warren Sigler. It must never be known that Doctor Antone and I permitted the body to leave Rio de Janeiro suspecting that the dead man had been poisoned."

"I understand." Edwin Berlett nodded. "I promise you, gentlemen, that the autopsy—if there is one—will be privately conducted. But I doubt very much that I shall have one at all."

"That is your own choice, *Senhor*," declared Dario, in a relieved tone. "We are your friends. We could not let you leave Rio de Janeiro without this information. It was also necessary, however, that we protect our own positions. If we can all three forget this entire discussion, all will be well."

"It is forgotten, gentlemen," affirmed Edwin Berlett. "Forgotten entirely. And now, Doctor Antone"—Berlett's voice was rising as he strolled to the door—"you have your papers. Since *Senhor* Dario and I"—he was opening the door—"have identified the body and signed the documents, the last formality has been completed. Good evening, gentlemen."

Standing in the doorway where Sigler could observe, Berlett extended his hand to Dario. Antone made a presence of fumbling with papers in his inside pocket. Then he, too, shook hands with Berlett.

The American lawyer conducted them to the outer door of the suite. As soon as the Brazilians had left, he turned to Sigler.

"I'm going down to the lobby," Berlett announced. "After that, to my room. Call me there if you have anything important."

"Yes, sir," responded the secretary.

"And in the meantime," added Berlett, "clear up here. There will be no more visitors, until the body is removed. Have everything ready for the removal."

"Yes, sir."

WHEN Berlett had gone, Sigler locked the door. Smiling, he strolled to the inner room, where The Shadow was still watching from behind the window. Stooping beside the bed which held the body of Torrence Dilgin, the secretary shoved his hand beneath the mattress and brought out two small bottles.

Sigler grinned shrewdly as he pocketed these objects. He pulled the key to his own room from his pocket and left the death room. The outer door of the suite closed behind him.

Darkness edged in from the window.

The form of The Shadow became visible. Like a tall specter of death, the eerie visitor advanced and viewed the corpse of Torrence Dilgin. A soft, mirthless laugh came from The Shadow's hidden lips.

The tall shape stalked across the room, passed through the outer portion of the suite and faded in the corridor. When Warren Sigler returned a few minutes later, he found no traces of The Shadow's brief visit.

ONE hour later, The Shadow was standing by the window of his room. He was again in the character of Lamont Cranston. A single desk lamp cast sufficient illumination to reveal his chiseled countenance.

There was a hawklike expression to that visage. Burning eyes, staring out toward Rio's splendor, were both thoughtful and predictive. Again, a laugh came from The Shadow. Motionless, the lips of Lamont Cranston delivered the whispered sound. This time, the laugh was tinged with mockery.

The Shadow had seen the justification of the suspicions held by *Senhor* Dario and Doctor Antone. He had watched Warren Sigler enter to remove the hidden arsenic bottles which he had not had opportunity to take away before tonight.

Sigler was a murderer; that was obvious. Dario and Antone were reputable Brazilians; their conversation had proven that fact. But Edwin Berlett, New York attorney who had come to talk with Torrence Dilgin, was a character of doubtful species.

Berlett's belittlement of Dilgin's dying statement; his crafty behavior in his conversation with Dario and Antone; his subsequent statements to Sigler—all were evidences of a cunning game.

Plans lay behind the lawyer's poker face. The Shadow, as yet, could not divine them; but he knew that Berlett was scheming for the future. The Shadow, though he needed more facts, was trying to ferret out the part that Berlett was playing in a game that had involved death.

Another laugh from steady lips. It was one of keen understanding. The Shadow had found his answer. He had formed a theory which enabled him to place Berlett. More than that, The Shadow had formed a plan of his own.

Edwin Berlett could wait, along with Warren Sigler. When the time for action had arrived, The Shadow would be capable of handling the clever lawyer as well as the stupid murderer.

CHAPTER V
AT PERNAMBUCO

DAYS had passed since The Shadow's arrival in Rio de Janeiro. The Steamship *Southern Star* had made its scheduled sailing from the Brazilian capital. Steaming more than a thousand miles northward, it had reached the final Brazilian port. The ship was at anchor in the harbor of Pernambuco.

Edwin Berlett was standing beside the rail of a stern deck. The lawyer was studying the wide-

Like a tall specter of death, the eerie visitor advanced and viewed the corpse of Torrence Dilgin. A soft, mirthless laugh came from The Shadow's hidden lips.

spread city, with its causeways connecting a central island with mainland and peninsula. Strolling across the deck to gaze out into the harbor, Berlett looked toward the open sea.

Somewhere in the direction of the ocean lay the hidden reef that served as protection to Pernambuco's harbor. Within a few hours, the *Southern Star* would be steaming through one of the navigable passages that pierced the reef, guided by a pilot who would know the hidden channel.

Passengers, standing by, were discussing the harbor, which had been improved to accommodate vessels the size of the *Southern Star*. Among them was a distinguished looking personage whose acquaintance Berlett had made. He was Lamont Cranston, wealthy New Yorker, who had come aboard the ship at Rio.

"Mr. Berlett."

The lawyer swung at the sound of his own name. Warren Sigler had approached. Berlett raised his eyebrows quizzically.

"What is it?" he demanded.

"I have completed all the work you gave me, sir," responded the secretary. "Is there any other duty?"

"Not at present."

WARREN SIGLER

While financiers in America saw their kingdom at the brink of ruin, Warren Sigler, secretary to Torrence Dilgin, within whose hands lay the power of saving this structure, was plotting for his own evil purpose. But the hand of The Shadow reaches far—even across continents!

"Then I shall go ashore, sir."

"For how long? The boat sails in three hours."

"I shall be back in one."

"Very well. Come to my stateroom when you return. No—I shall not be there. I am going down for a while; but after that I shall be in the smoking salon. Come there."

"Yes, sir."

Sigler walked away and descended by a companionway. Berlett remained by the rail to finish the perfecto that he was puffing. Unnoticed by the lawyer, Lamont Cranston left the group of passengers. He had overheard Berlett's conversation with Sigler.

FIVE minutes later, Edwin Berlett finished his smoke. He threw his cigar stump overboard and strolled along the deck. He stopped at a passage that led into the ship. Reaching a door, he unlocked it and entered a sumptuous cabin. Furnished in old-fashioned style, the stateroom was almost a combination of living room and bedroom.

The bed was large and comfortable. A huge wardrobe closet provided space that Berlett did not require for his limited supply of clothing. A writing desk was stationed in the corner. Upon it lay an opened box of cigars. Berlett advanced to fill his pocket with perfectos.

The lawyer stopped. Beneath the box was a sheet of paper, folded in peculiar, diagonal fashion. Berlett recognized that this must be a message. Unfolding the paper, he read the note.

A steady, crafty look showed on the lawyer's face. Berlett gripped the message between his hands. He tore it while he nodded; then smiled as he pulled the paper to shreds. Strolling slowly from the cabin, Berlett returned to his spot on deck.

Lamont Cranston had come back. Keen eyes were watching Berlett as the lawyer let fragments of paper drift into the harbor breeze. Fifteen minutes passed; then twenty. Berlett shifted to the shore side of the ship. He eyed the wharf as though expecting Sigler's return.

In contrast to his usual calm, Berlett seemed unusually anxious. When a half hour had passed, he left the deck and went into the smoking salon. Here he was greeted by a trio of card players who were whiling away the harbor hours with pinochle. In response to their insistence, Berlett joined the game.

IT was not long before Warren Sigler entered. The secretary had arrived back well within the hour. He saw Berlett at the card table and approached. The lawyer looked up from his hand.

"I have an appointment in fifteen minutes," he announced, glancing at a clock in the smoking salon. "It will be in my cabin. It is very important. I do not wish to be disturbed. Do you understand?"

"Yes, sir," returned Sigler.

"I shall return here afterward," added Berlett. "You will find me after my appointment. But do not come to my cabin while I am there. If anyone inquires for me, say that I am ashore."

The pinochle players were studying their hands. They thought nothing of the conversation. Berlett rejoined the game in casual fashion. Warren Sigler strolled from the smoking salon. His face wore a knowing smile.

The secretary made directly for Berlett's cabin. He found the door unlocked. He entered. He went to the wardrobe closet and stepped inside. He closed the door behind him. He was waiting, ready to be a hidden witness to the interview.

IN less than fifteen minutes, Edwin Berlett arrived at his cabin. He closed the door and seated himself at the writing desk. A few minutes passed. A cautious knock sounded. Berlett went to the door and opened it.

A tall, dark-visaged stranger entered. Berlett invited the visitor over by the desk and offered him a perfecto, which the arrival accepted.

Seating himself, Berlett faced his visitor. Both men were smoking; through clouds of smoke, Berlett studied the face of the man before him.

The stranger was evidently a Brazilian. Berlett did not seem surprised at that fact; indeed, his first statement, a question, indicated that he had expected a visitor of that nationality.

"You are Carlos Mendoza?" he asked.

"Yes," returned the stranger, "a fellow passenger from Rio."

"I have seen you on the ship."

"Only occasionally, I suppose. I have been keeping out of sight."

"So you mentioned in the note that you left here."

There was a pause. Mendoza was talking in excellent English, but it had the peculiar accent common to Portuguese and Brazilians.

"*Senhor*," announced Mendoza, "I shall tell you my exact purpose here. I was once a secret agent of the Brazilian government; I am now engaged in private investigation."

"So your note informed me."

"I took passage at Rio de Janeiro at the wish of *Senhor* Dario, the lawyer. He placed me here that I might afford you protection; and that I might also deliver you some important evidence."

"Regarding Warren Sigler?"

"Yes."

"Hm-m," mused Berlett. "I thought that Dario had told me all there was to know. He spoke to me the night before I left Rio."

"I know that, *Senhor*. But he did not tell you that I was working on the case. I was watching the room of this secretary, Warren Sigler. Let me tell you what the man did.

"After all had gone, he appeared in his room bringing two small bottles. He wrapped them in pieces of crumpled newspaper. A chambermaid was on the floor. He told her to empty the waste-basket, in which he had placed the hidden bottles."

"You saw Sigler do this?"

"No. I heard him instruct the maid. I went into his room and searched the basket. I found the bottles and removed them before the maid took away the waste paper. Those bottles, *Senhor*, I have with me, wrapped in cotton. They had contained arsenic inside; on the outside, they have traces of fingerprints which must be Sigler's."

"Why was I not informed of this?"

"I made my report to Dario just before the *Southern Star* left Rio de Janeiro. Dario ordered me aboard. I came as an ordinary passenger. I hold the evidence, *Senhor*."

"With you?"

"Yes, *Senhor*."

"Show me the bottles."

Carlos Mendoza arose with an apologetic laugh. He placed his hand upon his pocket, as though seeking to protect his prize.

"I cannot do that, *Senhor*," he announced, politely. "Unless you wish to—"

"Wish what?"

"To remain in Pernambuco."

"I don't quite understand."

"You should, *Senhor*," laughed Mendoza. "I am a Brazilian, like *Senhor* Dario. I must obey the law of my country. Should I give you this evidence, I must announce the fact to the authorities. That will mean the arrest of Warren Sigler. He will be held in Pernambuco."

"The same trouble as at Rio," observed Berlett.

"Exactly, *Senhor*," responded Mendoza, wisely, "but Pernambuco is the last port in Brazil. The ship sails after sunset. Once it has reached the open sea—"

"I understand. *The Southern Star* flies the American flag. It will be a case for my country."

"Yes. Should we be stopping at another port in Brazil, the captain would turn the case over to the authorities of that city. But we are leaving Brazil altogether, *Senhor*. Once I have given you the evidence, we can visit the captain. We shall demand the arrest of Warren Sigler."

Edwin Berlett pondered. Mendoza watched him shrewdly. The lawyer put another question.

"That will work," he decided, "but it still might make trouble for Dario and Antone—"

"No, *Senhor*. All is different now. Here is the story. I was hired by *Senhor* Dario simply to watch Warren Sigler, because Dario represented *Senhor* Dilgin, who died very suddenly. The night before the ship sailed, I found these bottles. I did not report until shortly before the *Southern Star* left Rio de Janeiro.

"I kept watching Warren Sigler, seeking to obtain fingerprints that would match those on the bottles. I failed, until after the *Southern Star* was leaving this harbor, Pernambuco. Obtaining the fingerprints, I was unfortunately beyond Brazilian law. That will be my story. What could I do but come to you, *Senhor*?"

"It sounds well," agreed Berlett, "but for one thing. You will have to get Sigler's fingerprints."

"I have them already, *Senhor*," laughed Mendoza, in a cunning tone. "I found a paper in the file which Sigler used in the Hotel Nacional. It had fingerprints that match those on the bottles. It was a blank sheet, *Senhor*.

"I shall say that I placed that sheet of paper in Sigler's cabin, here aboard the *Southern Star*. I shall add, *Senhor*, that it was not until the ship left Pernambuco that I obtained the impressions."

"Good." Berlett arose and clapped Mendoza on the back. "Your plan will work. It is justifiable under the circumstances. Sigler will have no comeback."

"Then I shall see you, *Senhor*—"

"In this cabin, after the pilot ship has left the *Southern Star* outside of Pernambuco harbor."

"Very good, *Senhor*. That will be our last contact with Brazil. But remember, you must be careful that Sigler does not suspect."

"That will be easy. Come here with your evidence. Bring your credentials. You can then tell me your story officially and present the evidence. We will go to the captain, with the evidence still in your possession."

"It is agreed, *Senhor*."

Edwin Berlett conducted Carlos Mendoza to the door of the cabin. He waited until the Brazilian had passed along the corridor. Then Berlett, himself, stepped from the cabin. As he turned to close the door, the lawyer stared back into his room. He smiled as he noted the door to the wardrobe closet, which was visibly ajar.

STROLLING to the smoking salon, Berlett seated himself in a chair and lighted a cigar. Five minutes later, Sigler appeared. Berlett was writing memoranda upon a sheet of paper when the secretary found him.

"Take care of these letters," ordered Berlett, passing his penciled items to Sigler. "Hurry them through and mail them ashore, by air mail. You have an hour yet, Sigler."

"Yes, sir."

The secretary thrust the notes in his pocket. He left the smoking salon. Edwin Berlett settled back in his chair.

Glancing about, he saw no sign of Carlos Mendoza. Edwin Berlett chuckled. Strolling from the salon, he reached the gangplank and also went ashore.

Carlos Mendoza had suggested a clever game as a follow-up of his note to Edwin Berlett. Warren Sigler had overheard the talk in full. There was a reason for Edwin Berlett's chuckle. The crafty lawyer could foresee a different outcome than the one called for in his conversation with Carlos Mendoza.

CHAPTER VI
OUTSIDE THE HARBOR

DYING light of day guided the *Southern Star* on the final stage of its passage through the Pernambuco reef. The ship had been delayed due to loading. The Brazilian pilot, however, had still gained sufficient daylight to reach the open sea.

Then night had arrived with the booming suddenness so common in the tropics. Edwin Berlett and other passengers were standing near the stern of the *Southern Star* gazing toward the distant lights of Pernambuco.

A hand plucked at Berlett's sleeve. The lawyer turned to see the steadied face of Carlos Mendoza. Berlett nodded. He spoke in a low tone.

"In fifteen minutes," said the lawyer, "in my stateroom. The door is open."

Mendoza stalked away. Warren Sigler, peering from a group of passengers, observed the Brazilian heading for a companionway. Sigler had overheard the words between the two men.

Edwin Berlett walked toward the steps that he customarily took to the smoking salon. Reaching another deck, he hurried along and neared the bow of the ship. There were no passengers in sight. Berlett glanced over his shoulder. Confident that he was unobserved, he descended by a companionway.

Picking a course which he had evidently chosen beforehand, Berlett reached the forward hold. He stepped through a bulkhead. Straight in front, he saw starlight glittering through the side of the ship. A coal hatch was open. Berlett reached his goal.

Below, the pilot ship was ready to cast off. It was nestled against the side of the *Southern Star*, resting in a calm sea. Calls from above indicated that the steamship was about to drop the pilot.

Directly below, two men were standing beside a heap of sacks near the stern of the pilot ship. Burlap showed almost white, in a blackened stretch against the side of the *Southern Star*. The sacks were less than ten feet below the spot where Berlett stood.

The lawyer gave a soft hiss. He could see the white caps nodding on the heads of the men just below him. Edging out through the coal hatch, Berlett half dropped, half sprang. He thudded softly on the pile of sacks.

The two men, roustabouts from Pernambuco, were quick to act. Stepping together, they formed a shield as Berlett dropped into a space beside the engine room of the pilot ship. Heaving sacks aside, the men let the burlap pile upon the lawyer. Each stooped and mumbled low words in turn. In response, Berlett's right hand slipped money into eager fists. The roustabouts seated themselves beside the sacks.

The pilot was aboard his ship. The little craft moved clear of the *Southern Star*. The big engines of the liner grumbled; the twenty-thousand-ton ship moved forward, while the pilot's boat swerved for its return through the reef to Pernambuco.

The coal hatch had closed in the side of the *Southern Star*. The last sign of Edwin Berlett's clever departure had been eliminated. Under the protection of the bribed Brazilians, the American lawyer was returning in safety to Pernambuco. With the harbor reached, his departure from the sacks that hid him would be a simple matter. Expectant roustabouts were counting on another bribe. Their lips were sealed. The story of Berlett's escape would remain unknown.

ABOARD the *Southern Star*, Warren Sigler was watching the fading light of the little pilot ship. The secretary's face wore a thoughtful smile. He was planning a surprise trip to Berlett's cabin. The time was here. Leaving his place by the rail, Sigler strolled, whistling, toward the companionway.

Three men by the rail—new passengers on at Pernambuco—stared as Sigler passed. A few minutes later, they left the place where they had been standing and entered the ship.

All this while, Carlos Mendoza was seated in a small cabin, waiting. Satisfied that the time for his appointment was nearing, the Brazilian arose and picked up a small bag that lay beside him. He left his own cabin, walked along deserted passages and reached Berlett's stateroom. He opened the door and entered. He laid his bag on Berlett's bed and unlocked the little grip.

Warren Sigler, watching from the end of a passage, had seen Mendoza enter. He had seen Edwin Berlett leave the deck sometime before. Evidently Sigler was not worrying about his new employer. Mendoza—the man with the evidence—was the arrival for whom Sigler had posted himself.

Sigler sneaked forward. Softly, he opened the door of the stateroom. He entered. He looked about for Mendoza. All that he saw was the open bag upon the bed.

Advancing, Sigler glanced about. Still no sign of his man. Puzzled, Sigler stood still. Then curiosity gained the better of him. He pounced upon the bag, only to find it empty.

A creepy laugh came from the corner by the open door. Sigler whirled. He shuddered at the form which he saw before him. Instead of Mendoza, he was viewing a tall being clad entirely in black. Cloaked and with broad-brimmed hat, this spectral figure was covering the astonished secretary with an automatic.

A crook by profession, the false secretary knew the identity of the being who trapped him. He was faced by The Shadow. Dully, he realized that the role of Carlos Mendoza had been but a disguise for this supersleuth. Living in Rio de Janeiro, Warren Sigler had thought but little of The Shadow, the grim fighter whose prowess was so famous in New York.

Tonight, he was learning that the arm of The Shadow reached far. Minion of a master crook, Warren Sigler was trapped aboard the Steamship *Southern Star*, less than an hour out of Pernambuco.

"Speak!" The Shadow's tone came in a shuddering hiss. "Speak, murderer—or die—"

The challenge ended in a whispered laugh. It brought stark terror to Warren Sigler; with terror came the futile frenzy that only horror can produce.

With a wild cry, Sigler leaped forward toward The Shadow. He was pouncing for that looming automatic. The Shadow did not fire. His free arm, swinging like a plunger, sent Sigler sprawling by the stateroom door. The man's cry, however, had served as a signal.

There were bounding footsteps in the passage. As The Shadow whirled out from the door, he was met by three men, two coming from one direction; one from the other.

Hired thugs from Pernambuco, Sigler had held them in readiness. The secretary had entered the stateroom to parley with Mendoza. With all passengers on distant decks, enjoying the welcome cool of the night, assassination had seemed an easy task.

THE SHADOW, in his whirl to the passage, met the two men first. His automatic thundered as these fighters raised revolvers to shoot him down. Two quick shots; the hired assassins sprawled wounded in the passage.

The Shadow whirled, dropping as he did. The third assailant had swung to aim. The man fired; his bullet whistled through the tip of The Shadow's slouch hat.

The Shadow's laugh came resounding as his black-garbed shoulders dived forward. Tripping over the plunging form, the third Brazilian went headlong upon his fellows.

The Shadow had played a daring game, counting upon the inefficiency of the would-be slayers. He could not have battled thus with New York gangsters. The hired South Americans, however, were of inferior caliber in a close-range fight.

One man was prone on the passage floor as The Shadow rose. The second, wounded, had struggled to his feet and was diving to the passage that led to the deck. With him was the unwounded man whom The Shadow had spilled.

The two men fired wildly as they hustled for cover. As they headed for the deck, The Shadow swung in pursuit. Trapped by the rail, the startled South Americans turned to aim back into the side passage as The Shadow came lunging upon them.

The Shadow had picked the unwounded man. Like a living avalanche he struck the thug before the man could fire. The automatic, swinging, dealt a glancing blow to the fellow's head. The South American sprawled to the deck as The Shadow whirled free.

The wounded man was shooting. His aim was wide. His shots missed the swiftly moving target; it was not until The Shadow swung upright that he gained a perfect chance to fire. As the man's nervous finger fumbled with the trigger, The Shadow loosed a slug from the automatic. The shot found the man's right wrist. Already wounded in the left shoulder, the fellow dropped his gun and fell groaning to the deck.

Again, The Shadow's laugh; with it a sudden shot from the passage. Warren Sigler, recovered, had dashed to the scene of the fray. Arriving at the deck, the frenzied secretary had staked all on a quick shot at the black-garbed figure that had whirled to a spot beside the rail, more than twenty feet away.

Sigler could handle arsenic better than an automatic. The bullet from his .38 whizzed through the sweeping fold of The Shadow's cloak and found its only lodging in the rail. Sigler steadied for a second shot that never came from his gun. It was The Shadow's .45 that boomed instead.

Aiming for a murderer who sought his life, The Shadow did not fail. His single shot was the final reward that Warren Sigler gained for treachery to a kindly master. The false secretary fell dead upon the deck.

Cries from above. Scurrying feet on the deck above The Shadow's head. The black-garbed victor made his quick return toward the inner passage. Leaping over Sigler's dead body he gained the inner passage before ship's officers arrived. Choosing an open course, he faded from view.

CONFUSION reigned aboard the *Southern Star*. Warren Sigler was found dead; also a passenger from Pernambuco. Two other South Americans, one wounded, the other stunned, were discovered on the deck.

Quizzing convinced the captain that these men were of criminal status. One hour later, all the passengers aboard the ship were assembled in the dining salon for a rigid checkup. Two were found to be missing.

One was a Brazilian named Carlos Mendoza, concerning whom no information was available. The other was Edwin Berlett, a prominent New York attorney, in whose stateroom the battle had begun, and whose secretary, Warren Sigler, had been killed.

There was but one conclusion. Despite the denials of the stunned South American who had come to his senses, it was decided that the armed thugs had thrown Berlett overboard. The ocean, too, was picked as the final resting place of Carlos Mendoza.

Because Mendoza was unknown, it was decided that he must have been a member of the crooked crew. A fight was pictured on the deck. Berlett, going over the rail, dragging Mendoza with him, while Warren Sigler—not suspected of treachery—battled to save his helpless master, Edwin Berlett.

The captured South Americans admitted that they had been hired to come aboard the ship; but they claimed that their orders had been gained from Rio. They had been told to aid a man who whistled; that was all. Their nationality was a point that incriminated the missing Carlos Mendoza as their leader.

LATER, a tall figure was standing alone near the stern of the *Southern Star*. The deck light revealed the steady, masklike features of Lamont Cranston. But the whispered laugh that floated across the propeller-churned tropical sea was the echoed mirth of The Shadow.

Alone, of those aboard the *Southern Star*, The Shadow knew the true story of Carlos Mendoza. The Shadow had booked two passages on this ship. He had come aboard twice; once as Lamont

Cranston, again as Carlos Mendoza. No one had suspected that a single passenger had played the part of two men between Rio and Pernambuco.

It was with faked talk of evidence that The Shadow had brought about a climax. His threatened exposure of Warren Sigler, based upon observations at the Hotel Nacional, had been sufficient to prepare a death warrant for the so-called Carlos Mendoza.

Also, The Shadow alone could have revealed the fact that Edwin Berlett had not perished. The Shadow knew that Berlett had followed through a clever scheme. He knew that the pilot ship, returning to Pernambuco, was the only way by which Berlett could have escaped from the *Southern Star*.

Why had Berlett fled? Why had he not remained to keep his appointment with Carlos Mendoza? The Shadow knew the answer. It was the note from Mendoza—not the interview with the pretended investigator—that had made Berlett decide upon his course.

The Shadow had not witnessed Berlett's reading of the note; but he knew that the clever lawyer, shrewd in the past, crafty in the thought of the future, had decided that refuge in Pernambuco would be better for his plans than a further voyage aboard the *Southern Star*.

Edwin Berlett had departed. More than that, he had gained a reputation that might help him. Presumably, Berlett was dead. Where crime lay in the offing, a living dead man might hold a real advantage.

The Shadow had triumphed tonight, in pitched battle with vicious foemen. He had delivered necessary death to Warren Sigler, a murderer who deserved a violent end. But the swift battle aboard the *Southern Star* and the check-up of the passengers afterward, had proven of aid to the schemes of some one other than The Shadow.

Edwin Berlett, safe in Pernambuco, had played his cards well. He had read between the lines of Carlos Mendoza's notes. He had played a crafty part during his interview with the pretended South American.

The Shadow, fighting for his own welfare and working in behalf of justice, had automatically performed another function when Warren Sigler had precipitated the struggle. The Shadow had abetted the cause of Edwin Berlett!

CHAPTER VII
NEW DEATH ARRIVES

DEATH aboard the Steamship *Southern Star*. This news, flashed by radio, created an immense sensation. Within a few hours after the fight on the liner, New York newspapers were running scare-heads based upon the meager reports from the northward bound vessel.

First announcements were followed by new details. The reported death of Edwin Berlett was blared forth by the journals. Radiograms dispatched to the *Southern Star* brought back terse replies. The ship was heading into Barbados. More details would be dispatched when it arrived in port.

Like an avalanche increasing in size and fury, the story of the fight on the *Southern Star* was magnified. To cap it came a new sensation. This was the burial, at sea, of a corpse that had been aboard the ship since Rio—the body of Torrence Dilgin.

The New York newspapers had not made much of Dilgin's death. The passing of an old, retired oil magnate, living south for his health, had not been considered important enough for heavy space in newspaper columns. But the reported death of Edwin Berlett had brought out the fact that the lawyer was bringing Dilgin's body back to New York. The captain of the *Southern Star*, like journalists in America, had taken an interest in the body that was stored aboard his ship.

Investigating, the captain had made the discovery that Torrence Dilgin's body had not been embalmed. He had taken an ice-packed corpse aboard the ship. This was entirely contrary to orders. The captain had exerted his authority as dictator of law aboard a ship at sea.

Funeral rites had been read above the coffin of Torrence Dilgin. The casket, with the remains of the millionaire, had been consigned to the ocean. The captain, firm in the belief that the disposal of this corpse was essential to the welfare of the passengers, had unwittingly disposed of the last evidence that could have pointed to Torrence Dilgin's murder.

But the burial itself was newspaper copy. The mystery of Dilgin's body; its hasty shipment from Rio; the fact that Edwin Berlett had been bringing it north without embalming—all were built into newspaper stories.

New York journals had their readers expectant. Each day was bringing new reports. Lester Dorrington, lawyer in charge of Torrence Dilgin's estate, was deluged by a flow of reporters. Testily, Dorrington refused interviews. He had no statement.

LATE one afternoon, a few days after the first reports had been received from the *Southern Star*, an old man was seated in a small, dilapidated office, scanning the early edition of an evening newspaper. The letterhead on a sheet of stationery that lay upon the man's desk announced his name and his profession:

HUGO VERBECK
ATTORNEY-AT-LAW

Verbeck's eyes were staring through the heavy lenses of rimmed spectacles. The old chap's hands were trembling with nervousness as they clutched the newspaper. Verbeck was devouring the gruesome details that concerned affairs aboard the *Southern Star*.

Some clever journalist had speculated upon Torrence Dilgin's death. Basing his column on the burial at sea, the writer had suggested that the millionaire's demise in Rio might be worthy of investigating. Reading this discussion, Verbeck rested his forefinger upon the name of Torrence Dilgin. He stared through his glasses at a photograph of the millionaire.

With a shake of his head, Verbeck laid the newspaper aside. He went to a safe in the corner of his old office. He opened the door, found a metal box and raised the lid. From the box he took the key to a safe deposit vault; also a folded paper of identification.

Verbeck left his office. He descended to the street and hailed a taxicab. He directed the driver to take him to the Paragon Trust Company. Arrived at the bank, Verbeck entered, showed his paper and was conducted to the safe deposit vaults.

The old lawyer used the key to unlock a box. He peered into space and saw a metal container that half filled the safe deposit box. Drawing the container forth, the old lawyer undid its clasps. He raised the lid. He stared in bewilderment.

The metal coffer was empty! Where Hugo Verbeck had definitely expected to find something of importance, he had discovered nothing.

A full minute passed while Verbeck blinked in owlish fashion. Then, with slow, methodical movement, the old attorney replaced the coffer and closed the door of the safe deposit box.

Verbeck was muttering as he left the bank. His lips were still moving as he called a cab and rode back to his building. When he reached his office, the old lawyer's face was a study in worry and perplexity.

Pacing back and forth across his little room, Hugo Verbeck was in a quandary. He mumbled incoherent words. He mopped his brow. He stopped at the desk and picked up the newspaper. Dusk had settled; it was too dark to read in the gloomy office, so Verbeck turned on the light, by pressing a switch at the door.

BLINKING in the light, Verbeck went back to the desk. He picked up the newspaper with apparent determination. He placed his forefinger upon another name mentioned on the front page. That was the name of Lester Dorrington.

Doubt registered itself on Verbeck's pinched features. Plainly, the old lawyer was perturbed about something that concerned Torrence Dilgin. From the reticence of his actions, it was apparent that he would have kept the matter to himself under ordinary circumstances.

Speculation on Dilgin's death and its aftermath had produced a different effect. Hugo Verbeck was beating down his own resistance. Whatever his secret—and plainly he had one—it was troubling him to the extreme.

Verbeck mumbled. He nodded. With sudden determination, he pounced upon a telephone book and hurriedly opened the pages until he found the name of Lester Dorrington. Verbeck's mind was made up; he was determined to call the attorney who was handling Dilgin's estate.

Verbeck gripped the telephone. He was facing the corner where the safe was located. He had not noticed that the door of the office had opened to the extent of two inches. Receiver in hand, Verbeck began to dial. It was then that a hair-streaked hand crept through the opening of the door and pressed the light switch.

As the office was plunged in darkness, Hugo Verbeck uttered a startled cry. He swung toward the door, which was opening to its full extent. The lawyer's body was silhouetted against the dull light of the window.

A revolver roared. Three shots came in quick succession, accompanied by bursts of flame that seemed like darts projected toward Verbeck's form. His cry ending in a rattled gurgle, Hugo Verbeck collapsed. His body fell across the desk; his convulsive fingers gripped the telephone book and dragged it with him. Hugo Verbeck sprawled upon the floor.

The door of the office slammed. A strange hush followed; it seemed to pervade the building as well as this single office. Then came calls; feet pounded in the hallways. Late stayers had heard the shots. Voices neared Verbeck's office.

Someone opened the door and turned on the light. Two men in shirt sleeves gasped as they observed the sprawled form of Hugo Verbeck. One man moved inward, mechanically. The other stopped him.

"Call—call the police from my office," the man stammered. "Don't—don't touch anything in here. It's—it's—there's been a murder. A murder!"

HALF an hour later, the police were in charge of Hugo Verbeck's office. A police surgeon was talking to a swarthy, stocky man who had just arrived. This fellow had an air of authority. It was natural, for he was taking charge of the case. He was Detective Joe Cardona, ace of the New York

OF ALL of The Shadow's agents, Burbank is the most unique. Always in the background; always hidden, even more so than his master, Burbank is the link which contacts The Shadow with all of his agents. Hour after hour, day after day, if necessary, Burbank's efforts are concentrated on the activities of The Shadow's compact organization. Every word is faithfully recorded and transferred to its proper destination; all reports are checked; all instructions expertly given. Not active, not meeting danger face to face, nevertheless he, too, serves—though he only waits in darkness.

force, at present serving in capacity of acting inspector.

Bluecoats watched while Joe Cardona stalked about the room. There was challenge in the dark eyes of the detective; there was determination in the firmness of his swarthy visage. To Joe Cardona, the solution of crime was a grim game.

One look at the body. Joe Cardona nodded. He turned toward the door and measured the distance. He strode to that spot and turned to face the desk.

"The killer knew how to handle a gun," declared Cardona, firmly. "Three bullets, doctor, every one a real hit. The man we want will turn out to be a professional with the rod."

Someone was approaching in the hall. Cardona turned to face a wiry, friendly faced chap. He recognized Clyde Burke, police reporter of the New York *Classic*. Cardona scowled; then laughed.

"On the job already, eh?" questioned the detective. "I suppose you heard what I said? Well—you can put it in your sheet. The killer didn't try to cover up what he was. We'd be dumb if we didn't pick him as a regular thug."

That was all. Joe Cardona walked to the desk. His keen eyes spied the newspaper that Hugo Verbeck had been reading. They wandered to the telephone book that had spread out when it reached the floor.

"All right," announced Cardona, suddenly. "That's all. We'll look for the killer."

Clyde Burke had watched Cardona's eyes. The reporter saw Cardona's glance at the newspaper; then at the telephone book. Clyde realized that the detective had gained a hunch. Clyde, himself, had caught an inkling of it.

Joe Cardona was wondering if a connection existed between the latest news sensation and the murder of Hugo Verbeck. Clyde Burke, a keen journalist, had naturally asked himself the same question. Clyde had caught the train of Cardona's thoughts.

"I'm going down to headquarters," announced the detective. "There's nothing else, Burke. You'll have to see me later… tomorrow—"

"All right, Joe."

Cardona lingered in the office, to gather routine data. Clyde Burke departed. When he reached the street, the reporter was smiling. He stopped in a cigar store and entered a telephone booth. He dialed a number. A quiet voice responded:

"Burbank speaking."

Clyde Burke began to talk. He was an agent of The Shadow. He was reciting facts concerning crimes to The Shadow's contact man.

"Report received," came Burbank's quiet announcement, when Clyde had finished his remarks. "Instructions: keep close to Joe Cardona. Report all new developments promptly."

Clyde Burke left the telephone booth. He was confident that The Shadow would have a real beginning in the game of tracking crime. Clyde was sure that his report was already being forwarded by Burbank. Perhaps it had already reached The Shadow.

For Clyde Burke had no inkling that The Shadow was not in New York. He did not know that Burbank was temporarily in charge of the active agents. Only Burbank knew the truth concerning The Shadow's whereabouts.

The contact man, stationed at a hidden post where Clyde and other active agents could report, was the only person who had the facts. Burbank alone knew that The Shadow was far away—a passenger aboard the *Southern Star* which tonight was steaming into Bridgetown, the principal harbor of Barbados!

CHAPTER VIII
THE MAN WHO FEARED

LATE the following afternoon, a chubby-faced man was seated at a desk by the window of an office high in the towering Badger Building. Complacent, leisurely in action, he was studying an evening newspaper which was spread on the desk before him.

A ring at the telephone. The chubby-faced fellow stretched out his hand and took the instrument. He spoke in a voice that was almost a drawl:

"Rutledge Mann speaking... Yes, Rutledge Mann, investments... Ah, yes, Mr. Brooks. I have arranged for the purchase of the securities that you require... Yes, they will be here at my office... Ten o'clock tomorrow morning."

The receiver clicked. Mann returned to his study of the newspaper. He seemed well suited to his chosen business. As an investment broker, Mann had an easy, unruffled manner that gained the confidence of his clients.

Early lights were twinkling in the dusk outside the window. Mann needed none, for his office, facing to the west, was still well illuminated by the setting sun. Apparently, Mann's work was finished for the day; but the investment broker showed no signs of leaving, nor did he look toward the window, to view the twinkling lights that were appearing in Manhattan's towers.

Drawing a pair of scissors from his pocket, Mann began to clip items from the evening newspaper. Certain paragraphs referred to Torrence Dilgin; others to Edwin Berlett; more, however, concerned the murder of Hugo Verbeck. Mann laid the clippings on his desk. He opened a drawer. From it, he produced other clippings. He placed the entire batch in an envelope.

From another drawer, Mann produced two yellow papers. One was a radiogram from the Steamship *Southern Star*; the other, a cable from Barbados, where the liner had docked this very day. Both messages referred to investments; both were signed Lamont Cranston.

Rutledge Mann was an agent of The Shadow. Serving in that secret capacity, he was a useful cog in The Shadow's anti-crime machine. Yet there was a puzzled look on Mann's face as the investment broker studied the yellow messages. Mann himself did not know their meaning!

RUTLEDGE MANN had received messages from The Shadow. Ordinarily, he would have supposed these to be such. But the securities mentioned were ones that Mann did not recognize. Hence, he supposed that the messages were for The Shadow—not from him. Even to such trusted agents as Mann, The Shadow remained a mystery.

Mann placed the messages in the envelope that held the clippings. Sealing the container, he arose from his desk. He left the office and descended to Broadway. There he hailed a cab and rode to Twenty-third Street. Strolling along the old-fashioned thoroughfare, Mann paused at the entrance of a dilapidated building. He entered.

Ascending a creaky stairway, Mann stopped before an isolated door that bore a name up its grimy glass panel. The title on the frosting read:

B. JONAS

Mann dropped his envelope in a mail slit. He left the door and descended to the street. His work was done. It was Mann's duty to forward clippings, messages and written reports to The Shadow. Mann had never seen anyone enter the office that bore the name of Jonas. Yet he knew that envelopes deposited there invariably reached The Shadow.

Minutes passed outside of the office with the grimy pane. The little hallway was illuminated by a flickering gas jet. Under ordinary circumstances, it would have remained deserted; for The Shadow used a secret entrance when he paid his visits to this secluded spot. Present circumstances, however, were not ordinary. The Shadow, despite Mann's belief to the contrary, was absent from New York.

Light footsteps sounded in the hall. A man appeared. He was of medium height. His features were obscured, not by design, but merely because the light jet was behind his head. The arrival drew a key from his pocket. He inserted it in the door marked "B. Jonas." The lock grated. The door whined as it opened inward. Cobwebs were wrenched from their moorings.

Rutledge Mann's envelope was lying on the floor just inside the door. The newcomer picked up the packet, retired to the hall and locked the door behind him. His face was again obscure as he departed, for he was looking at the envelope which he had gained. He thrust the packet in his pocket as he descended the stairs.

Dusk had settled when the man with the envelope reached the street. His countenance was still obscure in the intermittent light of streetlamps as he walked rapidly toward an avenue. Following the structure of an elevated, the man reached a quiet side street. He entered an old house and paused in the darkness of the vestibule. He bolted the door behind him.

The man ascended a darkened flight of steps. He reached a room on the second floor. Drawn shades made the place totally dark. Closing the door behind him, the man groped his way to a chair, and seated himself. He pulled a cord; a lamp light glowed above his head, behind his back.

The man was seated at a little table. In front of him was a switchboard. Beside him was a filing cabinet. A light was glowing on the switchboard; the man plugged in hastily and spoke in a quiet tone:

"Burbank speaking."

This was Burbank, contact agent of The Shadow! He, alone, knew that the chief was not in New York. Following complete instructions, this trusted operative was directing activities of other agents until The Shadow might return.

CLYDE BURKE'S voice came over the wire, in response to Burbank's statement of identity. This telephone was hooked up with a regular unlisted number. The Shadow's agents knew its number; it was through Burbank that they made their calls to be relayed to The Shadow.

"Report," ordered Burbank.

"Just left headquarters," informed Clyde. "Talking with Cardona when he got a call from the police commissioner. Cardona talked cagey because I was around. But he's leaving in half an hour, and he's going to meet the commissioner somewhere."

"Report received," returned Burbank.

The contact man pulled the plug from the switchboard. He waited; then formed a new connection. He dialed. A voice responded:

"Hotel Metrolite."

"Room 1412," ordered Burbank.

A few moments later, a man's voice came over the wire. Quietly, Burbank questioned:

"Is this Mr. Sully?"

"No," came the response. "This is Mr. Vincent—Room 1412—"

"Sorry," apologized Burbank. "My mistake."

In that call, Burbank had delivered a double message. He had actually wanted Room 1412 at the Metrolite, for that was the room occupied by Harry Vincent, agent of The Shadow. But Burbank had not wanted to give instructions over a wire on which an operator might be listening in.

Harry had recognized Burbank's tones. The giving of a false name was merely a signal that he was to call back to Burbank. There was a further significance, however. The name Sully began with the letter S. That meant that Harry should proceed southward from the Metrolite while on his way to make the return call. Thus Burbank was automatically heading Harry in the direction which he must later take.

Five minutes passed. During the interim, Burbank had drawn Mann's envelope from his pocket. He was reading the radiogram and the cable. Burbank's head was in front of the lamp; his face still remained hazy. But the messages that he was reading were lying in an illuminated spot.

Turning to the filing cabinet, Burbank drew out a folder. It proved to be a book of coded names. With its aid, Burbank was ready to decipher the messages that had come from The Shadow. Before he was able to start, a light glowed on the switchboard.

It was Harry Vincent. The active agent was calling from a pay station five blocks below the Metrolite. Burbank was terse in his instructions.

"Cover headquarters," he ordered. "Cardona leaving in less than twenty-five minutes. Report where he goes."

"Instructions received," came Harry's response.

The light went out. Ten minutes passed, while Burbank decoded the messages from the *Southern Star* and Barbados. The contact man was making penciled notations when a glow came from the switchboard.

"Burbank speaking," announced the contact man, as he plugged in.

"Marsland," came a steady voice over the wire. "Still out at the airport. The plane is late. Not expected for another hour. Thought I'd better send in word."

"Report received," returned Burbank.

THE contact man returned to his deciphering. These were not the only messages that he had received through Rutledge Mann. Previous radiograms had come from the *Southern Star*, bearing terse, condensed messages. But the code words used were parts of a remarkably complicated system. Orders to buy shares; to wait for fractional point risings; dates and names of securities—all formed a part in this cipher that permitted thousands of variations.

Men of wealth like Lamont Cranston frequently kept in touch with their investment brokers while inbound to New York. These messages could not possibly have excited suspicions. Burbank had sent one reply back through Mann. No more would be necessary. The cablegram from Barbados told that The Shadow was coming in by plane.

Thirty minutes—forty—the time passed while Burbank sat stolidly at his post. The contact man was slowly chewing on a stick of gum.

To Burbank, long, lone vigils were nothing. He was not a man of action; he was one of endurance. Prompt, precise and always dependable, Burbank had served The Shadow well. His post was the connecting link between The Shadow and the agents in the field. When emergency demanded, Burbank served as he now was serving. Instead of making calls to the deserted sanctum, he was issuing orders in The Shadow's stead.

The light showed on the switchboard. Burbank plugged in and spoke. It was Harry Vincent, announcing that he had trailed Joe Cardona, using taxis to follow the detective's car. Joe had gone in an ordinary machine, not in a police automobile.

The trail had led to an old house in the Nineties. Joe's car had parked alongside a limousine that Harry had recognized as belonging to Police Commissioner Ralph Weston. Harry was reporting the address.

The report received, Burbank turned to the files. He obtained a listing of telephones arranged according to street addresses. He found the one he wanted; with it was the name of Kelwood Markin.

Taking an ordinary telephone book, Burbank checked by finding Kelwood Markin's name in the big volume. But Burbank did not stop there. He ran down the list of Markins—which was a short one—and found this listing at the bottom:

Markin & Tharxell... attys... Bushkill Bldg...
DUblin 6-9438

There was no Markin listed as an attorney, under his own name. In the book, however, Burbank found the name of George Tharxell, listed as an attorney, in the Bushkill Building. Burbank made a penciled notation. Presumably, Kelwood Markin was the onetime senior of the firm, now no longer engaged in active work. Burbank filed this supposition for investigation on the morrow.

HARRY VINCENT'S trail had ended at the old house in the Nineties. Burbank had gone further; he had gained some useful data concerning the person who resided in that house. Between them, The Shadow's agents had learned much about the man whom Cardona and the police commissioner were visiting. But they had not been able to penetrate to the actual scene within Markin's house. Only The Shadow could have done such work as that.

Police Commissioner Ralph Weston and Acting Inspector Joe Cardona were seated in a comfortable living room, which seemed hushed by its dark-papered walls and heavy curtains. Before them was a stooped-shouldered man, whose eyes were keen despite the age that showed upon his withered face.

There was pleading in Kelwood Markin's eyes. His thin hands trembling as they clutched a small table before his chair, the old man was speaking earnestly.

"I am an attorney," he was announcing. "I know the law, Commissioner. I know that it is impossible to arrest a murderer without actual evidence against him. But this man is a double killer.

"Two persons have gone to their deaths at his order. I am sure of it, Commissioner. It was he who designed the killing of Edwin Berlett. He is responsible for the murder of Hugo Verbeck.

"But that is not all. This fiend"—Markin's lips quivered with the pronouncement—"will be sure to murder others. How many, I do not know; but I can promise you that one, at least, is marked for death."

"Do you know the name of the potential murderer?" inquired Weston.

"Yes," assured Markin. "But he is more than potential. He is actually a murderer."

"And the potential victim?"

"Yes. I know him also."

A pause. It was Detective Joe Cardona, weighing the duties of active inspector, who put the question that he thought most important.

"Who is the murderer?" demanded Joe.

"His name," announced Markin, raising a shaky hand, "is Lester Dorrington."

A look of incredulity showed on Cardona's face. Cardona knew Dorrington by reputation. The man was renowned in New York as a criminal lawyer. Cardona sat stupefied.

KELWOOD MARKIN

Old and retired, Kelwood Markin is one of the six lawyers who find themselves enmeshed in this story of intrigue and false trusts. Guarded in his uptown home, death threatens him, despite all precautions—the death which comes to three, and leaves three unharmed, of this lawyer group.

The old attorney had delivered the accusation in a hushed voice. His lips were quivering, now that he had named the man whom he suspected as a villain.

It was Commissioner Weston, unstunned by Markin's pronouncement, who put the next question. The commissioner's train of thought was different from Cardona's. Weston was looking beyond the murderer; anxious to foresee the menace of some coming crime.

"You have named the murderer," declared Weston, in a steady tone. "Tell us the name of the man whom you are sure that he will seek to kill. Who is to be his victim?"

Kelwood Markin turned at the question. His face seemed whiter than before. His hands had slipped to the table. Scratching fingers, wordless lips were testimonies of mute fear.

"The victim," quavered Markin, in a tone of senile terror, "is to be myself!"

CHAPTER IX
THE KEY

KELWOOD MARKIN had startled Joe Cardona when he had named Lester Dorrington as a deliverer of death. Markin's second statement, announcing himself as a potential victim, produced a similar effect upon Ralph Weston.

As Markin leaned forward in his chair, weary elbows on the table, pallid face turned pitifully toward these representatives of the law, Cardona and Weston sat staring in profound amazement.

If ever fear had been displayed upon a human countenance, Kelwood Markin showed it now. Noting the stupefaction that had fallen upon his listeners, the old lawyer raised his hands pleadingly. He seemed unable to voice a single utterance.

It was Commissioner Weston who broke the impressive silence. Rising from his chair, the official began to stride back and forth across Markin's living room. At last, Weston swung to Joe Cardona.

"When Mr. Markin called me this afternoon," announced the commissioner, "I knew from his tone that he was troubled. When I questioned him, he admitted that he could tell me facts that concerned crime now in the news. He spoke no further. That, Cardona, was why I summoned you here tonight. I had no idea that Mr. Markin's statements would prove so startling. I had not suspected this link in crime."

"I had," declared Cardona. "In Hugo Verbeck's office, I found a newspaper and a telephone book upon the floor. I mentioned those items in my report. I had a hunch that I did not mention.

"Verbeck had been reading the evening newspaper. He had decided to call someone. Who could he have called? Not Torrence Dilgin, nor Edwin Berlett. Both of them are dead. The only man whom Verbeck might have called was Lester Dorrington.

"That was just a hunch, mind you. It made me see a link between the crimes. But to consider Dorrington as the murderer—I can't see it, Commissioner. He's a man of reputation."

"Even though he does handle criminal cases," reminded Weston, dryly. "Do you realize, Cardona, that Lester Dorrington has a close association with members of the underworld?"

"In a legal way, yes—"

"And otherwise, perhaps. That, however, is not sufficient. This man"—Weston swung toward Kelwood Markin—"has a story to tell. Come!" He was addressing the old lawyer directly. "Let us hear it."

MARKIN'S countenance had changed. The old attorney had recovered from his display of fear. He was sitting silently in his chair. His keen eyes were steady as he surveyed the men before him.

"I told you when you came here," stated Markin, "that I could reveal the name of a murderer. In return, I wanted two things: action and protection. You have promised me neither."

"We cannot promise action without proof," insisted Weston. "Protection—yes—whenever you require it. But how can we promise action unless we know the facts?"

"Should I tell my story," declared Markin, "my own position may be jeopardized. Mind you, I have done no wrong. But a publication of the facts might place me at a schemer's mercy. Unless my testimony is kept in confidence until the proper time, it will be useless. Not only that, it may be disastrous to me."

"Your testimony will be kept confidential," snapped Weston. "Come, man! If new murder is in the offing, now is no time to tarry. Why do you suspect Lester Dorrington of murder? Why do you fear him?"

"Because of what was found in Verbeck's office," returned Markin.

"You mean the newspaper?" questioned Cardona. "Or the telephone book?"

"Neither," returned Markin. "According to the newspapers, Verbeck had been to the Paragon Trust Company, shortly before his death. That was why you stated that robbery might have been the motive for the murder. In Verbeck's pocket, you found—"

"A key!" cried Cardona, leaping from his chair. "The key to the safe deposit box."

"Exactly," returned Markin. His hand, now steady, drew open a drawer in the table. "That is why I fear death. That is why I know that I—like Verbeck—am in danger."

The old lawyer thrust a fist above the table. He opened his clenched hand. Something clattered upon the wood. It was a key to a safe deposit box.

"You mean," exclaimed Cardona, "that this is the duplicate of Verbeck's key!"

"I do not," declared Markin. "That key belongs to a safe deposit box in the Farley National Bank. What I do mean, gentlemen, is that I received this key under circumstances similar to those in which Verbeck received his key."

"Can you be specific, Mr. Markin?" questioned Weston, pausing in his pacing to resume his chair. "What is this riddle of the key? I can see no connection. Let us have the story."

Kelwood Markin bowed. He spread his hands for silence. In the hush that came with Markin's pause, Cardona and Weston stared intently at the old lawyer. With eyes that turned from one man to the other, Markin began his tale.

"SOME years ago," stated the old lawyer, "I was approached by a man named Rufus Gilwood. He came to my office in the Bushkill Building, where my partner, George Tharxell, is now conducting my former practice. Perhaps you remember Rufus Gilwood, Commissioner."

"I do," inserted Weston. "He was a cattle king, from Wyoming. He died a year ago."

"That is the man," affirmed Markin. "I had never seen him before he stepped into my office. He introduced himself, established his identity and proceeded to state the purpose of his visit.

"Substantially, Gilwood told me that he had placed certain funds in a safe deposit box at the Farley National. That money was intended for distribution to certain persons. Gilwood spoke of the funds as a gift. He asked me to be custodian until I heard from him again. Should he die—he specified that distinctly—I was to open the box and distribute the cash to the persons whose names I would find in the box."

"Gilwood gave you the key?" questioned Weston, sharply.

"Yes," responded Markin.

"And did you hear from him again?" quizzed Weston. "Did he call upon you before his death?"

"No" was Markin's answer.

Weston nodded wisely. He smiled. Markin saw his expression and nodded in return.

"Rufus Gilwood paid me one thousand dollars," explained Markin, "which I accepted as a retainer fee. He told me that he relied upon my integrity not to open the box until called upon to do so. He added, however, that another attorney knew of the transaction."

"Did he name the other lawyer?"

"No. I assumed that he mentioned the fact purely to impress me that my actions would be watched."

Commissioner Weston settled back in his chair. His smile broadened. He turned toward Joe Cardona. The acting inspector was displaying a perplexed expression.

"Don't you get it, Cardona?" questioned Weston.

"No," responded the sleuth.

"It's simple," explained Weston. "Markin, here, was duped by a scheme to avoid the inheritance tax. His possession of the key gave him access to the funds from the time when Gilwood visited his office."

"I expected Gilwood to return," added Markin. "He did not. When I learned that he had died, I was bound to deliver the gift funds to the proper recipients. The transaction was entirely clear of Gilwood's estate. There was no conspiracy on my part. Naturally, I decided to go through with the bargain."

"So you went to the safe deposit box," prompted Weston. "How much money did you find there?"

"You have struck the point of my story," replied Markin, solemnly. "When I opened the safe deposit box, I found a small iron coffer. I opened it. The coffer was empty!"

"A hoax?" demanded Weston.

"Hardly," responded Markin. "Gilwood had paid me a thousand dollars, a high price for a hoax. No, Commissioner. I knew the truth. That coffer had been rifled of its contents!"

"I see," nodded Weston. "I see the game now."

"Some lawyer," asserted Markin, "played Rufus Gilwood false. He had Gilwood put funds into that box. Probably the lawyer placed them there for him. Gilwood brought me the key. I found nothing after his death. The swindler had gained ill-gotten wealth. It was useless for me to tell my story. Such a deed would only have placed suspicion on myself. I could not describe the funds that had been taken from the safe deposit box."

"A smooth game," clucked Weston.

"One that made me fearful," added Markin. "I preserved silence; but I thought a great deal. I learned the name of the lawyer who had handled Gilwood's estate."

"Lester Dorrington!"

"Yes. But I could make no statement against him. I had no proof. The matter of Rufus Gilwood's empty coffer became a canker that troubled me. In fact, it was hopeless worry over the situation that brought about my retirement from active practice."

"I can understand it," agreed Weston, sympathetically. "Gilwood had relied upon your integrity. You felt yourself to blame; yet you were helpless."

"More than that," declared Markin, in a sober tone. "I realized that the swindler, with one soft game to his credit, would not have stopped with one scheme. I visioned other helpless attorneys like myself, holding keys to empty safe deposit boxes, all afraid to speak!"

"But if you had spoken—"

"I could not have proven my statements. Nor could others who might have risen with the same story. No, Commissioner, the swindler who planned that game chose an iron-clad proposition. The men whom he swindled were dead; the duped attorneys were helpless."

"But you are speaking now—"

"Because circumstances demand it. The schemer has struck a snag; one that he overcame only through the aid of some killer. Commissioner, I have kept track of the estates which Lester Dorrington has handled during the past year. My eyes were opened when I learned that he is handling the affairs of the dead oil magnate, Torrence Dilgin.

"A lawyer named Edwin Berlett went to Rio de Janeiro to see Dilgin. Why? Because Berlett was the corporation lawyer who handled the affairs of Dilgin's company. Why did Berlett go to Rio? Probably to discuss financial matters.

"Dilgin died about the time that Berlett arrived. Berlett disappeared from the Steamship *Southern Star* on the way home. When I read the news, I realized the truth. Torrence Dilgin was another man of wealth who had been swindled!"

AS Weston nodded, Joe Cardona joined in the sign of affirmation. Kelwood Markin licked his parched lips and resumed his theory.

"Dilgin must have told Berlett that certain funds had been stowed in a safe deposit box. Berlett was on his way to gain them. He was murdered by hired assassins. Then came the huge stories in the newspapers. They unquestionably brought doubts to a certain man—namely, the lawyer to whom Dilgin had given the key of a safe deposit box."

"You mean Hugo Verbeck!"

"Certainly. Verbeck went to the bank. He found an empty coffer. He was in the same dilemma that I had encountered. Ordinarily, he would have maintained silence; with murder involved, he probably intended to make the matter public. He was slain before he could do so."

"He was going to call Lester Dorrington," blurted Cardona. "I'm sure of it, Commissioner!"

"Verbeck was murdered," continued Markin, ignoring Cardona's interruption. "But his death has only added fuel to the flames. It has roused me to action; it has probably excited the suspicion and the fears of other attorneys whom Dorrington duped when he swindled his clients.

"I can picture it, Commissioner. Dorrington—talking to a client—persuading the man to entrust a key to a certain lawyer named by Dorrington—a way to avoid a tremendous inheritance tax.

"And I can see lawyers now—pitiful men like myself—realizing that Verbeck's death was a safety measure that may be applied to themselves. Perhaps they also know that Dorrington is the murderer."

"How can we find them?" questioned Weston.

"Only by waiting until they die," returned Markin, solemnly. "Unless they choose to speak, as I have spoken. Unless they call for protection and plead with you to apprehend a fiend who deals in murder."

"You shall have protection," asserted Weston. "Cardona, put two men on duty outside of this house. We will forestall any attempt upon Mr. Markin's life."

"You are protecting me alone," warned Markin, "but not the others whose lives may be at stake."

"We do not know who they are."

"But you know who seeks to kill them."

"This is in your hands, Cardona," decided Weston. "It's up to you to watch Lester Dorrington. Use all the men you need. If you gain sufficient evidence against him, we shall issue a warrant for his arrest!"

Rising, the commissioner waved Cardona to the telephone and instructed him to call headquarters to get two men for guards at Markin's house. Striding across the living room, Weston pulled aside draperies. The action revealed windows, closed with iron shutters.

"These look safe enough," declared the commissioner. "No one will come in by that route."

He opened a door at the rear of the room. It showed a small bedroom. Kelwood Markin, at Weston's side, explained that he could use the little room as sleeping quarters. He pointed to a window that was also shuttered.

"Very good," decided Weston. "What about your servants?"

"I have only one," returned Markin. "He is my secretary and attendant—Howland is his name—and he can be trusted."

"Where is he now?"

"In a little room at the end of the hall. I used to use it as a study. Ordinarily, Howland and I sleep on the second floor."

"Is there a telephone in the study?"

"Yes. This one is an extension."

"All right. Howland can occupy the study. What about visitors? Do you have many?"

"One only. Tharxell—my partner—comes here frequently in the evening."

"Can he be trusted?"

"Tharxell? Certainly."

"Very well, then. Conduct your affairs as usual. Two men will be on constant duty outside of the house. Your statement will be kept secret, Mr. Markin. Rely upon us to follow the clue that you have given regarding Lester Dorrington."

WHEN Commissioner Ralph Weston and Acting Inspector Joe Cardona left Kelwood Markin's home a half hour later, two men from headquarters were on the job. Patrolling the street outside of Markin's, they were on the constant lookout for suspicious characters.

The man with the key had told his story. Joe Cardona, on his way to headquarters, was planning immediate measures to keep tabs on Lester Dorrington. A motive had been found for the murder of Hugo Verbeck; more than that, a definite suspect had been uncovered.

Joe Cardona was satisfied that prompt observation would prevent the murders that Kelwood Markin believed were due to come. In person, the acting inspector was going out to Long Island to keep a watch on Lester Dorrington's secluded mansion.

Cardona, thinking over Markin's statements, had become convinced that Lester Dorrington was the man to watch. With that belief in mind, Cardona had a hunch that Dorrington's Long Island home would be the spot from which crime orders would be issued. He believed that his vigilance would prevent new murder.

Little did Joe Cardona realize that new crime was due tonight. His trip to Long Island was to prove a useless journey. Murder—planned ahead—was scheduled for Manhattan. Joe Cardona was traveling from—not toward—the spot of its beginning!

CHAPTER X
SWIFT DEATH

FLOODLIGHTS were brilliant at the Newark airport. Watching eyes were turned toward the sullen sky. A plane from the south was long overdue. The ship had lost its course, but was reported safe. It was bringing passengers from South America.

Among the watchers at the airport was a stalwart man whose face was marked by ruggedness. He was standing by the side of a coupé, at the limit of the field. This was Cliff Marsland, agent of The Shadow.

The thrum of motors came above the fainter murmur of automobiles that were passing on the Lincoln highway. Highlights picked out the shape of a huge trimotor plane. It was the ship from the south. Watchers saw it pass above the field. It circled; then made a perfect landing.

The ship came almost to a stop. Circling on the ground, it taxied toward the hangars and finally came to a standstill. Spectators followed the attendants who raced up to the big plane. Cliff Marsland left his coupé and followed the small throng.

Among the passengers who stepped from the ship was a heavy man of medium height. On the ground, this arrival studied the people whom he saw. His eyes peered from beneath bushy brows. Bags were on the ground; he stepped over to identify his luggage and spoke to a waiting attendant.

"This is my bag," he declared. "The name is on the tag. Edmund Talbot. I want to go by cab to the Hotel Goliath, in New York City."

"Yes, sir," replied the attendant.

Cliff Marsland turned and strolled back to his coupé. He was unobserved by the man who had landed. Cliff's face wore a grim, satisfied smile. He had discovered the man whom he had come to seek. He knew the destination which the fellow had chosen.

Cliff Marsland knew that the name of Edmund Talbot was a false one. He had been informed by Burbank that the stranger would not give his true identity. The man whom Cliff had sighted from the crowd was Edwin Berlett, arrived directly from Pernambuco.

When people had left the field, Cliff went into the waiting room and found a telephone booth. He put in a call for the special number that he knew. Burbank's quiet voice responded. Cliff gave his report.

"Arrived," he stated tersely. "Identified. Assumed name, Edmund Talbot. Hotel Goliath."

"Report received," returned Burbank. "Instructions: go to the Goliath; learn the room number and register on the same floor, close by."

"Instructions received," acknowledged Cliff.

CLIFF'S coupé made good time Manhattanward. The Shadow's agent sped along, a mile or more behind Berlett's cab. Cliff was not attempting to overtake the taxi. He did not sight a cab even from the heights of the huge spans across the Passaic and the Hackensack rivers; but he did see one entering the tube as he neared the Holland Tunnel.

Passing under the Hudson River, Cliff reached Manhattan and took a swift course uptown. He reached the street where the Hotel Goliath was located and grabbed a bag from the floor beside him. He entered the hotel just as a cab was drawing up to the door.

It was Berlett's taxi. Strolling toward the desk, Cliff allowed the lawyer to pass him. He saw the man register under the name of Edmund Talbot. He heard the clerk give the room number: 2036. Berlett followed the bellhop who took his bag.

"How about something around the twentieth?" questioned Cliff, casually, as he registered.

"I'll give you a nice room," assured the clerk. "Front, boy!" He pounded a bell. "Show Mr. Marsland to 2012."

The rooms were not as close as Cliff had hoped. The twentieth, nevertheless, was Berlett's floor. Cliff decided that he would look the place over before calling back to Burbank.

Room 2012 was near the elevators. That was a point. The night was sultry; a partly opened door might well be intended for a breeze. Seating himself by the window of his darkened room, Cliff found that he could watch the elevators with ease. That was a decided advantage, even though Berlett's room was on the opposite side of the hotel.

In Room 2036, Edwin Berlett was standing in his shirtsleeves. His bag was opened on the floor beside the bed. The supposedly dead lawyer was staring from the window. He seemed to be contrasting the pinnacled skyline of New York with the crescented stretch of illumination that he had observed in Rio de Janeiro.

A ring at the telephone. Berlett stepped back from the window. He picked up the receiver and spoke. A smile appeared upon his face.

"Yes..." Berlett paused. "Yes... This is Mr. Talbot... Yes, I arrived later than I expected. Ship delayed... All is arranged? Good... I'll be here. Staying close to the hotel... Yes... Tired after the trip. Of course... Of course.

"You'll call me tomorrow... Good... Everything is working out as planned... Yes, of course... I understand... Yes, I'm marking down the number..." Berlett's hand began to inscribe figures on a pad beside the telephone... "I'll call you if I need quick service..."

Berlett hung up the receiver. He folded the slip of paper on which he had written and tucked it in his watch pocket. A crafty, satisfied smile appeared upon his face as Berlett turned out the light. A few minutes later, the creaking of the bed announced that the lawyer had retired.

CLIFF MARSLAND, not long after, passed through the corridor outside of Room 2036. The Shadow's agent saw darkness at the transom above Berlett's door. Returning quietly, Cliff entered his own room and called Burbank. He reported Berlett's arrival and the fact that the man had evidently turned in for the night. Burbank's instructions were to remain at the Goliath until Harry Vincent came as relief.

Logically, Edwin Berlett would have supposed that no one knew of his presence in New York, other than the man who had called him on the telephone. The caller, addressing Berlett as Talbot, was evidently a participant in a prearranged plan.

But The Shadow, knowing that Berlett would not tarry in Pernambuco, had radioed through Rutledge Mann to have an agent on the lookout for the lawyer. From now on, an agent of The Shadow—either Cliff or Harry—would be stationed close at hand to Berlett's room. Chance visitors, should they appear upon this floor, would be followed by The Shadow's men.

One man whom old Kelwood Markin had picked as a person murdered by Lester Dorrington's design was still alive, namely Edwin Berlett. The other—Hugo Verbeck—was most certainly dead. The newspapers had suggested no connection between the two lawyers; but Kelwood Markin had done so, naming Dorrington as the link between. Markin had declared himself a dupe, along with Verbeck. He had suggested that there might be others of the same sort. It was a correct belief.

A DREARY-FACED man was seated in the smoking room of the Tarpon Club on Forty-sixth Street. Chewing at the end of a half-smoked cigar, he was reading the latest reports in the final newspapers. The subject that interested him was the death of Hugo Verbeck.

In a parallel column, this solemn man had spied the name of Lester Dorrington, mentioned in connection with the death of Torrence Dilgin. The newspaper stated that Dorrington was still withholding statements regarding the millionaire whose estate he was handling.

The dreary man came to life. He cast the newspaper aside. He walked out into the small lobby of the club and entered a telephone booth. There was a purpose in his action; in a sense, it resembled the futile phone call that Hugo Verbeck had tried to make.

The dreary man, however, did not put in a call for Lester Dorrington. Instead, he called detective headquarters. When a gruff voice responded, the caller spoke in a worried tone:

"Hello... This is Clark Durton speaking... Clark Durton, attorney... I am calling from the Tarpon Club, on Forty-sixth Street...

"No, no. There's no trouble here... I want to speak to one of your inspectors... Not just any one—a particular man—an acting inspector..."

Durton paused to recall a name that he had read

of in connection with the death of Hugo Verbeck. Before he could speak again, the gruff voice suggested Joe Cardona.

"That's the man," responded Durton. "Cardona... Yes... Is he there?"

Again an expectant pause. Then, in a disappointed tone, Durton resumed:

"I see... You expect him in shortly... No, don't have him call me... I'm coming down to headquarters. I'll see him in person."

Durton hung up the receiver. He went through the lobby, gained a gray overcoat and hat of the same color and continued to the street. He stood on the gloomy sidewalk and looked for a passing cab.

There was something conspicuous about Clark Durton. He was holding a cane that he had obtained with his hat and coat. He was swinging the walking stick with his right hand, tapping it against his left palm. This was a habitual action of Durton's.

A low-slung touring car was parked across the

Bullets spattered the wall ... the lawyer collapsed without a murmur ...

street, a trifle to the west. As Durton stared in hope of hailing a cab, the touring car moved forward. As the driver shifted into high, he swerved directly toward the curb where Durton was standing.

THE lawyer leaped back, fearing that the automobile was about to mount the curb. Against the stone front of the Tarpon Club, his gray-clad figure stood like a living target. An order hissed within the touring car.

Then came the rattle of a machine gun. Bullets spattered the wall; other slugs raked Durton's standing form. The lawyer collapsed without a murmur. His cane clattered across the sidewalk and rolled toward the spot where the touring car had been.

But the automobile had not lingered. Gathering speed, it was whirling down the street, making for the green light that showed by the nearest avenue. The speeding car had passed the crossing before shouts arose in Forty-sixth Street as bystanders sped to the spot where Clark Durton lay.

Kelwood Markin had spoken true. He had told of approaching death. He had expressed the fear that other men held keys to empty safe deposit boxes. He had warned that a wholesale slaughter was impending.

Clark Durton, attorney-at-law, had gone the same voyage as another member of his profession: Hugo Verbeck. The owlish old lawyer had been riddled by bullets from a killer's gun; this dreary-faced victim had taken a dozen slugs from the muzzle of a machine gun.

Swift death had struck. It had come from gangster minions of the insidious plotter who had chosen murder as his course. The perpetrator of gigantic swindles was wiping out all lawyers who might remain to end their testimony in the exposure of his evil scheme for wealth!

CHAPTER XI
THE CONFERENCE

THE next afternoon had ended. Acting Inspector Joe Cardona was at his desk in headquarters. A frown on his swarthy face, the star sleuth was reading new accounts of death. The murder of Clark Durton outside the Tarpon Club had been welcome fodder for the presses.

"Guy outside to see you, Inspector." The announcement came from a detective who had opened Cardona's door. "It's that fellow Burke—the newshound from the *Classic*."

"Hello, Joe." Clyde Burke, shouldering his way past the detective at the door, was prompt with a wave of greeting. "What's the idea of keeping us out? Getting snooty on this inspector's job?"

There was banter in Clyde's tone. Cardona smiled sourly and waved the detective from the door.

"It's all right," ordered Joe. "I said keep the reporters out. That doesn't include this bird. He's no reporter."

"You're right, Joe," laughed Clyde, as the door closed. "I've graduated. I'm a journalist!"

"You're a pest!" growled Cardona. "Listen, Burke. There's no use of coming in here until I send for you. I've given you breaks before; I'm not going to let you down. But you hit it when you spoke about this inspector's job. There's no time to chew the rag here at headquarters. I've got two dozen men out on the street. There's no telling what may turn up—"

Cardona broke off as the telephone rang beside him. Lifting the receiver, the sleuth growled a hello. Then his tone changed.

"Yes, Commissioner..." Cardona's voice was easing. "I understand... Yes, I can drop up there again... In an hour? Very..."

"I guess Weston's worried," remarked Clyde as Cardona hung up the receiver. "How's he acting, Joe? Tough?"

"Yeah," returned Cardona. "That's his way. I saw him last night. Nothing important. Just put me on the fire because I hadn't grabbed the gorilla that bumped off Verbeck. Suppose I'll get the same dose on this Durton case."

"Got the dragnet working?"

"On its way. But the birds we're after are pretty foxy. We're not grabbing a lot of small-time crooks wholesale just yet. They haven't had time to wise up to who's done the jobs. Scram now, Burke—I've got to check up on a batch of reports before I leave."

Clyde strolled from the office. He reached the street. Arriving at a cigar store, he entered and put in a call to Burbank. Definitely, Clyde assured the contact man that Joe Cardona was making a trip uptown, evidently to the same destination that he had chosen on the previous night.

IN his secluded switchboard room, Burbank sat patiently after receiving Clyde Burke's call. Tonight, the contact man had no instructions for Harry Vincent. Apparently, Burbank was not planning to put a trailer on the job. Ten minutes passed. A light glowed on the switchboard. Burbank plugged in and gave his statement:

"Burbank speaking."

A quiet voice responded. It was a tone that Burbank recognized at once.

It was the assumed voice of Lamont Cranston.

The Shadow had arrived from Barbados. Burbank had expected this call. He had checked with a call to the Newark airport. He had learned that the plane from the south was due on time tonight.

Burbank's response was brief. The contact man knew that time was pressing. He told The Shadow the location of Kelwood Markin's house in the Nineties. He stated that Joe Cardona would be there within the hour. When his report was ended, Burbank gathered papers and thrust them in an envelope. Rising, he extinguished the light above his head, donned hat and coat and departed from the darkened room. He was on his way to Twenty-third Street to drop accumulated data through the mail slit in the office that bore the name B. Jonas.

FIVE minutes before Joe Cardona was due to arrive at Markin's, a cab stopped at the nearest corner to the old house. The driver turned to speak to the passenger. A ten-dollar bill floated through the window and landed in his hand. Staring into the back of the cab, the driver saw that his passenger was gone.

Chuckling, the cabby drove away. He had gained full fare and a large tip for his rapid trip in from the Newark airport. The jehu gave no further thought to the startling disappearance of his passenger.

A cloaked shape was gliding along the street where Cardona's men were watching. The Shadow seemed to sense the presence of observers. He stopped at a deserted house a few doors from Markin's. He spied a loose grating in the basement window.

With swift precision, The Shadow removed the yielding bars. He slid downward, invisible in the blackness. Finding a stairway, he ascended. The path was clear to the top floor. There The Shadow, using a flashlight, spied the outlet that he sought—a trapdoor in the ceiling.

A gloved hand opened a door; then a second one close by. The two barriers came well together. They made an excellent support. The Shadow raised his lithe form atop the doors. With a jimmy, he pried the trapdoor loose. Rising through the opening, he reached the roof.

With rapid strides along the housetops, The Shadow arrived on Markin's roof. He worked with the jimmy and pried a trapdoor upward. He dropped through to the deserted upper floor; then headed for a stairway distinguishable by a light below.

As The Shadow began his descent, there was a ring at the front door. A stocky man appeared, on his way to answer the summons. As his figure disappeared in the vestibule, The Shadow gained the ground floor. On his left he saw an open door—the entrance to Markin's living room.

The Shadow saw that the chamber was empty. Gliding into the partly lighted room, he spied a pair of hanging draperies at the front. He slipped between the curtains and gained a vantage spot upon the broad sill. He was not a moment too soon. The stocky man, returning, came through the living room and rapped at a closed door.

"What is it, Howland?" came a querulous voice.

"Two visitors, sir," responded the secretary. "Commissioner Weston and Inspector Cardona. They have come in with me, sir."

Weston and Cardona were entering the room as Howland spoke through the closed door. They had arrived outside almost at the same time. As they stared toward the door of Markin's temporary bedroom, the barrier opened. The old lawyer, his face drawn, stepped into view.

"You can go, Howland," said Markin. "Remain in the study."

"Yes, sir."

MARKIN sat down with his visitors. The lawyer chose the spot behind the table. His face, though it showed tenseness, also carried an expression that indicated justification of his fears.

"I am glad that you have come," declared Markin, in a steady tone. "New misfortune has proven my theory. I think that you will agree that my qualms were not merely the meanderings of an old man's mind."

"Quite right, Mr. Markin," asserted Weston. "I learned that you had called my office. I arranged to come here, and I ordered Acting Inspector Cardona to join us. I thought, perhaps, that you might have gained new information."

"How?" queried Markin, with a spread of his hands. "What else can I say? I told you that other lawyers might be on the death list. I hoped that you might have information."

"We have," declared Cardona. "We found the key to a safe deposit box among Durton's effects. None of his family could identify it."

"He is one of us," nodded Markin. "Let us hope that there are none others beside myself."

"The key is the only piece of evidence," stated Weston. "It supports your statements, Markin. I believe that Clark Durton received that key from a millionaire. I am sure that he, like yourself and Verbeck, found the safe deposit box empty. But there the trail ceases."

"It would," said Markin. "In Verbeck's case, it seemed certain that he received the key from Torrence Dilgin. I have already stated that I gained mine from Rufus Gilwood. But there is only one man who can tell you who gave the key to Clark Durton. That man is Lester Dorrington."

"If we knew how many millionaires were swindled," suggested Cardona, "we could figure how many lawyers are slated for the spot. I'm putting four men on guard here, Mr. Markin. There was only one killer who went after Verbeck, but a bunch bumped Durton."

"That is something gained," decided Markin, in a wise tone. "You have learned definitely that the slayers are gangsters. But have you followed my suggestion of checking upon Lester Dorrington?"

"I covered his house last night," returned Cardona. "I had three men with me on Long Island. Dorrington was there all the while."

"He would be!" exclaimed Markin, pounding his fist on the table. "If your visit here tonight, gentlemen, is in hope of gaining information, I can give no more than I have already. I told you how I received a key from Gilwood; how his dodge to escape the inheritance tax failed. Dorrington appropriated those funds from Gilwood's box at the Farley National, just as he took the cash which Verbeck was supposed to find at the Paragon Trust.

"You have the information; what you need is advice. Here it is: remember that Lester Dorrington is crafty. He is too wise to form contact at his home. His plans have undoubtedly been made in advance. There is only one course for you to follow. Look for crooks whose cases he handled in court. They are the ones who will be in this game."

"That's right, Cardona," agreed Weston, turning to the ace sleuth. "That limits your hunt. Get the stool pigeons on the job. Keep away from the dragnet. These killers are men who are working from some hideout."

"I've got the stools working," insisted Cardona. "I've been looking up facts on Dorrington, too. I haven't used the plan that Mr. Markin here suggests we—"

"Use it then," interposed Weston, "and pass the word tonight. Others murders may be in the making. Two have come in two nights. One may be on its way even now."

Rising, the commissioner extended his hand to Kelwood Markin. The retired lawyer received the shake. As Weston and Cardona turned toward the hall, he uttered words of thanks, particularly because four men were now on duty outside his house.

"There is no use in trying to deceive Dorrington," declared the old lawyer. "He has watched others; he will be watching me. He must certainly know by now that you are guarding this house. He knows that I have spoken.

"That, in a sense, is unfortunate. It may mean that Dorrington is all the more anxious to kill off other persons who may testify against him. I am still fearful, gentlemen. You can appreciate my qualms. By gaining your protection, I have unquestionably made Dorrington all the more desirous of killing me."

Weston nodded from the door. This angle of the case was serious. Yet the commissioner expressed the assurance that four men outside the house, with Howland inside, should be sufficient for Markin's safety.

The visitors departed. Markin summoned Howland. He gave the secretary brief orders for the morning. The old man entered the bedroom and locked the door behind him. Howland turned out the lights in the living room, but did not lock the door.

Curtains stirred. The Shadow emerged from his hiding place. Crossing the living room he reached the hall and gained the stairs. He went up through the trapdoor and across the roof; when he descended through the deserted house, he found a side door that opened into a narrow alleyway. He used this as his exit.

LATER, the blue light shone in The Shadow's sanctum. A soft laugh sounded as the master sleuth studied the gathered clippings and reports. By his trip to Markin's, The Shadow had, since his arrival, gained the real facts in the secret that lay behind a chain of deaths.

Facts, undisclosed while The Shadow was in Rio, were pointing the way to the measures which must be taken to aid the law. By his actions aboard the *Southern Star*, The Shadow had sought to end the run of crime. Yet murder had followed in New York, and The Shadow had learned why.

Piecing the remarks which Markin, Weston and Cardona had made concerning their previous conversation, The Shadow had gained a practical knowledge of Markin's revelations. The hidden listener at the conference tonight was the one who had profited through the discussion.

New murder might be on its way. Another lawyer—as yet unknown—might be the next victim set for murder. When crime struck, The Shadow would be there to meet it. He had gained the ground that he required to overtake new bursts of violence.

Earphones clicked. A light glowed upon the wall. Burbank's voice came across the wire. The Shadow responded, in his whispered tones.

"Instructions to Marsland" were his words. "Go to the Pink Rat. Await written orders that he will receive there."

"Instructions received."

Earphones clattered; hands disappeared from the light. When they returned, they were carrying folders that were identified by names. The Shadow began to study reports on crooks—definite data which he had produced from his exclusive files.

Half an hour passed while The Shadow engaged in research. Then came a click of the light. A laugh crept through the darkened sanctum. The Shadow was departing. He was on his way to the underworld.

There he would form contact with Cliff Marsland. The Shadow and his agent, independently, would seek the information that was needed. The Shadow had taken the same advice that Joe Cardona had received from Kelwood Markin.

On this, the first night of his arrival in New York, he was seeking firsthand information concerning the whereabouts of crooks who had been legal clients of Lester Dorrington.

CHAPTER XII
A CLIENT ADVISES

ON the following afternoon, a tall, cadaverous man entered the lobby of the Bylend Building. He purchased a newspaper at the stand; he paused to glance at the headlines. The murders of Hugo Verbeck and Clark Durton were still in the news, but no new killings had been reported.

The tall man was Lester Dorrington. He was returning to his offices after lunching at his club. His expressionless face revealed nothing of his thoughts as he strolled toward the express elevator that awaited passengers for the twentieth floor and those above that level.

When Dorrington's footsteps clicked along the corridor of the twenty-fourth floor, a door opened across the way from the lawyer's suite. Peering eyes watched Dorrington pass. A detective, stationed by Joe Cardona, was watching the lawyer's return.

From the time that he had left his house that morning, during the lunch period that he had spent at the club, Lester Dorrington had been under police surveillance. Yet there was nothing in the lawyer's attitude that indicated suspicion of that fact.

Arriving in his inner office, Lester Dorrington began to study papers that were upon his desk. While the solemn-faced attorney was thus engaged, a ring came from the private telephone. Dorrington went to the little cabinet in the corner. He brought out the telephone and answered the call.

"What's that?" he questioned, sharply, as he recognized the voice over the wire. "Ace Feldon? I didn't tell him to come to see me... I see... He wants to talk to me, eh? Put him on the wire... What's that? Well... All right... Send him down..."

Dorrington deposited the telephone in the cabinet. He strode swiftly across the luxurious private office and locked the door that led to the outer rooms. Dorrington had half a dozen workers in his general office, with lesser associates in private rooms of his extensive suite. He did not want to be disturbed by any of them.

Coming back to the corner by the little telephone cabinet, Dorrington unlocked the door of a closet. He pressed a shelf upward. A click followed. A panel raised in the rear of the closet.

The opening showed a spiral staircase.

DULL footsteps were clanging down the stairway. Dorrington stepped back into the office. A hard-faced, big-fisted man appeared from the open panel. His thick lips wore a pleased smile.

"Hello, Dorrington," growled the arrival.

"Hello, Feldon," responded the lawyer, dryly. "Sit down. I shall talk with you immediately."

As the hard-faced man sauntered to a chair, the lawyer stepped into the closet and closed the panel. He left the door open, then came back to his desk. Taking his swivel chair, he stared coldly at his visitor.

"Hope you ain't sore because I dropped in," began "Ace" Feldon. "Say, Dorrington—that staircase is a swell gag. I knew most lawyers have got a good way out of their offices. You've got a couple here on this floor. But that office upstairs is the best stunt yet."

"This was the first time you used it," reminded Dorrington. "Your previous visits, Feldon, did not require secrecy."

"That's right," nodded Feldon. "You always told me, Dorrington, that if I wanted to see you on the q.t., all I had to do was drop in on a guy named Loven, who has his office on the floor above this. But I never figured that you'd have a way between. It's a pip, Dorrington, that staircase is."

"I appreciate your commendation," declared Dorrington. "Now that we have discussed the staircase, let me hear the reason for your unexpected visit."

Ace Feldon shifted in his chair. Hard-boiled though he was, this toughened fellow was ill-at-ease as he met Dorrington's searching gaze. Feldon fumbled with a hat that he was holding in his hands. Then, with a tone that indicated final decision, he put a definite question.

"Listen, Dorrington," he growled. "What's the idea of picking Whitey Calban to do your bumping for you? What was wrong with me?"

"Calban?" questioned Dorrington, in apparent surprise. "I haven't seen the man for months, Feldon."

"That ain't the point," retorted Ace. "Maybe you haven't seen him; but you're using him."

"For crime?"

"Yes. For murder."

Dorrington smiled slightly as he shook his head. The lawyer was accepting the statement as preposterous.

ACE FELDON, now that he had begun, was not ready to desist.

"Listen, Dorrington," he stated, "you've represented Whitey Calban and you've represented me. Both of us are smooth workers. The bulls don't mean nothin' in our sweet young lives. If you wanted anythin' done—along our line—it's a sure bet that either Whitey or I would pull it for you."

"Granted," agreed Dorrington. "Murder, however, is something which I have found entirely unnecessary so far as my business is concerned. I have represented killers; but I have never hired them."

"There's a difference between Whitey Calban and me," resumed Feldon, steadily ignoring Dorrington's statement. "I'll tell you what the difference is. I'm a square shooter, but Whitey Calban ain't. I've got it in for that guy Calban."

"So I have heard," remarked Dorrington. "Feuds between gangleaders are not unusual. It seems to be part of the racket."

"I ain't one that goes out of my way to find trouble," retorted Ace Feldon. "There's just one reason why I've got it in for that louse Calban. He's a double-crosser, that's why. And when a guy like Calban begins to slip one over on a friend of mine, I do somethin' about it. Savvy?"

"I take it, then," observed Dorrington, mildly, "that you have come here to discuss certain activities of Whitey Calban's."

"You've got me right, Dorrington. Dead right. Listen; if I'm workin' for a big shot and usin' a bunch of gorillas to help me with the jobs, I ain't goin' to spill nothin' to the heels in my mob, am I?

"You bet I'm not. Neither is any other guy that's on the level. But Calban ain't a straight shooter. He's been blabbin' to the crew, lettin' his gorillas know who's hirin' him. That ain't good policy, particularly when the work ain't finished yet. Calban's the mug who bumped Verbeck an' Durton."

"Quite interesting."

"It ought to be—to you—since Calban's spilled it to his mob that he croaked those lawyers because you told him to!"

Lester Dorrington sat rigid as a statue. Not a muscle twitched upon the lawyer's cadaverous face. Dorrington's eyes were fixed steadily upon Ace Feldon. The gangleader nodded sourly.

"Calban let it slip," he insisted. "He yapped the facts to his gorillas last night, down at their hideout. Told 'em last night was a layoff but tonight there'd be another job. Then he got mouthy and spilled your name as the guy that's backin' him."

"Quite odd," observed Dorrington. "Quite odd, Feldon, that you should tell me this."

"Tell you that Whitey Calban's a double-crosser? Put you wise because you're a friend of mine?"

"No. That part of your story is plain. What puzzles me is how you happen to know so much concerning Calban and his gang."

"That ain't no riddle," snorted Feldon. "I ain't never liked Whitey Calban; but that wasn't no reason why I should try to make trouble for him. It was reason enough, though, for me to want to watch the guy.

"There's a fellow named Steve Quigg who used to work for me when I had my squad of gorillas. Calban never knew that Quigg was with my crew. When I busted up the outfit, he signed with Calban. But Quigg sees me right along. He knows that Calban is a louse. That's why he tips me off to what Whitey's mob is doin'."

"So Quigg serves you as undercover man?"

"Right. But I ain't never tried to pull nothin' on Calban. Just keepin' a line on him, that's all. When Steve Quigg calls me up today an' tells me that Calban's told his mob about you, I figured it was time you knew it.

"Suppose that job goes sour tonight. Suppose the bulls grab Calban. He's goin' to blab, ain't he? He'll tell the bulls that you're the guy that hired him. But he'll never admit he squealed. He'll lay it on some of the gorillas that he talked to.

"I'm tellin' you—Calban's a double crosser. You've got the proof of it right now. You've treated me good, Dorrington. I'm your friend an' you know it. I'm puttin' you wise."

LESTER DORRINGTON was leaning upon his elbows. Staring squarely across the desk, he spoke firmly to Ace Feldon.

"Thank you for the information," stated the poker-faced lawyer. "I can assure you, however, that it is unnecessary. Outside of the legal case in which I represented Whitey Calban, I have had nothing whatever to do with the man."

A buzzer sounded as Lester Dorrington ceased speaking. The attorney waved his hand toward the closet. It was the sign for Ace Feldon to depart. Someone in the outer office required an interview with Dorrington.

"I ain't askin' nothin'," declared Feldon as he rose from his chair and slapped his hat upon his head. "But I'm tellin' you, Dorrington, it works both ways. If Whitey Calban is workin' for you, he's pulled a fast one, talkin' to those loud-mouthed gorillas.

"If he ain't workin' for you, he's a real double-crosser. A louse like him ain't fit to live. You're a real guy, Dorrington, an' I'll leave this with you: anythin' that I may be doin' will be on your account. Savvy?"

The gangleader had reached the closet. There were knocks at the panel of Dorrington's office door. The lawyer had no time to reply. He shoved Ace Feldon through the panel and pulled down the shelf that locked the secret barrier. Closing the door of the closet, he went to answer the knock at the outer door.

Important clients were awaiting. Within five minutes after Ace Feldon's departure, Lester Dorrington was engaged in prolonged conference. Afternoon waned, while the discussion continued. Dusk settled; lights were turned on; it was six o'clock when the conference was ended.

Alone, ready to leave his office, Lester Dorrington stood by his desk. He was recalling his interview with Ace Feldon; for once, doubt seemed to register itself upon Dorrington's cadaverous countenance. The attorney was pondering upon the situation as Feldon had outlined it.

At last, a knowing smile traced itself faintly on Lester Dorrington's lips. The lawyer shrugged his shoulders, turned out the light and departed from his office. He told a secretary that he was going to his home on Long Island; that he could be reached there in case of urgent messages.

On his way to the Pennsylvania Station, Lester Dorrington was trailed by two of Cardona's men. The lawyer did not appear to notice the stalking sleuths. Close-mouthed, crafty in every dealing, Lester Dorrington showed no concern regarding events that were to come.

CHAPTER XIII
CLUES IN THE DARK

"WHERE'S Cardona?"

"Out."

Clyde Burke was the man who asked the question at headquarters. The one word answer was all that he received from a laconic detective who was sitting in the acting inspector's office.

Something was in the wind, but Clyde could not uncover it. Cardona had been absent all afternoon. It was nine o'clock in the evening, still the acting inspector had not returned. Clyde strolled from headquarters, wondering where Cardona could be.

Clyde's supposition that Cardona was engaged in special sleuthing was not an idle one. At the very moment when the reporter was leaving headquarters, Acting Inspector Joe Cardona was alighting from an elevated train at a station near the Bowery.

Descending the steps, Cardona assumed a shuffling gait. Coat collar up around his chin, the acting inspector headed toward a narrow street. He followed the thoroughfare for several blocks, turned his course and reached an alleyway. Here he paused to light a cigarette.

The night was windy. Each match that Cardona used seemed to flicker automatically. With a disgusted grunt, the ace sleuth stepped into an opening between two dilapidated buildings. When he had reached this vantage point, however, he made no new effort to light a match. He waited until a whispered voice came from behind a broken barrel by the house wall.

"Joe!"

"O.K., Gummy. What've you got?"

"Nothin' much." A hunched figure shifted in the darkness. "Whitey Calban is the guy you want; but I ain't been able to spot his hideout."

"Seen any of his gorillas?"

"No; but they've been around. Listen, Joe. Calban's the only guy that could've pulled those jobs the way they was done. He wasn't seen nowhere three nights ago; the next day the guys in his mob ducked out."

"But they've been back—"

"Not enough for me to spot 'em."

"All right, Gummy. Scram."

Joe Cardona waited until footsteps had shuffled back toward the barrel. Lighting his cigarette, the sleuth emerged from between the buildings and resumed his progress. He slouched past the entrance to an underworld dive known as the Pink Rat. Joe did not enter.

The acting inspector had no desire to be seen in this locality. He knew that "Gummy" had covered the Pink Rat. Of all the stool pigeons in Manhattan, Gummy was the most dependable. The man had been a find. Cardona had kept him undercover. When Gummy spilled information, it was always at meetings somewhere within the confines of scumland.

Gummy had attributed two murders to a gangleader named Whitey Calban. Joe Cardona felt sure that the reliable stool had gained the facts. But there was no way of tracking Whitey to his present lair. Cardona's face showed grimly in lamplight as the sleuth neared the borders of the underworld.

This would mean the dragnet. Tonight, from headquarters, Joe would have to pass the word for a complete search of the underworld. Skulking criminals would be hauled before the law. Those most liable to suspicion would receive the third degree. Someone, Joe felt sure, would squawk on Whitey Calban, even though the gangleader might himself escape the mesh.

JOE CARDONA had passed the Pink Rat. Even had he entered the dive, he would not have learned more than Gummy the stool had told him. For the Pink Rat sheltered a cagey lot of ruffians. Little of importance was spilled within its walls.

Rat-faced mobsters—men who had managed to dodge suspicion of the police—were assembled in the smoke-filled room that formed the chief portion of the Pink Rat. Bottles were pounding upon tables. Glasses were clinking. Oaths came in gnarling, raspy tones.

The Pink Rat was not a healthy place for strangers. Not more than three stool pigeons outside of Gummy would dare to enter its portals. But hardened, recognized denizens of the underworld were welcomed in this dive. It was the hangout for the toughest.

A fellow with a chiseled-face came sauntering

through the door. Hands were raised in greeting as this newcomer—better dressed than most of the other patrons—sauntered to a table by an inner door.

This was Cliff Marsland. The Shadow's agent was regarded as a killer by those of the underworld. He belonged to a class of super gorillas. He was a fighter whom any gangleader would have chosen for a lieutenant.

No one suspected Cliff's real mission in the badlands. None of the denizens of the Pink Rat would have believed that Cliff was working for The Shadow. They did not know that Cliff, tonight, had just completed an intensive tour through the tenderloin, searching for Whitey Calban's hideout.

The Shadow's agent had learned as much as Gummy—no more. His discoveries, however, had been shared by another. The Shadow had also been sojourning in scumland. He, like Cliff, had picked Whitey Calban as the probable killer of Hugo Verbeck and Clark Durton.

THE waiters in the Pink Rat were an odd lot of aproned ruffians who looked as tough as the patrons. Every one was a capable bouncer. All were ready to pounce upon stools, battle with police or mix it with unruly mobsters should occasion demand. New faces constantly appeared among their number. The waiter who thumped a bottle on Cliff's table was a long-faced fellow whom The Shadow's agent had never seen before.

The waiter was apparently left handed. As his fingers still encircled the bottle, Cliff Marsland stared. Upon the third finger of the left hand, The Shadow's agent spied the flashing sparkle of a strange gem that flickered changing hues beneath the light. It was The Shadow's girasol—the strange fire opal that was an unmatched jewel.

Cliff had been instructed to report here to The Shadow. With him, Cliff had the data that The Shadow needed. It was in a small envelope—a list of the places where Cliff had been in search of Whitey Calban.

Moistening his thumb upon his tongue, Cliff followed the action by placing his hand in his pocket. He found the flap of the little envelope; dampened it; then pressed it against the flabby surface of a banknote. Drawing a roll of currency from his pocket, Cliff peeled off the bill that held the envelope. He stared straight at the bottle as he laid the banknote—a ten spot—on the table, with the envelope beneath.

The girasol glimmered as the waiter's hand moved from the bottle. The hand crunched the ten-dollar bill. Cliff, glancing upward, saw a stoop-shouldered form shambling through the opening at the back of the Pink Rat.

Five minutes later, the waiter reappeared. His hand laid bills and change upon the table. Grasping the crinkling one-spots, Cliff could feel a little envelope among them. He thrust the money in his pocket.

Cliff knew that The Shadow, like himself, had been searching this district. Cliff had gone to certain places at The Shadow's order, which Cliff had gained through Burbank. Both searches had been futile. Hence this rendezvous at the Pink Rat.

The Shadow had added Cliff's list to his own. Striking off the places that had proven worthless, The Shadow was ordering a new search. The Shadow would go to certain spots; Cliff to others.

Cliff's new list had reached his pocket with the money. Watching, Cliff saw the stoop-shouldered waiter nearing the door that led outside. That barrier was at the opposite end of the Pink Rat. Cliff knew that The Shadow was leaving.

Cliff's gaze wandered. It would be his turn to depart shortly. The Shadow's agent pushed bottle and glass aside. He was about to rise from his chair when he heard a sharp challenge from the other end of the room. Buzzing conversation ended as mobsters stared toward the other end of the smoke-filled dive.

Two regular waiters had blocked the path of the one who had neared the outer door. They were arguing with him. They did not recognize him as one of the regular waiters at the Pink Rat. They were not satisfied with his explanation that he had come on the job tonight.

"Yeah?" a beefy-faced waiter was demanding. "So you want to scram, do you? Well, you ain't goin' to. There's been too many stools around this joint lately. We ain't lettin' nobody like you get out."

In response, the stoop-shouldered waiter released a sudden jab to the beefy face before him. The challenger collapsed as the sock reached his jaw. The other challenger let out a yell as he pounced upon the false waiter. With one accord, the patrons of the Pink Rat were leaping to their feet to join in the fray. As the brawlers struggled by the door, burly mobsmen sprang to block the barrier.

THE Pink Rat was lighted by three sets of ceiling lights. Those at each end of the basement dive were clusters. The central illumination came from a single frosted bulb set in the middle of the ceiling.

Each set operated from a different circuit. One switch was by the outer door, the other was close to the table where Cliff Marsland sat. The third—the central switch—was in back of an improvised bar.

As mobsters, anxious for strife, were leaping to their feet, the false waiter sent his second antagonist sprawling from a vicious wallop. The challenger rolled across the floor.

The fake waiter did not pause. His left hand shot to the light switch near the outer door. Before mobsters could stop him, he had pressed the switch. At the same instant, his right hand came from the side of his smudgy apron. An automatic boomed; the aim was perfect. The bullet shattered the big light in the center of the dive.

Cliff was acting as The Shadow fired. No eyes were in his direction. With a quick grasp, Cliff yanked the switch by the inner door. The smoky dive was plunged in darkness; with it came the jeering, strident tones of a weird laugh.

The Shadow! Mobsters knew with whom they had to deal. The odor of powder mingled with the aroma of tobacco as revolvers barked wildly toward the spot where the enemy had last been seen. Flashlights glimmered; they dropped as booming shots from an automatic picked the hands that turned lights toward the door.

The mobsters at the entrance were pouncing in the dark. Fierce hands were grasping for the invisible quarry. The Shadow, close to the wall by the door, was eluding them. He had drawn a second automatic in the darkness. Swinging this weapon, The Shadow was clearing the path.

His adversaries were at a hopeless disadvantage. They were gripping for one among several; but to The Shadow all forms were those of enemies with whom he could deal.

Slugged gangsters staggered. Others, in the middle of the dive, blazed shots toward the door, unmindful of the fact that others of their kind might receive the bullets. Shooters were out to get their enemy at all cost.

It was Cliff Marsland who provided prompt diversion. Springing to the side wall of the room, Cliff was knocking tables from his way while he punched through the darkness toward the outer door. He had drawn a pair of automatics; with these weapons, Cliff delivered quick shots across the darkened dive.

Wild shots stopped the men who were aiming toward the door. This attack from their very midst sent gangsters dropping for the cover of tables. The Shadow had thrown aside the last blockers. Cutting in by the wall, he had kept them between himself and the interior of the dive. Bullets intended for The Shadow had clipped the intervening mobsters.

As Cliff's fire spelled an interval; as mobsters turned in the dark to aim for the unseen henchmen, The Shadow loosed shots from his second automatic. These bursts came from the door itself. The rapid fire ended as quickly as it had begun. Gangsters, dispatching slugs toward the door, were shooting only at the spot where The Shadow had been.

CLIFF had ceased fire. A light came on. Someone had pressed the switch at the inner door. Chaos showed in the Pink Rat. Groaning mobsmen and crippled waiters were lying on the floor. A cluster of crumpled forms showed by the exit to the alley.

Oaths rang through the joint as mobsters saw that their quarry had escaped. There was no sign of the stoop-shouldered waiter. Someone shouted the suggestion of following to the street. Half a dozen ruffians sprang toward the exit.

Cliff was among this throng. His smoking automatics marked him simply as participant in the fight, not as The Shadow's aide. Battering past tables, Cliff had traveled well toward the outer door. He was at the heels of those who sought The Shadow's trail.

Flashlights showed the alley empty. Swiftly, The Shadow had traveled from the outside street. Shrill whistles were sounding, less than two blocks away. A policeman had heard the gunfire. He was summoning other officers to the scene.

"Scram," came a growled suggestion.

Grunts of acknowledgment. One mobster leaped back to the Pink Rat to pass the word to those within. The others began to scurry along the alley. Cliff joined in the departure.

Staring back from the corner, The Shadow's agent witnessed a general exodus from the Pink Rat. Whistles—distant sirens—told that the police were closing in. Cliff darted for another alleyway and made good his escape.

FIVE blocks away, Cliff pulled the envelope from his batch of bills. Near a streetlamp, he read the names of four localities that The Shadow had chosen for investigation. Cliff knew that The Shadow had taken other places for himself.

The nearest was an old, deserted house on the border of Chinatown. Cliff knew the place well; but he had not figured it as a hideout. Nor had The Shadow, until after more likely spots had proven barren.

Cliff lost no time in heading for this first place on his list. He felt that success was improbable. When he reached the dingy building, he saw no lights among its broken windows. The back door offered possible entry. Cliff found the rear entrance in the darkness. Suddenly, The Shadow's agent dropped beside a pair of battered steps.

Footsteps were coming toward the back of the house. They mounted the steps; a soft knock sounded on the door. Cliff could almost feel the swish as the door opened inward.

"That you, Steve?" came a voice from inside the house.

"Yeah" was the cautious response from the man on the steps. "What's the lay, Hunky?"

"Stick here," ordered the inside man. "Whitey's coming up with the mob. They're all in the cellar."

"We're startin' out?"

"Yeah."

"Where to?"

"Jake's joint, where we've got the cars parked. Then up to Eighty-fifth Street, in back of the old Budwin Garage. We'll get together there. The job's near the place."

"O.K., Hunky. I'll mooch over to Jake's. I'll be waitin' there."

"We'll be along in ten minutes."

Footsteps descended. The door closed. One minute passed. Cliff Marsland arose and moved stealthily from beside the steps. Reaching the street, Cliff traveled one block and reached a dilapidated drug store where he found a battered phone booth.

The agent was calling Burbank. Through the contact man Cliff would get much-needed word to The Shadow. There was no time to stop men of crime from leaving on their mission; but there was a chance to meet them at their goal.

Cliff Marsland, following The Shadow's tip, had located the hideout of Whitey Calban, five minutes before the murderous mobleader and his crew of killers were leaving to deliver another stroke of death!

CHAPTER XIV
MOVES TO A FINISH

HALF an hour after Cliff Marsland had sent the tip-off to Burbank, a man was answering a telephone call at the Hotel Goliath. It was Edwin Berlett, in his room on the twentieth floor.

"Hello..." The lawyer's crafty face showed a smile. "Yes... This is Mr. Talbot... Good... Good... That means tonight will finish it... Yes... I'll handle it from now on... Certainly. I understand..."

The lawyer hung up the receiver. Satisfied, he laid the telephone aside and strolled to the window. As Berlett stared toward the lights of Times Square, his face showed the pleased expression of a man who was concerned with well-completed plans.

SINGULARLY, another individual was making a telephone call at the very time Berlett was talking. This speaker was Lester Dorrington. The criminal lawyer was standing in the spacious study of his home on Long Island.

"Stay on the job, Squeezer," Dorrington was saying in a cautious tone. "Watch him, but don't get too close... That's right. There may be trouble if he spots you... I know. He won't suspect I've got you watching him, but he might turn dangerous if he knew... No, no. It doesn't matter if he does talk. He can't talk, Squeezer... That's right... It would mean trouble for him if he said too much. More trouble for him than for me... Tomorrow... Yes... Loven's office..."

These were not the only telephone calls in which lawyers were participating. Seated by the table in his living room, Kelwood Markin was also speaking across the wire.

"Very good," the old man was saying. "If you've found the identity of the killer, you should be able to stop the murders... Yes, I feel safer than before; but I shall be even more satisfied after you have acted... Yes, that may be true; at the same time, Dorrington may have more than one weapon in his arsenal... Gangsters... Yes, if they are eliminated, Dorrington's teeth will be gone... But he may still find a way to bite..."

The men who had telephoned were secluded, away from approaching crime. There were others, however, who were about to deal in action. A group of men were clustered in a darkened spot behind the old Budwin Garage on Eighty-fourth Street. They were awaiting the arrival of their leader.

"Here he is," whispered one of the gang.

A man was stepping from the sidewalk to join the crew. It was Whitey Calban, notorious gangleader, ready to give orders to his murderous cohorts.

"Listen, mugs," growled Whitey. "Remember all I've told you. After tonight, the guy we're working for won't need us. You can show your pans wherever you want. I've paid you off. I'm taking a trip.

"The job's mine tonight. I've got you birds along just to make sure it goes all right. Six houses down the street; that's where I'm going. I'm ringing the front door bell and I'm going in. But I want you guys to stick around by the front door. If you hear too many shots, pile in. Got it?"

"How about the back, Whitey?" came a question from one of the crew. "Maybe that'd be a good spot to watch."

"A good idea, Steve," commended the gangleader. "You take the back. You can duck out after you hear me fire."

"You'd better give me time to get there, Whitey. I've got to double around the block."

"All right, Steve. We'll wait."

Steve moved from the group. The waiting mobsmen heard his footsteps click upon the sidewalk. Steve was walking past the garage, toward the corner of an avenue. His figure, however, was not the only one that left the blackness of the garage wall.

A figure that moved as silently as night itself had taken the opposite direction. Detached from a darkened portion of the garage wall, this shade moved softly along the sidewalk. Six houses from the garage, the phantom form paused. Keen eyes spied a passage that ended between buildings. The shape entered the opening and merged with the darkness of a bay window.

ON the avenue, a hard-faced mobster was moving toward Eighty-third Street. Steve Quigg, the gorilla who had practically appointed himself as guardian at the rear, was on the way to take his post. As he sauntered rapidly, Steve made a motion with his right hand.

A man stepped from an entry and followed him. At the next turn, this fellow moved up and joined Quigg. The two talked in cautious tones as they headed toward the rear of the house that Calban had chosen.

"We've got to work quick, Ace," informed Steve. "Calban gave me five minutes to get posted."

"All right, Steve," came Feldon's response. "We'll jimmy that back door in no time. Which house is it?"

"The sixth. You made good time, Ace."

"Thanks to you, bo. That was smart stuff, calling me before you met the crew at Jake's."

The two men found an opening that suited their liking. Their talk ceased as they moved toward the rear of the house that Calban had picked for crime. It was only when they neared the door that they wanted that Ace Feldon put a whispered question:

"Anything more about Dorrington?"

"No," responded Steve. "But what's the difference? He spilled it once. The gorillas are all wise."

ON Eighty-fourth Street, a man had begun a steady pace from the direction of the garage. It was Whitey Calban. The mobleader had left his crew. He was strolling along in the manner of a regular pedestrian. Reaching the sixth house, the killer mounted the brownstone steps. He rang the doorbell.

A timid-faced servant answered. He peered suspiciously at the visitor. Whitey's face was a tough one.

"I want to see Mr. Keith," announced the mobleader. "I've got an appointment with him."

"Yes, sir," responded the servant. "You must be the gentleman whom he is expecting. Come in, sir. Mr. Keith will see you."

The servant ushered Calban into a dim parlor. He went upstairs to announce the visitor. Whitey caught the tones of a wheezy voice; then the servant came down, followed by a middle-aged man who looked like a recluse.

"Good evening, sir," said the middle-aged man, as he peered through gold-rimmed spectacles. "You are the gentleman who called me this afternoon?"

"Yes."

"Your name, please?"

"Calban."

"I am pleased to meet you, Mr. Calban; I am Kingsley Keith, attorney-at-law. From your conversation this afternoon, I presume you were coming for legal advice?"

"That's right."

"Thaddeus"—Keith turned to the servant—"turn on the light in the office. I shall talk with Mr. Calban in there."

The servant went to a door just beyond the entrance to the parlor. He stepped into a darkened room. He pressed a light switch; then stepped aside while Keith and Calban entered. Thaddeus left the room, closing the door behind him. Kingsley Keith occupied a seat behind a massive table. Calban took a chair at the other side.

This room was furnished in office style. Except for the bay window at one side, the walls were lined with bookcases that towered to the ceiling. Huge buckram-bound volumes loaded the heavy shelves. Calban looked about the room.

"Nice lot of books you've got here," remarked the gangleader. "Never saw so many in any other lawyer's joint."

"My work is almost entirely research," explained Keith. "That is why I have my office here in my home. These volumes constitute but a small portion of my law library. I have rooms filled with books throughout the house."

"You don't get many visitors, then?"

"No. Most of my clients are other attorneys. I was surprised to receive your call this afternoon, Mr. Calban. What brings you here?"

Calban had been stalling for time. He was studying the layout of the room. There were three doors: one from the hall, which Calban and Keith had entered; a second, to the left of the rear bookcase that Calban was facing; the third, to the right of the same shelves.

The door at the left, Calban decided, must lead either to a rear hallway or another room. The one at the right—this barrier was obscured by the shadow of the bulky bookcase—was probably the entrance to a closet. The shades were drawn at the windows. This was a factor that Calban relished.

"My business?" Calban's face wore a peculiar leer. "I can tell it to you in a hurry. Have you been reading the newspapers, Mr. Keith?"

"I have not," returned the lawyer. He stared in puzzled fashion at the blond-haired ruffian before him. "I must confess, Mr. Calban, that I seldom peruse the daily journals. My research work requires constant reading of law reports and briefs. I am not interested in current events."

"Well," declared Calban, "I'm here to tell you about a couple of guys who were bumped off. They were lawyers, like yourself. Hugo Verbeck was one guy; Clark Durton was the other. Did you know them?"

"Hugo Verbeck"—Keith shook his head. "No. I have met Clark Durton; indeed, I believe that I did some research work for him, a few years back. Did I understand you to say that these men were dead?"

"You bet they're dead," responded Calban. "Plugged. Murdered. That's why I'm here."

"Regarding their murders?" Keith's eyes opened wide behind his spectacles. "Do you mean"—the lawyer paused as he studied Whitey's leering face—"that you know who killed them?"

"Sure," rejoined Whitey. "I'm the bimbo that croaked those birds."

Kingsley Keith pressed hands to tabletop. He stared in amazement. He half rose from his chair; his face betrayed horror.

"I do not handle criminal cases," he announced. "You must go to some other lawyer, Mr. Calban. My advice, moreover, is that you be more cautious in your opening remarks when you discuss this matter with a criminal lawyer."

"Wait a minute." Calban snarled the order as he came to his feet. "I didn't come here to get advice. I've got business with you, Keith. I'm the guy that croaked Verbeck and Durton. I'm the guy that's going to croak you!"

With this insidious announcement, Calban yanked a .45 revolver from his pocket. He jammed the muzzle close to Kingsley Keith's ribs. He delivered an evil laugh as the lawyer sank back into his chair.

"You're getting a slug from this smoke wagon," jeered Calban. "You're the third guy that's on my list. Verbeck—Durton—now it's your turn."

KEITH'S hands dropped to the arms of his chair. The bespectacled attorney was horror-struck. Leering at his immediate victim, Whitey Calban placed his forefinger upon the trigger of the .45.

"Curtains for you," he gibed, staring toward the lawyer. "Curtains—and then I'm on my way."

Calban backed as he spoke. Petrified, Keith made no move. Faced by death, the research lawyer expected the shot of doom. But as he stared, Keith was amazed to see a look of terror creeping over Whitey Calban's face.

The mobleader's hand was trembling. His eyes were fixed on a spot beyond Keith's head. A slight sound had made the killer stare in that direction. His trigger finger had been stayed by the menace which now loomed before him.

Blackness had moved forward from the door on the right. Before Calban's bulging eyes, darkness had taken living shape. A being clad in black had materialized itself. Burning eyes were staring from beneath a hat brim. A fist that protruded from an inky cloak was holding a huge automatic.

The muzzle of the gun was straight toward Whitey Calban. The would-be killer was at the mercy of the being who held the gun. Fear gripped the gangleader. He had been caught on the verge of brutal murder by a foeman who showed no mercy to men of evil.

Twitching lips, blinking eyes, shaking hands—these were proofs that Whitey Calban had recognized the relentless enemy who had him covered. Helpless, the killer was staring into the eyes of The Shadow!

CHAPTER XV
CROOKS UNITE

TRANSFIXED by sight of that weird shape before him, Whitey Calban could make no utterance. In dulled fashion, the murderer realized that The Shadow must have learned his plans. The master of vengeance had entered this room by the bay window. He had chosen a darkened spot to lie in wait for the coming killer.

Curtains! Calban could see them for himself. Whether he tried to kill the lawyer or whether he made a futile effort to do battle with The Shadow, Calban knew that the result would be the same. Covered by The Shadow's automatic, Calban realized that he had no chance. The Shadow would surely beat him to the shot.

Kingsley Keith was still trembling. The lawyer was bewildered by the change that had come over his murderous visitor. He could grasp no explanation for Calban's sudden weakening.

There was another, too, who wondered at Calban's fright. The door at the left of the bookcase had opened. Ace Feldon, with Steve Quigg at his elbow, was peering into the lighted room. The gangleader who despised Whitey Calban had a gun in readiness.

"Plug him, Ace," Quigg was whispering. "Now's your chance."

"I'm lettin' him get the lawyer first," returned Ace, also in a whisper. "That's what he's here for. But I can't figure it, Steve. Look. He's standin' there like a dummy—"

Ace eased the door that Steve might see. The minion stared in wonderment. Neither Feldon nor Quigg could see The Shadow. Conversely, The Shadow could not observe the door through which the armed men were peering. Kingsley Keith was within Feldon's view, however. That was why the gangleader could not understand Calban's sudden terror.

Before Ace could make further comment, the startling situation was explained. A sound came from the book-lined office. Hollow tones made Whitey Calban quiver; they brought a grim look to Ace Feldon's face.

The Shadow, moving forward, had delivered his mocking laugh. Rising whispers rose to a shuddering, chill-provoking taunt. It was The Shadow's answer to the threat that Whitey Calban had handed Kingsley Keith. It was the token that presaged swift death to a murderer who deserved such fate.

Death! Calban saw it in the glint of The Shadow's eyes. The crook dropped his gun arm as he cowered away from the muzzle of The Shadow's automatic. The advancing form loomed like a mammoth of vengeance as The Shadow closed the space between himself and the table beyond which Whitey Calban stood.

FROM his hidden post, Ace Feldon saw The Shadow. In that brief instant of recognition, the watching mobleader was gripped with furious hatred. Ace, like Whitey, was of the underworld. The Shadow, common enemy of gangdom, was the one enemy whose presence could unite all crooks. Ace Feldon's feud with Whitey Calban was forgotten.

Tigerlike, Ace sprang into the office. As he flung the door inward before him, the fuming mobleader brandished his gat and aimed point-blank for The Shadow. With an oath upon his lips, Ace was set to kill the foe whom all scumland feared.

The Shadow whirled instinctively. As his eyes saw the gleaming muzzle of Feldon's revolver, the master fighter dropped as he twisted. This was the fadeaway that he had so artfully performed before the gun barrels of other gangland foes. In Ace, however, The Shadow had met an adversary who was prepared for such an action.

Despite his frenzied eagerness, Ace had swung to a direct aim. His finger paused upon the hair-trigger of the revolver, while his hand swung the gun along with The Shadow's sidewise, downward shift. Ace was aiming low, confident that with his advantage he could surely beat The Shadow to the shot.

A factor intervened. The Shadow, instinctive in the face of danger, had chosen more than a mere change of position to aid him in this unexpected emergency. In his whirling fadeaway, he disappeared from Feldon's view, just beyond the seated form of Kingsley Keith.

In this action, The Shadow was seeking to save the lawyer's life, not to jeopardize Keith's safety. Well did he realize that this new intruder was out to get his own life, not Keith's. The Shadow knew that Feldon would not waste bullets on a helpless man while seeking to finish the menace of the underworld.

The Shadow was right. Feldon's finger stopped at the very point of firing. Keith was in the path of the turning gun muzzle just as Ace was about to loose his shot. With a swift spring, Ace headed for the table, to get his aim beyond the angle of Keith's seated body.

The act was his undoing. The Shadow, too, was moving, in the direction opposite to Feldon. But where the gangleader, a dozen feet from Keith, was following an arc that might have represented the rim of a wheel, The Shadow was using the lawyer's body as a hub. His gun-filled fist swung into view from the lawyer's right as Ace still aimed beyond Keith's left. The Shadow fired.

The shot winged Feldon. The gangleader's leap ended in a lurch against the table. Ace sprawled across the surface, poised upon the far corner and went crumpling to the floor. His gun, flying from his hand, skidded past the spot where Whitey Calban stood.

Whitey had been rigid. The Shadow's drop had caught his eye; then he had turned to see Ace Feldon's surge. The burst of The Shadow's automatic brought him to his senses. Whitey, much though he sought The Shadow's death, had all the stubbornness of a mechanical killer. He was anxious to get Kingsley Keith, the man whom he had come to slay.

DROPPING toward the floor, he planked his right arm on the table, to loose quick shots in the direction where both The Shadow and the lawyer were located. Where Ace had failed by seeking The Shadow only, Whitey was ready to reach the black-clad warrior by first mowing down the blockading human who sat between.

The Shadow had not forgotten Whitey. He was coming up as the gangleader dropped. The automatic thundered through the room. The Shadow had picked the quickest target—the gleam of Whitey's gun. He did not hit the bull's eye, but his shot sufficed. The bullet clipped Whitey Calban's forearm.

Whitey fell backward, groaning. Instinctively, he clapped his left hand to his right wrist, leaving his revolver useless on the table. Beyond the heavy piece of furniture, the crippled gangleader was out of The Shadow's range. The black-garbed victor did not attempt to follow up his shot. There was another man with whom he had to deal.

Steve Quigg had not seen the reason for Ace Feldon's inward surge. Steve, playing a two-way game, had purposely kept out of sight to avoid Whitey Calban, who did not know Steve was Feldon's spy. When Ace fell and Steve saw Whitey aim, the situation changed. Jumping in from the door, Steve turned toward the bookcase in back of Kingsley Keith just in time to see the flash of The Shadow's .45.

Steve leaped for The Shadow, swinging his gun as he sprang. Rising upward and forward, The Shadow swung his right arm like a mallet, in swift, backhand fashion. It was his quickest method of dealing with Steve's coming aim. Just as the mobster was pressing the trigger of his gun, the automatic smashed against the revolver. Steve's shot whistled past The Shadow's shoulder and bored deep into a buckram-bound book upon the nearest shelf. An instant later, the revolver dropped from the gangster's numbed fingers.

The force of The Shadow's blow had carried his hand past Steve's body. Wildly, the mobster grabbed for The Shadow's arm. Powerful, quick as a tiger, Steve Quigg locked in a forceful struggle with the enemy who had diverted his shot. The mobster's body swayed back and forth in the grip of The Shadow's binding arms.

Kingsley Keith was on his feet, howling for Thaddeus. The lawyer's cries ended with a gasp. Whitey Calban had come up in front of the table. Grimly, the wounded mobleader was gripping his revolver with his left hand. Elbow flopped upon the table, Whitey took unsteady aim for the struggling forms of The Shadow and Steve Quigg.

The Shadow, swinging Steve against a book shelf, caught a glimpse of the mobleader's action. But The Shadow observed more than the mere deed. He saw Whitey's good wrist sagging. He knew that the gangleader, weakened, could never steady for the aim he needed. Nevertheless, the situation called for a prompt finish to the struggle with Steve Quigg.

With a mighty surge, The Shadow caught Steve in a jiujitsu grip. The mobster's heavy body rose upward like an effigy of straw. As Steve struggled helpless, The Shadow bent for a mighty heave. The leverage that he employed was calculated to hurl Steve clear across the table, squarely upon Whitey Calban's wavering form.

Steve made a frantic clutch toward the wall. Just as The Shadow began a springlike snap, the helpless gangster clutched the end of a bookcase. As The Shadow delivered his terrific twist, an entire section of the bookcase came ripping from the wall with a resounding crash. Buckrammed books poured downward in an avalanche as Steve's form shot head forward to the floor. The Shadow, like the gangleader, was buried in the deluge that came from the laden shelves.

A lucky break had given Whitey Calban a chance; the gangleader was still too weak to take it. He could no longer see The Shadow; his loose hand was wavering. It was Kingsley Keith who provided the very opportunity that Whitey required.

THE lawyer was terrorized by the sight of the wobbling gun. Showing action for the first time, Keith came up from his chair and shot his arms across the table. Had he performed the simple action of wresting the weapon from Whitey's shaky hand, all would have been well. But the frightened lawyer behaved in a most stupid fashion.

He grabbed Whitey's wrist with both hands. He sought to beat the killer's forearm on the table. In so doing, he turned the muzzle of the gun directly toward himself. Whitey pressed the trigger.

A report. Keith's hold relaxed. The lawyer staggered back from the table, rammed his shoulder into the bookcase behind him, sidled to the right and sprawled among the pile of books from which The Shadow was emerging. Whitey Calban, a glassy glitter in his eye, leered as he saw the lawyer's fall. With a frenzied return of strength, the killer managed to steady his hand for another shot.

This time, Whitey's target was to be The Shadow. He tried to turn the muzzle of his gun, for direct aim toward the form in black. The Shadow ended his opportunity. Half crouching among the scattered piles of books, The Shadow aimed his automatic and fired a single shot. This bullet was dispatched with vengeance. Whitey slumped from the table, carrying his gun along. The gangleader rolled over on the floor, a bullet through his heart.

Rising, The Shadow cleared the heaps of law books and headed expectantly toward the door to the hall. He was none too soon. Continued gunfire had alarmed Whitey's henchmen. A police whistle from down the street had added to their

apprehensions. One gunner had fired warning shots toward an advancing bluecoat; then the entire crew had smashed through the front door.

As The Shadow reached the hall, he saw two men advancing. He gave no quarter to these rats. An automatic in each hand, he opened fire. One man sprawled; another dove for the parlor. A third ruffian, covering Thaddeus, ran back into the vestibule.

Whistles sounded from the front. The Shadow's laugh resounded. The gorilla in the vestibule was firing toward the street. The police had arrived. Whirling as Thaddeus scurried to the safety of the stairway, The Shadow moved across the office. He gained the bay window. Shade and sash came up together. The Shadow's tall form swung out into the dark.

Police were coming toward the office. Steve Quigg, crawling bewildered from among the books, grabbed up Whitey Calban's gun. Before he could aim toward the door, a bluecoat entered. The officer shot down the lone gunner who remained. Other shots were barking in the hall and outside the house. The law was taking charge.

Bluecoats had driven the last remaining mobsters into the house. The space between the building and the house next to it was unguarded. It was through this opening that The Shadow glided. His swift steps, unseen, unheard, carried him from the vicinity.

A solemn, whispered laugh sounded in the gloom of a side street, three blocks from Kingsley Keith's. There was no mirth in the repressed shudder of the tone. The Shadow had gained a victory; with it, a loss.

He had dealt death to Whitey Calban, the murderer whom he had come to meet. But fate had tricked The Shadow. Though dead, Whitey Calban had accomplished his design. The killer had slain Kingsley Keith.

CHAPTER XVI
CARDONA MAKES A CALL

IT was the following afternoon. The newspapers had made huge stories of the fray in which Kingsley Keith had died. Photos of the dead lawyer; pictures of the house; diagrams of the downstairs room—all had provided excitement for eager readers.

Seated at the big desk in his private office, Lester Dorrington was digesting the reports. The cadaverous lawyer was nodding as he rubbed his chin. The police had hinted at a feud between Whitey Calban and Ace Feldon. Dorrington knew that for once they were right.

A ring from the private telephone. Dorrington answered it. Tersely, he ordered the speaker at the other end to send the visitor down. Unlocking the closet, he opened the panel. A wiry, wise-faced fellow stepped from the stairway.

"Sit down, Squeezer." Dorrington waved the visitor to a chair. "Let's talk this whole business over."

"It looks bad," said the wiry man, in a whiny tone. "Trailing's my business. You know how I tagged Berlett when he took the plane to South America. But snooping in—seeing what's happening—well, that ain't so easy. Last night, for instance—"

The speaker paused as a buzzer sounded. Dorrington frowned slightly. He pointed back to the closet.

"It must be something important," declared the attorney. "Duck, Squeezer. I don't know who's out there; it wouldn't be good policy to keep a visitor waiting today."

Squeezer nodded as he sidled for the closet. Dorrington closed the panel and locked the door. He strolled across his office and opened the door as a secretary appeared. The girl was followed by a stocky, swarthy-faced man. Lester Dorrington recognized Detective Joe Cardona.

"Step in," invited the attorney. "I'm glad to see you, sir. It is a privilege to receive a visit from one whose time must be quite fully occupied."

Cardona sensed the sarcasm. Dorrington was closing the door. He went to his desk, waved Cardona to a chair and offered the acting inspector a cigar.

"What can I do for you?" questioned the lawyer.

"Two crooks were killed last night," asserted Cardona, bluntly. "One of them, Whitey Calban, murdered a lawyer named Kingsley Keith."

"So I have learned from the newspapers."

"We think that Calban killed Hugo Verbeck and Clark Durton."

"So I understand."

"Well"—Cardona stared steadily as he spoke—"you've handled cases for both of those crooks. What can you tell me about them?"

"I represented them before the law," stated Dorrington, in an even tone. "The facts are in the records. I can produce testimony from my files."

"I'm talking about the present, not the past. Someone was in back of Whitey Calban. Somebody wanted those three lawyers to die."

"Probably. Your theory sounds logical."

"Can you suggest anyone who might be a suspect?"

Lester Dorrington allowed a smile to flicker upon his face. He puffed at his cigar before he answered. When he spoke, his tone was calm.

"Certainly," declared the lawyer. "I can name such a person."

"Who?" queried Cardona.

"Myself," responded Dorrington.

THE detective gaped. He had come here, in his capacity of acting inspector, to parry with Lester Dorrington. Using the attorney's legal connection with the dead man, Cardona had seen a golden opportunity for a visit.

To Cardona, Kelwood Markin's suspicions of Lester Dorrington had been justified. But Joe had never expected the criminal lawyer to fall in line with his thoughts.

"I have named myself as a suspect," stated Dorrington with a smile, "purely because of certain circumstances. I note by the newspapers that all of Whitey Calban's mobsmen battled the police in stubborn fashion. As a result, not one of the so-called gorillas survived.

"Therefore, you failed to obtain a blind clue which you might otherwise have obtained. There is still a chance that you may get it from some pal of one of the dead gorillas. Had you used the dragnet, Inspector"—Dorrington emphasized the title with which he addressed Cardona—"I believe that you might have heard some mention of my name."

"We got Calban," said Cardona, gruffly, "even if he wasn't dead, for his mob is done. We didn't need the dragnet."

"So I have saved you trouble," nodded Dorrington. "I would prefer to have you hear my name mentioned by myself than from some rat who knows nothing of the facts."

Joe Cardona sat dumfounded. This interview was staggering him. He stared at Lester Dorrington. The lawyer's face was solemn and inscrutable. Joe could not guess what might be in his mind.

"Yesterday," declared Dorrington, "I received an unsolicited visit from Ace Feldon. The gang-leader came to this office and spoke to me in confidence."

"We didn't see—"

"I know," smiled Dorrington, as Cardona paused abruptly. "You mean the dicks who were covering this office didn't see Ace Feldon. That merely proves the incompetence of the average detective. You should make a note of it, Inspector. Pass it along to the police commissioner.

"But to resume. Ace Feldon came to warn me about Whitey Calban. Ace seemed to think that Whitey was a double-crosser. He told me that Whitey had killed Hugo Verbeck and Clark Durton. He was sure that Whitey intended to continue his career of murder."

"Where did Ace get that dope?" questioned Cardona.

"From a man named Steve Quigg," replied Dorrington. "He told me that Quigg was his man; that the fellow was one of Calban's crew."

"Say!" exclaimed Cardona, forgetting his antagonism toward Dorrington, "that explains how Ace Feldon horned in on the trouble."

"Yes," agreed Dorrington, "but let me proceed, Inspector. Ace Feldon told me something else. He declared that Whitey Calban had told his outfit that I was the man in back of the murders. That was the real reason why Ace Feldon came to me."

"What did you do about it?" demanded Cardona.

"Nothing," assured Dorrington calmly. "Really, I regarded Feldon's visit as a consultation. As his attorney, I could keep his statements to myself. I am speaking today only because Feldon is dead.

"But at the same time, I doubted the veracity of Feldon's story. I knew that Feldon thought he was speaking true, but I was not at all sure about the unknown factor—Steve Quigg—nor could I see any reason for the actions and the statements attributed to Whitey Calban.

"I felt sure that Feldon was either totally wrong or totally right. Since I knew that Calban was not operating under my direction—the idea was preposterous—I assumed that he was not operating at all. I decided that Ace Feldon was merely filled with hatred toward Whitey Calban; that Steve Quigg, to play in with Feldon, had made damaging reports concerning Whitey Calban."

JOE CARDONA was nodding unconsciously. He was feeling the persuasive force of Dorrington's quiet tones. The lawyer was using the same easy manner of speech that had proven effective with doubtful juries. The effect was almost hypnotic.

"Today, however," stated Dorrington, dryly, "I learned that Whitey Calban had actually murdered. I read that the bullet from his gun matched the one that slew Hugo Verbeck. I read that you inferred Clark Durton to be the in-between victim. I knew that Steve Quigg had told Ace Feldon the truth regarding Whitey Calban's actions.

"Therefore, I argued that he had told the truth in the matter of Calban's statements. Absurd though it seemed, I was forced to believe that Calban had told his thick-headed gorillas that he was working for me. The whole crew was dead; but some of them might have let out the word. Therefore, your visit pleased me. It enabled me to anticipate rumors that you might have gained."

"You haven't explained the reason why Calban laid it on you," announced Cardona suddenly.

Dorrington leaned his head back against the chair. He chuckled. Cardona's statement seemed to strike his sense of humor.

"Why should I know about that? quizzed Dorrington. "I have already told you that I did not believe the statements. Nevertheless, I have formed a theory. Would you like to hear it?"

"I would."

"For some reason—one that I cannot satisfactorily explain—Whitey Calban was out to murder a trio of lawyers. He did one job himself; he called in a crew for the second, which involved the machine gun. Obviously, he wanted the mob around when he pulled the third job.

"Gorillas are an odd lot. One-tracked minds; one-celled brains would be a better definition. Calban killed a lawyer. They knew it. He killed a second attorney. The gorillas wondered why. With a third member of the legal profession lined up for the spot, Calban evidently decided that an explanation was in order. He didn't want his mob to think he had gone crazy.

"So he probably decided to tell them that he was working for someone. He wanted to name a person whose name they would recognize; he also wanted to make his false statement sound logical. So Calban—whom Feldon justifiably described as a louse—picked my name as the best one to use. His gorillas knew that I had represented him. Probably they thought that I was taking payment for legal work on a barter basis."

Cardona had no answer. The story fitted. The longer that Dorrington talked, the less confident Cardona became. The acting inspector made one feeble effort at a challenge.

"What about Ace Feldon?" he demanded. "Why did he go to get Whitey Calban? Did you know he was going to mix into the mess? Did you send him?"

"Too many questions," returned Dorrington, coldly, "and the last one is uncalled for. Had I sent Ace Feldon to get Whitey Calban, I would certainly not be telling you that I had talked to Feldon yesterday.

"Remember this, Inspector. I am an attorney and a highly paid one. I represent criminals; I never employ them. To think that I would summon a crook to my office to give him orders is as preposterous as to suppose that you would issue instructions to gangsters while giving a third degree.

"Ace Feldon had it in for Whitey Calban. When such feuds exist, they usually result in death. It was not my business to worry about a crook's plans. Ace was gunning for Whitey. Steve Quigg was with Ace. It was natural that Steve would tip Ace off to the coming job. That was the logical time for Feldon to have his battle out with Calban."

"But he let Calban get away with murder!"

"Why not? What did Keith mean to Feldon?"

"Nothing, I guess," admitted Cardona.

"You're wrong," snapped Dorrington, with a suddenness that jolted the acting inspector. "Feldon was fool enough to believe that Calban was actually working for me. Therefore, Feldon assumed that Keith was a man whom I wanted killed. That's why he let Calban do the job before he stepped in to fight it out with the man he hated!"

AGAIN, Cardona was lost. Dorrington had come through with another unexpected statement. The attorney had switched his conversation in bewildering fashion. His theories fitted with a remarkable perfection.

"Cardona," suggested Dorrington, in a serious tone, "you should spend more time in analyzing the criminal mind. As a detective—still persisting in your stupid third degree—you have committed the blunder of meeting single-tracked brains head on.

"I understand the real working of the thinking machines that crooks possess. Of course, I have a decided advantage. Such clients as Whitey Calban and Ace Feldon invariably confide in me. Perhaps, sometime, I may be able to give you definite advice in the correct way to deal with such fellows. Frankly, I should be pleased to do so."

Cardona arose from his chair. He felt that the interview was due for a prompt ending. He could not tell whether Dorrington was using sincerity or sarcasm. As Cardona turned toward the door, the lawyer joined him and conducted the sleuth to the outer office.

"Call me in advance next time you wish to see me," suggested Dorrington, in a friendly tone. "I shall then be able to give you a definite appointment, with more time at our disposal.

"Of course, if you must see me on short notice, I can always spare you time. Either here or at my home on Long Island. You will always be welcome, Inspector."

Cardona received the lawyer's extended hand. The shake completed, the acting inspector turned toward the hallway, while Dorrington went back into his office. Quietly, without a click, the lawyer turned the key in the well-oiled lock.

Lester Dorrington's cadaverous face was placid. In matter-of-fact fashion, the brainy lawyer went to the cabinet, removed the private telephone and dialed Loven's office on the floor above.

"My visitor has left," announced Dorrington, in an even tone. "Tell Squeezer to come down. I can talk with him without further interruption."

Dorrington hung up. He unlocked the door of the closet; he raised the secret panel. Returning to his desk, the solemn-faced lawyer helped himself to another cigar. He lighted the perfecto with nonchalant ease and drew long puffs while he awaited the arrival of Squeezer.

CHAPTER XVII
THE BAIT

"I WAS a sap, that's all."

Joe Cardona was rueful as he made the admission. Two listeners heard his statement. One was Commissioner Ralph Weston; the other was Kelwood Markin.

The trio had assembled in the old attorney's living room. Though it was not yet five o'clock, the room was illuminated by lamps. Closed shutters and hanging draperies cut out all daylight.

"I went back to headquarters," said Cardona, "feeling like a fool. I was ready to choke a reporter who butted in while I was there—Burke of the *Classic*. Then I got your call, Commissioner, saying to meet you here."

"I thought it wise to hold conference with Mr. Markin," declared Weston, "even though we did have to disturb his afternoon nap. The death of Kingsley Keith most certainly appears to be another link in the chain of crime. Particularly since you found a safe deposit key in Keith's office."

"One that Thaddeus could not identify," nodded Cardona. "It belongs to a box at the University Trust Company. So far as I can see, Keith was another of the dupes."

During the short, gloomy silence that followed, Ralph Weston's face clouded. The commissioner stared hard at his ace detective.

"You had a good reason for seeing Dorrington," said Weston to Cardona, "but your results were by no means satisfactory. Let me see that report again, Cardona. You are sure that you remembered all the details of your conversation?"

"Just about," returned Cardona, bluntly. "If I was trying to ease it for myself, I wouldn't have left it as raw as it is. Dorrington twisted me just the way he wanted. I wasn't in his office to accuse him of murder. He talked suspiciously about himself. Had the jump in everything he said."

"Dorrington is crafty," asserted Markin, wisely. "That is why I fear him. This house, Commissioner, is my citadel. I have not been out of it since murder began. My only visitor has been George Tharxell, the one man I can trust, excepting Howland."

"You're sure of them?" quizzed Cardona.

"Yes," stated Markin. "Nevertheless, I feel ill-at-ease even though I am protected—"

The old lawyer broke off. A ring at the door had made him start. The three men sat silent; Weston ceased reading the report that Cardona had given him. A rap at the door; Howland entered at Markin's summons.

"Mr. Tharxell," announced Howland. "Shall I show him in, sir?"

"At once!" exclaimed Markin. "I had not expected him so soon. Perhaps he has the information that I told him to get."

A QUIET man of methodical appearance was ushered into the living room. Markin introduced Tharxell to Weston and Cardona. He pointed his partner to a chair. Tharxell sat down, produced a folded sheet of paper and handed it to Markin. The old attorney's face lighted.

"It's here!" he exclaimed. "It fits!"

"What's that?" quizzed Weston.

"Dorrington's activities in handling estates," replied Markin. "I told Tharxell to look up the records. Dorrington is a criminal lawyer. Estates are not ordinarily in his line. During the past five years he has not handled more than a dozen of any consequence.

"It occurred to me, Commissioner, that I had opened Rufus Gilwood's safe deposit box less than one week after the old millionaire had died. Verbeck did the same with Torrence Dilgin's box. Tell me"—Markin turned to Cardona—"what about Durton's key? What about Keith's? Did you find out when they were used at their respective banks?"

"Yes," returned Cardona. "The banks told me the particular dates on which each of those keys were brought with papers of identity. Keith's is there in the report, Commissioner—"

"Twelfth of December, two years ago," announced Weston.

"And Durton's was used in June of the same year," recalled Cardona. "June the ninth, as I remember it."

"Let's see," chuckled Markin, running his forefinger down the list. "Ah! Here we have them. Parkinson Watts, the importer, died on the fifth of June that year. Hector Mell, Wall Street wizard, died on the seventh of December."

"Then Watts," exclaimed Weston, "was the man who gave the key to Durton. Mell was the dupe who handed one to Keith!"

"It appears so." Markin passed the list to Weston. "It seems more than mere coincidence, Commissioner. There are not many estates in Dorrington's list."

"A lucky point," decided Weston. "It looks like malice aforethought. A criminal lawyer—like Dorrington—handling a few choice estates. Why would millionaires have gone to him?" Weston's nod was the answer to his own question. "This is a useful point, Markin. It bears out your beliefs regarding Dorrington."

Handing the list to Cardona, the commissioner arose and paced the floor. He made no objection to George Tharxell's presence. Since Markin had taken his partner into confidence, Weston did the same.

"Your visit was a bull," said Weston, to Cardona. "Nevertheless, it has done no harm. I should like to talk to that man, Dorrington. I should like to hear him speak."

"Why not call on him, Commissioner?" questioned Markin. "He is crafty enough to know that he is under suspicion."

"Never invade the enemy's terrain," declared the commissioner, "until you are sure that his defense is weakened. Make him come to you."

"Request him to come to your office."

"No. He would be too well prepared."

"Meet him somewhere, then. Place him in a position where he is at a disadvantage. If you could only force him to join you at one of those places where crime was done at his bidding!"

"Verbeck's or Keith's!" exclaimed Cardona. "Say—there's a real idea. I'd like to talk to Dorrington like I would to any crook—"

"To try the third degree, I suppose," interposed Weston, coldly. "Very tactless, Cardona. Very. The suggestion is absurd. Nevertheless, it has the germ of an idea. If we could coax Dorrington to talk with someone who could match his cunning, under circumstances that would hold him at disadvantage in—"

"How about here?" broke in Cardona. "Get him here to talk with Mr. Markin!"

CARDONA swung toward Markin. The old lawyer's face was a study. It showed eagerness to get at Dorrington; but with the expression came evidence of fear. The latter reaction gained predominance.

"No!" protested Markin. "No! It is most unreasonable. I am the one man who could testify to Dorrington's undoing. He needs my death more than Verbeck's—more than Durton's—more than Keith's—"

"But his fangs are gone," interrupted Weston. "Whitey Calban is dead. So is Ace Feldon."

"He may have other underworld connections," warned Markin. "Should he come here, with assassins at his heels to—"

"He would betray his own guilt."

Markin's trembling ceased at Weston's quiet, emphatic statement. A gleam of prospective hope showed upon the old attorney's face. Sagely, Markin nodded.

"That is true," he agreed. "Your men outside are my protection. Yes—Dorrington would enter alone; the others would have to follow. I would like to talk with him. The idea appeals to me—if only you could both be here. That, however, is impossible."

"Do you want us present?" put in Cardona. "Or would it do if we were listening in?"

"How would you listen in?"

"With a dictograph."

"Where?"

"In the bedroom."

Markin shook his head. He looked toward the closed door at the end of the room.

"Dorrington would suspect," he protested. "The bedroom would not do."

"How about the study?" asked Weston. "The place where Howland sleeps?"

"It's close enough," added Cardona. "We could be in here inside of five seconds if any trouble started."

"That would do," agreed Markin, in a thoughtful tone. "Yes it would be an excellent arrangement. I see merit in the plan. Real merit. There is only one objection."

"What is that?" questioned Weston.

"The mental hazard," responded Markin. "I cannot let Dorrington know that I fear him. I must feel confident that he is not accompanied by thugs."

"We'll be here; a squad will be outside."

"I know. But if Dorrington sees that I am virtually in hiding, he will be contemptuous. He must not find me cowering in this room. He must not know that I am afraid to leave the house.

"Suppose, Commissioner, that I arrange an appointment with Lester Dorrington. Suppose I managed to bring him here—to this very room. Could you call first and take me out with you? Could we watch the house, to make sure that Dorrington came unaccompanied?"

"Certainly."

"I could have Tharxell here meet Dorrington. Howland could usher Dorrington into this room. The door is thick. You, Commissioner, could enter with and join Inspector Cardona in the study at the end of the hall."

"That would enable you to overcome the mental hazard?"

"I believe so."

"Good. Then you are ready to follow our suggestion."

"Yes."

AS proof of his decision, Kelwood Markin reached for the phone book. He found the number of Lester Dorrington's office. He dialed and asked to speak to the attorney. It was after five o'clock, but Markin evidently learned that Dorrington was still at his office, for the old lawyer's face showed a pleased gleam.

"Hello..." Markin's tone showed but the bare trace of a quaver... "Mr. Dorrington?... This is Kelwood Markin, attorney... Yes, of Markin and Tharxell... I have a matter to discuss with you, Mr. Dorrington... No, no, not a criminal case. This concerns an estate... A deceased client. It is a matter of long standing, yet one that I feel should be taken up between us.

"Tomorrow?... At your office?... Hardly, Mr. Dorrington. I am retired... Yes, living at my home. I seldom go downtown. I thought perhaps you might come here to see me... Good... Could you come this evening?... Excellent... At eight o'clock, if you can make it... Not later than half past eight... I invariably retire before half past nine. I'm getting to be an old man, Mr. Dorrington..."

The receiver clicked. Kelwood Markin, his face elated despite the excitement which had gripped him, was staring toward Weston and Cardona.

"That will bring him!" exclaimed the old lawyer. "I shall discuss the Gilwood case with him. I shall get into ground that will prove treacherous to him. You must place the dictograph at once,Inspector.

"Can you call for me before eight o'clock, Commissioner? Good. I shall give instructions to Howland. As for you, Tharxell, you must also arrive about eight o'clock. You will receive Lester Dorrington. We can discuss business for a few minutes after I come in. Your presence will give me confidence. Then you can leave at my bidding."

Kelwood Markin arose. The others followed suit. George Tharxell departed. Weston and Cardona prepared to leave. The detective said that he would send up the men with the dictograph at once. He remarked that they would come in a telephone company car. The men outside would be instructed to let them pass.

"You stay here, Cardona," decided Weston. "See that the job's done right. Call headquarters and give the orders to the men."

"All right, Commissioner."

Weston left the room. Howland showed him to the door. Markin beckoned to Cardona.

"You can call from the study," suggested the attorney. "Then you can also arrange the room for your occupancy. After that, we can come back here and pick the place for the microphone."

The two men left the living room. Howland returned from the front door and went back to the study. Silence prevailed within the confines of the living room. Then came a rustling of the curtains by a window.

BLACKNESS came from the heavy hangings. The form of The Shadow stood revealed. Gliding forward, the cloaked intruder crossed the living room, reached the hall and noiselessly ascended the stairs.

The Shadow had been tipped off by Clyde Burke. He had arrived here secretly; he had been an unseen listener during the conference. He was leaving by the exit in the roof, for the empty house some doors away.

The bait had been set for Lester Dorrington. Kelwood Markin, veteran lawyer, was to meet with the attorney upon whom suspicion rested. The law would listen in while the two men talked.

Half past eight. The Shadow must return before that appointed time should he, like Weston and Cardona, intend to hear the details of the coming conference. Kelwood Markin had become the bait; Lester Dorrington the fish; but in the offing was a hidden danger: Edwin Berlett.

Where Weston and Cardona counted upon a duel of wits between two keen-brained lawyers, The Shadow could foresee the entrance of a third. Brutality—gang murder—was an epoch of the past.

Strategy and hidden cunning were the factors that must bring the climax. Markin had accepted a definite course of action. Dorrington, playing his intelligent part, had agreed to the appointment. Berlett, to figure in the game, would have to make a move.

Three keen attorneys: one, retired; the second, active in his practice; the third, a man supposedly dead. These were the men whose cards would be played tonight!

CHAPTER XVIII
DORRINGTON RESPONDS

"HELLO... Yes... This is Mr. Talbot."

The speaker was Edwin Berlett. He was standing in his room at the Goliath Hotel. Evening lights of Manhattan were visible through the window.

"Yes..." The lawyer's face showed an intense gleam. "Yes... I have the information you sent... I understand... Yes. That's all I need..."

Berlett hung up. He went to a closet and obtained hat and overcoat. For the first time since his arrival in New York, Edwin Berlett intended to leave the Hotel Goliath. Until tonight, his longest trips from the room had been no further than the hotel lobby.

Berlett walked from his room. He reached the elevators. While he was waiting for a car, a young man strolled into the hall. It was Harry Vincent. To Edwin Berlett, The Shadow's agent appeared to be an ordinary guest.

Reaching the lobby, Berlett strolled out to the street. He hailed a taxicab. Harry, following, called a second vehicle. As Harry entered his cab, a third taxi shot past. A few seconds later, the three vehicles were speeding forward in procession, Harry's at the rear.

"Where to?" the driver was asking.

"Turn right," ordered Harry, as he observed

Berlett's cab swing up the nearest avenue. "Keep going until I give you another order."

Three blocks up the avenue, the trio of cabs threaded their way through traffic. Harry's cab was almost up to the one that seemed to be following Berlett's. Suddenly, the lawyer's cab swung right into a narrow street. Harry snapped an order to his driver.

Berlett's taxi had gained by the maneuver. It was half way down the block before the second cab made the turn, with Harry's close behind. Suddenly, Berlett's taxi came to a stop. Stepping from his vehicle, the lawyer entered a building. The cab pulled away.

The second jehu ground his brakes. As Harry's cab swept up, The Shadow's agent saw a man leap from the stopped cab and dash in pursuit of Berlett. Harry ordered a quick stop. He tossed a bill to the driver and hurried into the building.

It was the arcade of an office building. Though open at night, the place was deserted. Far ahead, Harry glimpsed Berlett leaving by the door on the next street. He saw a wiry pursuer hustling on the lawyer's trail. Harry walked swiftly. Reaching the further door, he stopped.

Out on the sidewalk, the wiry man was staring toward the avenue. Harry could not see the fellow's face, but he knew what must have happened. A single cab had been waiting at the rear entrance of the arcade. Berlett had gained the vehicle; he was again on his way. The wiry trailer had no chance to follow. Harry saw the man clench his fists, then walk toward the avenue.

Harry, too, had lost the trail. His one satisfaction was that Berlett had also slipped the unknown man. Harry walked back through the arcade. His job was to return to the Hotel Goliath and report to Burbank.

SOME minutes later, a taxi stopped at an avenue near Kelwood Markin's. Edwin Berlett alighted. He chose the street in back of Markin's home. Between two buildings, he could see dim lights in the lawyer's house. Berlett sidled along, studying other buildings.

He found one to his liking. He had made the same choice as The Shadow. Moving through a passageway, Berlett stopped beneath the boarded windows of an empty house. He looked upward, breathed tensely in the dark, then looked and found a rear door.

Cautiously, Berlett tried the knob. The door gave, almost at his touch. The lawyer hesitated; then entered. He produced a pocket flashlight and picked his way through a dusty hallway toward a flight of steps.

Berlett, apparently, was thinking that this house might have the same layout as Markin's, for he inspected the doorways that he passed. He reached the top floor and threw the beams of his torch along the ceiling. He saw the trapdoor.

Peering into a room, Berlett spied an object in the corner. It was a curtain rod, made of wood. He obtained the rod and carried it to the hall. He poked against the trapdoor. It yielded as easily as the back entrance. With the rod, Berlett had no trouble in shifting the trap door off from the opening.

Replacing the curtain rod where he had found it, the lawyer returned to make the ascent. Berlett had proven his agility in his flight from the *Southern Star*. He gave new evidence of his physical ability. He opened a door, gripped the top with his hands and drew his feet up to the knobs. Raising his right, he caught the edge of the opened trap. His left hand followed. Berlett swung free

EDWIN BERLETT

Of the six lawyers involved in this plot, Edwin Berlett seems to be the biggest, most important. He is counsel to the corporation which becomes involved in this fight, the man who has been confided in by many.

and kicked the door shut. With a strenuous effort, the lawyer reached the roof.

Crouching, Berlett moved toward Markin's. His feet crunched on cinders. Reaching the house he wanted, Berlett worked upon the trapdoor that he found. This barrier should certainly have been tightly in place. Yet it gave when the lawyer hoisted.

Smiling at the ease with which he had conquered obstacles, Berlett dropped boldly into Markin's house. He had left the trapdoor overlapping. Moving softly along a thick carpet, he discovered a stout table in the corner. Using this piece of furniture, he mounted to close the trap. Putting the table back in the corner, he stole to the stairs.

When he reached the gloomy first floor hall, Berlett spied the yawning entrance to the living room. Darkness lured the intruder. Berlett moved into the living room. He spied the thick dark mass of draperies.

Again choosing in The Shadow's fashion, Berlett moved to the curtains and found a hiding place upon the window ledge.

Minutes ticked by. Something swished in the outer hall. Berlett did not hear the sound, nor did he see the form that glided in from the hall. The lawyer did not know that another intruder had arrived. The Shadow, following the very route that Berlett had picked, was in Kelwood Markin's living room.

THE SHADOW was stealthy, even in the darkness. He seemed in no haste to gain his usual hiding place. Hence, he was not far inside the door when a sudden dingle announced a visitor to the house. Swerving silently, The Shadow headed for the door of Markin's bedroom. His action was well chosen.

Hardly had The Shadow gained this temporary hiding place before Howland arrived and turned on the living room lights. The secretary looked about in methodical fashion, then continued to the front door. The Shadow, quartered in the gloom of Markin's temporary bedroom, decided to remain.

He picked a hiding place behind a huge chair that was close to a fireplace. The chair was halfway on the hearth; evidently the gas log in the fireplace was seldom used by Kelwood Markin.

George Tharxell entered the living room with Howland. The junior partner took a chair; Howland left and went back into the study. Tharxell, awaiting the arrival of Lester Dorrington, sat alone, totally unconscious of the fact that two observers were close at hand.

OTHERS were awaiting the arrival of Dorrington. In a parked car across the street from the old house, Ralph Weston and Kelwood Markin were on the alert. In addition, four men from headquarters were posted at vantage spots.

Five minutes passed. A cab rolled along the street. It stopped in front of Markin's. A man alighted and went up the steps. It was Dorrington, alone.

"Wait," whispered Markin, nervously, as he and the commissioner saw Howland admit the visitor.

Another tense five minutes. Markin opened the door of the parked car. He stepped to the sidewalk. Weston followed. Both knew that the coast was clear. Dorrington had brought no aides. Together, Weston and Markin crossed to the house. The old lawyer rang his own doorbell.

Howland answered and motioned Weston toward the rear. The commissioner tiptoed past the closed door of the living room. Markin and Howland followed slowly, talking as they came. With Weston safely past, Markin opened the door and stepped into the living room. He was greeted by Lester Dorrington.

"Ah!" exclaimed Markin. "I am the one who is late. My apologies, sir. I was out for a short walk. How long have you been waiting, Tharxell?"

"About five or ten minutes before Mr. Dorrington arrived," replied Tharxell. "I can go, sir. If you wish, I can return later."

"No need, Tharxell. Here"—Markin drew an envelope from his pocket—"I have gone over these papers in regard to the Stevenson claim. I can make no criticism of your work, Tharxell, although I have added a few marginal comments. You intend to see Stevenson tonight?"

"I can see him if necessary."

"Do so. Call me afterward. That is, if you finish the business before ten o'clock. Not after ten, Tharxell. I shall be sleeping soundly by that time."

Tharxell departed. Markin took his position behind the table and looked toward Dorrington. The visiting lawyer made a comment.

"You are still engaged in practice, I take it," remarked Dorrington, "even though you do not go to your office."

"My name is still on the door," returned Markin. "Tharxell, however, is in full charge. I have been actually retired for a full year."

"I see," nodded Dorrington. "Then you want to see me regarding an old matter. One of long standing, I suppose."

"Yes," declared Markin. "It concerns the affairs of Rufus Gilwood, deceased. You, I understand, handled his estate."

"I did," said Dorrington.

"I have something here that will interest you."

Markin opened a table drawer. He searched without result. "Hmm. What did I do with it? Wait here, please. I must go to my study. I believe I left it there."

MARKIN went to the door and opened it. He entered the hall and closed the door behind him. He continued to the rear and opened the door of the study. He placed his finger to his lips as he looked toward the three men who were seated there.

"The key," whispered Markin. "The key of the safe deposit box. Where is it?"

"I left it at headquarters," returned Cardona, in a low tone.

"Do you have one of the others?"

"No."

"Here is a key"—the interjection came from Howland. "It is one of your own, sir. Will it do?"

Markin nodded as he clutched the key. Howland had brought the object from a desk drawer. Pacing back to the living room, Markin entered and closed the door. Dorrington was puffing a cigar.

"This is it." Markin went behind the table and let the key clatter as he spoke. "This, Mr. Dorrington, was given to me by Rufus Gilwood."

"How long before his death?" inquired Dorrington, curiously.

"A year or more," recalled the old attorney. "I received it in confidence. Gilwood told me that he might return for it. If he did not, I was to open the safe deposit box and distribute the funds that I found there. They were to go to people named."

"Well?"

"Gilwood never returned to my office. I opened the box after his death."

"What did you find there?"

"Nothing."

Dorrington puffed calmly at his cigar. He made no comment. It was Markin who was forced to speak.

"I knew that you were the attorney in charge of Gilwood's estate," asserted the old lawyer. "But I hesitated to tell you of the matter. The box was empty. What could I do about it?"

"Old Gilwood was an eccentric sort," mused Dorrington. "That may have been his idea of a joke."

"He paid me a thousand dollars as a retainer," returned Markin.

"That makes it different," declared Dorrington. "It placed you under obligation. Under the circumstances, you should have come to me at once. Why did you not do so immediately after Gilwood's death?"

"Because the box was empty. I was its sole custodian. I might have been accused of theft."

"Of theft?" Dorrington snorted. "Accused of something, Markin, but not of theft. The facts of this case are evident. You and Rufus Gilwood were technically guilty of conspiracy to defraud the government and the commonwealth of inheritance taxes."

"Not so!" challenged Markin. "We did not discuss such matters. Moreover, there proved to be no funds involved."

"The intent for conspiracy was present. You have proven it by your own statement. I was the attorney who represented the estate of Rufus Gilwood. You should have brought the key to me before the box was opened!"

With this assertion, Lester Dorrington arose from his chair and stepped toward the door. Kelwood Markin stared, his hands clinching the edge of the table.

"You handled the estate," spluttered the old lawyer. "You knew about me—about this key. You are to blame, Dorrington—"

"I?" Dorrington laughed. "Talk facts, Markin, not fancy. You have admitted that your first negotiations with Rufus Gilwood were of doubtful quality. Your failure to communicate with me regarding the key points to conspiracy. Your silence since Gilwood's death is a bad factor in itself; your belated statement of your actions is final proof of the guilt on your conscience.

"I handled Rufus Gilwood's estate in a manner both legal and commendable. I do not care to have the dealings of a shyster foisted upon my enviable record. If you value your own position, Markin, you will keep your silence. Your statements are a discredit to you and to the profession which I represent and you belittle."

Plucking hat and overcoat from the chair where they were lying, Dorrington walked haughtily from the room. He left the door open behind him. He went out through the front while Howland, in response to Markin's call, was peering from the study.

Seeing the secretary, old Kelwood Markin clicked out the light in the living room and hastened along the hall. He joined Weston and Cardona. The old man was spluttering with rage as he closed the door of the study.

THE SHADOW was moving from the bedroom. Silently, unseen by Edwin Berlett, the phantom intruder gained the hall. He moved to the door of the study; merging with darkness, The Shadow listened. He could hear the tones of Markin's indignant voice.

A few minutes later, Edwin Berlett came stealing from the living room. As the departing lawyer neared the steps, The Shadow, hearing the sound of tiptoed footfalls, turned in that direction. Even in the gloom, sharp eyes could distinguish Berlett's dark countenance.

Then came a click from the study. The door opened outward. The Shadow swinging to the wall beneath the stairs, was out of sight behind the swinging barrier. Berlett, on the stairs, continued upward.

The intruding lawyer was on his way from Markin's. His mission here was ended. But The Shadow remained. Hidden behind the opened door, he awaited the events that were to come.

CHAPTER XIX
DEATH FAILS

"He tricked me!" Markin's tone was querulous as the old lawyer stood by the living room door. "His method proves his scheming. Dorrington accused me to cover his path of crime. The man has cunning beyond all measure!"

"He's a fox all right," agreed Joe Cardona. "I never met one like him. He made a sap of me. He made it tough for you, too, Mr. Markin."

"Stamping out of here in indignation," snorted the old attorney. "Accusing me of conspiracy. I should have known it, however"—the old man's tone was pitiful—"because of Dorrington's amazing shrewdness. I tell you, Commissioner, the man's methods are ironclad. There is only one way to thwart him; that is through his arrest."

"We still lack evidence," affirmed Weston. "All we can do, Mr. Markin, is afford you the same protection that you have had in the past. You should, however, feel relieved. You remain unharmed despite the fact that Lester Dorrington was here."

"I fear him more than ever," declared Markin, nervously. "I sensed a menace all the time that he was here. The living room seemed charged with a living threat. I am afraid. Terribly afraid."

"My men are on guard."

"I fear danger from within. This house is not safe. I have only Howland with me."

"Put a man inside, Cardona," ordered Weston. "Meanwhile, we'll get ready with a campaign to smoke out this man Dorrington. He's got something that he's covering. I could tell it by his tone, over the dictograph. I'm going home, Cardona."

"All right, Commissioner," responded the ace. "I'll be here another hour, going over those notes that Howland took. I'll put a man inside before I leave."

Weston departed. Markin, reassured by the promise of an inside guard, retired to his bedroom. Joe Cardona and Howland went to the study. They left the door open. Seated by the desk, Cardona had a view of the entire hall. Until his departure, the acting inspector was serving as Markin's guard.

IT was half past nine. While Howland typed off his shorthand notes of the talk between Markin and Dorrington, Cardona strolled into the living room. Turning on the light, Joe pried behind the curtains. Just as he finished his inspection, he heard Markin call through the bedroom door.

"Who's there?"

"Cardona," returned Joe. "Everything all right in there?"

"Yes," called Markin. "I'm going to sleep. Don't forget the man is to be on duty."

"I'll remember."

Cardona strolled back to the study. He sat at the desk and drummed while Howland typed. A monotonous half hour went by. At three minutes past ten, the telephone rang. Howland answered it.

"Hello..." began the secretary. "Oh, yes... Mr. Tharxell... Can you call in the morning? Mr. Markin has retired... Perhaps we had better not disturb him... Very well, sir, if the Stevenson case has been settled, Mr. Markin might be pleased to know it... Yes, I shall call him..."

The secretary left the study. Cardona watched him enter the living room. He could hear the dull sound of Howland's taps upon the bedroom door. Then came a wild shout. Leaping to his feet, Cardona dashed toward the living room.

Howland had turned on the light. Gaining no response to his knock, the secretary had opened the tight-fitting door to the bedroom. From the hall, Cardona saw Howland struggling to drag Markin from his bed. The smell of illuminating gas was coming from the inner room.

Cardona joined in the rescue. Together, he and Howland dragged Kelwood Markin to the front hall. Cardona yanked open the front door and gave a whistle. Two detectives came on the run.

Howland was reviving Markin. The old lawyer's eyes were bulging. His hands were moving feebly. Nevertheless, he was still alive. Gratified by that fact, Cardona dashed into the gas-filled bedroom and turned on the light. Holding his breath, the detective heard the hiss of escaping gas. He swung toward the fireplace. Stooping, he plucked at the handle beside the gas log and turned off the flow.

Back in the living room, Cardona gasped fresh air. On his next trip to the bedroom, he managed to unbar the iron shutters. As the detectives joined him, Joe sent one to call Commissioner Weston. Stooping by the fireplace, Joe began an examination of the gas log.

It was then that he uttered a startled exclamation. Clamped to the side of the gas log was a device that captured the sleuth's attention. It was a small, clocklike mechanism that issued dull, almost imperceptible ticks.

FROM the device projected an arm that ended in a tiny clamp. This had been attached to the key controlling the gas jet. Someone had placed the mechanism to do its deadly work. The set-up was so simple that it could not have required more than two minutes to affix it.

Joe unclamped the telltale machine and carried it to the door of the living room. The detectives arrived at his call, one bringing the news that Commissioner Weston was coming to the house at once. Kelwood Markin, recovered, but pale-faced as he leaned on Howland, also came in from the hall.

"Look at this!" cried Cardona. "It was set to turn on the gas jet. It must have been timed for ten o'clock—after you were asleep, Mr. Markin!"

Eyes stared in amazement. Yet there was one onlooker who experienced no surprise. The Shadow had glided from his hiding place behind the door to the study. Gazing from the hallway, he saw Cardona exhibit the deadly clockwork. Then, with a silent swing, The Shadow moved to the stairs and ascended toward the darkness of the second floor.

Ten minutes passed. Kelwood Markin sat slumped in a living room chair while Joe Cardona talked to the detectives. Then came a ring at the doorbell. Howland answered. Two men entered. One was Commissioner Weston; the other, George Tharxell. The two had arrived simultaneously.

"What's happened?" demanded Weston, as he strode into the living room and saw the pallid face of Kelwood Markin.

Joe Cardona told the story. He displayed the clockwork instrument. Weston walked in and took a look at the fireplace. He returned to the living room.

"That was put in here tonight!" stormed the commissioner. "Who was the man that did it?"

"Only three persons were in this room," asserted Cardona. "We've got two of them right here now. Howland and Tharxell."

"What brought you here?" demanded Weston, turning to Tharxell.

"I called just after ten," replied the lawyer. "Howland told me he would awaken Mr. Markin. Then the call was interrupted. I heard shouts across the wire. I came here at once."

"That's right," said Cardona.

"I found the receiver off the hook when I went to call you, Commissioner," said a detective. "I had to juggle to get the operator. The receiver's on now."

"One minute, commissioner," asserted Cardona. "I heard that telephone call. It clears both of these men from suspicion. The fellow who clamped this machine on the gas log intended to kill Mr. Markin. The clock is set for ten. All the murderer had to do was leave it. In the morning, we'd have found Mr. Markin dead."

"Go on—"

"Well, Tharxell called up right after ten o'clock. He wanted to talk to Markin. If Tharxell had set this device, he wouldn't have called up, would he?"

"Mr. Markin expected me to call tomorrow," put in Tharxell. "I happened to get through with Stevenson early—"

"That's right," interrupted Weston. "We heard it over the dictograph. Proceed, Cardona."

"Howland here," resumed Cardona, "told Tharxell over the phone that Mr. Markin was asleep. He could easily have insisted that Tharxell hold the call until morning, like he was supposed to do. Instead, he went to rouse Mr. Markin.

"What's more, I don't think Howland was in the living room alone at any time. He helped me plant the dictograph here by the door. More than that, while we were looking for places, we happened to take a look at that fireplace in the bedroom. This gimmick"—Cardona raised the mechanism as he spoke—"wasn't there at seven o'clock. I'd have seen it if it had been."

"Which leaves us one man," announced Weston, sternly. "Lester Dorrington. Was he alone in the living room?"

"Yes," rejoined Cardona. "When Mr. Markin came to get the key—"

"That's it!" cried Weston. "The fellow was too bold for once. He thought he was alone with Markin. He didn't know that we were listening in. Well, Markin"—the commissioner turned to the old attorney—"I'm sorry that this happened. But you've pulled through it—a few minutes of gas didn't hurt you. You're lucky; and what's more, we're lucky."

Seizing the mechanism from Cardona's hand, Weston held it before the eyes of all. The commissioner was impressive as he spoke.

"We're going to Dorrington's with this!" decided Weston. "This is the time the fox will answer questions. Here is the evidence of crime. Come, Cardona; we will take the witnesses with us to Dorrington's home!"

Five minutes later, Weston and his companions had departed from the house. A light had been left on in the hall. It revealed the figure of The Shadow, coming from the stairs. The phantom shape merged with the darkness of the study.

A dial clicked a number on the telephone. Then came an eerie, whispered voice. The Shadow, speaking to Burbank, was giving orders to the contact man. The black-cloaked master was planning his own climax for the scene to come at Dorrington's.

CHAPTER XX
ATTORNEYS SPEAK

"STATE your case, Markin."

Commissioner Weston was the speaker. He was the central figure in a group that occupied the study of Lester Dorrington's Long Island home. Weston had taken the chair behind the lawyer's desk. On his right front sat Kelwood Markin; on the left, Lester Dorrington himself.

Joe Cardona was on guard at the central door, directly opposite Weston. Tharxell and Howland were seated in a corner. The study, a paneled room with luxurious furnishings, had been turned into an inquisition chamber.

"There lies the evidence." Kelwood Markin pointed emphatically toward the desk, on which lay the mechanism found in the old man's fireplace. "It proves that an attempt was made upon my life.

"I am a lawyer who was approached by a client of Lester Dorrington's, namely, Rufus Gilwood. I was given the key to a safe deposit box that presumably contained funds for distribution. That box was empty after Gilwood's death.

"Three lawyers have been murdered. Verbeck, Durton, Keith—their deaths indicate that they, like myself, were approached by clients of Lester Dorrington. We have even decided upon the particular clients in question. You, Commissioner, hold the threaded facts in this astounding case.

"I affirm that Torrence Dilgin, who died in Rio de Janeiro, was the last of the clients whom Dorrington swindled. I believe that Dilgin tried to speak before he died—to name Verbeck as the man who held his key. I believe that Edwin Berlett, returning to America, was murdered before the other victims.

"Lester Dorrington is a master schemer. He sent his clients to different lawyers, each with a key to a safe deposit box. Dorrington robbed those boxes. I, like the other lawyers, was duped. In Dilgin's case, however, Dorrington feared exposure, because of the notoriety which involved the death of Edwin Berlett.

"Forced to slay Hugo Verbeck, he decided to continue. He used a gangleader, Whitey Calban, to do his dirty work. When Calban was killed, he had no other agent. He was forced to use measures of his own to do away with me. We know that Dorrington must have placed the mechanism in my fire place. I demand his arrest. I state the charge. Murder!"

GRIM silence succeeded. Lester Dorrington had not flinched. Virtually a prisoner, he seemed waiting for Kelwood Markin to be done. After the tense pause, he turned to Weston.

"You may speak," ordained the commissioner.

"These facts are interesting," announced Dorrington, in an easy tone. "They bring out points that had previously puzzled me. Kelwood Markin is right. There is a master schemer who has designed death. A crooked lawyer swindled millionaires by robbing their safe deposit boxes and letting other attorneys be the dupes."

Howland was taking down the statement in shorthand. Dorrington did not appear to be perturbed. He paused impressively; then resumed.

"The crook was evidently a remarkable schemer," declared Dorrington. "Our friend Markin has reasoned well; but his chain of thought ceases too abruptly. Let us picture this human spider, spinning his web. He chose innocent lawyers to whom he sent millionaires. But he did not stop there.

"He foresaw the danger of exposure. He feared that the men who held the keys might testify against him. So he went further than Markin has stated. He was too wise to handle the estates of the millionaires whom he swindled. He gave them advice; they followed it. He sent each of them to a different man so far as the keys were concerned; but he sent all of them to the same lawyer to handle their estates!"

Profound silence greeted this persuasive sally. Dorrington's cold logic was a refutation to Markin's accusations. The criminal lawyer proceeded with his case.

"I was the attorney whom the schemer picked to make out the wills. I, too, was approached by clients whom I did not expect. I, an attorney who handled criminal cases, was amazed when such men as Parkinson Watts, Hector Mell, and Torrence Dilgin came to me regarding their wills.

"I knew that someone must have sent them. I could not place the man. They gave me no information. So I accepted their fat fees and felt grateful. But all the while I was looking for a game. I was trying to find the hidden lawyer who stood behind the scheme.

"Torrence Dilgin died suddenly in Rio. Then came murders in New York. Ace Feldon told me that Whitey Calban was spreading my name among gorillas. I realized that the slain lawyers might be concerned somehow with the mysterious estates. Knowing nothing of the safe deposit boxes, I could not fathom the actual game. I appreciated but one important fact: namely, that my own safety was in danger.

"I was to be the goat for murder. I handled my cards as best I could. I had my suspicions, but my story, should I tell it, would have seemed more astounding than Markin's. All the while that I have been maintaining silence, I have been looking for the real crook in the game."

AGAIN, Dorrington paused. This time, he looked from man to man and finally steadied his gaze upon the commissioner. He put a question to Weston.

"May I count," he asked, "upon no interruptions, no matter how absurd my story may seem at its beginning?"

"Yes," came the assurance.

"Very well." Keenness showed on Dorrington's cadaverous countenance. "I wondered until recently why Torrence Dilgin had made me attorney for his estate. Dilgin already had the services of a competent corporation lawyer, namely, Edwin Berlett.

"When the Dilgin Corporation sent Berlett to Rio, he did not seem pleased with the assignment. I called upon an ex-stool pigeon—Squeezer Tifkin, to whom I had been of service—to make sure that Berlett actually departed on his plane.

"Berlett went to Rio. Then came the news of Dilgin's death; following it, the report of Berlett's assassination and the burial of Dilgin's body at sea. The two occurrences made me think. A boatload of passengers saw the lowering of Dilgin's coffin, but not one had seen the South American killers throw Edwin Berlett overboard.

"Sigler, old Dilgin's secretary, was slain in the fight that was supposed to have spelled the end of Edwin Berlett. I saw an answer. Sigler may have known too much. Maybe he was the man the killers sought to slay. Who hired the killers? I knew the answer. Edwin Berlett!"

Gasps came from about the room. There was logic in Dorrington's revelation. None could deny it. The smooth-talking lawyer, however, had not yet finished. Wagging an emphatic finger, Dorrington declared:

"Edwin Berlett never left Pernambuco. I was sure of it. I knew that he was crooked, even though I did not know his exact scheme. When murders began, I felt that he was in back of them. I was sure that he had arranged crime before leaving New York.

"Following my theory, I had Squeezer on the job, watching planes that came in from the South. One night, Squeezer came back to Manhattan because a plane was overdue. He went out to the airport later, but too late. The passengers had landed. Nevertheless, he found names and listings. He learned that a passenger calling himself Edmund Talbot had gone to the Hotel Goliath.

"Squeezer watched the hotel lobby. He caught a glimpse of this Talbot. He recognized the man as Edwin Berlett. Tonight, Berlett left the hotel. Squeezer lost his trail. Berlett has not yet returned; but I am positive that he will be back. I had not intended to inform the police of Berlett's presence in New York, until I was sure that the man was performing crime. Tonight was the first time that he was at large.

"Under present circumstances, however, I am forced to release my accusation. I agree with Kelwood Markin. An insidious crook swindled millionaires and made attorneys his helpless dupes. My plea is this: I am the greatest dupe of all. To offset that, I have named the murderer. Edwin Berlett."

COMMISSIONER WESTON sat as stolid as a statue. Not a breath stirred within the paneled room. Berlett's own actions, particularly his pretended death aboard the *Southern Star*, were damaging accusations. Weston could see that the whole case rested on a single deed: the capture of Berlett himself.

"What's the room at the Hotel Goliath?" demanded the commissioner. "We'll watch the place for Berlett's return. We'll get him and we'll make him talk. Six men, Cardona—"

The commissioner stopped short as a voice came from the side of the room. A door in the paneling had stood ajar. None had noticed it during the past few minutes. That door had opened.

Upon the fringe of the rug stood a stocky man whose eyes were peering from beneath heavy brows. In his hand, the newcomer held a revolver. From the spot where he stood, the muzzle of his gun covered the entire group.

It was Lester Dorrington who announced the man's identity. Weston and the others gasped as they realized that for the second time tonight, an accused man faced his accuser. Quivering, his calmness gone, Dorrington blurted forth the name:

"Edwin Berlett!"

CHAPTER XXI
THE SHADOW SPEAKS

"I HAVE heard these accusations," came Berlett's unruffled statement. "In return, I demand that my story shall be heard. Do I have your assurance on that score, Commissioner?"

"You—you have," stammered Weston, as he stared into the gun muzzle.

"Very well." Berlett calmly thrust his revolver into his pocket. "I am here to speak, not as a criminal nor as a dupe, but merely as a chance person who can provide the solution to your problems.

"I held nothing against Lester Dorrington in the past. I never approved of him as Torrence Dilgin's personal attorney. I did not send Dilgin to him; nor did I send the other clients. I can see why

Dorrington suspected me of so doing, for as a corporation lawyer, I have contacts with many big men of industry. But Dorrington was wrong.

"All I ever did against Dorrington was to instruct my man Morgan to keep an eye on him while I was in Rio. I doubt that Morgan did so. Morgan is somewhat incompetent. Moreover, he thinks that I am dead."

Preliminaries ended, Berlett resumed with a more steady tone. His voice came without interruption. Hushed listeners were swayed by the persuasive words of a story that was fully as convincing—despite its incredible features—as those which had been told before.

"In Rio," stated Berlett, "I was present at the deathbed of Torrence Dilgin. The old man gasped words about a key. He named the sum of one million dollars. He tried to state the identity of a living person. He failed.

"Before leaving Rio, two Brazilians—one an attorney, the other a physician—told me that they feared Torrence Dilgin had been poisoned. They suspected Warren Sigler, the secretary, as the murderer. I decided to feign ignorance. In fact, I did everything I could to make Sigler feel that I was not concerned.

"I arranged prompt shipment of the body. I avoided embalming, for I wanted an autopsy when I reached New York. I thought that I could trap Warren Sigler here—not in Brazil—and in that way bring the matter to a rapid head."

BERLETT paused. As he came to the next portion of his story, he seemed to be picturing scenes aboard the *Southern Star*. At last, he faced the eyes that scanned him.

"In Pernambuco," related Berlett, "I found a note in my cabin. It warned me that Warren Sigler intended to murder me; that thugs were coming aboard the ship, to do their evil work outside the harbor. The note told me how I could avoid death. I was to rouse Sigler's suspicions—the man had never trusted me—by meeting the writer in my cabin. There, I was to discuss Sigler as a murderer.

"I went to the cabin. I met the writer of the note, a man who called himself Carlos Mendoza. Sigler had hidden himself in the cabin—his method was crude—and he overheard all that was said. When the *Southern Star* left Pernambuco harbor, I went back in the pilot ship. Mendoza had arranged the ruse.

"Sigler and his thugs were beaten in their fight. I came on to New York, by plane, still following Mendoza's instructions. When I arrived at the Hotel Goliath, under the name of Edmund Talbot, I received a call from a man named Burbank, who was evidently an agent of Mendoza.

"Burbank told me all would be well. He had men watching me, to see that I was safe. I knew that Mendoza would somehow arrive in New York. Burbank assured me of that fact. I knew that Sigler had been in the employ of some swindler who had duped Torrence Dilgin. Therefore, I still needed protection.

"Meanwhile, lawyers were slain—two of them—while my benefactor, Carlos Mendoza, was still aboard the *Southern Star*. Just before the third death, Burbank informed me that Mendoza had reached New York; that soon, I would be called upon to play a part in return for the aid that had been given me.

"Tonight, the opportunity arrived. Burbank instructed me how to leave the Hotel Goliath. He told me how to avoid pursuers; he even stated that one of Mendoza's men would make sure of my safe departure. He also told me where to go—along a strange path that Carlos Mendoza had arranged for me.

"Tonight"—Berlett paused emphatically—"I entered the home of Kelwood Markin, by coming through the trapdoor in the roof. I descended to Markin's living room. I lay behind the curtains of the window. I saw all that took place within that room."

A hush; then a sudden statement from old Kelwood Markin. The gray-haired lawyer was seizing upon Berlett's words to make a new thrust.

"He must have seen Dorrington—"

"Berlett placed the death machine." It was Dorrington who spoke. "This sounds like a confession—"

"Let him speak!" thundered Weston.

"I saw George Tharxell produce that device that lies upon the table," stated Berlett, simply. "I saw him return without it. Lester Dorrington is innocent!"

EYES toward Tharxell. The man was quivering. Edwin Berlett's tones began again.

"Through Carlos Mendoza," declared the third accuser, "I learned the truth concerning crime. Mendoza pieced the riddle. I am but his spokesman; He is the one who saw through the cunning game.

"A master schemer planned gigantic swindles. He spoke to millionaires. He showed them how—through his device—they could avoid inheritance taxes. Each gave the schemer a large sum—Dilgin's contribution was a million—and he in turn sent each man to a duped lawyer. Those poor chaps held the keys, to boxes already empty. For the crook kept their money for himself.

"He had the millionaires go to Lester Dorrington as the lawyer to handle their estates.

Dorrington knew none of the men who held the keys. Thus conspiracy was avoided. The vicious schemer, however, chose Dorrington with a purpose. He knew that in an emergency, he could sign up some killer whom Dorrington had represented—for instance, Whitey Calban—to slay the lawyers who held the keys.

"How was he to protect himself? There lay the deepest measure of his cunning. By naming himself as an extra dupe. By pretending that he, too, had been approached by a wealthy man whose estate had been handled by Lester Dorrington. He, like his victims—Verbeck, Durton, Keith—was ready to hold up a key and cry for pity!"

No name was needed. The accusing words told the final story. All eyes turned toward Kelwood Markin.

The old lawyer's face was purple. With clawlike hands upon the arms of his chair, he was trying to rise while his lips sputtered vain epithets.

"It fits!" exclaimed Dorrington, leaping to his feet. "Berlett is right! Markin never received a key from Rufus Gilwood! I remember now—I had known Gilwood slightly before he came to me to make his will. He was not one of the mystery clients."

"You did well, Dorrington," commented Berlett, from the door. "Markin failed to pin the murders on you. That is why he had Tharxell plant the mechanism in the fireplace."

"Tharxell called up so we'd stop the gas," broke in Cardona, suddenly. "The game is up, Commissioner. We've got our man—"

As Cardona pounced toward Markin, the old lawyer leaped to his feet. He yanked a revolver from his pocket with amazing speed. Wildly, he aimed toward the man whom he had come to hate the most—Edwin Berlett.

Caught off guard, Berlett responded as quickly as he could. He reached for his own gun, but his action was belated. Markin's aim was ready as Berlett's hand came in view. To those who watched, Berlett seemed doomed to the death that he had escaped.

THEN came an unexpected roar. An automatic flashed from the darkness beyond the opened door. A whistling bullet, aimed past Berlett's arm, found its mark. That shot spilled Kelwood Markin on the floor. Writhing, the unmasked fiend coughed out his evil life.

With that shot came the weird rise of a taunting laugh. The triumph of The Shadow sounded through the paneled room. As Tharxell, yanking a gun, was beating Cardona to a shot, a second roar was followed by a cry from the man who had aided Markin. Tharxell's arm dropped while the laugh broke into its high crescendo.

As Howland also yanked a revolver, the smoking muzzle of the automatic turned straight toward the secretary. The third shot, however, was unnecessary. As The Shadow's laugh produced its shivering echoes, Cardona pounced upon Howland before the man could gain an aim.

As Edwin Berlett stepped inward, the men on their feet were staring toward the door. They saw nothing more than blackness. A gloved hand was dropping the automatic beneath the folds of a cloak. A swishing form was already making its departure. The Shadow had spoken—with bullets.

Joe Cardona understood. He knew why Markin's schemes had failed. The old man had told Calban to tip off his gorillas with the false story regarding Dorrington. Scramming, Calban would have left the others for the dragnet.

It was The Shadow who had spoiled that scheme. He had begun the fight that had ended in the wiping out of Calban's mob. Again, he had spoiled Markin's last bet by placing Edwin Berlett as the witness of the old fiend's final scheme of treachery.

JOE CARDONA knew that Edwin Berlett's incredible story must be true. For Joe knew the identity of the personage who had worked as Carlos Mendoza. The Shadow! His uncanny power; his mighty hand—these had brought justice as the final outcome.

Tharxell and Howland, pitiful tools who had known but shreds of Markin's game, were blurting out their stories. Tharxell had formed contact with Whitey Calban. He had carried orders to the killer.

Howland confessed a knowledge of the swindles. Berlett and Dorrington smiled in grim satisfaction as the secretary stated that Markin, a miserly hoarder, had stowed away the funds that he had gained. The keys to deposit boxes that Howland kept in the study would open the old fiend's hidden coffers.

A million would be gained to save the Dilgin Refining Corporation. Edwin Berlett and Lester Dorrington, friends at the finish, could arrange the financial aid that the great company required.

But these discoveries were mere words to Acting Inspector Joe Cardona. The star sleuth was finding answers to his mental questions. He could picture The Shadow listening in at Markin's, finding a clue to crime as he heard the statements of the cunning fiend.

Murderers had struck while The Shadow was absent. Another crime had succeeded through the victim's own blunder. These had been triumphs for the insidious schemer, Kelwood Markin; but the final victory had been The Shadow's.

As he stared at the dead form of the fiend before him, Joe Cardona could still hear echoes of The Shadow's laugh. Whispers of triumphant mirth still seemed to linger as tokens of the vanished conqueror.

Righteous men had been cleared of suspicion. Millions would be restored to their proper owners. A murderous monster had perished. Justice had prevailed—through The Shadow!

THE END

INTERLUDE by Will Murray

This Shadow volume focuses on the most mysterious member of the Dark Avenger's stealthy group of agents.

Known only as Burbank, The Shadow's night contact man was never given a first name, although one story revealed his first initial—L. Introduced in the second novel, *The Eyes of The Shadow,* as a radio operator and television expert, and operating as a jack-of-all-trades in subsequent exploits until the murder of original day contact agent Claude Fellows in *Gangdom's Doom,* Burbank was promoted to telephonic contact agent in the seventh story, *The Silent Seven.* In that tale, he served as an attendant at a lunch counter in Grand Central Station, but this cover position proved too cumbersome to be practical, and Burbank was soon operating from a switchboard at an undisclosed location. From time to time, as he did in the 1933 novel, *The Death Triangle*, Burbank might be called upon to do some field surveillance, electronic or otherwise.

Burbank was one of The Shadow's oldest agents. Almost nothing is known of his background. Maxwell Grant invariably described his face as solemn, but youthful, and perpetually in shadow. Not even the other agents ever beheld his features. Burbank never teamed up with another active agent, as so often did Harry Vincent and Clyde Burke, or Cliff Marsland and Hawkeye, to give two recurring examples. Throughout the series, Burbank remained quiet and colorless. In *The Killer*, Gibson mentions his only personal habit—he methodically chewed gum during the long hours at his post.

Rarely did Walter Gibson shine any type of spotlight on Burbank. In our lead novel *The Key*, he broke that taboo. In this unusual story, while The Shadow is out of the country, the responsibility for managing day to day operations fell upon Burbank's capable shoulders The explanation for this may be as simple as the novel coming in short at the climax, and Gibson going back to build it up. He once explained:

> The hardest page, of course, is the first. But I've found a way around it. Instead of fussing with it I begin to write anyway. If it's bad I figure to come back to it at the end and fix it.

Over the years, Burbank popped up in some unusual situations, taking a position as an elevator operator in *Vanished Treasure* or getting involved in the climactic gunfight in *Crime Over Miami*. No doubt we will be dedicating another *Shadow* volume to him in the future.

The Key was submitted under the title of "Death Millions" in October 1933 and published in the June 1, 1934 issue of *The Shadow Magazine.*

By contrast, *The Case of Congressman Coyd* was written in December of '34, and published a year later in the December 15, 1935 issue. Here, The Shadow temporarily relocated his base of operations to Washington D.C., and in a rare move, Burbank went with him. For an aide whom Gibson often dubbed an "inactive agent"—that is, he was seldom called into the field—this was a huge break from Burbank's secluded communications nest.

Shadow novels set in the nation's capitol form a distinct subset of the Master Avenger's cases.

Burbank as visualized by Edd Cartier

The first was 1934's *The Embassy Murders*, which we'll no doubt reprint one fine day.

Then came *The Plot Master,* which introduced Senator Ross Releston. The lawmaker from an unidentified state grew to become The Shadow's unofficial official Washington liaison.

The Case of Congressman Coyd reunites Releston with Harry Vincent, who posed as his confidential secretary in the earlier tale. In fact, many of The Shadow's main agents are called in on this case. For this sensitive operation, *Evening Classic* reporter Clyde Burke reactivates his DC-based National City News Association, which played a major role in *The Embassy Murders*. Also joining the investigation are Cliff Marsland and Hawkeye.

With so many active agents in the DC area, Burbank's participation is mandatory. We don't want to spoil the story in any way, but Burbank plays an interesting and very different role in this remarkable novel. No wonder Walter Gibson considered relocating the center of The Shadow's operations to Washington. It was a rich backdrop for his investigative skills.

In the years since the demise of *The Shadow Magazine,* popular fiction and movies have been populated by the descendants of this hard-working master electrician, wiretapper and radioman. Electronics wizard Barney Collier in TV's *Mission: Impossible* is a perfect example. Today, they are called communications experts, computer geeks and go by other colorful job descriptions, but they all derive from this solitary man who toiled tirelessly in service of The Shadow behind what is now an obsolete telephone switchboard.

As for the faceless and enigmatic Burbank himself, Walter Gibson revealed in later years his true first name: Luther! For he was named after the famous plant botanist Luther Burbank, Why? Gibson never said.

In an early cut drawn by an anonymous S&S staff artist, Burbank's face was carefully concealed. But in later years, illustrator Edd Cartier, perhaps not knowing Maxwell Grant's original intent, presented readers with a full-on portrait, finally showing the countenance that until then had always been wreathed in shadow....

Now, proceed to *The Case of Congressman Coyd*, one of the better cases extracted from the private files of The Shadow. •

Burbank (portrayed by André Gregory) at his communications hub in the 1994 film, *The Shadow*

Like a jagged thunderhead out of a clear sky came a blast of evil to hover over the nation's capital. But The Shadow struck—and then came the solution of

The Case Of Congressman Coyd

A Complete Book-length Novel from the Private Annals of The Shadow, as told to

Maxwell Grant

CHAPTER I
AT THE CAPITOL

A COLD drizzle had settled upon Washington. The massive bulk of the Capitol building showed hazy in the dulled afternoon light. The high dome of the great building was barely discernible against the foggy sky. Atop the dome, the resplendent statue of Armed Victory formed a shrouded figure amid the swirl of mist.

A taxicab was rolling in from the Union Depot. Arriving at the Capitol grounds, the cab pulled up at the east entrance. A wiry passenger alighted, bundling the folds of his raincoat about his chin. Paying the driver, this arrival turned toward the many steps that led into the Capitol.

Huddled visitors were coming down those steps, anxious to regain their cars and escape the increasing rain. Swinging in out of the rain, head down and in a hurry, the wiry man bumped squarely into a chap of larger build. The jostled man grunted angrily; then stopped short and clamped a heavy but friendly hand upon the wiry fellow's shoulder.

"Burke!" exclaimed the man who had been jolted. "Clyde Burke! When did you breeze into town?"

"Hello, Garvey," grinned the wiry man, as he pulled down the collar of his raincoat and thrust out a greeting hand. "Glad I bumped into you. I just landed in town and intended to look you up later."

"Opening the news bureau again?"

"I expect to. I'd like to get the old office in the Wallingford Building if it's still empty."

Garvey nodded, then, in an impetuous fashion he drew Clyde Burke toward the inner wall of the portico. It was plain that Garvey had something to talk about; and Clyde showed every indication of being interested.

This fact was not surprising. Both men were journalists; Clyde, a New York reporter—Garvey a freelance newshawk who preferred Washington. A few years ago, Clyde Burke had opened a bureau of his own, called the National City News Association; Garvey had coined welcome cash supplying him with stories.

The very success of the bureau had made it short-lived. Clyde Burke, as a news gatherer, had figured in the exposé of a criminal ring in Washington. The New York *Classic*, his old sheet, had offered him a fat salary increase because of his exploit. Clyde had returned to Manhattan; and many of his Washington friends had regretted his departure. Chief among them, Garvey.

"You've picked a ripe time to come down here, Burke," informed Garvey, as the two went into conference. "This burg is hot with news. Congress is just winding up its session, but that's only the beginning of it. Special reports, investigations, committee meetings—they're all in the making. Boy! I'm glad you blew in!"

"Any special lowdown, Garvey?"

"Sure. Remember that recent story—the cancellation of lumber contracts?"

"Of course. The government found them phony and ended them. Going to use their own lumber, instead, from the national forest surplus."

"That's it. Well, Burke, there were millions of dollars involved in that clean-up; but it's just the first. Smart gyps are finding it tough to shove any new rackets past these legislators. The committees are on the job."

GARVEY paused to consult a watch that he drew from his vest pocket. He uttered a grunt of satisfaction; then clamped Clyde's elbow.

"Come along," suggested Garvey. "There's still time for a look-in. See things for yourself, Burke."

"Going up to the Senate chamber?" queried Clyde, as his companion led him through a door beneath the portico.

"No," responded Garvey, turning toward a corridor that led beneath the rotunda. "We're heading for the south wing. Nothing doing in the Senate today. We'll take a look at the monkey house."

Clyde smiled slightly at Garvey's slang term for the House of Representatives. Then he voiced a question.

"Galleries are apt to be jammed, aren't they?" asked Clyde.

"They would be," chuckled Garvey, "if it wasn't for the rain. That kept most of the gawks away. We'll find plenty of space; and you'll get a chance to see the Honorable Layton Coyd in action."

"That's something," nodded Clyde, as they stopped at a south wing elevator. "Congressman Coyd is supposed to be a real orator, isn't he?"

"A windjammer, if you ask me," confided Garvey. "But what's more, despite all his bluster and eccentricity, he's capable. Individualistic—takes orders from nobody—but he lines up followers on all the best measures."

Garvey's talk came during the elevator ride. Reaching an upper corridor, the two journalists entered a swinging door and arrived in the gallery of the representatives. Garvey nudged Clyde as they took their seats.

Clyde nodded; below, a man was speaking. The ringing tones of a strong, oratorical voice indicated that Congressman Layton Coyd held the floor.

Peering down, Clyde made a mental study of Coyd. The famed congressman was a man of sixty, who stood with erect shoulders and high-tilted head. Coyd's grayish face was smooth as parchment; but his profile showed a ruggedness.

A huge shock of jet-black hair topped his straight forehead. His nose was wide and somewhat flattened. His chin was rounded; and Clyde could discern a curved scar, conspicuous because of the tight flesh.

As Coyd turned, the bushiness of his eyebrows was more apparent; also a peculiar squint that seemed to be Coyd's permanent expression. Gesturing as he spoke, raising both hands with fists half clenched, Coyd showed a tendency to tilt his head toward one shoulder, an oddity that contrasted with his erect bearing.

CLYDE had never seen the Hall of Representatives so quiet. But as he caught the import of the congressman's words, Clyde realized the reason for the spell that the man had cast.

"Tyranny shall end!" Coyd paused, with one fist uplifted, as he delivered his tirade. Then, his voice dropping to a deep pitch: "Yes, tyranny. Deep, insidious tyranny, worse than that of ancient autocrats who openly enslaved their peoples.

"The tyranny that we have today is masked. It is cloaked by pretended beneficence!" Coyd's tone had boomed; suddenly it quieted and the orator spoke with sarcasm as he spread forth his hands. "A beneficent tyranny, gentlemen, prepared to delude the simpleminded.

"To us, as to little children, come these gift-bearing tyrants." Coyd paused, his set lips twisted into an ironic smile. "Bell-ringing Kris Kringles, one on every corner, each clamoring for our confidence. Ah, yes, we believe in Santa Claus. We believe in fifty of him."

A buzz of laughter sounded in the gallery. It subsided suddenly as Coyd, half hunched and bending forward, straightened and thrust forth a commanding fist.

"These tyrants have ruled!" boomed the orator. "Ruled because we failed to look for jokers in their contracts! But we are gullible no longer! The schemes of speculators; the falsified books of money grabbers; the exorbitant profits of swindlers who pretend that they are working for the commonweal—these will be ended! Ended for us and for posterity!"

Coyd was dynamic, all his energy thrown into one titanic gesture. Watching, Clyde saw a tremendous relaxation seize the man. Coyd's whole body shrank; he subsided into his seat and huddled there, running long fingers through his tousled hair.

APPLAUSE roared from the house. The gallery echoed it while representatives scrambled forward to clap Coyd on the back and shake his hand. The black-haired man was lost amid a flood of congressmen.

"How did you like that diatribe, Burke?" queried Garvey. "Coyd means that stuff—and he sells it. What's more, he's right. If you doubt me, take a look at that guy over on the other side of the gallery."

Clyde looked to see a long-faced man who was seated just in back of the rail. There was something of the rascal in the fellow's gaunt features. His lanky figure reminded Clyde of a spidery creature. The man was glaring as he chewed his distorted lips.

"Who is he?" queried Clyde.

"Tyson Weed," returned Garvey. "The most persistent lobbyist in Washington. A bird that still hopes to sell the government a carload of gold bricks."

Weed was rising as Garvey spoke. Clyde saw the lobbyist move dejectedly from the gallery. He was about to speak to Garvey when the free lance grabbed his arm and pointed out another man who was preparing to leave.

This individual had an imposing air; his face, though somewhat flabby, showed distinction. His bearing was one of self-importance; there was something dramatic in his manner as he picked up a gray hat, a cane with a huge gold head, and a sporty overcoat that resembled a cape.

Below his full chin, the man was wearing a piccadilly collar, adorned with a flowing artist's necktie. The oddity of his attire was ludicrous; it indicated the conceited type of person who sought to attract attention.

"Montgomery Hadwil," informed Garvey. "Thinks he's the greatest character actor in the profession. A swellhead, if ever there was one. Come along—we'll head him off."

"What for?" queried Clyde, as he followed Garvey from the gallery. "Why does a ham actor rate important?"

"Because," chuckled Garvey, as they made for a stairway, "Montgomery Hadwil is the fiancé of Miss Beatrice Rydel, who, in turn, is the daughter of Dunwood Rydel, who is a steel, coal, lumber magnate—and a dozen other things."

"So Montgomery Hadwil is going to marry into the Rydel millions?"

"Into the Rydel family—not into the dough. Old Dunwood Rydel has promised to disinherit his only daughter the moment she becomes Mrs. Montgomery Hadwil."

Garvey was hurrying toward a stairway to reach the rotunda.

"What's Hadwil around here for?" Clyde queried. "Will that get him in right with the old man?"

"The answer is simple," returned Garvey. "Coyd is in the limelight, and whenever there's a glare, Montgomery Hadwil wants to bask in it, too. The fellow's a ham, I tell you. Wait until you hear me rib him!"

THEY came to the rotunda and spotted Hadwil crossing to leave by the east exit. They overtook the actor on the drizzly steps. Hadwil looked annoyed as he recognized Garvey. He did not slow his long, stalking pace.

"Statement for the press, Mr. Hadwil," suggested

The Shadow, weird creature of the night, scourge of the underworld! A splotch of black, with gleaming eyes of fire, tapering, white-fingered hands that were clad in black gloves when The Shadow was in action; other times, revealed in their grace and strength, with The Shadow's girasol—a fire-opal unmatched in all the world—a stone of ever-changing hue that betokened the mystery of The Shadow.

The name of The Shadow had become a fixture throughout the underworld. The power of his hand had been felt in every center where organized crime was fostered. In London, in Paris, in Berlin—even in Red Moscow—The Shadow had won amazing victories over fiends of crime. But the center of his vast activities was New York. Here, The Shadow was the lone fighter who swung the balance in favor of the law when champions of justice seemed overwhelmed with unconquerable odds.

The Shadow!

Gasping, dying lips had cried that name. Rats of the bad lands had uttered it with convulsive efforts. Others—those whose cause was just—had blurted it forth with thanks; for The Shadow, in his ceaseless war against those who deserved to die was equally vigilant in his actions of saving those who had the right to live.

The Shadow was a being of amazing prowess. A supersleuth, he detected the inroads of crime where others saw nothing beneath the surface. A master of disguise, he had the ability to assume new identities with chameleon rapidity. An indomitable fighter, his mammoth automatics had blazed their way to safety for himself and those who were under his protection.

These rôles were portions of The Shadow's strategy. He adopted them as occasion suited. Yet to the underworld and the police as well, The Shadow, in his moments of greatest power, appeared as a phantom clad in black. As such, he materialized himself from darkness. His mission accomplished, he returned to enshrouding gloom, leaving only the echoes of a strident, mocking laugh as token of his victory.

The Shadow seemed superhuman. His weird accomplishments had left their mark. The denizens of the underworld—toughened, growling mobsters—who spat their contemptuous desire to meet this mighty being were the first to quail when they gained the desire that they had expressed. Through his supernatural measures, The Shadow gained an advantage that served him well. Often had steady trigger fingers trembled when their owners faced The Shadow's blazing eyes. Hesitation had cost more than one hardened gangleader his life. For The Shadow never paused when a death combat loomed. His finger was one that never faltered.

Police reports—particularly those made by Detective Joe Cardona—contained no mention of The Shadow. Until his identity had actually been discovered, this superfighter must be considered as unknown. Yet Cardona knew that The Shadow was no myth; and his opinion was verified by supercrooks throughout Manhattan. The very name of The Shadow was provocative of awe.

The Shadow had never been traced. His entries and departures from scenes of danger were too well timed for that. It was suspected that The Shadow had agents who aided him in his affairs; but the bridge between the men and their master seemed unpassable.

This was because The Shadow chose to fight alone. He utilized his operatives when he searched for crime; in final combats, however, their parts were purely subordinate. There were crooks who had sought The Shadow's agents, just as they had tried to find The Shadow himself. Some of those crooks had gained their objectives, but only temporarily. Death had been their final lot. They had gone to deserved graves from which they could not speak to warn their fellows in crime.

In all his dealings with his agents, The Shadow used the same surprising secrecy that he adopted in his affairs with the underworld.

Garvey. "What about your coming plans for matrimony? Can you give me an idea when the day will be?"

Hadwil stopped at the bottom of the steps. He tilted back his head in conceited fashion, tapped the sidewalk with his cane.

"I leave for Europe, shortly," he announced. "There I shall devote myself to further study of the drama. Despite the envy with which my fellow Thespians regard me, I still feel that I have not yet attained perfection.

"After my return, I shall consider the plan for my marriage to Miss Rydel; all arrangements, however, will remain with her. As for my voyage—I shall be absent from America for at least six months."

A huge limousine rolled up while Hadwil was speaking. A square-faced chauffeur opened the door; the actor entered and the car rolled away, leaving Clyde and Garvey standing in the drizzle.

"That limousine," informed Garvey, "is one of half a dozen cars owned by Dunwood Rydel. I suppose his daughter Beatrice inveigled papa to let her sweetie ride about in it while he is in Washington. Well, Burke, let's hop a cab and go down to locate that office of yours."

The reporters hailed a taxi; the driver took a course for Pennsylvania Avenue. Speeding along, he passed the limousine in which Hadwil was riding. Neither Clyde nor Garvey gave that car notice. The actor, however, was keen-eyed enough to spot the reporters in their cab.

Reaching for the speaking tube, Montgomery Hadwil spoke to the chauffeur. There was an odd tone in the actor's voice, a strange, venomous snarl that seemed at variance with his pose.

"Don't forget, Mullard," Hadwil informed the chauffeur. "Tell the chief about my meeting those newshounds. So he will know that I've spilled the story."

A nod from the chauffeur. Montgomery Hadwil's lips showed a twisted leer as the pompous actor settled back on the cushions. Up ahead, Mullard's face showed a hard, knowing grin. Both occupants of the limousine had registered deep malice.

Evil was afoot in Washington. There had been purpose in Hadwil's visits to the Capitol. Yet neither Clyde Burke nor his old pal Garvey, both on the trail of news, had suspected any motive beneath the surface of Montgomery Hadwil's self-conceit.

CHAPTER II
THIEVES THRUST

NEARLY two weeks had elapsed since Clyde Burke's arrival in Washington. Congress had ended its session, yet tension existed at the Capitol. As Garvey had predicted, there would be news. Clyde sensed it in the air. For Clyde Burke was in Washington with a mission. His reopened National City News Association was a blind. Actually, his purpose was to report doings at the Capitol to a hidden chief located in New York. For Clyde Burke was an agent of The Shadow.

It was common knowledge that certain interests had lost millions of ill-gotten dollars because of the alertness of a competent Congress. Personal investigations and cooperative committee work had disclosed many ills. Other evils were soon to be corrected. If crooks could block or counteract such measures, they would surely do so. That was a fact which The Shadow recognized.

Clyde Burke, summarizing his own findings, was forced to admit that he had accomplished but little.

In two weeks Clyde had learned but little more than he had gained on his first day. Congress had closed; Coyd was busy with committee reports, to be arranged for the next session. It was obvious, to Clyde's observation, that Coyd represented the right.

There was another man in Washington who rated even more importantly than Layton Coyd. That was Senator Ross Releston, chairman of various committees in the upper legislative body. Releston was a great factor in the Senate; and Coyd was aping Releston's example. That policy had won him favor; for Releston was so greatly esteemed that anyone who adhered closely to the senator's beliefs was due to gain ready followers. But Coyd had been wise enough to act in an independent fashion. Hence he was regarded as a power in his own right, a sort of Releston in a lesser field.

Looking for opposition to these men, Clyde could see it coming from two quarters. First, the lobbyists, who were in Washington to get all they could. Chief in this ilk was Tyson Weed, whom Clyde had seen off and on since that first day at the Capitol. Second, those men who had interests to protect. Towering from this group was Dunwood Rydel, magnate of many interests. Clyde had seen Rydel twice; the man was big and portly, gruff-voiced and glowering. There had been no interview. Rydel had refused to make any statement to the press. He and his daughter lived in a large house with a group of servants and kept to themselves.

AT that point, Clyde's speculation ceased. Had it gone further, he might have made a surprising discovery. But Clyde had eliminated as a nonentity one man whom he had actually seen and should have watched: Montgomery Hadwil, the character actor whom Rydel—so people said—did not want as a son-in-law.

On Clyde's very desk were clippings that pertained to Hadwil. The reporter was actually fingering them as he stared absentmindedly from the window. The clippings showed Hadwil's saggy features and stated that the middle-aged actor had gone abroad to gain new appreciation of the drama. They added that Hadwil's marriage to Beatrice Rydel had been postponed until after his return.

So Clyde let the clippings drop to the desk as he continued to wrinkle his brow and ponder. It was not until the door opened that Clyde's reverie ended. Swinging about, Clyde saw Garvey grinning from the opened barrier that bore the title:

National City News Association.

"Hello, Burke," greeted Garvey. "How's the old N.C.N.A. coming along? Any chance to sell you anything?"

"What have you got?"

"Nothing—except guesses. The market's good for them, I know, but these are bum ones."

"I can't use them then."

Garvey came in and stretched himself in a chair. He helped himself to one of the Clyde's cigarettes and began a résumé.

"Regarding Mr. Coyd," he remarked. "I should say the Honorable Mr. Coyd. Well, he's overworked. Jittery, contradictory, blunt with his best of friends—the reporters. I saw him two days ago, and I saw him yesterday. The first time he was haggard and worn out. The second time he was purple and angry. Never twice alike."

"What did he have to say?"

"Nothing much. He gave some halfway interviews last week; but none this week. His daughter is coming on to Washington to visit him. His two secretaries are up to their necks in work. That's all."

"Have you seen Senator Releston?"

"No. He gives no interviews, except by occasional appointment. Don't ask me if I've seen Dunwood Rydel. I haven't—that is, not to talk to. Nobody sees him. He's a sulker."

"What about Weed?"

"Say—there's something, Burke. That guy's been bobbing in and out of town like a jack-in-the-box. Seeing the people he's lobbying for, I guess. You can't figure Weed—"

Garvey paused as the telephone rang. Clyde answered the call; a voice asked for Garvey. Clyde handed over the instrument; Garvey talked abruptly, then hung up.

"Come on!" he exclaimed. "That was Tuft, of the Interstate Press, giving me a hot tip. Senator Releston has reported a burglary up at his place. He's ready with an interview for all reporters. Let's go!"

THEY hurried from the office. In a taxicab, en route to the senator's home, Garvey gave more details, also supplying facts that he had meant to mention previously.

"Foster Crozan just arrived in town," stated Garvey. "He's a man with a lot of money, mostly inherited, who's gone in for politics. He's taken the best way to do it; going in for investigations that will help the congressional committees."

"Didn't Crozan help to uncover those lumber contracts?" inquired Clyde. "It seems to me he was mentioned prominently."

"He did," acknowledged Garvey, "and he's handed more good dope to the right people since. He's due to run for the Senate from his home State; and he's done plenty to talk about in his campaign. He's a friend of Releston's. Crozan has visited Releston before; and he's on again to learn things that will make him useful when he gets elected."

The cab had pulled up in front of the Hotel Barlingham, an old but conservative edifice which Senator Releston had chosen for his Washington residence. Garvey kept quiet as he and Clyde sauntered through the lobby, then entered the elevator.

They alighted at the sixth floor and went to a corner suite. There they entered a lounge room; a secretary ushered them through a hallway and into an office. They found half a dozen newspaper men facing Senator Releston, who sat behind a large desk.

THE senator was a man of somewhat rugged features but his face was mild in expression. Gray hair added to the dignity of his appearance; and Releston's eyes were kindly, almost curious, as they surveyed the new arrival. Recognizing that Burke and Garvey were new representatives of the press, Releston proceeded with the statement that he had been about to read.

SENATOR ROSS RELESTON — suspicions evil brewing and calls The Shadow to Washington.

"Early this afternoon," stated Releston, quietly, "one of my secretaries, Donald Lanson, went into my room to discover two men rifling the drawers in my filing cabinet. The thieves locked Lanson in a closet, and it was twenty minutes later that he managed to get free.

"None of these documents, however, were originals. They were merely duplicates. So, gentlemen, the theft, while indicating real villainy, was of no serious consequence."

With that, the senator arose. It was plain that he intended to make no further pronouncement. The reporters helped themselves to copies of the statement from a ready stack on the desk. Then they filed from the office, Clyde and Garvey among them.

"What do you make of it?" queried Clyde, as they rode away in a taxi. "Sounds like a straight statement, doesn't it?"

"Releston always talks straight," returned Garvey, absently. "I'm wondering though—just wondering about when it happened. It may have been earlier than Releston said."

A pause; then Garvey added:

"Foster Crozan came in this morning. The senator probably met him. If crooks were watching, that's the time they would have picked to step into the place."

"What about Crozan?" asked Clyde. "Where was he when we were there?"

"Somewhere in the apartment, probably. Releston didn't want him to be bothered with an interview."

"You don't think this burglary was more serious than Releston indicated?"

"No. Chances are that the papers were duplicates, just as the senator said. The intent was bad; but the results nil."

GARVEY dropped off before they reached the Wallingford Building; but Clyde kept on to his office. At his desk, The Shadow's agent found a pad of telegraph blanks and began to prepare a wire. That dispatch was to carry a secret to The Shadow, in New York.

In response to this wire, The Shadow would come to Washington. His presence here was needed; a rift had come into the serenity of the scene. Completing the message, with its hidden plea for his chief to visit the Capitol, Clyde reached for the telephone. As he did, the bell began to ring.

Impatient at the delaying call, Clyde snatched up the receiver, intending to be as abrupt as possible. He snapped his opening words into the mouthpiece:

"Clyde Burke speaking."

A change came over Clyde's countenance as a voice responded. Strange, whispered tones, commanding words that held Clyde speechless. His telegram had been anticipated; the speaker on the line was The Shadow.

But Clyde's chief was not calling from New York; by The Shadow's own statement, Clyde understood that these instructions were being given from a local telephone in Washington.

Clyde hung up, baffled. The Shadow knew about the theft at Releston's. How had he learned of it? How had he arrived in Washington so soon?

Then truth dawned; and with it, Clyde gained full realization of how consequential the crime at Releston's might prove to be.

The summons that had brought The Shadow had been dispatched to him direct. Its sender, though not an agent of The Shadow, had reason to know the value of The Shadow's prowess. The man who had sent the important request was Senator Ross Releston himself!

CHAPTER III
THE SHADOW PREPARES

HALF an hour after Clyde had received his call from The Shadow, a taxi driver pulled up in front of the Hotel Barlingham. The driver glanced askance into the rear of his vehicle, wondering whether or not he still had his passenger.

The driver grunted his relief as the rear door opened and a tall figure came into the light of the hotel front. The first inkling of his presence in the cab had been when the driver had heard a voice order him to go to the Hotel Barlingham.

The tall stranger did not appear formidable when he entered the hotel lobby. He was dressed in a dark suit. His face was of chiseled mold. Masklike features, dominated by a hawkish nose; thin, inflexible lips; eyes that were steady—these were elements of physiognomy that made the arrival's visage bear a masklike, unemotional expression.

On the sixth floor, the stranger entered the lounge of Senator Releston's apartment. Lanson was in charge there; the secretary was wan-faced and suspicious-eyed. The visitor gave him a card; Lanson nodded and smiled.

"Go right in, Mr. Cranston," said the secretary. "Senator Releston told me not to keep you waiting."

PASSING through to the office, the tall visitor found Senator Releston at his desk; opposite the gray-haired solon was a tall, middle-aged man who had the physique of an athlete. Sharp-eyed and alert, this individual turned a frank, square-jawed face toward the new arrival.

"Ah, Cranston!" Senator Releston spoke in hearty welcome as he came to his feet and extended his hand. "It is good to see you. Meet Foster Crozan, who arrived today. Crozan, this is Lamont Cranston."

Crozan delivered a strong handshake that brought the semblance of a wince from Cranston. On his feet, Crozan was tall and well-built; a powerful man who seemed much younger than his gray-streaked hair would indicate. Crozan watched Cranston seat himself leisurely in a convenient chair; then sat down himself.

"I did not mean to summon you to Washington, Cranston," apologized Releston. "My wire merely requested you to communicate with me by long distance. I was surprised when you wired back that you were coming here."

"Purely a coincidence, Senator," remarked Cranston, his voice a level tone that held a slight drawl. "I had intended to leave for Florida tomorrow. My luggage was all ready for shipment; so I came ahead today."

"You will leave tomorrow then?"

"Yes. A few weeks in Miami; then on to Havana. After that, Brazil and the Amazon country. A six-months sojourn on this expedition."

Releston nodded.

"Cranston is a globe-trotter," he explained to Crozan. "He has been everywhere. I was fortunate to locate him at his club in New York."

Crozan looked puzzled as he watched the visitor. He saw Cranston extracting a cigarette from a gold-and-platinum case. He watched the visitor lazily insert the cigarette into a holder; then produce a lighter in lackadaisical fashion. Crozan could not withhold comment.

"You go in for big-game hunting, Mr. Cranston?" he asked.

"Certainly," drawled the visitor, pausing to puff at his cigarette. "A pursuit of yours, also, Mr. Crozan?"

"No. I was simply wondering—"

"At my lack of energy? I thought that puzzled you, Mr. Crozan. Well, I am often quite as deliberate in aiming at an elephant as I am at lighting a cigarette. Leisurely action, Mr. Crozan, is quite different from hesitancy. I make it a policy to never become excited—"

"Exactly what I told you, Crozan," put in the senator, with a nod. "That is why I felt that Cranston's opinion would be a useful one to us in this critical situation that we are facing."

CROZAN nodded his agreement. He was beginning to be impressed by Cranston's lack of energy. A pleased smile showed upon his open features.

"Cranston," declared Releston, "today, thieves rifled my filing cabinet. They stole important papers that pertained to committee investigations. Those papers were only duplicates; nevertheless, their loss may be serious."

"Because of the information which they contain?"

"Exactly. Some of them were old data, such as the lumber statistics which Crozan gathered some months ago. But others concerned unfinished subjects: mining, manufactures, utilities which we are investigating. Except, fortunately, some recent material which Crozan was to send me; but brought with him instead. That data had not as yet been filed."

"And just how serious is their loss?"

"Very serious. Because they will tell the new owners exactly how far we have progressed with our investigations."

Releston paused emphatically. He leaned upon the desk and added this explanation:

"You see, Cranston, the great value of these committee investigations lies in keeping certain interests in a state of quandary. If they knew that they were going to be regulated; if they knew that they were to be given a clean bill of health—in either case they would act accordingly and—"

"And defeat the investigations," put in Crozan. "They could sell or buy, according to the future that they knew was coming; and in that manner show huge profits that they could not otherwise gain."

"So serious is it, Cranston," affirmed Releston, "that if Congress were still in session, I would move the dismissal of the committees as a better course than keeping them. Nevertheless, we still have one strong hope."

CRANSTON'S face looked inquiring. Releston raised a solemn finger and drove home his point.

"Washington is filled with rumors," declared the senator. "So many, in fact, that no credence will be given to any statement unless it comes from an authoritative source. Unless I, for instance, made some statement that would bolster the facts that these thieves have learned, the investing public would not rally to support the rogues."

"Then your course, Senator," came the quiet response, "is to avoid all statements that might serve as indicators."

"A policy which I intend to maintain," assured Releston. "Unfortunately, I am not the only authority concerned. Every iota of information that I possess is owned in duplicate by Congressman Layton Coyd."

"Our new Daniel Webster," added Crozan. "A

golden-throated orator who likes to be heard. A windbag on most occasions; but one whose warbles would gain listeners now that certain information is at large."

"It is no jesting matter, Crozan," rebuked Releston. Then, in a solemn tone: "You see, Cranston, Coyd is an individualist. He takes orders from no one. He has the right to speak if he chooses; just as I have the right to preserve silence.

"Moreover, he is eccentric. His efforts during the past session threw him into a high pitch of nervousness. He is really ill, under a physician's care. Yet he persists in further effort. If I could only see him, I might handle him tactfully; but he will not keep his appointment.

"That is why I wished to speak to you. I need some man to serve as intermediary. A special secretary, appointed by myself to deal directly with Coyd. To wait on him, to suit his convenience. A man who can bring back information. One who can be trusted. You can supply that man."

"I presume that you mean Vincent."

"I do. Harry Vincent, whom you once recommended to me in the past and who served me with intelligence and loyalty.* I knew of no way to reach Vincent except through you. My hope, Cranston, is that he may be available."

"He is. I shall wire him in Michigan tonight, Senator. You may expect him within forty-eight hours."

Leisurely, Lamont Cranston arose. Senator Releston was smiling with relief. He raised his hand, however, to restrain his guest. Taking pad and pencil, the senator scrawled a note and folded it. He passed the message to his visitor.

"Send that telegram, Cranston," he suggested. "In my name, so that Vincent can come here direct. Unless you prefer to wire him yourself. It is optional. Well, Crozan"—Releston was turning as he spoke—"this may enable us to bolster our own forces. Our one worry from now on will be to single out our foe."

"We have done that already," asserted Crozan. "Dunwood Rydel is the rogue with whom we have to deal. He wants to recoup his losses from those lumber contracts. What is more, he may have interests in half a dozen of the enterprises which were named in your stolen papers."

"I am not so sure that Rydel is the culprit, Crozan," stated Releston. "He is on the defensive, not likely to deliver such an open thrust as thievery. I am inclined to suspect Tyson Weed."

"Weed is a mere lobbyist. Capable of sneaky measures and tactics. Not nearly so dangerous as Rydel, Senator."

*See *The Plot Master*, reprinted in *The Shadow* Volume 21, available from Sanctum Books.

"He is a schemer, Crozan. We must not underrate him. He has money; he maintains sumptuous quarters at the Hotel Halcyon."

"Quite true, Senator. But do not underrate Rydel. He has millions; and much of his wealth is at stake."

Releston nodded as he considered this suggestion. The senator's face was troubled; Crozan looked serious. Cranston, however, seemed to have lost interest. He shook hands in blasé fashion and strolled out through the lounge, where he obtained his suitcase from Lanson and made a departure.

"What did you think of Cranston, Crozan?" inquired Releston, after the visitor had gone.

"A weary fellow," responded Crozan. "Frankly, Senator, I feel that you hold an exaggerated impression of his capacities. All I can hope is that Vincent will represent the picture you have painted of him."

"Cranston does seem to have slipped," acknowledged Releston, in a troubled tone. "But I feel confident that Vincent will be as alert as usual. After all, he is the man for whom we must depend on contact with Coyd."

WHILE Releston and his guest were discoursing thus, the subject of their conversation was riding in a taxicab, through secluded cross streets. His suitcase was open in his lap. An electric light was throwing its glare upon a metal mirror.

The cover of the case was toward the driver; he could not see the face of Lamont Cranston as it bent down into the suitcase. Long fingers were at work upon that face; they were molding it, changing its contours, applying dabs of puttylike makeup.

The transformation ended. A hawkish visage remained; but it was not the physiognomy of Lamont Cranston. A soft laugh whispered from above the mirror; the light went out as the lid of the suitcase dropped shut.

Five minutes later, the cab stopped in front of the pretentious Hotel Halcyon. The transformed passenger alighted, paid the driver and handed his bag to the doorman. Entering the hotel, he registered; but not under the name of Lamont Cranston. Instead, he signed as Henry Arnaud.

Casually, the new guest inquired for Tyson Weed, only to learn that Weed was away. Being a resident of the hotel, however, Weed would be back within a few days. His suite number, for Mr. Arnaud's information, was 1012. The suite to which the clerk assigned Henry Arnaud chanced to be 808.

After establishing himself in his new quarters, Henry Arnaud turned out the lights in the little parlor of his two-room suite. He opened his suitcase; this time no light blinked. That bulb belonged only in the special makeup tray. Arnaud had opened the tray along with the lid.

Cloth *swished* in the darkness. The folds of a cloak settled over shoulders. A slouch hat pressed upon a head; hands drew on black gloves. A soft laugh sounded as a figure approached the window. Another transformation had taken place. Henry Arnaud had become The Shadow.

A spectral figure, this cloaked shape swung across the sill. A gloved hand adjusted a square box that The Shadow had taken from the suitcase, clamping the container safely beneath the cloak. Strong fingers—their grip would have amazed Foster Crozan—were firm as they clutched a projecting cornice.

Beetlelike, yet indiscernible against the brick side wall of the high hotel, The Shadow poised above space. With a calm precision—a worthy tribute to the deliberate calculation of which he had boasted when guised as Cranston—The Shadow swung his body to the right and coolly caught a neighboring cornice with one freed hand.

Another swing enabled The Shadow to thrust his hand farther upward and grip the iron posts of a projecting balcony, one of a dozen ornamental contrivances that graced the broad wall of the Hotel Halcyon.

ONE minute later, The Shadow swung across the rail. His gloved hands pressed the pane of a blackened window, to discover that the sash was locked. A prying strip of steel clicked its message; The Shadow loosened the catch without leaving any telltale marks. He dropped into the room within. A tiny flashlight flickered.

The Shadow had entered Suite 1012. He spent a dozen minutes in the rooms reserved for Tyson Weed; then emerged and locked the window behind him. High above the tiny lights of the street, The Shadow swung back along the cornices. He clung with one hand while he hooked a length of threadlike wire above the final cornice. Finally he swung back into the window of 808.

Gloved fingers clicked a table lamp. Then, into the light, came the folded piece of paper that Senator Releston had given to Lamont Cranston. Unfolded, the paper read:

> WHILE VINCENT WILL PROVE USEFUL, OTHER AID IS MORE URGENT. IF POSSIBLE, ARRANGE FOR THE SHADOW TO COME TO WASHINGTON AND REMAIN THROUGHOUT THE COMING CRISIS.

To his friend Lamont Cranston, Senator Releston had given this plea. For Senator Releston knew that somehow Lamont Cranston could contact that mysterious fighter who had aided the government in the past. He was sure that Cranston could bring The Shadow to Washington.

Even Releston had not identified the pretended personality of Lamont Cranston with the mysterious figure of The Shadow. Like others, the senator would believe that Cranston had left Washington for Florida.

Beneath the light, The Shadow's hand began inscribing messages. One was a summons to Harry Vincent; the others were coded orders to additional agents. The Shadow was bringing a small but competent corps of workers to Washington, there to aid him in the protective measures that Senator Releston required.

Today, two suspects had been mentioned; Tyson Weed and Dunwood Rydel. For the present, The Shadow was prepared to concentrate on one, Tyson Weed. Should the lobbyist prove inconsequential, an investigation of the magnate would be in order. Tyson Weed was due to be covered by The Shadow.

CHAPTER IV
HARRY REPORTS

THREE days after The Shadow's conference with Senator Releston and Foster Crozan, a sedan pulled up in front of an old brownstone house in the northwest section of Washington. The car belonged to Senator Releston; the young man who alighted from it was a brisk, clean-cut chap who had but recently come to town.

This was Harry Vincent, gaining his first view of the old mansion which Congressman Layton Coyd had chosen as a residence. Entrance was gained to the house by a pair of crumbling brownstone steps. Harry ascended them and rang the bell.

A weary, doubled-up servant admitted the visitor. The fellow blinked weakly at Harry, not recognizing him. Then came a man's voice, brisk from the hall:

"If it's Mr. Vincent, Mose, step by and let him enter."

Mose saw Harry nod; wearily, the ancient servitor allowed him to enter. In a spacious, gloomy hallway, Harry found himself face to face with a well-groomed young man, who extended his hand and delivered a pleasant smile. This chap's expression was friendly.

"My name's Jurrick," he stated. "Don Jurrick. One of Mr. Coyd's secretaries. The congressman received Senator Releston's telephone call. He says that he can see you."

Jurrick led the way toward a flight of stairs. They went upstairs and turned toward the front of the house. They came into a huge room, across it a doorway that opened into a bedroom. This was Coyd's present quarters; the place was a medley of living room, reception hall and office.

SEATED by a desk was Layton Coyd, garbed in dressing gown, his legs wrapped in a blanket.

Harry noted the weariness of the man's grayish face. He also observed what Clyde had noticed; the parchmentlike texture of Coyd's skin, with the crescent scar that marred chin and cheek.

But Harry was not impressed with the ruggedness of the congressman's profile. For Coyd's features were relaxed; they seemed weather-beaten rather than well-molded.

Beside Coyd was a tall, sallow-faced man with black hair and a pointed mustache. This individual had an air of self-assurance; his attire was immaculate, his poise seemed somewhat foreign. Jurrick introduced Harry to Coyd. The congressman shook hands without rising; then introduced Harry to the sallow-faced man, whom he named Doctor Borneau.

"Has Mr. Coyd been sick?" inquired Harry in an undertone.

"The congressman has suffered from heat strokes and nervousness," replied Jurrick. "Doctor Borneau happened to be in Washington and arranged to act as consultant. He's been on the case several months. He happens to remain in Washington as he is preparing a series of speeches on Oriental diseases."

Before Harry could add a comment to the conversation, another young man joined the group. He had shocky, red hair and a freckled face; he shook hands with Harry awkwardly.

"Hugh Tabbert, my fellow secretary," stated Jurrick. "Tabbert comes from the congressman's home state, while I'm an extra hand here in Washington. Tabbert knows all the hometown politicians by their front names. That's where he had the edge on me."

Jurrick's tone was jocular and friendly; but Tabbert seemed to resent it. Harry took that as an admission of inferiority on Tabbert's part; for Jurrick had obviously meant the remark as nothing more than a mild jest.

"Tabbert!" Coyd snapped the order from his chair. "Come here. Doctor Borneau wants to question you about my medicine."

TABBERT approached the pair; Borneau, taking the congressman's pulse, questioned him mildly, in a foreign accent.

"You have been exact with the doses?" inquired the physician.

"Just as close to the dot as I can make them, sir," returned Tabbert.

"That is good." Borneau nodded. "Yes. Very good. We shall keep them on. Maybe perhaps one little change—"

He paused and drew a pad from his pocket. He made notations and handed them to Tabbert; then glanced at his watch and nodded.

"I'm tired, Doctor," complained Coyd, his tone showing irritability. "What good is medicine—treatment—if everything continues to annoy me? My mind seems bewildered—whirling—"

"Too much of the overwork," interposed Doctor Borneau, with a smile. "*Ma foi, m'sieu'*! Of what good can be the medicine if you do not give the cooperation?"

"I suppose you're right, Doctor," grumbled Coyd. "By the way, Tabbert"—Coyd addressed the dull-faced secretary, who was stirring a glass of liquid—"what have you heard from Lucian? When does he intend to have that bust finished?"

"In a few days, sir," responded Tabbert. "He will bring it here, sir, for your approval."

"Be sure he does so." Coyd glowered angrily. "Bah! Such delay! I was afraid he had broken another cast and would want me to go through another of those plagued sittings. Such things annoy me!" Coyd's voice had become harsh; his fists were upraised and twitching. "Confound it! Everything annoys me! This place is becoming a madhouse—"

Coyd was coming to his feet, gesturing wildly as he flung aside the blanket that encircled his legs. Doctor Borneau sprang forward and gripped the congressman's arm. At a gesture from the physician, Tabbert set down the glass and lent his aid. Under their combined pressure, Coyd subsided. He huddled in his chair, muttering as he thrust his fingers through his shocky, black hair.

Harry Vincent had watched the quick changes that had come over the congressman; then looked toward Jurrick. Something in his glance made the friendly secretary realize that an explanation was necessary; for Jurrick gave one in an undertone.

"Mr. Coyd seldom has such outbursts" was Jurrick's whisper. "Certain matters arouse his anger; the matter of the bust is one of them. The native sons want a bronze bust of Mr. Coyd for the state capital. They have been pestering him for its delivery."

"And the bust is nearly ready?"

"Yes. A sculptor named Lucian is molding it from a plaster cast. That is what is causing the delay. A few months ago, Lucian took a mask impression direct from Mr. Coyd's face. It was accidentally broken, and he had to take a new one. That irritated Mr. Coyd, and justifiably—for those sittings were a nuisance. But the bust is almost done at last—"

Jurrick broke off and turned toward the door. He bowed and advanced to meet an attractive girl, who was entering from the hall. Harry heard the secretary address her as Miss Coyd; he knew that this must be the congressman's daughter.

COYD opened his eyes wearily, then smiled pleasantly as his daughter approached. An attractive brunette, trimly attired, the girl had arrived as a welcome visitor. She leaned forward and kissed her father's forehead; then sat down in a chair which Tabbert clumsily placed beside the congressman's big chair.

"Hello, Evelyn," said Coyd, slowly. "You seem very cheerful today, dear. Are you all ready for your vacation in Virginia?"

"The lodge is opened, Daddy," returned the girl, brightly. "The servants are just waiting for us to come there."

"For us?"

"Certainly. You are going with me, Daddy."

Coyd shook his head. The girl turned appealingly to Doctor Borneau. The physician spoke to Coyd.

"A trip to Virginia would do you good, sir," declared the doctor. "It is part of my prescription. At the same time, Miss Coyd, I believe that it would be for the best if your father should rest before the journey."

"That's right," rumbled Coyd, becoming more active. "Run on down to Virginia, Evelyn. Stay there at the lodge. I shall join you later."

"Very well." The girl paused after giving agreement. Then: "Would you mind, Daddy, if I took a friend to Virginia with me?"

"A friend? Who?"

"Beatrice Rydel."

COYD came upward in his chair. He glared angrily at his daughter and began to pound his fist upon a table that was beside him.

"Dunwood Rydel's own daughter!" stormed Coyd. "Why should you be friendly with her, of all persons? Her father and I are enemies, Evelyn—"

"But Beatrice and I are friends."

"Perhaps. Nevertheless, that is no reason to invite her to visit you."

"Please, Daddy, don't stir yourself into another temper. Beatrice won't annoy you if she visits with me."

"Maybe not." Coyd settled back in his chair. "After all, the girl is nothing but an empty-headed chatterbox; and I've put up with many of that sort in the State legislature. Very well, Evelyn; take her to Virginia with you."

That matter settled, Coyd glanced across the room and spied Harry Vincent. He had practically forgotten the stranger's presence. Coyd decided that it was time to discuss business.

"I welcome your visit, Mr. Vincent," he declared. "Senator Releston tells me that you are to serve as his own representative. An excellent plan, for it will enable me to keep better contact with the senator. I agree on the point that he and I should cooperate.

"There is nothing, however, for us to discuss today. My mind is burdened with troublesome details; after they are cleared, I shall send for you, Mr. Vincent. Good day, sir, and my regards to Senator Releston."

It was an abrupt dismissal, yet not intended as a rude one. Harry understood that Coyd's thoughts were hectic at present.

GOING down the brownstone steps, Harry engaged in a flurry of thoughts. He had learned trivialities in this first visit to Coyd's; yet in that mass of chaff there might be some point of value.

Coyd's indisposition, Doctor Borneau's presence, the congressman's irritability over the matter of the delayed bust—these were facts worth noting. Most important, however, was the information that Beatrice Rydel was to be Evelyn Coyd's guest at the country residence which Congressman Coyd had take in Virginia.

This would be of interest to The Shadow, thought Harry, as he entered his sedan and drove away. Convinced in that impression, he was too occupied to notice present points that he should have observed.

One was a face that appeared at an upstairs window—Coyd's bedroom—and watched The Shadow's agent drive away. That countenance was Hugh Tabbert's; and the face was much more alert than Harry would have believed possible.

The other factor that escaped Harry's observation was a parked coupé across the street. From behind the steering wheel of that vehicle, a thick-faced man with a heavy, black mustache had been watching the front of Congressman Coyd's home.

With glaring eyes, this mustached observer watched Harry drive away; then grunted with satisfaction as he settled back in his seat and resumed his observation of Coyd's residence. With stubby fingers, the spy noted down the license number of Harry's car.

Events were brewing about the mansion wherein Layton Coyd resided. Cross purposes were at work; and the very atmosphere presaged the coming of the crisis that Senator Releston had anticipated. Senator Releston had been wise in his request for The Shadow's aid.

CHAPTER V
TWO CAMPS

DUSK had followed afternoon. Lights were agleam in a stately mansion that stood back from the traffic of a Washington avenue. This was the

Washington colonial residence of Dunwood Rydel, the millionaire magnate who felt that his interests commanded his stay in Washington.

Behind the huge colonial mansion, the garage formed a wide, squat building. It had once been a stable; now it housed the half dozen cars that formed Rydel's fleet of automotive vehicles. Back of the garage was a high, thick hedge; it was from this barrier that a sidling figure entered the grounds, unseen against the blackness of the hedge itself.

Heedless of the patrolling servants who kept watch for prowlers, this prowler glided along the side wall of the garage and reached a small door at the front corner. A gloved hand turned the knob; a shrouded figure entered a darkened passage. The visitant found another door and opened it inch by inch.

The sound of voices came from the big storage room of the garage, where four cars were parked in a row.

The Shadow had seen the lights through the rear windows. He had stopped at the garage to listen in on any conversation that might prove of interest. The voices that he heard were those of two chauffeurs in Rydel's employ. One was standing ready to enter a large imported coupé.

"I guess the master's ready and waiting, Chet," declared the chauffeur by the car. "I'd better not keep him waiting. He's got an appointment this evening."

"Where's he going, Bill?" queried the idle chauffeur. "Down to the Lotus Club?"

"Yeah, for dinner. That's why he's starting early. He always goes there when Miss Beatrice is away. Say—is Mullard driving clear down to that place in Virginia?"

"No, He just took Miss Beatrice into town to meet her girlfriend. Won't be back for a while, though; he's probably getting those new tires for the limousine."

Bill clambered aboard the coupé and backed it from the open door of the garage. Evidently Rydel had been waiting Bill's appearance.

The Shadow swung suddenly about as Chet came toward the little door where he was stationed. The chauffeur was whistling; the trill announced his approach. The Shadow moved out through the little front door and blended with blackness against the wall. The move was a wise one, for Chet stepped into view a moment later. The chauffeur paused to light a cigarette.

Forced to delay his departure, The Shadow waited. He had no further purpose here; as soon as Chet was gone, he intended to glide along. But before the chauffeur could step away, a flashlight glimmered. One of Rydel's inspecting servants arrived to talk to the chauffeur.

"Hello, Whitey," greeted Chet. "Giving the grounds a look-over like the boss wants?"

"Yeah," growled Whitey. "Fine job for a butler, ain't it? Like Toby, being a valet, and doing his bit on the other side of the house. Scouring the shrubbery."

"Hubert and Tobias," chuckled Chet. "Great monikers for a couple of guys like you fellows. Well, I'll still call you Whitey and Toby—"

"Here's Toby now," interrupted Whitey, swinging toward the gravel drive. "Hey, Toby—"

WHITEY'S greeting ended as a harsh exclamation came from Toby. The approaching watchman had pressed the button of his flashlight. Purely by accident, the glare had focused on the wall of the garage; there it had revealed the blackened outline of The Shadow. Toby had seen the living shape.

Hard upon Toby's discovery came action. Before the servant had opportunity to catalog the physical appearance of this black intruder, The Shadow's swift form surged forward. Toby swung hard with a lead-weighted club that he was carrying. A gloved hand plucked his descending wrist.

With a sharp cry, Toby spun upward; his body was heaved into a somersault. His fingers lost their clutch upon the club; his flashlight went spinning through the air. Toby flattened on the gravel and rolled over into a helpless sprawl.

Two reserves were springing into action; Whitey, with a club and flashlight; Chet, yanking a revolver that he carried while about the garage. As Whitey's torch cleaved the darkness, a black form hurtled in to meet him. Gloved hands found their grip as The Shadow joined in swift grapple.

Flashlight and club went flying. With a grunt, Whitey sagged beneath choking fingers that clamped his throat. Then The Shadow flung the husky guardian to the gravel; coming up to hands and knees, Whitey paused, half dazed beside the groggy form of Toby.

Chet had snatched the flashlight from the drive. Away from the garage, he circled the gleam, frantically trying to spot the intruding fighter. A sudden exclamation of success came from the chauffeur as a figure sprang suddenly into the light. Chet swung the revolver, seeking quick aim.

A gloved fist *swished* through the glare. Buffered knuckles clipped Chet's chin. The chauffeur reeled backward; then thudded to earth. Torch and revolver slipped from the chauffeur's loosened grasp while The Shadow swished past the garage and gained the hedge beyond. Silent, mirthless, he was gone when the half-groggy servants came clambering dizzily to their feet.

AT the Lotus Club, Dunwood Rydel was seated at a corner table in the grillroom, confining his diet to a bowl of milk and toast while he growled to a companion opposite. Big, portly and glowering, Rydel seemed in ill sorts. His friend, a quiet, mild-mannered man, was shaking his head in disapproval.

As Whitey's torch cleaved the darkness, a black form hurtled in to meet him.

A stranger entered the grillroom and seated himself at a table opposite. His features were the hawklike guise of Henry Arnaud. Departing from Rydel's terrain, The Shadow had headed for this club that he had heard the chauffeurs mention. His manner of entry had been simple. He had used a letter of introduction signed by Lamont Cranston, whose name was known in all exclusive clubs.

"You're a lawyer, Wimbledon," The Shadow heard Rydel say. "You ought to agree with me. I tell you, there's not been fair discrimination."

"You are wrong, Rydel," returned the mild-mannered man. "True, you have suffered through certain investigations. The findings, however, justified."

"But why are they pressing on me all the time? Striking at interests which concern me? Why don't they let up? Why don't they pick on other big-money men?"

"They will," assured Wimbledon. "Give them time, Rydel. Many investigations are under way."

"Humph."

With this utterance, Rydel pushed aside his bowl of milk and toast and delivered a sour expression that befitted his dyspeptic nature.

"Why stay in Washington?" queried Wimbledon. "You have business in New York. Why not spend your time there, Rydel?"

"I'll have to go to New York," grumbled the magnate. "But I'll be back here, Wimbledon. I'll tell you why. Foster Crozan is here—has been, off and on, for weeks. He's staying at that hotel where Senator Releston lives."

"You don't like Crozan, do you?"

"Why should I? In order to boom his campaign for next fall, he's stirred things up in that state where he lives. He wants to be a senator; that's why he pushed himself into the investigation of the lumber contracts."

"That shows no personal animosity on his part. You merely chanced to be a contract holder."

"I don't trust Crozan. He's out to win more than that Senate election. He blackened me once; he will try it again. He's jealous of my wealth."

"Preposterous, Rydel. Crozan is a millionaire in his own right. True, he has ambitions; but they are honorable ones. Take my advice as a friend, Rydel; do not let your animosity carry you too far against a man of integrity such as Crozan. Your own malice will boomerang and injure you instead of him."

THE two men arose and left the grillroom, en route to some business conference. The Shadow followed. Through this brief observation he had gained a definite idea of Dunwood Rydel. He had heard enough to know of the man's prejudices; but he had recognized also that he had seen but the surface of Dunwood Rydel. Later, when the occasion might demand it, The Shadow could learn more.

Another point gained by The Shadow: he knew that Rydel's servants had not informed him of the affray out at the house. Evidently they had decided that their report of a mysterious prowler could wait until their master returned.

In the easy fashion of Henry Arnaud, The Shadow left the Lotus Club. He entered a taxi and told the driver to take him by the shortest route to the Hotel Halcyon. As the cab rolled along, The Shadow glanced at his watch. His whispered laugh betokened satisfaction.

It was nearly eight o'clock, an important hour in The Shadow's plans for tonight. For The Shadow—as Arnaud—had learned today that Tyson Weed was due back in Washington, scheduled to arrive at eight this evening.

A soft laugh came from The Shadow's disguised lips. While waiting for Weed's return, he had looked in on one camp; that of Dunwood Rydel. At present, he was on his way to investigate the other headquarters.

Within the next few hours, The Shadow intended to learn some inside facts concerning Tyson Weed's business in Washington.

CHAPTER VI
THE DOUBLE DEAL

WHEN The Shadow alighted at the Hotel Halcyon, he still affected the easy guise of Henry Arnaud. It was a part less leisurely than the languid role of Lamont Cranston; nevertheless, his actions as Arnaud gave no appearance of great haste.

Perhaps that was why The Shadow, glancing casually across the street, managed to spy a hunch-shouldered figure sidling from view beyond the railed front of an old, darkened house. The man whom The Shadow noted had not expected observation from so casual an arrival as this one who had stepped from the cab.

A thin smile showed on The Shadow's lips, as he entered the hotel. The man whom he had spied was one whom only the keenest eyes could detect. That huddled figure was "Hawkeye," one of The Shadow's own agents, a trailer whom The Shadow used on numerous occasions.

Inside the hotel lobby, The Shadow observed a husky, well-built man seated in a corner chair. This chap looked heavier, more rough-and-ready than Harry Vincent; at the same time, his features were clean-cut, and he was quite at home in the gilt surroundings of the Hotel Halcyon. This was Cliff Marsland, another of The Shadow's agents.

Across the lobby, lounging by a cigar counter, was a thick-faced man with heavy, dark mustache. Swarthy of countenance, wise of manner, this individual was wearing a Derby hat tilted down over his sharp, almost glaring eyes.

Though not conspicuous, the mustached man came immediately within The Shadow's keen range of observation. While pausing at the news stand to make a purchase, The Shadow, mild in his guise of Arnaud, found opportunity to study the fellow at close range, without the man knowing it.

Walking toward the elevator, The Shadow noted Cliff Marsland watching the man in the Derby. It was not surprising that Cliff should be making such observation on his own initiative. The fellow with the mustache had the air of a private detective. Cliff, knowing the ways of such worthies, had not been lax in noting it.

REACHING 808, The Shadow entered a darkened room. He spoke in a whisper; a quiet voice answered from the corner. A man was stationed there in the darkness, earphones clamped to his head.

His stooped shoulders were barely visible in the light from the window. This was Burbank, The Shadow's contact man; he had been summoned on from New York to take up his post here during The Shadow's temporary absence.

A buzz sounded from beside the table where Burbank was seated. The contact man removed the earphones and picked up the telephone while The Shadow waited. Burbank held a brief, even-toned conversation; then hung up and reported to The Shadow in the darkness.

"Weed has arrived," stated Burbank. "Marsland recognized him from Burke's description. Weed has gone up in the elevator. Marsland also reports a man loafing by the cigar stand who looks like a dick. The fellow took an interest in Weed's arrival."

His report given, Burbank again donned the earphones. The Shadow turned on a light above another table. He opened an envelope that was lying there; from it he produced a coded report. This was from Harry Vincent; it told the details of Harry's recent trip to Coyd's.

Harry's report, however, made no mention of the mustached man in the coupé; for Harry had not spied that watcher outside of Coyd's. Such mention would have been illuminating had it been included in Harry's report. For the man with the Derby hat whom The Shadow and Cliff had noticed in the lobby was the very fellow who had been acting as spy outside of Coyd's.

The telephone buzzed; again Burbank answered it. This time he held the earphones above his shoulder as he hung up the telephone receiver with his other hand. Methodically, he reported:

"Marsland again. Man by the cigar stand went up alone in an elevator. Indicator showed tenth-floor stop. Looks like a visitor for Weed."

The Shadow donned the earphones. Half a minute followed. Then he heard a sound of muffled knocking. Dragging footsteps; a door opened, then closed. After that came voices.

Cliff was right; Weed was receiving a visitor. Those earphones which The Shadow wore were picking up all sounds from Suite 1012, thanks to a tiny microphone that The Shadow had planted on his visit a few nights ago.

A WHINY voice reached The Shadow. It was Weed, greeting the visitor. The tone fitted the description that Clyde Burke had given of the long-faced, sneaky-looking lobbyist. Weed's whine, though peevish, also carried a tinge of authority.

"Well, Walbert?" came the lobbyist's query. "What about it? Where's your report?"

"Right here" was a gruff response, that fitted the man with the Derby. "Take a squint at it. There's lots for you to lamp. I was parked across the street from Coyd's most of the afternoon."

Weed spent time in perusal; finally, he spoke, as peevishly as before.

"This doesn't help me, Walbert," declared the lobbyist. "None of these details give me anything. Doctor Borneau has been to Coyd's before."

"But not this other fellow," observed Walbert. "I checked the number of his license. He was driving Senator Releston's bus."

"Get his name. It might be useful. But if he's from Releston, he'd be hard to deal with. That's obvious, Walbert. No, you haven't brought me much."

"What about Coyd's daughter being there? That's something, ain't it?"

"Listen, Walbert." Weed's tone was querulous. "I didn't hire you just to watch Coyd's house. This is no ordinary gumshoe job. Any cheap dick could do what you've done. I want something that will give me an opening.

"You know what I'm up against. I've got to reach either Senator Releston or Congressman Coyd. Both of them have given me the grand bounce. All I can hope for is to get something on one of them. Releston's a tougher proposition than Coyd; that's why I'm concentrating on the congressman."

"Maybe there's nothing you can get on Coyd. He's supposed to be mighty honest."

"Perhaps he is; but the odds are he isn't."

"What about that sculptor guy that I saw going in there once?"

"He doesn't know anything. Just a goof that's

making a bust of the old guy. What you've got to spot, Walbert, is some bird from Coyd's own state. Some yahoo that's come to Washington looking for a favor. That kind always likes to tell things that they remembered when some senator or congressman was just a small-time legislator in his home state."

"All right, Mr. Weed; I'll keep my eyes peeled. Nobody spotted me outside of Coyd's today. I'll go back there tomorrow. Maybe I can pick up some dope on Coyd, from guys around town."

"Get what you can, Walbert. Let me know if you spot anything. That's all for tonight."

Conversation ended. The Shadow spoke to Burbank; not in the tone of Henry Arnaud, but in a low-voiced, commanding whisper.

"Call the desk" was The Shadow's order. "Ask the clerk to look for a message."

Burbank did as ordered; he received word that there was no message in box 808. As soon as Burbank hung up, the telephone rang. It was Cliff. He had seen the clerk look in the pigeonhole marked 808. He knew that Burbank wanted him; the signal had been prearranged.

"Hawkeye to trail Walbert, the man who visited Weed," ordered The Shadow, quietly.

Burbank repeated the order to Cliff. Through the earphones, The Shadow could hear the sounds of Walbert's departure. There was ample time for Cliff to stroll out and tip off Hawkeye, giving the little agent the name that The Shadow had learned. Hawkeye was going on the trail of a man whose identity was now known.

TWENTY minutes passed. The Shadow had given the earphones back to Burbank; suddenly, the contact man took them off and raised them toward his chief. Listening, The Shadow heard new voices. One was Weed's again; the other was abrupt and harsh.

"Let's read it, Quidler," came Weed's comment. "I hope you've got something this trip."

"I have," was the reply, in the clipped tone. "You said you wanted a real operative—not a dumb dick. Well, I'm the bozo you was after."

"Say—this is something, Quidler! Coyd's daughter has gone on a trip to Virginia and Beatrice Rydel is along with her. How did you grab off that dope?"

"I'll tell you how. I stuck around the back of Coyd's house. There I met Mose, an old half-blind servant of Coyd's. I pumped him a good deal. He told me that Coyd has been rather sick lately, that Evelyn Coyd and Beatrice Rydel were going to Virginia on a vacation. Then there was this fellow Vincent who came from Releston—"

"All right, Quidler," Weed cut in. "That's enough. Sit down and help yourself to a drink while I review the details."

The Shadow spoke to Burbank. The contact man picked up the telephone and put in another call to the desk. He wanted to be sure about the expected message. The clerk finally reported that he had made another look. It was not there.

TWO minutes later, Cliff called the room. Prompted by The Shadow, Burbank asked about any suspicious-looking persons who had recently entered the lobby. Cliff stated that a tall, slouchy-looking fellow had gone up in an elevator. Cliff described him as a long-nosed, peak-faced individual who had looked like a salesman.

"Watch for him," stated Burbank, methodically. "If he comes down shortly, you'll know that he is the man now visiting Weed. His name is Quidler. He's another dick like Talbert. Trail him."

Sounds of departure came through the earphones. The Shadow removed the instruments; he picked up a briefcase which he found in the darkness. Leaving Burbank, he strolled out into the hall. Still as Arnaud, he walked in the direction of the elevators.

When The Shadow reached the lobby, Cliff Marsland was gone. The Shadow knew the answer. Quidler had descended in a previous car; Cliff had spotted him and was on the fellow's trail. With a slight smile on his fixed lips, The Shadow walked out to the street. He reached a darkened spot; there a transformation took place. Henry Arnaud became The Shadow.

A whispered laugh sounded amid darkness; prophetic as well as understanding. The Shadow had learned the game that Tyson Weed was playing. It was a double deal, involving two private detectives. Weed had signed up two dicks, independently; both had been assigned to get something on Congressman Layton Coyd.

The Shadow had matched the lobbyist's double deal. On Walbert's trail he had dispatched Hawkeye; he had sent Cliff after Quidler. Burbank was still covering Weed, thanks to the dictograph hookup between 1012 and 808.

That accomplished, The Shadow was free to roam alone; to pass unseen through the secluded byways of Washington, seeking objectives of his own. Phases of the game were opening; The Shadow was seeking further indications of the moves that lay ahead.

CHAPTER VII
COYD'S SECRET

FOUR days had passed. They were uneventful ones, stalemated at every point. Senator Ross

Releston and Foster Crozan had expressed no opinions to Harry Vincent.

Tyson Weed had received no reports from his detectives. Hawkeye and Cliff had trailed the dicks, but to no avail. All had proven empty. Dunwood Rydel, however, was at home; a newspaper mentioned that he was confined to bed by a slight illness. All seemed quiet on the surface.

Meanwhile, Congressman Coyd was ill at ease; but he managed to keep his burden to himself. He was about to dismiss Tabbert when Jurrick entered to announce that his daughter had arrived unexpectedly from Virginia.

This gave Coyd his opportunity to dismiss both secretaries. A few minutes later he was alone with his daughter and his physician. Evelyn began to talk; her father listened with an indulgent smile.

"You are coming to Virginia," affirmed Evelyn, emphatically. "This very afternoon, Daddy. No excuses this time."

"Is Beatrice Rydel still there?" inquired Coyd. "That might be the only excuse that I needed."

"She is still at the lodge, Daddy, but that makes no difference."

"Very well, my dear, I shall come down to see you tomorrow."

"Today, Daddy."

"No. Tomorrow."

Evelyn persisted no longer. She knew when her father's mind was made up. Evelyn closed the door when she left the living room. As she walked through the upstairs hall, she saw someone stepping into a doorway. The girl stopped with a sharp exclamation. Sheepishly, Hugh Tabbert stepped into view.

"Sorry to have startled you, Miss Evelyn," apologized the red-haired secretary. "I—I was just passing along here when—"

"A poor excuse," interposed the girl. "You were listening to our conversation, Tabbert. I would report you, if it were not for my father's nervous condition."

"Honestly, Miss Evelyn, my duty is to—"

"Your duty does not include listening outside of doorways. See that it does not happen again, Tabbert."

On the stairs, Evelyn met Jurrick. The sleek-haired secretary had heard words uttered above; he gazed inquiringly as Evelyn approached. The girl spoke to him quietly.

"Tabbert is behaving oddly," she explained. "It would be best for you to watch him, Don. I rebuked him; but I did not want to report the matters to father."

"Certainly not, Miss Evelyn," responded Jurrick, solemnly. "You may rest assured that I shall maintain your confidence."

"Thank you, Don," smiled the girl; then, with a twinkle in her eyes: "Very few people call me Miss Evelyn. Most everyone addresses me either as Miss Coyd or just as—"

"Evelyn?" inquired Jurrick.

The girl nodded.

"Remember it," she remarked, as she turned to walk toward the front door.

Jurrick smiled. He watched the girl's departure, feeling pleased because Evelyn chose to meet him on less formal terms. Upstairs, however, Tabbert was staring downward; his fists clenched, his teeth gritted.

Tabbert had known Evelyn for years; for he came from her father's hometown. An adoring swain, secretly in love with the congressman's daughter, he resented the favor that she had shown to the smooth-mannered Jurrick.

WHILE this bit of drama was in progress, Congressman Coyd had chosen to discuss more serious matters with Doctor Borneau. Seated in the living room, Coyd was explaining his present trouble.

"I feel better, Doctor," he stated. "Much better; and yet, in a sense, I am worse. Physically, I am comfortable; but my brain is in a whirl. It has been, for the past two days."

Reaching to the table, Coyd produced some newspaper clippings and handed them to the physician. They were interviews, given the day before. Borneau read them solemnly.

"These show lucidity, Mr. Coyd," decided Borneau. "Your statements are proof of your good reasoning. Simple facts regarding the amount of time it will take to complete investigations."

"The statements were all right, doctor, when *I* read them."

"When *you* read them?"

"Just this, Doctor. I don't remember having given those orders. I rested from dinner until supper. But when I read those clippings this morning I was amazed. I questioned my secretaries, tactfully, of course. They told me that at four-thirty I had gone down to interview the reporters. I can't understand it. I can't even remember going downstairs."

Doctor Borneau shook his head and smiled seriously. He waved a warning finger. "The overwork again, Mr. Coyd."

"Is my condition serious, Doctor?"

"No. It's merely a state of temporary aphasia. To explain it would involve a lot of medical terms, but it is not dangerous."

"But will it become worse, Doctor?"

"Not if you are careful. Do not worry. Above all, do not discuss it with persons."

"But if I should have another interview, if I say things without realizing it—"

"Ah! You are worrying already!" Doctor Borneau smiled triumphantly. "You see what I mean? What I have told you, you must do. Do not worry. That is my advice, Mr. Coyd. Tomorrow you will start on your vacation. It will do you good."

There was a rap at the door; Coyd called to enter. Jurrick entered, bringing a square box that formed a heavy weight. Coyd smiled.

"Open it, Jurrick," he ordered. "It must be the bronze bust for the State capital."

"One moment," remarked Doctor Borneau. "The medicine must first be taken. Go, young man, and prepare it."

Jurrick went to the medicine chest and began to remove the bottles. He paused; then turned doubtfully, just as Tabbert arrived from the hall.

"Which ones do I use, sir?" inquired Jurrick. "Just what is the mixture? How much of each?"

"Tabbert will prepare the medicine," responded Coyd. "You open the box in the meantime, Jurrick."

TABBERT took over Jurrick's task. He had completed the mixing of the medicine just as Jurrick finished opening the box. The bronze bust came into view while Coyd was gulping down the contents of his glass.

"It flatters me," grumbled Coyd. "It is too healthy-looking. It has my scar"—he rubbed his chin—"but the face is fuller than mine."

"It was taken from your own casts, sir," reminded Jurrick. "You have not changed so greatly in these few weeks."

"You look unusually well, sir," added Tabbert, comparing Coyd's face with that of the bust. "You do change, though, Mr. Coyd. Sometimes you look quite differently—even on the same day, sir—"

"That is enough," interrupted Doctor Borneau. "Do not worry my patient. Indisposition makes the face become hard; sometimes, it will give a relax, very strongly, afterward."

"Put the bust on the mantelpiece," ordered Coyd, rising and stretching his arms. "Keep it up here, where reporters never come," he yawned; then laughed: "I don't want those pests bringing troublesome photographers here with them."

Coyd started toward the bedroom. Tabbert put a question as the congressman reached the door.

"You intend to take a nap, sir? What if the reporters should come this afternoon?"

"Come up," replied Coyd, "and if I am awake, tell me that they are here. If I am asleep, do not disturb me."

With that, Coyd entered the bedroom and closed the door behind him. Doctor Borneau accompanied the secretaries downstairs; then left the house. As the physician stepped into a taxicab, a man across the street eyed him from a parked coupé.

It was Walbert; the watching dick made a note of the time, then leaned back behind the wheel to wait. Nothing to be gained, he thought, by watching Coyd's house when no visitors were there. In fact, Walbert was convinced that nothing was due to happen within that house today.

In that guess, the dick was wrong. Already, important events had brewed. Deep-laid plans of schemers had gained proven strength. The crisis that Senator Releston feared had arrived. A thrust that involved millions of ill-gained dollars was ready for delivery, with all its staggering consequences.

CHAPTER VIII
THE INTERVIEW

GATHERING clouds had brought an overcast sky during the period of Doctor Borneau's visit at the home of Congressman Layton Coyd. As hours lapsed, heavy gloom enveloped the old mansion, as if the very elements were themselves presaging ill.

Swirling wind, pattering rain; these obscured the outside scene. To Walbert, watching Coyd's house from his rain-swept coupé, the house lights were splotches amid the dull mass of darkness formed by the brownstone house front.

Noting that the lower story alone was aglow, the mustached dick began to speculate on the possibility of further visitors.

If others came, Walbert realized that it would be difficult to recognize them, without parking closer to the house. He preferred to remain where he was, at an angle, across from Coyd's residence. Muttering angrily, Walbert shifted in his seat. As he did, he fancied that he heard a scraping sound from the back of the car.

Shifting, jolting up and down, the dick tried to gain a repetition of the sound. There was none; instead, the driving of the rain became more apparent. The windshield and the windows were clouding; Walbert was feeling warm. So he pulled a handkerchief from his pocket and began to polish the mist from the glass, at the same time tossing his Derby hat to the seat beside him.

INSIDE Coyd's mansion, the atmosphere was morose. The lower hall was poorly lighted; the stairs were obscure; while the passage that led beyond the stairway was almost totally dark. A loud-ticking grandfather's clock was pointing to twenty-five minutes after four when Tabbert, a book beneath his arm, emerged sleepily from the front library on the ground floor. The red-haired secretary strolled toward the stairs.

"Tabbert! Where are you going?"

The hail came from the passage beyond the stairway. Tabbert paused as Jurrick came into view. Pausing, Tabbert scowled; then decided to reply.

"Upstairs," he reported, curtly. "To see if Mr. Coyd is awake. It's nearly time for the reporters."

"I know that," smiled Jurrick. "So does Mr. Coyd. That is why he came downstairs while you were daydreaming in the library. He is in his study; he wants to see you there."

Sourly, Tabbert followed Jurrick through the dim passage. Jurrick knocked at the study door; a response coming, he and Tabbert entered. They found Coyd seated behind a large desk; he was wearing an old smoking jacket and was puffing at a rank-odored stogie, his favorite type of cigar.

Coyd, quite alert, noted Tabbert's expression and rapped severely upon the desk.

"Come, come!" he exclaimed. "This is no time for petty jealousies. This afternoon is important; I have an interview to grant when the reporters arrive. Jurrick, type these notes"—Coyd picked up a sheet of pencil-scrawled paper—"and you, Tabbert, be ready to receive the reporters. Leave the door open so I can call you."

Jurrick took the penciled notes to a typewriter in the corner. Tabbert went out into the hall and loafed there, listening to the click of the machine. Soon the doorbell rang. Mose appeared to open it; he admitted a bevy of rain-coated reporters. Tabbert conducted the newshawks into the study.

As the reporters began to take their chairs, others arrived. Soon there were ten in all, among them, two who had been present yesterday for the first time. These were Clyde Burke and Garvey.

Another ring at the doorbell; Tabbert followed Mose to answer it. Harry Vincent stepped into the hall, shaking the rain from his hat and poncho. He hung the garments on a hat rack, along with the dripping coats of the reporters; then followed Tabbert into the study. Meanwhile, Jurrick had finished typing the notes. The handwritten ones he tore up and put them into the basket.

"Gentlemen"—Coyd looked over the top of his spectacles to note the last arrival, then reverted to his notes—"I have a statement that is both definite and important. It concerns munitions and their regulation."

An audible buzz came from the reporters. It stifled as Coyd shot an annoyed glance toward the group.

"Munitions have been regulated," announced Coyd, "and the rulings will stand. The committee of investigation came unanimously to that decision. Present embargoes that concern warring countries will be maintained; the same will apply to new conflicts and to nations wherein revolution threatens."

HARRY VINCENT shifted uneasily. So far, the congressman's statement was merely one of generalities; but Harry feared that more drastic expressions were coming. Harry's dread was justified.

"In making appropriations for munitions and armament," continued Coyd, pounding his fist upon the desk, "we have decided to take the profit out of war. No American manufacturer"—Coyd was on his feet, his voice rising to the forced oratory that Clyde Burke had heard him use before—"no countryman of ours shall ever again gain fortune through sales of war supplies to our government.

"Congress will set the price; Congress will also force a refund should any profits result. The supplying of materials for war will be made a patriotic duty; not a business enterprise. That, gentlemen, is final."

Coyd paused. But the congressman's statement was not finished. A bombshell was coming.

"A patriotic duty," repeated Coyd, his voice lowered, his clenched fist half loosened and wagging slowly. "Patriotism, gentlemen, concerns one's duty to his own country; not to others. Should American manufacturers choose to supply war materials to foreign governments that are under no embargo, they will be free to do so.

"Such sales will not be subject to congressional price regulation. We do not consider them—for the present—to be within our sphere of attention. Later, a new committee will be formed to deal directly with that subject. The appointment of that committee, however, will not be discussed until the next session of Congress."

Voice modulated, the speaker seemed spent in effort. Watching Coyd, Clyde Burke saw him slump into his chair, exactly as he had sagged after his speech in the House of Representatives. There was something dramatic in the action; it was difficult to guess whether the weariness was genuine or feigned.

Then Coyd removed his spectacles and faced his audience, with head tilted to the right.

"That is all, gentlemen," he announced, quietly. "You may go and print this interview."

Reporters came to their feet. Some were buzzing; the wiser ones were nudging them for silence. They moved from the study in a pack, Tabbert following, to usher them out.

BACK in the study, Harry Vincent was staring at Coyd's slumped figure.

"I am sorry, Mr. Coyd," stated Harry, "that you did not tell me of your intention to give this interview. You had opportunity to do so when I called up at noon. Because of your calmness, I assured Senator Releston that you would make no special statements to the gentlemen of the press—"

"I changed my mind," snapped Coyd, angrily. "Confound Releston—and you, too, Vincent!" With these words, Coyd's fist smashed against the desk. "Who am I that I should toady to Releston? The Senate committees are his business; those of the House are mine!"

"But their interests are identical—"

"They are not! They run parallel; but each is independent. I have never told Releston what he should or should not say."

"You might at least have called him. But since you did not, I shall."

Harry was on his feet, reaching for the telephone that stood on Coyd's desk. An arm shot forward; quick fingers clamped Harry's wrist; The Shadow's agent found himself staring into glaring eyes that were fierce beneath Coyd's heavy brows.

"You will make no call from here," Coyd's lips hissed furiously. "If you wish to talk to Senator Releston, go and see him. Remember your place, Vincent!"

Jurrick stepped over and gripped Harry's arm in friendly fashion. At that moment, Tabbert arrived at the door; his eyes narrowed, glowering, as he saw Coyd rise to his feet and shake a heavy fist in Harry's face.

"Get out!" stormed Coyd. "Out, I tell you! Go back to Releston! Tell him what you wish!"

"I'll tell him plenty," assured Harry, grimly, as he let Jurrick draw him toward the door.

"You'll tell him lies!" Coyd's voice was a wild scream, his gestures frantic. "Lies! I shall need a witness to them. Go with this fellow, Tabbert. Hear what he says to Releston. Bring back what the senator tells you!"

Tabbert nodded; roughly, he gripped Harry's other arm and dragged The Shadow's agent from the room while Jurrick was aiding with mild pressure on the other side.

"Keep steady, old man," suggested Jurrick, as they marched through the hall. "You couldn't help breaking loose the way you did. I understand."

"What's that, Jurrick?" demanded Tabbert, savagely, his face enraged. "You are turning against Mr. Coyd? Against our employer? Against the one whom we should admire and respect?"

"Lay off, Tabbert," pleaded Jurrick. "I'm just seeing Harry Vincent's viewpoint—"

"You lack loyalty. You—you traitor! A scummy traitor, Jurrick, that's what you are! When Miss Evelyn hears that you—"

"Do not bring Miss Coyd's name into this, Tabbert. Remember, you are going along with Vincent. It would be best for you to realize that he has a duty to Senator Releston, as important to him as yours to Mr. Coyd."

TABBERT subsided. They had reached the front door; the enraged secretary followed Harry to don hat and poncho. Sullenly, Tabbert picked up garments of his own. A voice spoke from the hallway; Tabbert and Harry turned with Jurrick to see Congressman Coyd standing wearily at the stairway.

"I am going to my bedroom," announced the congressman, wearily. "I am going to rest. My effort is spent; I did not expect so much confusion.

"Jurrick, see Tabbert and Vincent off. Then station yourself in the library. If there are any callers, have Mose bring them to you. I want you to talk to them, Jurrick. I shall rest until dinner time."

Jurrick nodded. Harry and Tabbert preceded him through the front steps. Jurrick pulled the door shut, but kept his hand on the knob while he watched Harry and Tabbert walk to the sedan. They appeared to be arguing; but their animosity had lessened.

Jurrick saw the sedan roll away; then he turned to enter the house. Hence, he did not observe the coupé that started from the other side of the street, after Harry's car had passed it. Walbert had seen someone come out with Harry; the dick was tailing the sedan.

Jurrick, halfway in the house as Walbert started, regained the hall and closed the big front door. Congressman Coyd was no longer by the stairway. Jurrick went into the front library; there he found Mose, carefully rearranging books upon their shelves.

"Mr. Coyd went upstairs, Mose?" inquired Jurrick, seating himself in a comfortable chair.

"I guess so, Mr. Jurrick," responded the servant. "I hain't seen him, though, since them reporter men were here. This is where I've been all along. Here in the library, fixing all these here books."

"All right, Mose," laughed Jurrick. "I'll help you by reading one of the books while I'm here. You won't have to put it away, then."

"Thanks, Mr. Jurrick."

THE big hall clock was chiming five. The only light within Coyd's residence was that of the widely spaced electric incandescents; for the outside gloom had greatly increased.

Of all spots where premature darkness had thickened most effectively, those passages between Coyd's house and the neighboring buildings seemed most favored. They were almost completely blackened.

A movement occurred near the rear of one passage. A dark-garbed, rain-swept figure merged with the darkness that was beneath the shelter of an overhanging roof. Keen eyes peered from the gloom. The Shadow had arrived at the home of Layton Coyd.

The Shadow had reached the old house less than ten minutes after Harry Vincent's departure. The reason for his quick arrival was a telephone call that he had received from Clyde Burke, while Harry was still engaged in stormy session within Coyd's study.

Immediately after the brief interview, Clyde had found some pretext to call The Shadow from a drugstore near Coyd's. Clyde had accomplished this in an offhand fashion that had passed with Garvey.

Keeping close to the house, The Shadow followed the passage to the front, till he arrived at the door.

The Shadow tried the door and found it locked. He produced a probing tool; his tiny flashlight glimmered from beneath the folds of his cloak. The door yielded when The Shadow jabbed a thin, flat piece of steel between frame and door.

ENTERING the house, The Shadow found himself in a gloomy entry. He went up a few steps and came into the rear halls. On his left was the door of Coyd's study. The Shadow opened it and entered. He closed the door and turned on the light. He found a folded sheet of paper on the desk. Opening it, he read the notes that Jurrick had typewritten.

Remembering a point of Clyde's report, The Shadow looked in the wastebasket and found the original penciled paper. The Shadow fitted eight fragments together. He found that Jurrick had copied the notations exactly. The papers fluttered one by one into the wastebasket, until seven had dropped. The Shadow still held the eighth. He folded it and placed it beneath his cloak.

Moving from the study, The Shadow reached the front hall. Stealthily, he peered into the library; there he saw Jurrick reading by a lamp. Mose had finished arranging books; the servant was slowly gathering up old newspapers and dumping them into wastebaskets.

Softly, The Shadow glided away from the door. He gained the stairs and ascended; his footfalls silent, no swish from his rain-soaked cloak. The door of the upstairs living room was open. The Shadow entered that apartment. Large windows at the front gave the living room a bit of outside light. Objects were discernible.

The Shadow saw the bronze bust on the mantel. He approached to study it. He could tell that it was a perfect replica of a face mask, for no effort had been made to smooth the roughness of the profile. Even the scar upon the chin was prominent in this metallic likeness of Congressman Layton Coyd.

With a soft, whispered laugh, The Shadow moved away. He reached the closed door of the bedroom and opened it softly. He entered and approached a large four-poster bed. There he saw Coyd, stretched out in slumber.

The congressman was garbed in a dressing gown. His face was toward the window; the haggard features showed a pallor in the fading light. Coyd looked like a man whose health was irregular. The lines of his face seemed deeper than those of the bust. His closed eyes looked more sunken.

Gliding from the bedroom, The Shadow softly closed the door behind him. His form was barely visible in the gloom; his sharp eyes, however, could still espy all objects. A wastebasket stood by a table.

Reaching into it, The Shadow found torn letters and crumpled papers. The latter impressed him most. Removing them, The Shadow carried his trophies to the window.

Examining each, he rejected them until he came to one that bore a penned scrawl. It was a brief note, the handwriting characterized by oddly shaped letters. Coyd had written it to his daughter Evelyn; the congressman must have heard from her before mailing it; hence he had thrown it away.

The Shadow kept this letter, but dropped the others back into the wastebasket. He laughed softly as he moved toward the thick darkness of the windowless hall. Silently, he descended the stairs; there he turned toward the rear passage. He stopped suddenly and pressed against the wall by the stairway.

THE door of Coyd's study was opening; a glimmer of light came from that room, which The Shadow had left dark. Then Mose appeared; wobbling as he walked, the old servant was carrying out the wastebasket. Mose passed The Shadow; the menial's dim eyes never noticed that blackened shape against the wall.

The Shadow watched Mose add the wastebaskets to others that were standing near the doorway to the living room. Then Mose started upstairs. Listening to his creaky footsteps, The Shadow knew that the servant was going up to get other wastebaskets to empty with those that were on the ground floor.

With a swift move, The Shadow gained the passage to the outside door. He left the house, carefully latching the door behind him. Passing through the deepening darkness, he reached the rear street, followed it for a block and came upon the entrance of a deserted store. Moving into the doorway, The Shadow removed his cloak, hat and gloves. He bestowed them in a briefcase that he opened into enlarged form.

Donning a soft gray hat, he strolled from the storefront. His gait was that of Henry Arnaud. One block on, The Shadow reached an avenue. Standing in the drizzle, he formed a plain figure as he hailed a passing cab. Entering the vehicle, he ordered the driver to take him to the Hotel Halcyon.

A soft laugh came from the lips of Henry Arnaud as the cab wheeled through the rain. That repressed mirth was both reminiscent and prophetic. It also carried keen understanding. A crisis had come, despite The Shadow. But the aftermath had been of The Shadow's own making.

CHAPTER IX
THE ANTIDOTE

TEN o'clock the next morning found Senator Ross Releston at his desk. Spread before the senator were copies of many metropolitan dailies; the headlines on their front pages made a mass of screaming print. The munitions story had broken with a bang. Releston's countenance was troubled.

Across from the senator was Foster Crozan; his face, too, showed glumness. Like Releston, Crozan knew how terrific the consequences of Coyd's interview could be; but he was not discussing the matter with the senator. Both were waiting for a visitor.

Lanson entered. Releston looked up eagerly and put a question to the secretary.

"Mr. Rydel is here?"

"No, sir. Vincent has not yet returned with him. It is Mr. Cranston who is here, sir."

"Mr. Cranston? I thought he had gone to Brazil?"

"Apparently not, sir. He said—"

"Show him in, Lanson. Show him in. Cranston can speak for himself."

Half a minute later, Releston was on his feet welcoming his millionaire friend. The Shadow, again in the guise of Lamont Cranston, had entered in his usual languid fashion. Releston's greeting ended, The Shadow shook hands with Crozan.

"My Amazon expedition is off," remarked The Shadow, quietly. "It fell through while I was in Havana. So I am heading north instead. I decided to stop off and see you, Senator."

"I am glad you did, Cranston," acknowledged Releston. "Of course, you have seen the newspapers. Our worst expectations have been realized."

Before The Shadow could make comment, two men appeared at the door of the room. One was Harry Vincent; the other Dunwood Rydel. Harry stepped aside to let the magnate enter. Rydel advanced to meet the challenging glare of Releston, who waved him to a chair. The senator made no further introduction. Instead, he opened hostilities immediately.

"Rydel, I demand an explanation," stormed Releston. "I am confident that the story in today's newspapers is your work. I want to know why you forced it into print!"

"My work?" queried Rydel, savagely. His eyes were beady as he turned his glare from Releston to Crozan. "Where did you get that impression, Senator? From Crozan?"

"Yes." Crozan spoke boldly for himself. "It is obvious that you were behind it, Rydel. I know your methods. Dollar-grabbing is your specialty."

Rydel was about to fume a reply when Releston silenced him. The stern-faced senator continued his accusation.

"IT was believed," stated Releston, "that restrictive measures might be placed upon the sales and price of all munitions, including those to be shipped to foreign countries. To enforce that last measure, however, we needed to await the next session of Congress.

"It was our plan to form a special committee at that time; to have it cooperate immediately with the present committee, which is not—unfortunately—permitted to interfere with exports that are free from embargo.

"We had hoped to keep that fact to ourselves. We knew that hidden interests were buying up the stock of idle munitions plants; but that they were afraid to operate while the committee report was pending, because they thought their profits might be seized.

"Coyd's statement has ended their doubt. Already the shares of those munitions companies are shooting skyward. Speculators, tipped to what was coming, are primed to make millions. During the next few months, factories will work at full capacity, pouring American-made munitions into foreign lands.

"A golden harvest, through steel and powder that will later bring blood and strife. That is the terrible part of it, Rydel. Lust for wealth has inspired those behind the game; and I accuse you as the leading instigator!"

Another might have wilted under Releston's salvo; but not Rydel. The portly magnate showed challenge in his heavy-jowled face. He came to his feet and glowered across the desk.

"Rubbish!" he snarled. "Plain guff; poor talk from a man of your intelligence, Senator. I have no interests in munitions, sir. The stocks that I hold in such companies are few; and most of them are in large concerns that have already promised full cooperation with the government!"

"What about proxies?" demanded Crozan.

"Proxies?" queried Rydel, with a laugh. "Find any if you can. Prove that I have been buying munitions stocks, in my name or in any other."

"We know you could have covered it, Rydel."

THE magnate delivered a contemptuous growl. An ugly smile showed on his pudgy face as he resumed his chair. Thumbs tucked in vest sleeves, Rydel leaned back as if to welcome further query.

"Perhaps," decided Releston, "the profit to your basic interests will sufficiently reward your scheming, Rydel. We realized that you would be in a position to defy us. I merely wanted you to know the greatness of the misery that your selfishness may produce.

"Europe is in ferment. Increased armaments and munitions purchases may cause destruction there. We, who think of the welfare of the world as well as that of America, felt sure that we could do our part to prevent foreign strife. Our hopes have been shattered."

"Not by me," announced Rydel. "Look here, Senator—now that you're talking quietly, why don't you listen to common sense? Somebody's in back of the munitions game; but I'm not. I'm not an ugly octopus, trying to swallow everything.

"I wouldn't be fool enough to mix into the munitions racket, even if I were mean enough to want to. You've singled me out, Senator, simply because you've been prejudiced against me."

Rydel paused; then glared viciously at Crozan. He continued:

"How could I have been in back of it?" demanded the magnate. "Coyd did the talking, didn't he? He has it in for me just like you have. How could I have reached him? Answer that!"

"I can tell you." Foster Crozan spoke steadily, as he arose from his chair and towered above the seated magnate. "Congressman Coyd has a daughter, who is a great influence in his life. She has visited her father at recent intervals, coming to Washington from Virginia. You, too, have a daughter, Rydel. She is Evelyn Coyd's closest friend. Do you deny that at present your daughter Beatrice is staying in Virginia with Evelyn Coyd?"

Instead of replying, Rydel bounded to his feet. He clenched his fists. Crozan dropped back, expecting a threatening gesture; but Rydel merely pounded his fists against the side of his own head and began to stalk the room, laughing like a madman. Near the door, he stopped and faced the others.

"My daughter!" he giggled. "My daughter! Mixing into politics—my daughter, with no thought in her empty head except a crazy infatuation for a conceited, penniless actor. Jove! Have the two of you gone as insane as Coyd? One would think it, to hear you advance such an absurd theory as—"

He stopped, tilted back his head and delivered another laugh.

"Perhaps," asserted Releston, dryly, "you can suggest a better method of our learning who influenced Congressman Coyd to his ill-timed statement."

"I can," assured Rydel, sobering. "Go to Coyd and ask him about it. But don't annoy me with any more of this kindergarten stuff. I am leaving for New York; I shall return in a few days, Senator. Perhaps then you will have realized the absurdity of your theory."

RYDEL turned on his heel and stalked from the room, leaving Releston and Crozan speechless. The Shadow, quiet through the tempest, was performing the Cranston gesture of inserting a cigarette in a holder.

"Perhaps you were wrong, Crozan," remarked Releston. "The link does seem flimsy. Rydel's daughter could not be intelligent; if she were she would never have become infatuated over that ridiculous actor, Montgomery Hadwil."

"That does not follow, Senator," disagreed Crozan. "Love and intelligence are different mental processes. Beatrice Rydel may be quite bright. Moreover, I can see a reason why she would lend aid to her father's cause."

"To gain his consent to her marriage to Hadwil?"

"Exactly. Senator, I think Rydel bluffed us. He is on his way to New York, he says, and he is probably going there to meet others of his kind. They will gloat over their victory."

"Shall I have Secret Service operatives cover him?"

"What good would it do? He has committed no crime. You cannot arrest him. He has no conscience. More than that, Rydel has left us helpless."

"Not quite," observed The Shadow, in the calm tone of Cranston. "On the contrary, he has given a very excellent suggestion; one that may lead to real results. One, in fact, that may provide the antidote for this poison that has been released."

"What was that?" queried Releston, eagerly, while Crozan stared, puzzled.

"Rydel told you to see Coyd," returned The Shadow. "It was true advice, whether he intended it as such or not."

"You are right," agreed Releston. "Come, let us start for Coyd's." Then, to Harry, at the door: "Have the car ready at once, Vincent."

FIVE minutes later, Harry was piloting the sedan toward Coyd's. Senator Releston was riding in the back, between The Shadow and Foster Crozan. As the car spun along an avenue, the senator remembered something which The Shadow had said.

"By the way, Cranston," he remarked. "You said something about an antidote. Is there a cure for this crisis, Cranston?"

"Perhaps," replied The Shadow. "We shall see."

That cryptic statement ended The Shadow's discussion. The sedan had reached Coyd's. Three passengers alighted; they ascended the brownstone steps. Releston first; then Crozan; after that, The Shadow.

Firm, disguised lips held the semblance of a smile that the others did not see. The Shadow, his keen brain at work, had found an answer to a problem.

CHAPTER X
COYD AGREES

THEY found Congressman Coyd in his upstairs living room. His table resembled Releston's desk, inasmuch as it was piled high with newspapers. With Coyd were Jurrick and Tabbert; also a man of professional appearance, whom The Shadow knew must be Doctor Borneau.

Coyd was glum, almost apologetic as he greeted the visitors. He stared seriously at Releston when the senator sat opposite him. Yet in Coyd's eyes was the semblance of a glare; the natural mistrustfulness that went with the man's self-styled independence.

"Let us come to facts, Mr. Coyd," asserted Releston. "We do not require privacy. All present know the reason for my visit. I have come to ask you about the interview that you gave yesterday. Just what was its purpose?"

"I cannot answer you, Senator," groaned Coyd, wearily. "Please do not plague me with useless questions. My mind is burdened. I am leaving for a rest."

"To Virginia?" inquired Crozan.

"Yes," replied Coyd. "Doctor Borneau has advised it. I wish, gentlemen, that I had gone there sooner."

"Then," stated Releston, "I take it that you have regretted yesterday's interview."

Coyd's eyes blazed. The congressman towered as he rose from his chair and raised his fist dramatically. His face took on a fullness; it showed its true likeness to the bronze bust on the mantelpiece.

"I regret nothing!" cried Coyd, reverting to his oratorical complex. "I stand upon my own record! I take no orders from others! Not from you, Senator Releston, nor from any man at all—"

"Even though you have done great harm," interposed Releston, with a sad shake of his head. "Have you considered that, Mr. Coyd?"

The congressman subsided. The sorrow that was evident on Releston's face was something that Coyd had not expected. Despite his love of independence, Coyd was sympathetic. He subsided into his chair.

"Frankly, senator," he declared. "I may have made a mistake. You must realize, though, that my urge is one of progress. I represent the people; it is their right to know of certain facts."

"And your constituents include those rogues who are already reaping their evil harvest?"

"You mean that rogues were awaiting my statement regarding munitions control?"

"Exactly. They have probably bought up shares of stock for trivial sums. The market in such securities has started to rise. Tomorrow—or in a few days—it will be soaring. Scamps knew the truth; they were prepared."

COYD slumped and bowed his head in his hands. His voice came in a mutter; when he looked up his whole countenance showed haggard.

"Whatever I can do, Senator—whatever I can do—"

"Your mistake cannot be rectified. You can, however, tell me one fact that may aid us in finding the culprits. What caused you to issue your statement to the press?"

Coyd shook his head seriously.

"I do not know, Senator," he declared. "Oddly, I cannot answer the question."

"Did anyone approach you?"

"Certainly not! You know that I would never listen to outside suggestions!"

"Something must have persuaded you. Can't you remember?"

In response to Releston's question, Coyd shifted uneasily. He glanced appealingly toward Doctor Borneau. The physician nodded and stepped forward.

"You have named the ailment, Senator," declared Borneau, quietly. "Mr. Coyd cannot remember."

"Cannot remember?"

CONGRESSMAN LAYTON COYD— powerful figure in Washington, he denounces the lobbyists.

"His mind has been overtaxed. He is subject to a mild form of aphasia. Not a serious condition; but one which causes a hiatus in his memory."

"You say it is not serious!" exclaimed Releston. "Not serious, when it leads to such results as this?"

Emphatically, Releston picked up one of the morning newspapers and pointed to the headlines. Doctor Borneau smiled.

"I speak as a physician," he reminded. "Not as a politician. I say that Mr. Coyd's condition is not serious, Senator, because his brain is lucid. Read his statement; you will agree with me that it shows the efforts of a healthy mind."

Releston looked puzzled. It was Coyd who tried to help the senator out of his dilemma.

"Yesterday," Coyd explained, "I took a rest. I awoke from my nap shortly after four. I came downstairs; I met the reporters and gave the interview. I had words with Vincent, which I am forced to regret. Then I went back to nap and did not awaken until seven."

Coyd paused, half pitifully. He looked toward Doctor Borneau, who delivered a prompting nod. Coyd pushed his fingers through his shock of black hair; then turned appealingly to Releston.

"Frankly, Senator," he admitted, "I cannot remember waking between those two naps."

"Perhaps, Mr. Coyd," Releston stated dryly, "your mental condition is so precarious that your best policy would be to resign the chairmanship of your committees."

"Never!" retorted Coyd. "Hear what Doctor Borneau has said! My faculties are not below normal! I am alert, despite my nervousness. I can assure you of this; my statement yesterday was a clear one. I must have had reason to give it!

"Since I no longer recall the episode, I naturally have forgotten my reason also. That is a logical consequence. I can assure you, however, that I must have acted on my own. I take orders from no one!"

"What do you think of it, Crozan?" inquired Releston. "Should I insist upon this matter?"

"It will do you no good, Senator," stormed Coyd, suddenly. "No one can force me to abandon my normal rights. I shall retain my position of authority!"

"Suppose Mr. Coyd should resign," suggested Crozan, speaking straight to Releston. "Who would head the committees? Is there anyone competent to replace him?"

"No!" exclaimed Coyd, bursting into the discussion. "Matters would be worse, Releston. Three or four men would be required to fill my place. There would be conflict; moreover, Congress has ended its session. Who would appoint those committee heads?"

CROZAN appeared troubled; he was impressed by Coyd's statement. So, for that matter, was Releston. Worried, the senator looked to The Shadow, who was leaning by the mantel, puffing a cigarette that extended from its long holder.

"What do you think, Cranston?" questioned the senator. "You have shown good analysis of this situation. Is there not some answer to our problem?"

"Mr. Coyd can supply the answer," replied The Shadow, casually. He looked straight toward the congressman as he spoke. "Moreover, I think he may be willing to do so."

"How?" queried Coyd. He was impressed by the magnetism of those focused eyes. "I am willing, sir, to listen to any reasonable request from Senator Releston. But when he tries to label me as a madman—"

"Senator Releston admits that he is wrong," interposed The Shadow, quietly. "He accepts the statement made by both you and your physician. Your mental faculties are active. It is wise that you should continue in your high service to the government."

Coyd was on his feet, his chest swelling as he listened to these flattering statements. The Shadow smiled solemnly.

"At the same time," he added, "Senator Releston cannot ignore your own admission of poor memory. An admission, Mr. Coyd, that has also been backed by your physician. So, in full fairness to Senator Releston, you should take precautionary measures to offset any future lapse of memory."

"How can I do that?"

"By agreeing to let Senator Releston read any public statement before you make it; and to discuss its wisdom with him. That, Mr. Coyd, would be a courtesy."

Releston spoke up promptly.

"A courtesy which I shall gladly return," he assured. "I shall inform you of any public utterance which I intend to make, Mr. Coyd."

Coyd nodded slowly. His expression showed that he had been conciliated.

"I agree," he declared, emphatically. "But suppose I should forget? My memory is really bad—"

"You can instruct your secretaries," interposed The Shadow. "Have them remind you that Senator Releston is to be informed beforehand of your statements."

"Vincent can help with that," added Releston, quickly. "If he could be here more regularly—more often—"

"Very well," interrupted Coyd, abruptly. Then, to his secretaries: "You hear that, Jurrick? Tabbert? Jove! Why didn't the two of you jolt me yesterday?"

"I was afraid to, sir," confessed Jurrick. "When I was copying your penciled notes, I wondered about them—"

"And I was puzzled when I heard you read them, sir," broke in Tabbert. "But I knew that Jurrick must have copied them exactly. I saw you hand them to him, sir; I knew how quick you always are to catch any error in a copy."

"I understand," nodded Coyd. "I know that I must have written that statement and delivered it verbatim. But I cannot explain my folly. Jove, Releston! Is there no way to stop it?"

RELESTON shook his head; Crozan copied the senator's example. The Shadow, however, spoke in slow, deliberate fashion. His even-toned words were definite.

"My understanding of the present situation," he remarked, "is that the congressional committees are authorized to regulate the sales and purchase of all munitions that our government may require. Am I correct, Senator?"

"Absolutely," returned Releston. "But we cannot control exports, Cranston. We can only lay down the law in reference to government purchases."

"I understand. I have heard also that Congress made a large appropriation for American armament, to be supplied as occasion may demand, bringing this country up to its treaty limitations. Am I correct again?"

"You are, Cranston. One function of the present committees is to determine when that appropriation shall be made; and how the moneys shall be spent."

"Very well." The Shadow's smile was fixed. "Suppose that you, Senator, and Mr. Coyd, issue a joint statement. Tell the public that the committees may recommend that the entire appropriation be spent at once; that all munitions available should be purchased immediately, with the price fixed barely above cost. And then—"

The Shadow paused, his smile unchanging. Senator Releston had grasped the idea. The solon's stern face was lighted with enthusiasm.

"Marvelous, Cranston!" cried Releston. "You have the answer! These factories will be working overtime, rushing their foreign orders, knowing that our present committees cannot stop them.

"But we control supplies needed for the American government. We can make the factories store away their output; we can deny them the privilege of export on the grounds that we control all munitions that the American government may want. We can make them wait for our refusal before they ship their munitions. Until we say that we will not buy, they cannot unload elsewhere!"

"And when you decide that you will not buy," remarked The Shadow, "Congress will again have been in session. The new committees will have been formed, empowered to control—to ban—all exports of munitions."

"Munitions on hand, with no sale," ejaculated Releston, his face beaming. "The only possible purchaser would be our own government. It would buy at cost—"

"But it never will," assured The Shadow. "Once your statement has been made, Senator, with Mr. Coyd's approval, the whole game will be spiked. Those rising stocks will slump back; the factories will never open."

RELESTON nodded. He turned to Harry Vincent and pointed to a typewriter in the corner of the room.

"Take this statement, Vincent," said the senator, briskly, "direct on the machine. A joint statement by the congressional committees on munitions, of the Senate and the House—"

The Shadow had stepped forward; Releston saw a slight restraining gesture of his hand. The senator understood; he turned to Layton Coyd.

"It is your privilege, sir," bowed Releston. "You have heard the plan, Mr. Coyd. I shall concede to you the honor of delivering the words for this epoch-making statement."

It was the perfect stroke. Coyd, when the cause had seemed hopeless, had expressed his willingness to follow Releston's lead. He could not withdraw from it; in fact, a statement from Releston alone would be sufficient to spike the scheme by which swindlers hoped to use munitions makers as a step to wealth.

Even though he might have shown reluctance, Coyd was committed, now that The Shadow had shown the way. But if Coyd were forced to play second fiddle at this time, future relations might be strained between him and Releston. Knowing that, The Shadow had gestured to the senator; Releston, wise in all circumstances, was stepping aside for Coyd.

In grandiloquent fashion, Coyd stepped forward. Bombastically, he delivered his statement, one hand tucked beneath his coat in Napoleonic fashion.

The statement finished, Coyd relaxed. He seemed to shrink as he always did, when an effort had been ended. As Coyd groped his way back to his chair, Harry pulled out sheets of paper and their carbons. He brought the triplicate copies to Releston, who pointed toward Coyd. Harry brought the papers to the congressman. Coyd signed each one with a flourish.

At the bottom of each sheet, Releston wrote the words: "Approved in full"; then added his own signature. Coyd saw the action and smiled. He knew that the glory was all his. Speaking quietly, his tone filled with friendliness, he said:

"I leave the rest to you, Senator. I am too tired to interview the press. I am starting for Virginia within an hour. Doctor Borneau assures me that after a brief rest, I shall be myself again."

"Call the newspapers, Vincent," ordered Releston. "Tell them to have representatives at my apartment within fifteen minutes. This news will reach New York by wire in time for the noon editions. It will stop that forced rise of munitions shares, before the closing rush at the market."

THE visitors left Coyd's. Harry took the wheel of the sedan. Senator Releston occupied the center of the rear seat, clutching two of the precious papers that bore Coyd's signature and his approval. The senator was bubbling with enthusiasm. Foster Crozan, on his right, was nodding, his lips wreathed with a steady, set smile.

The Shadow, his disguised lips straightened, was looking from the window on the left as the sedan pulled away from the brownstone house. Enthusiastically, Releston turned and thumped his hand upon The Shadow's back.

"Grand work, Cranston!" approved the senator. "You gain the credit. You were right; the poison was given—a big dose to the public, the interview that Coyd gave yesterday. But you found the antidote, old fellow. You found it and the cure will be complete."

A slight smile formed on the lips of Lamont Cranston. Releston thought that The Shadow's expression was a response to his own enthusiasm. The senator was wrong; The Shadow had smiled because of something that he had seen, not heard.

The Shadow had noticed a coupé parked across the street as the sedan rolled by. He had spotted the man hunched behind the wheel; he had recognized the mustached face of Walbert. But The Shadow had seen even more. He had noticed a slight lift of the rumble seat; he had caught a momentary glimpse of a wizened face ducking out of view, within the back of the coupé.

Hawkeye, the artful trailer, had been clinging close to the mustached dick. The little spotter had chosen the cute system of riding everywhere within the confines of the rumble seat at the back of Walbert's coupé.

CHAPTER XI
WEED GAINS FACTS

"WALBERT has arrived."

Burbank's hand came up over his shoulder as his voice spoke these words. The Shadow received the earphones in the darkness. Quiet reigned in 808 as the chief and his agent waited in the blackness. Evening had replaced daylight.

Voices came through the earphones. Tyson Weed was querulously interrogating Walbert.

"So you saw Releston come and go," remarked the lobbyist. "And you saw Coyd leave alone, in a hired hack. You trailed him twenty miles down in Virginia; then you guessed he was going to see his daughter, so you came back. So what?"

"So what?" queried Walbert, gruffly.

"That's what I said," retorted Weed. "What does any of this mean? Borneau, Vincent, Crozan—all the rest of them—what have you got that's new? Then this about Coyd?"

"I've given you all the facts about Coyd—"

"But not the kind I need. Go back on the job and keep your eyes open. Maybe you'll land a break if you persist long enough."

"Want me to go down to Virginia and watch his nibs?"

"No. He's taking a vacation; incidentally, the newspapers mentioned that also. There's no good of keeping tabs on Coyd while he's taking the rest cure. Wait until he comes back to Washington."

Sounds of Walbert's departure came. The earphones went back to Burbank. The Shadow moved toward the window; his keen eyes stared out above the lighted city.

WAITING at the window of 808, The Shadow was confident that Quidler should soon arrive in 1012. Both dicks had had appointments with Weed on that preceding night. It was likely that both would be here again. Walbert had come and gone; Quidler, by rights was due. As The Shadow mused, Burbank spoke:

"Quidler has arrived."

The Shadow took the earphones. He heard Quidler's clipped tones, which Burbank had promptly recognized. Like Walbert, Quidler had brought a written report. The Shadow listened.

"Say!" The exclamation was Weed's. "You're sure about this, Quidler?"

"Sure about everything I've written," informed Quidler, snappily. "It's more than a guess when I say a guy has been trailing me. I've wised to it a couple of times. What's more, I've seen that coupé parked in front of Coyd's too often—"

"Forget it," interrupted Weed, impatiently. "That's not the part of the report I'm talking about. I'm interested in this business about Coyd himself. You're sure you saw him outside the house?"

"Sure. Two days ago I spotted him coming in just after I got there. Along around four o'clock. He got out of that limousine and went in through the side door of the house."

"Leaving the limousine waiting for him?"

"Out back. Just like my report says. He'd been somewhere, Coyd had. Well, he came out again half an hour later, and the chauffeur drove him away."

"You should have had a cab ready to trail him."

"I know that, Mr. Weed. But I muffed it that time. It took me too long to get a cab; and I chased all over town trying to locate the limousine. And it was while I was chasing around that Coyd must have hopped back home."

A pause. Weed was evidently consulting the report. The Shadow listened keenly at the earphones. This expedition of Coyd's was something that had happened while Cliff had not been watching Quidler.

"Coming to yesterday," Quidler remarked suddenly. "It was pouring rain. I didn't think Coyd would slide out again. I kept going back and forth; and he must have left his house while I wasn't there. Because along after four, when I got there again, the limousine was waiting on the back street.

"Not conspicuous, you know. It had pulled away from Coyd's house. But I knew it by the license plate; and I'd looked the number up, like my report says."

"Tell me this," demanded Weed, "you're positive that the limousine belongs to Dunwood Rydel?"

"You bet it does," returned Quidler, "and that chauffeur is one of the monkeys who works for Rydel. Listen: it was about quarter of five when Coyd comes barging out of the side door, like he was in a hurry. Leastwise I think it was Coyd; it was too dark for me to make sure. Anyway, he took the limousine.

"I had a taxi waiting around the corner. I grabbed it and trailed the big bus to that old apartment I tell about, there in the report. The limousine waited there about ten minutes. I couldn't see

TYSON WEED—high-powered lobbyist haunting the corridor of the capitol buildings.

nobody get out; but maybe Coyd did. It's likely he got back into it again, if he was out, because he probably had to get back to his house."

"But you lost the trail?"

"Yeah. The taxi driver skidded going around a corner and wound up on the curb with a flat. I paid him and beat it, because I didn't want to be around if some cops showed up and started an argument."

"You went to Rydel's later?"

"Sure. To see if the big limousine showed up there. It did. What's more, I found out that sometimes the chauffeur parks it at the old F Street garage; and the chauffeur's name is Mullard—"

"Wait a minute."

WEED evidently took time out to make a final perusal of Quidler's report. When he spoke again, the lobbyist was sharp in tone.

"Look at this newspaper," he ordered. "This account says that Coyd has gone away for a trip."

"Sure he has," chuckled Quidler. "That fits my report, don't it? Look what I've got to say about this afternoon. I went around to that apartment and did some gumshoe work. Kept looking through transoms until I spotted the place I wanted. There was Coyd, big as life, smoking a stogie and reading a newspaper. Had the light on—the shades drawn—"

"Hold on, Quidler. The newspapers have more to say about his trip. They state that he went to Virginia."

"They're wrong. He's here in Washington. I saw him this afternoon."

"But I'm sure that he was driving down through Virginia at noon. Twenty miles south of Washington."

"Maybe he was. He could have doubled back. I've seen too many pictures of that guy's mug to be mistaken."

"That doesn't follow, Quidler. Look at these photos." Newspapers rustled; Weed was exhibiting the morning dailies, with their story of yesterday's interview. "See? They're all different."

"They're all funny-looking. Like Coyd, himself. Maybe the galoot does look one way when he's swelled up and another when he's tired or sick. But that mush of his is a giveaway. Nobody else has a mug just like it. That scar of his, those eyebrows, that shaggy hair. Don't tell me, Mr. Weed. I know."

"Humph."

Another pause after Weed's utterance. Then came an ejaculation from Quidler:

"My report! You're burning it!"

"I am," rejoined Weed, with an ugly chortle. "It's dynamite, Quidler. I want to get rid of it."

"You mean—you don't think—"

"I'm thinking plenty. I don't want to carry this paper; I don't want anyone else to see it."

"I get you," Quidler chuckled.

"Never mind, Quidler. You've done well. We can pass up a discussion of the details."

"You mean you've got enough on Coyd to make him talk turkey. Well, I hope you remembered the address of that apartment. That's where you'll find the old bozo."

"I've remembered it. That is where I'm going, Quidler."

"To talk with Coyd?"

"Maybe. Maybe not. I've put two and two together, Quidler. Maybe it will make four; maybe two and two will be twenty-two. Anyway, you've done your part. Slide along; and stay away from that apartment."

"You're going there right away?"

"Not for a while. I'm waiting in case of a long-distance call from New York. But there's no rush. The bird will still be in the nest when I look for him."

SOUNDS indicated Quidler's departure. A chuckled laugh followed; it was Weed's expression of a deep understanding. The lobbyist was comparing Walbert's report with Quidler's, much to his satisfaction. The Shadow knew that Weed had gained even more results than before.

Earphones went back to Burbank. The Shadow strolled from the room. As Henry Arnaud, carrying a briefcase, he reached the lobby and took a seat there. From this post, he could witness Weed's departure and take up the crafty lobbyist's trail.

As for Walbert and Quidler, their work was done for tonight. Hawkeye and Cliff could still watch them, however, in hope of chance developments. The future boded well for The Shadow. Only some wild freak of chance could hinder his present quest.

So reasoned The Shadow; and he reasoned wisely. For even while he waited in the lobby of the Hotel Halcyon, bad luck was on its way. Before this night had ended, The Shadow would have his share of trouble.

CHAPTER XII
TWO DICKS TALK

THE SHADOW had deliberately delayed his departure from 808 to give Quidler time to leave the Hotel Halcyon. The Shadow was positive that Cliff Marsland was waiting outside to take up the dick's trail; and The Shadow had been right.

Quidler had taken a cab outside the hotel. Another taxi had followed him. The trail had led to a frequented street just north of Pennsylvania Avenue. There, Quidler had alighted to enter an old but popular hotel, the Nayland House.

Cliff had followed the dick into the thronged lobby. He had watched Quidler enter the taproom. The place had but one entrance; Quidler would have to come out through the lobby. So Cliff sat down and waited.

The Nayland taproom was crowded and noisy. Cliff had decided that Quidler could not have chosen it for an important meeting; and he was right. In fact, Quidler had simply decided to celebrate. Weed had slipped him a fat roll of cash; the dick had cause to be jubilant.

It was entirely by chance that Quidler happened to bump into an old acquaintance. Shouldering his way to the jammed bar, the beak-faced dick jostled a long-necked rowdy who was standing there. The fellow swung about with an angry snarl. Quidler recognized a sallow, rattish face.

"Hello, Jake," chuckled the dick, with a friendly grin. "Bumped into you, didn't I, huh? How're you, old fellow. Last guy I expected to see here was Jake Thurler."

"Hello, Quidler," rejoined Jake, a leer forming on his leathery lips. "What're you doin' in town? Still in the gumshoe racket?"

"Sure. It's gravy. Washington's a good spot. What're you doing, though? Running booze down through the dry South?"

Jake shook his head.

"Out of that racket," he informed. "Too hot for me. Too hot for any guy that's got brains. I'm working for Stew Luffy, the big shot that's runnin' a classy gamblin' joint across the Potomac. Steerin' suckers down there is my job. Plenty of saps loose; an' I'm the guy to spot 'em."

"You're workin' tonight?"

"Sure. This is a good place to draw from." Jake was speaking in a low, confidential tone. "Sometimes I fix the squawkers, too. Stew don't like howls about his joint. But say"—the ratty fellow raised his tone—"here's a guy you'd like to know, Quidler. He's in the gumshoe racket, too."

JAKE leaned back so Quidler could look past him to see a glum-faced fellow who was wiping foam from a big black mustache. The man was wearing a Derby hat tilted over his forehead; but Quidler could see an angry look in his eyes when Jake nudged him roughly.

"Snap out of it, Walbert!" snorted Jake. "Wantcha to meet an old pal of mine. He's a Sherlock, too. Shake hands with Quidler over here."

Walbert extended a flabby paw and received Quidler's hand grip. Then, the mustached man swung away and began to drink again, while Jake Thurler turned to chat with Quidler.

"Who is the guy, Jake?" queried Quidler, in an undertone. "Looks like a dumb cluck to me. Who's he working for?"

"Keep it under your hat," confided Jake. "I'm the only bird he's mentioned it to. Ever hear of a bozo named Weed? Tyson Weed?"

"Walbert's working for Weed?"

"Sure. And it ought to be a good racket. Weed's got dough, they say."

"Edge out, Jake. I want to talk to Walbert."

Jake consented reluctantly. He whispered a warning as he moved away. Quidler gave him a wise look; then slid in beside Walbert. The mustached dick studied him rather sourly.

"Ease down to the end of the bar," remarked Quidler. "I got something to tell you, Walbert. A lot to tell you."

Walbert hesitated; then followed instructions. Something in Quidler's manner impressed him. As they reached the deserted spot, Quidler came right to the point.

"Listen, bozo," he informed, "a guy that tries to trail me is wasting his time. I'm no palooka. Get me?"

"Who are you talking about, fellow?" demanded Walbert, with a growl. "You mean me?"

"I mean that when I'm working on a case, the bird that hires me don't need to check up on what I'm doing."

"Yeah? Well, who's been hiring you lately?"

"A fellow named Tyson Weed."

WALBERT'S jaw dropped. For a moment, the mustached dick stared so sharply that his very manner was a giveaway. Quidler chuckled hoarsely.

"Tyson Weed," he repeated. "He's the guy that hired me. To keep a lookout on a congressman named Coyd. You know all about it, Walbert. You're the guy I've seen out front of Coyd's, parked in a coupé."

Quidler's eyes were flashing eagerly. He was not sure about Walbert having been the man in the coupé. But the blink of the eyes beneath the Derby hat made Quidler know that his guess was a good one.

"All right," parried Walbert, realizing that he had slipped. "Suppose I was out front of Coyd's? What does that mean? Where were you?"

"Out back of Coyd's. Does that mean anything to you?"

"Not a thing. I was never anywhere but out front. Say, Quidler; it looks like you're the second fiddler. Keeping an eye on me, eh?"

Quidler grinned sourly. Walbert's return thrust had been a good one. He clapped the fellow roundly on the shoulder.

"Not bad, Walbert," he approved. "Only you did some tagging once in a while. Hopping cabs to follow the ones I was in. Picking up my trail; then dropping it."

"Hopping cabs?" quizzed Walbert. "Say—what do I want with them when I've got my own buggy? Let's get this straight, Quidler: do you really think I've been trailing you?"

"Somebody has. I told Weed so tonight and he said to forget it."

"You were up at Weed's tonight?"

"Sure. I just came from there."

Walbert brought his empty glass down with a thud.

"The louse!" he ejaculated. "So that's why he told me to vamoose. After he'd said get there early. Didn't want me to know he had another guy working on the same case."

"Weed told me just when to get there," admitted Quidler. "Say, fellow, maybe we're getting somewhere. I'm putting it straight; I never knew that anybody else was supposed to watch Coyd. Did you?"

"No. That's straight, Quidler."

"So Weed took us both for saps."

"Looks like it."

Quidler chuckled. After all, it was Weed's business to do as he liked. A grin on his peaked face, the dick called for drinks. Walbert indulged in a broad smile. He saw the situation identically with Quidler.

"Looks like our stunt is to pal up," decided Walbert. "Hand Weed the ha-ha. Working together, we can do a better job. How does it hit you, Quidler?"

"Not a bad idea. Well, you didn't know I was watching you; and I thought you were watching me. We were both wrong."

"Which makes us both right."

Quidler, gulping from a glass, stopped short. He turned to Walbert, with a serious stare.

"Somebody was watching me," he declared. "Maybe not at Coyd's; but at other places. Say—there couldn't be a third guy working for Weed?"

"Not a chance. Finish your drink. The next is on me."

Quidler complied; then made another comment:

"There is a guy, though. He's working for somebody different than Weed. Guess he didn't spot you, Walbert; but he trailed me."

"If he trailed you, he's liable to trail me. Especially if we team up on the q.t."

"You said it. It's something we ought to find out about."

"I'm going to."

QUIDLER turned and spied Jake. He beckoned to the fellow and Jake came over. Quidler spoke confidentially.

"There's a guy been trailing me, Jake. How about getting a line on him? Could you help me?"

"Sure. It's a cinch. Want me to bag him?"

"Can you do it?"

"Soft. I got everything outside. A phony cab for the saps; a touring car to cover. All you got to do is start out in a cab of your own. The phony will pick up the bird you want."

Walbert interposed.

"You don't need a cab, Quidler," offered the mustached dick. "Ride with me in my coupé. Which way will we head, Jake?"

"Over the Potomac bridge. Duck off the road and douse the glims. My man in the hack will do the rest. You can come on back."

"What about the mug?" inquired Quidler. "We got nothing against him, you know."

"We'll make him squawk," assured Jake. "It don't take much. Leave that to us."

"Sure," grumbled Walbert. "Jake knows his stuff. He'll handle the bird."

"You bet I will," leered Jake. "Out at Stew Luffy's joint. Wait a couple of minutes, while I fix things. Then go out and get in your buggy." Jake departed.

FIVE minutes later, Walbert and Quidler set down their empty glasses. Buzzing as they left the taproom, they went through the lobby and out to the street. Cliff Marsland saw them pass. Calmly, The Shadow's agent followed.

Walbert's coupé was parked a hundred feet down the street. The dicks boarded it; Walbert started the motor, and the car drew away. Cliff spied it from the curb; as he looked for a taxi, one shot into view from the other side of the street. Cliff boarded the cab and ordered the driver to follow the coupé.

The two cars crossed the Potomac. Walbert took to a curving boulevard; then found a little-traveled road and chose it. Cliff, crouched forward in the taxi, pointed out the path to the driver. The fellow nodded; but lagged slightly. Up ahead, the coupé swung a curve.

"Here's a good spot," said Walbert, to Quidler. He pulled the coupé to the side beneath some trees. "We'll douse the glims and watch what happens."

Out went the lights. The dicks watched from darkness. As they did, the top of the rumble seat opened cautiously. A wizened face poked its nose into view. Hawkeye looked about; then gazed toward the road as he heard a car approaching.

It was Cliff's taxi. Hawkeye watched it pass; he heard the chuckles from the dicks. The cab was slowing, a hundred yards ahead. Then, from around the curve, came a swift touring car. As Hawkeye peered over the rear fender, he saw the larger machine overtake the cab, just as the taxi stopped.

Watching, Hawkeye saw men pile from the touring car and drag a figure from the taxi. Walbert started the coupé; the car swung about and started back toward Washington. Hawkeye, high out of the rumble seat, could see the taxi turning to come back; the touring car was going on ahead.

Boldly, the little spotter swung clear of his hiding place. Clinging to the right fender, he pushed his face up toward the open window. He could hear comments despite the rattle of the car. The dicks were chuckling.

"The guy was trailing you, right enough, Quidler."

"Yeah. Thanks for helping get rid of him, Walbert. He'll talk plenty when he gets out to Luffy's joint."

"Jake's taximan must have shoved a gun in his face. Covered him unexpected and made it soft for the other guys."

The car was near the Potomac bridge. Lights showed a gasoline station. Hawkeye dropped from the running board as the coupé slowed. With loping gait, he hurried toward the service station. There, Hawkeye found a telephone.

THREE minutes later, The Shadow saw the clerk at the Hotel Halcyon look into the box marked 808. Rising from his lobby chair, The Shadow went to a telephone. He called the room. Burbank's quiet voice gave the news.

"Instructions," declared The Shadow, in Arnaud's easy tone. "Hawkeye to cover Weed."

"Instructions received" was Burbank's response.

The Shadow strolled from the lobby. He walked straight to a parking space; there he entered a coupé that was parked there in the name of Henry Arnaud. Behind the wheel, he started the car and slowed at an inconspicuous corner of the lot. Swiftly he donned cloak and hat, from his briefcase.

Hands thrust automatics beneath the black

cloak. Gloves slid over long fingers. A foot pressed the accelerator as hands gripped the wheel. The car roared as it sped along a clear street. The speedy coupé reached the Potomac bridge.

The car passed a cab on the bridge. Not the one that had carried Cliff; that had already reached Washington. This was one that Hawkeye had called from the service station. The shrewd spotter was speeding back, to serve as The Shadow's substitute.

For The Shadow had given up his plan to follow Tyson Weed in person. His mission was one of emergency; a rescue that had become most pressing. Hawkeye had learned the vital facts by listening to Walbert and Quidler.

The Shadow knew the location of "Stew" Luffy's notorious gambling dive, an undercover establishment that persisted in defiance of the law. Minister of vengeance, he was speeding thither to aid Cliff Marsland, trapped by men of crime!

CHAPTER XIII
THE SHADOW'S SUBSTITUTE

FIVE minutes after The Shadow had left the Hotel Halcyon, Tyson Weed appeared in the lobby. Luck had tricked The Shadow tonight. The chance meeting of Walbert and Quidler had forced an issue that the dicks, individually, would not have pressed. Cliff Marsland's capture had been the result of a cooperative plan.

Drawn to an immediate quest, The Shadow had been forced to leave an open time period. Chances were that Weed would not choose those few minutes for his trip to the old apartment house that lay somewhere in Washington; but again, the short odds won. Weed was leaving the hotel while Hawkeye was still on his way in from the Potomac bridge.

Outside the hotel, Weed hailed a cab. About to enter it, the lobbyist paused. A newsboy, coming along the street, was shouting out the headlines as he sold the bulldog editions of a morning journal. Weed paused to buy a newspaper. He fumbled for the change and found it.

A penny slipped from his hand as he paid the newsboy. The coin rolled across the sidewalk and disappeared through a grating. Snatching the newspaper roughly from the boy's hand, Weed turned toward the cab.

"Say, mister—"

The newsboy's plaint was wistful. He had not even touched the coin that the man had dropped. Weed snarled angrily.

"Fish it out for yourself," he told the boy, pointing to the grating. "I haven't time to waste."

"But it's down the grating—"

Weed shoved the boy aside; but before he could enter the cab, the driver slammed the door. Leaning from the front seat, the taximan took the boy's part.

"A hurry, eh?" he barked at Weed. "Not in this cab, you ain't. Pay the kid the cent you owe him, or you don't ride in this hack."

"Move along. I'll just take another cab."

"Yeah? Not while I'm around. It'll be tough for the hackie that gives you a lift."

The cab driver showed a pair of threatening fists. He made a gesture that indicated further pugnacity. For a moment, Weed thought that he intended to step to the street. Huddling back, the lobbyist fished in his pocket; finding no pennies, he tossed the newsboy a nickel and snarled for him to keep the change.

"Thanks, mister!"

WEED paid no attention to the newsboy's remark. Expediency, not generosity had forced Weed to the deed. The cab door was being opened by the grinning driver. Weed stepped aboard and snapped out his destination, telling the cabby to hurry. The taxi shot away.

But at that very moment, another cab had swung around the corner. Sharp eyes from its interior had spotted the lanky figure of Weed, hopping spider-like into the waiting cab.

Hawkeye, just in time, was quick to nudge the driver and tell him to follow Weed's cab. The fuming lobbyist had been in luck; now the situation had changed. Weed's own stinginess over a dropped penny had delayed him long enough for Hawkeye to snag his trail.

Unfortunately, the driver of Weed's cab was a man who held no malice. Even though he expected no tip, he drove with speed and precision. Cutting through the weblike maze of Washington's streets, he picked shortcuts and sudden turns that were confusing to Hawkeye's driver.

It was the little spotter, not the cabby, who managed to keep an eye on the cab ahead. But at last, the game failed. Hawkeye's cab swung a corner, sped a block and crossed Q Street. Hawkeye could see no taxi ahead. He knew that the trail had been lost. Telling the driver to stop, he shoved a bill in the fellow's hand and dropped from the cab.

Hawkeye was going on the theory that perhaps Weed's destination had been nearby. If so, the lobbyist had alighted and dismissed his cab. There might still be a chance to trail him. If Weed had gone on, there would be no use trying to pick up his course. Hawkeye was hoping for the only chance.

Weed's cab had stopped. It had turned down Q Street and had halted before an obscure building, while Hawkeye's cab was crossing the thoroughfare. Weed had scowled as he paid the driver.

Finding the tip omitted, the driver had laughed and driven on. Weed had turned into the entrance of an old apartment. Both the cab and he were out of sight when Hawkeye's came back to Q Street. The building that Weed entered was actually an old house converted into an apartment. Once it had been well managed; the name board showed push-buttons and bell. But the bell-button bore a scrawled paper that said "Out of Order" and Weed decided that the door might be unlocked. It was.

Entering, the lobbyist went up one flight. He came to a door marked 2D. He paused there, staring at the lighted transom; then went to the end of the hall where he found an opened window that led to a fire escape. Stepping out, Weed found a darkened window that he was sure opened into the apartment that he wanted.

Again, luck was his. The window was unlocked; evidently the occupant of the apartment feared no intruders. It was dark here on the fire escape, with an empty building in back and a little alleyway between.

... the top of the rumble seat opened cautiously. A wizened face poked its nose into view.... Watching, Hawkeye saw men pile from the touring car and drag a figure from his taxi.... He could hear comments.

Weed opened the window and slid into the room. He was breathing tensely as he felt his way through darkness, toward the crack of a lighted door.

Arriving at the barrier, Weed paused; then, with a jolt, he shoved the door open and plunged into the room. He grabbed the door and closed it behind him. Looking across the room, he saw a man rise excitedly from a chair. Weed grinned as the fellow threw a newspaper aside.

The lobbyist was staring at the glowering face of Congressman Layton Coyd.

ATTIRED in smoking jacket, the surprised occupant of the apartment was too perturbed to make a move. Weed saw his lips twitch; that fact gave the lobbyist confidence. He motioned toward the chair and bowed with sarcasm.

"Sit down, Congressman," he urged, in wheedling fashion. "Excuse my unannounced arrival. Since I am here, we may as well be friendly."

"Who are you?" The question was hoarse-toned. "Why have you come here?"

"You don't remember me, Mr. Coyd?" Weed smiled meanly as he remembered statements in Quidler's first report. "Well, well, I had forgotten that your mind was troubled. Loss of memory, perhaps."

All of Coyd's dignity became apparent as the shock-haired man drew himself erect and pressed his hand against his scarred chin. Then came a shake of the shaggy head.

"What?" quizzed Weed. "You don't remember Tyson Weed? Your pet lobbyist? The prize pest, as you used to call me?"

Coyd's figure relaxed. The expression that came over his face was partly one of anger; at the same time, it showed relief. It was like the dawn of recognition, followed by a nod.

"I remember you now, Mr. Weed. Sit down. Tell me the purpose of your visit. I am rather surprised that you learned I was here."

"No wonder." Weed grinned as he took a chair. "The newspapers stated that you had gone to Virginia."

"Yes, they did." Coyd's words came reluctantly as the unwilling host resumed his chair. "Tell me, you possess this information exclusively as your own."

"Yes," replied Weed, blandly, "and that fact, Mr. Coyd, leaves us clear to form a friendly agreement."

Twitching fingers pushed their way through shaggy, black hair, that glistened in the lamplight. Weed watched the expression on the tight-skinned face.

"An agreement," came Coyd's ponderous tone. "Just what do you mean by an agreement, Mr. Weed?"

"Just this." Weed was on his feet; his hissed tone lacked its whine. "I represent various interests, Mr. Coyd. I have been paid to see that their rights are given fair consideration by Congress; that needed appropriations are made for them."

"And you are even empowered to use bribery to obtain votes. Am I right, Mr. Weed?"

"I have never attempted bribery."

"Because you knew that you were dealing with honest men. You want the government to purchase worthless timberlands; to grant money for the reopening of useless canals. You are ready to advocate the draining of marshlands, to further speculative real estate developments."

"What of it? Such things have been done before."

"I have never been party to them."

WEED watched a change come over Coyd's expression. The shaggy-haired man came to his feet; he was pompous as he thrust one hand beneath his smoking jacket in Napoleonic pose.

"You have proven yourself a nuisance, Weed," came the accusing tones. "In the past, I have refused to see you. Your visit here is uncalled for. There is the door. Go."

"Not yet." Weed grinned wisely as he faced his challenger. "I have a purpose here, Mr. Coyd. Tell me: why did you make that statement regarding munitions? Why were you responsible for an attempt to aid speculators?"

"A whim on my part. A mistake. One that I rectified after I realized it."

"You take the credit? Come, Coyd—I am too wise to fool. Senator Releston forced the issue."

"You are wrong, Weed. Read the newspapers—"

"I have read them. Between the lines. I know that your scheme went sour. You fooled Releston; but not me. I know what's coming. Something bigger than munitions."

There was no reply. Coyd's features were purple; but Weed noted that clenched fists were twitching helplessly. The lobbyist thrust a pointing finger beneath the congressman's flattish nose.

"Here are my terms," affirmed Weed. "You back the things I want; in turn, I'll keep my mouth shut. I won't visit your house; instead, I'll see you here, by appointment. While you're pulling your own big deals, you can slip mine by in the rush."

"Impossible." Coyd's head shook emphatically. "After all, Weed, why should I listen to your preposterous requests? Why do I need your silence?"

"Why? Because it would do you no good if it were known that you, the self-styled paragon of justice, had chosen to live in a hideout here in Washington."

"A hideout? Absurd! My physician has ordered a rest. I chose this apartment for that purpose. It is quiet here."

WEED licked his lips. His face was gloating, his chuckle deep in his throat. He had found his chance; he used it.

"Suppose, Mr. Coyd"—the lobbyist was sarcastic as he pronounced the name—"suppose that I should inform Senator Releston of your present whereabouts? Suppose I told him that Congressman Layton Coyd so requires rest that he has chosen to take it in two places simultaneously?

"What if I told him that you were living in this apartment and also dwelling in your comfortable lodge, some seventy miles away, in Virginia? What would Senator Releston think of such miraculous eccentricity?"

"I'm not at the hunting lodge, Weed. I'm right here, in Washington."

"Certain persons, if promptly quizzed, might swear that you were at the lodge. For instance: Miss Evelyn Coyd; and also Miss Beatrice Rydel. If Senator Releston should call the lodge, by long distance, this very evening—"

"One moment, Weed. You actually intend to see Releston?"

"I do. And if he requires a counter witness, there is a man named Mullard—one of Dunwood Rydel's chauffeurs, I believe—"

"You know more than I thought you did, Weed. Say nothing further. I am ready to talk terms."

The blatant tone had ended. Weed smiled as he saw the look of resignation that had come over the tight-skinned face. His point was won; he listened for his victim's next statement.

"Go back to your hotel," came the slow pronouncement. "Say nothing of your visit here. I have a conference tonight with a certain man—one whose name you have probably guessed—and I shall tell him that I intend to support your enterprises.

"After all, such a course may be advisable. It will carry attention away from other matters. Since I am deemed eccentric, it is preferable that I should play the role in full. On second thought, Weed, I believe that your visit here has been a fortunate one.

"You will hear from me tomorrow." Advancing, the speaker clamped a friendly hand on Weed's shoulder. "I shall call by telephone and arrange a definite appointment. Meanwhile"—he was drawing Weed to the door while speaking—"you can prepare your own plans. Use wisdom. Arrange a systematic campaign whereby your requests will come at intervals. We must cooperate in this game, Weed."

The lobbyist nodded. His shaggy-haired host opened the door and urged him into the hall. Weed thrust out a hand and received the firm shake that was characteristic of Congressman Coyd. The door closed; the lobbyist strolled toward the stairs.

Inside the room, a vast change had come over the countenance of Congressman Layton Coyd. The apartment dweller was listening to the departure of Weed's footsteps. Satisfied that the lobbyist was gone, he wheeled about and hurried to the telephone. Hastily, he dialed a number; when a voice responded, he spoke in quick, abrupt terms:

"Weed was here... Tyson Weed, the lobbyist... Yes, he's wise... Yes, I handled him. He's gone back to his hotel... Expects to hear from me tomorrow...

"You'll handle it? Good! That's best. In person; then no one will know... What's that? The other hideout? Yes, you're right... I'll start there at once... Yes, I can call Mullard myself, at the F Street garage..."

A look of elation showed on the tight features of Congressman Coyd. A quick hand hung up the receiver; a rapid finger dialed a number. In disguised tone, the speaker asked for Mullard; when the chauffeur answered, he gave abrupt orders to come at once.

OUTSIDE the old apartment building, Tyson Weed had paused to light a cigarette. The match showed his grin; then, as he puffed his smoke, the lobbyist strode along Q Street. His lanky figure was moving at its customary gait. Weed came beneath a lamplight; his leering figures showed.

Eyes spotted him from across the street. A watcher saw Weed turn the corner. A hunched form edged toward the old apartment building. It was Hawkeye. The Shadow's agent had seen the tall man come from the house; upon recognizing Weed, Hawkeye knew where the lobbyist had been.

Crossing the street, Hawkeye entered the converted apartment house. He looked about the first floor; then sneaked up to the second. Staring along the passage, he saw the opened window to the fire escape. Hawkeye went in that direction. Peering from the window, he saw the opened window of apartment 2D.

Hawkeye eased out to the fire escape. He slipped into the window of the bedroom. He saw the glimmer that edged the farther door. Imitating Weed, Hawkeye did a sneak in that direction. He reached the door; just as he laid his hand upon the knob, the barrier was yanked open. Hawkeye stopped short; he found himself staring into the livid countenance of Congressman Layton Coyd.

This time, it was the intruder who was surprised;

moreover, Hawkeye was of a different ilk than Weed. Before The Shadow's substitute could make a move, a fierce oath came from Coyd's spread lips. Strong hands shot for Hawkeye's throat.

The grapple that followed was a swift one. Hawkeye was gripped by an antagonist to whom fury had lent unexpected strength; at the same time, The Shadow's agent was as slippery as an eel. He twisted to the living room; there, they banged about, upsetting furniture in the struggle. As they bowled against a table, Hawkeye twisted free.

Dropping back to a corner near the bedroom door, Hawkeye yanked a revolver from his pocket. He covered his foe with the weapon; he heard a snarl, then saw the look of terror that flashed upon his enemy's dried countenance. Hawkeye grinned, more wisely than had Weed. It was the spotter's turn to talk terms with Congressman Layton Coyd.

As Hawkeye puffed for breath, a sound made him turn. He was just in time to see the door from the hall swing open. On the threshold was a man in chauffeur's uniform: Mullard.

The fellow's face was set in an ugly grimace. Mullard had arrived to hear the crash of conflict; he had opened the door with a duplicate key. He had yanked a revolver, to deal with the intruder.

Covered by Mullard's gun, Hawkeye had only one course: self-preservation. He did not lose an instant in taking it. With a quick spring, Hawkeye dived for the bedroom. Mullard fired viciously, but too late. The chauffeur's bullet whistled wide of The Shadow's substitute.

LOPING through the bedroom, Hawkeye gained the window and dived for the fire escape. He was just in time. Mullard had reached the bedroom; two shots stabbed from the chauffeur's gun.

Hawkeye twisted through the rail and clung there to take aim; but Mullard had reached the window. The chauffeur saw the whiteness of Hawkeye's wizened face and jabbed shots at the fugitive.

As the first bullet whistled past the tip of Hawkeye's ear, the spotter dropped from the fire escape. Wise was his move; for Mullard's second shot zizzed past the very spot where the little trailer had been.

Gasping a wild cry as he fell, Hawkeye plopped to the mud of the alleyway and rolled beneath the hinged ladder of the fire escape.

Mullard had heard Hawkeye's gasp. The chauffeur thought that he had crippled his quarry. Windows were banging upward in the apartments on other floors.

Mullard swung about, snatched a big suitcase from the floor and dashed through the living room. He saw his companion waiting; whiteness registered on Coyd's tight features.

"I bagged him," growled Mullard. "Let's get away, in a hurry. Who was he?"

"Some thief" was the reply. "Weed was here; the fellow must have found the window that he opened."

Footsteps clattered as the two men dashed down the front stairs. Outside, they leaped into the limousine which Mullard had parked a few doors below. As yet, excitement had not reached the front of the building. Mullard shot the big car from the curb.

Just as the limousine wheeled away, a wizened face poked from a corner of the old house. Hawkeye's sharp eyes saw the departure; the spotter knew that pursuit was hopeless. No vehicle was handy to take up the chase. Sidling away, Hawkeye scurried along Q Street, anxious to get away from this terrain before police arrived.

The Shadow's substitute had done his best; but the breaks had been against him. Too late to spot Weed's entry, Hawkeye had reached the hideout only to encounter trouble. Instead of gaining a triumph for The Shadow, the little substitute had been lucky to save his own hide.

Tonight, success had been in the balance. Had The Shadow, himself, been present to trail Tyson Weed, the schemes that involved Congressman Coyd would have been nipped in the bud. Had The Shadow witnessed that interview, evil purposes would have been revealed.

Fate had decreed otherwise. The game was still on; and with it, crime was due. The flash of opportunity had passed. New tasks would confront The Shadow.

CHAPTER XIV
MURDER BY NIGHT

HAWKEYE'S experience had been a rough one; but the little spotter had twisted free from his trap. In that, Hawkeye had been fortunate—much luckier than another of The Shadow's agents. For while Hawkeye, free and unhurt by his drop to the muddy alley, was sidling away from Q Street, Cliff Marsland was experiencing the tight close of a trap from which he could see no escape.

Bound to a chair, his arms crossed behind his back, Cliff was blinking at the single light of an underground room. Windowless, whitewashed walls surrounded him; between Cliff and the only door stood the quartette of ruffians who had brought him here. Chief of the four was Jake Thurler, a venomous, snarling inquisitor.

As Hawkeye paused for breath, a sound made him turn. He was just in time to see the door from the hall swing open.

"Not squawking, eh?" came Jake's quiz. It was a reference to the stolidness that Cliff had maintained. "Well, that ain't going to last forever. Get that hunk of lead pipe, Pete. Shove it in them ropes behind this mug's back."

Pete complied. Jake, glaring, was about to issue another threat when a sharp rap sounded at the door. Jake gestured to another rowdy. The fellow pulled back the bolt and admitted a squatty man in evening clothes.

"Hello, Stew," laughed Jake. "Want to see me put the heat on this bozo?"

"What are you going to do?" queried Stew. "Maul him?"

"Not yet," leered Jake. "Too many taps on the konk makes a mug goofy. Sometimes they ain't able to squawk even when they want to. I got a better way."

"What's the lay, Jake? When you brought this bird in the back way, I said use your bean about him. What's he been pulling?"

"Trailin' a pal of mine, Stew. I said I'd find out what his racket was—who he was workin' for."

"And your pal said to give him the heat?"

"No. But two fellows said to nab him; and they left it up to me. Maybe they'd be soft enough to yap if they saw me workin' on this guy; but they ain't here."

STEW looked doubtful. Cliff watched the gambler's callused face; for a moment he was hopeful. Not that he saw any mercy in Stew Luffy's expression; on the contrary, the gambler's hard countenance was more merciless than Jake Thurler's ratty face.

Cliff's hope was that Stew might consider it poor policy to make a torture chamber out of this room beneath his gambling joint. For a moment, Stew seemed inclined in that direction. It was Jake who turned the trend.

"This mug was around the Nayland House," he informed. "That's the best spot I got, Stew, for snaggin' the saps that I bring out here. Maybe he was watchin' me, too. I gotta find out, don't I?"

Stew nodded.

"Better make him talk," decided the gambler. "The place is yours, Jake."

Jake grinned as the gambler turned about and went to the door. Stew had decided to wash his hands of the cutthroat crew. Jake and his ruffians had proven useful at times.

"Coming down later, Stew?"

"Maybe," returned the gambler, in response to Jake's question. "If the guy's got anything to spill, I'd like to hear it."

As soon as the door was closed, Jake spoke to Pete. The underling had shoved the lead pipe into the ropes. Another hoodlum took the opposite end of the bar. Together, they twisted. Cliff winced as the tightening ropes jerked back his shoulders. He felt as if he were in a straitjacket.

"Hold it that way," rasped Jake. "Let him get used to it. Slap another turn when I give the word."

Stew Luffy, upon leaving the cellar room, had gone up a flight of stairs to reach another door. There, the gambler rapped. The door opened; Stew faced a big, pock-faced rowdy who served as bouncer in the gambling joint. The pair stood in a little hallway, with a door opposite. Stew gestured down the darkened corridor.

"Anybody on the back door, Frank?"

"Yeah," returned the bouncer. "Muggsy is out there. He let Jake and them other guys come in."

"I'll send some of the boys around from the front," decided Stew. "We need more than one man there. If there's a raid, we'll need time to tip off Jake. He's putting the heat on a guy. Wanted me to come back and watch."

"Going down again, boss?"

"Me? Not a chance. I'm going in and watch the suckers lose their wads. Say—there'll be a fifty-grand take tonight. No sap has a chance in this joint."

"Not with that gaffed roulette wheel. Say, boss—you've fixed this racket great."

"It's just started. If it stays quiet for a couple of weeks, we'll all be sitting pretty. That's why I'm letting Jake put the heat on the guy he grabbed. Maybe the bird knows too much. It's best to find out."

With that, Stew opened the door opposite the cellar. Frank grinned as he saw the boss depart, en route to the gambling room where gullible players were losing their money on a fixed roulette wheel. Frank's chuckle indicated his admiration for Stew; but the bouncer's gloating was due for a sudden finish.

Something moved amid the blackness of the back door corridor. Like gruesome tentacles of night, two outstretched arms came forward. Then darkness became a living shape.

A cloaked figure followed the arms; a silent, living avalanche swooped hard upon Frank, before the big bouncer realized what was arriving.

IT was The Shadow, swift, noiseless and expert in his overwhelming attack. Frank, gasping, stared bulge-eyed into fiery optics as gloved hands pressed his throat.

Frantically, the bouncer struggled, clutching at a twisting form that managed to wrench from his grappling arms. All the while, thumbs pressed hard against the big fellow's windpipe.

Frank slumped. The hands released their grip. The bouncer rallied for a struggle; but arms were clutching him for the final stroke. A lithe, powerful figure snapped backward; the bouncer hurtled head foremost to the floor. His skull cracked the wall. Frank lay half stunned.

Snapping away the fellow's belt, The Shadow bound Frank's hands behind his back. This was his second swift victory. Entering the back door of the gambling joint, he had clipped "Muggsy" on the chin and left that victim senseless, bound and gagged as well.

The Shadow finished his job with Frank by gagging the bouncer with the fellow's own handkerchief. That done, The Shadow unlocked the cellar door.

In the improvised torture chamber, Cliff Marsland had experienced the agony of a second twist. His back was tight against the rear of the chair; the topmost rung was cutting against his spine. The strain upon his shoulders was even worse. His arms felt ready to wrench from their sockets.

Cliff realized what torture the next twist would bring. He foresaw permanent injury should he be wrenched to a worse position and held there. Yet Cliff was grim in his defiance. He was ready to hold out, despite the fact that rescue seemed hopeless. Cliff did not know that Hawkeye had been a witness of his capture.

"Spill it, mug," oathed Jake Thurler, his ugly face close to Cliff's. "Who told you to tag Quidler? What's the trouble? Not comfortable enough? I'll fix that. Go ahead, you guys. Give it another twist—"

Jake broke off and held up his hand to stop the torturers. Someone was rapping at the door. Jake nodded to the hoodlum stationed there. The fellow pulled back the bolt and swung the barrier inward.

"It's Stew," chuckled Jake. "Come to lamp the fun. I thought he'd be back—"

Jake blinked suddenly. For a moment, he saw only the blackness of the cellar. Then, to his astonishment, the gloom moved inward. A *swish*, a sudden change of shape. Blackness had become a living being. A whispered laugh echoed through the cell-like room. Jake gasped his recognition:

"The Shadow!"

A FIGURE cloaked in black, burning eyes that glared from beneath the brim of a slouch hat. Mammoth automatics, thrust forward by gloved fists. Those were the impressions that held vicious crooks staring.

Jake stood helpless; so did the cutthroat at the door. Pete and his companion loosed their grip upon the lead pipe; their hands came upward.

Cliff Marsland grinned weakly as he tugged forward. The bar revolved among the ropes. The strain ended. Cliff's muscles responded with more than normal strength. He gave a powerful twist, vainly hoping to break a rope; his success was different than he expected.

The side of the chair back broke. As the wood crackled, the rope slid from it. Cliff drew one arm free; then used it to tug the other free. Rising, he twisted and pressed down upon the broken chair as he pulled his ankles clear from the lower ropes. That job was easy, once he had gained a standing position.

There was no need to talk. Jake and his crew had learned who Cliff's chief was. Their realization that they were faced by The Shadow had been a stunning blow. But Cliff's regaining of freedom was to produce a change.

Jake was maddened at the thought of the captive being clear to demand vengeance. Insanely, the rat-faced rogue made a wild leap for The Shadow.

The move would have been suicidal but for the actions of the others. As maddened as Jake, they, too, went berserk. The hoodlum at the door snatched out a gun. So did the torturers behind the chair. Cliff was between them and The Shadow; he was their shield, and knowing it, they leaped for the released prisoner.

The Shadow had caught the moves in a twinkling. Instead of blazing a shot at Jake, he wheeled suddenly from the wild crook's path. He shot one hand upward and pressed the trigger of its automatic. Flame spurted toward the single light in the ceiling; the bullet shattered the huge incandescent.

While glass was clattering amid the sudden darkness, an automatic blazed in the direction of the door. A cry—a groan—The Shadow had clipped the guard who had been posted at the barrier. He had picked the rowdy's exact position in the dark.

Cliff parried the swing of wild arms in the dark. Free from the broken chair, he dived across the room, heading for the door. He knew that The Shadow wanted him clear of the fray. He was responding to that wish. The Shadow heard Cliff stumble over the prone form of the wounded crook.

Revolvers were barking wildly; in response came automatics, their blaze from an unexpected inner corner. Jake and his two pals saw the spurts; wildly, they fired in that direction, forgetting the door in their effort to down The Shadow. Cliff, stumbling through, gained the stairway.

AUTOMATICS spat in earnest. His unarmed agent clear, The Shadow had no longer need to tarry. Ever shifting, he had moved away from telltale spots where his guns had flashed; but crooks, with their spurting revolvers, had forgotten the need for motion in the dark.

Ripping bursts were thunderous in the stone-walled room as The Shadow dispatched scorching slugs toward living targets.

His laugh, triumphant, quivered mockingly through the torture chamber as The Shadow whisked through the doorway and followed Cliff's path. Groans and oaths, belated shots—those alone pursued the master of darkness. The Shadow had felled every member of Jake's crew, including the rat-faced ruffian himself.

Cliff had reached the upper hallway to find Frank's outsprawled figure. A revolver was bulging from the bouncer's pocket. Cliff snatched the weapon; and none too soon.

Cries came from the end of the hallway. Stew's door crew had come around the building, to find Muggsy bound and helpless. Entering, they had spotted Cliff.

The Shadow's agent opened fire. As he did, the cellar door swung outward. From the crack between the door and the frame, a fresh automatic blasted quick shots down the hall.

Cliff heard a hissed order; he dived for the door that led into the gambling rooms. He was no longer a target when the men at the back door found the range.

The cover-up crew was advancing; the progress stopped as the invaders met The Shadow's withering cannonade. Under that barrage, they faltered. As the foremost ruffians staggered, those behind them turned and scrambled for the safety of outdoors. The Shadow, *swishing* out from behind the door, delivered final bullets. The corridor cleared, he followed Cliff's path.

Straight into the gambling room. There, Cliff had stopped short. Tuxedoed men and gowned women had heard the gunplay; they were scurrying for side rooms, while frightened croupiers were gathering up money from the roulette table.

Stew Luffy, revolver in hand, was standing in the center of the room. Alone, he was ready to shoot it out with any comer.

HURTLING in from a passage, Cliff took the challenge. As Stew blazed hasty shots, Cliff answered with bullets that skimmed the gambler's coat sleeves. Recognizing the prisoner whom he had failed to favor, Stew feared further quarrel.

As croupiers burrowed their way behind slot machines along the wall, Stew dived past the roulette table. Behind its bulk, he popped up with his gun.

Cliff, taking a shortcut, had reached the near side of the table. Dropping as Stew came up, Cliff hoisted the table with a mighty heave and toppled its entire bulk upon his foe. Stew, scrambling back, was too late.

The table flattened him; his revolver clattered across the carpet as his head thudded the floor. Money scattered everywhere; the roulette wheel jolted loose and rolled to a stop, exposing the wiring of the electrical equipment that had been used to gyp the customers.

A shot blazed from the front door. A bullet sizzled past Cliff's ear and shattered the glass front of a slot machine. Cliff swung to respond; he saw two bouncers aiming from the door. Then came roared flashes from the passage by which Cliff had entered. The Shadow had arrived; his timely bullets clipped those aiming gun arms.

The staggered bouncers dived shrieking from the exit. The Shadow swept after them; and Cliff dashed forward behind his cloaked chief. They gained the outside air; there, The Shadow clamped Cliff's arm and dragged the rescued man through the darkness. Across the driveway, they reached The Shadow's coupé, parked among other cars.

The coupé shot along a curving drive. Shouts arose, as Stew's reserves, rounding the building, spied the fast-moving car. Revolvers spoke wildly; then their users dived for cover as The Shadow leaned from the window and blazed answering bullets from the muzzle of a .45.

As they skirted the side of the old mansion that Stew had converted into a gambling hall, Cliff caught the sound of bedlam. Cheated customers had peered out from the side rooms to see the ruined roulette layout.

The fixed wheel had raised their wrath. The patrons of Stew's joint were scrambling to grab money from the floor, overwhelming the resisting croupiers who tried to stop them.

Horns were honking; a siren was wailing from the distance. Local authorities had been summoned. They would find the crippled rowdies whom The Shadow had left amid the wreckage. Stew Luffy's gambling racket was ended. The Shadow's laugh, weird from the blackness beside Cliff Marsland, was a tone of parting triumph.

HALF an hour later, a cloaked figure emerged from the coupé, in an obscure corner of the parking lot beside the Hotel Halcyon. Cliff Marsland followed The Shadow to the ground; he saw no sign of his chief after he alighted. Grinning, despite his weariness, Cliff strolled away. He was going to join Hawkeye, in their own quarters.

The Shadow, reaching a deserted doorway below the hotel, had undergone a transformation.

When he stepped into view, he was again Henry Arnaud, carrying a briefcase. Entering the Hotel Halcyon, The Shadow traveled up to Room 808.

Burbank was ready with reports amid the darkness. The contact man had heard from Hawkeye, in detail. That report given, Burbank had one of his own. It concerned Tyson Weed.

"Nine minutes after Hawkeye reported," informed the contact man, "Weed arrived in 1012. He put in a long-distance call to New York. Informed someone there that he had fixed everything.

"Three minutes afterward, Weed turned on the radio. He kept it loud for about five minutes; then turned it down. It is still tuned in on Station WIT, which has not yet finished its half-hour orchestra program."

The Shadow took the earphones. The only sound that he could hear from 1012 was that of the radio orchestra. It was tuned very faintly; yet the melody contained a variety of instruments, indicating that at full strength, the sound must have been deafening.

With a significant whisper to Burbank, The Shadow again donned his cloak and hat. He raised the window and swung out into the darkness of the night. Swinging precariously along the wall, The Shadow followed that angled route that he had used on his first visit to the Hotel Halcyon.

He reached Weed's balcony; there, he forced open the window and carefully lifted the lowered shade. A moment later, The Shadow eased into the room. A spectral figure, he stood amid the mellow light from a table lamp, gazing toward the floor.

FOUR feet from the softly tuned radio lay Tyson Weed. The lobbyist was staring face upward; his body, fully clad, was sprawled in grotesque pose. Weed's vest was opened; blood stained his shirtfront. The lobbyist was dead; shot through the heart.

The Shadow entered the opened door of the bedroom. Through darkness, he made his way to a door that opened into the hall. That barrier was unlocked; it swung lazily inward as The Shadow pulled it. The door had been pried open with a jimmy.

Returning to the living room, The Shadow reconstructed the scene. Calculating the time element, he knew that a call must have been made from that old apartment that Weed had visited. Someone had come here while the chauffeur was on his way to the hideout that Hawkeye had later visited.

The unknown intruder had arrived before Weed. He had hurriedly cracked the door from hall to bedroom. Burbank had not heard it; a proof that the connecting door between the bedroom and living room had been closed. Nor had Weed noticed it; for the bedroom entrance was farther down the passage than the door which Weed would logically use; namely, the entrance from hall to living room.

Weed had made his telephone call. When he had finished talking to New York, he must have turned to find an intruder who had silently entered the living room from the bedroom. Weed had made no outcry; he must have simply stared at sight of a leveled gun. The intruder, covering Weed, had turned on the radio.

Burbank had heard the ear-splitting cadence of the loud orchestra. Hence he had failed to hear the shot that must have come while the radio was blaring loudly. Weed had fallen; one bullet had killed him. The murderer himself had toned down the radio, then departed.

A cool, calculated crime; yet every detail was plain to The Shadow, thanks to Hawkeye's report and Burbank's vigil at the earphones. Hawkeye had reported two men at the apartment on Q Street: Coyd and a chauffeur. Neither of these could have come to the Hotel Halcyon in time to deliver death.

Some one else had performed lone murder. The killer had disposed of Weed because the lobbyist had learned too much. There had been thievery at Releston's; The Shadow had encountered hand-to-hand fighting at Rydel's; there had been gunplay at Stew Luffy's place this very night.

WEED'S death, however, marked the first stroke of outright murder. The Shadow, himself hidden, had challenged hidden crime; luck, alone, had blocked his narrowing quest. Here, in defiance of The Shadow, lay the corpse of a murdered victim.

Crime's fangs were fully bared. Those behind it had shown their willingness to stop at nothing. New efforts by The Shadow would be urgent. Calm in the face of this confirmed knowledge, the master of blackness moved out to the little balcony. Locking the window as he had done before, he swung back down the trail to 808.

Burbank was seated with dead earphones. Coiled wire fell to the floor; with it the microphone, for The Shadow had brought the instrument from Weed's room. No longer needed, that tiny device would be a bad clue to leave in a place where murder would soon be discovered by the law.

Doffing the useless earphones, Burbank heard a sound amid the darkness. It was a whispered laugh, suppressed but sinister; a restrained mirth that came with grimness. Burbank had heard that tone before; he knew its meaning. The Shadow's laugh boded ill for those fiends who dealt in heinous crime.

CHAPTER XV
BEFORE THE STORM

THREE days had passed. Bright afternoon pervaded Washington. The sunlight was pleasant in Layton Coyd's upstairs living room. Seated in the comfortable warmth, the congressman showed healthy cheerfulness as he chatted with two visitors: Senator Ross Releston and Foster Crozan.

Doctor Pierre Borneau was smiling as he noted the improved health of his patient. Harry Vincent, here with Releston and Crozan, was also impressed by the change which had come over Coyd. Jurrick and Tabbert, moving in and out of the room, seemed to have forgotten their old grudges.

"Three days of complete relaxation," commented Coyd, driving his hands against his swelled chest. "A tonic, gentlemen, that I recommend to any one whose nerves have been bad. Of course, I must still give some credit to Doctor Borneau's medicine. I took my kit of bottles with me; my daughter saw to it that I missed no doses. But it was sunshine, freedom from worry, that brought about my full recovery."

"You have our congratulations, Mr. Coyd," assured Releston. "Let us hope that you will not plunge into overwork. That is one thing to be avoided."

"I can't promise you that," remarked Coyd. "I have work to do and I intend to do it. If I tire, I shall take another rest. But I promise you this, senator. I shall give no interviews to the press."

"You have decided definitely to make no public statements regarding committee procedures?"

"Not exactly, Senator. Two days from now, I intend to speak before the National Progress Society, at their semiannual banquet. My speech will be broadcast over a national network. However, I shall give you a full copy of it beforehand and—"

"Do not be too optimistic, Mr. Coyd," put in Doctor Borneau. "Remember, sir, what I told you. Starting once again at the hard work may mean a strain. It is for me to say if you can go to the banquet."

"Of course, Doctor," nodded Coyd. "Of course, if I am not well, I shall not attend the banquet. In that case, I shall broadcast from here. Those at the banquet will hear my speech over the loudspeaker. That can all be arranged, doctor."

"You have a good physician, Mr. Coyd," stated Releston. "Doctor Borneau and I met at dinner last Wednesday night."

"Where, Senator?"

"At the French Embassy. We were together all evening, in fact until long after midnight. Incidentally, Doctor, I have not forgotten all those facts that you mentioned regarding nervous ailments. I was greatly impressed by the tremendous scope of your knowledge and experience."

"Thank you, Senator," observed Borneau, with a bow; then, twisting the points of his mustache, he added: "I must return the compliment, *m'sieu'*; your knowledge of the government exceeds that knowledge which I have of medicine and—"

"Wednesday night!" interposed Coyd. "That was the night that someone murdered that fellow Weed. I am sorry that he met with such sudden death; but I must also express gratification that there is one less lobbyist in Washington. He pestered you, Senator, just as he did me."

"I HAVE not seen Weed for several weeks," recalled Releston. "The last time was before you arrived, Crozan. Let me see—Weed was never about since you have been stopping at the Barlingham."

"No," returned Crozan. "Not unless it was during that short interval that I went home to obtain those documents on the mining investigation. I arrived back here just after the robbery at your apartment."

"Yes. Of course, Weed was not about at that time. If he had been, I would have blamed him definitely for the theft of those duplicate papers. Do you know, Crozan, this murder makes me wonder about that matter."

"You mean that Weed might have been slain because he had the papers."

"Yes. It is quite a possible theory. I have not mentioned it to the police, however, as I did not want to stir up new comment."

"Of course not. You told the press that the papers were of little consequence. Incidentally, the newspapers said that Weed's suite showed no signs of having been rifled."

"The murderer might have known where he had the papers."

"Yes. That is true—"

Crozan paused as Jurrick entered. The secretary had been downstairs. He was coming in to announce a visitor. Something in his expression indicated surprising news. Jurrick spoke to Coyd:

"Mr. Rydel is here, sir."

"What!" exclaimed the congressman. "Dunwood Rydel? What does he want?"

"He did not say, sir."

"Show him up."

EXPECTANT silence still held the group when Dunwood Rydel entered. The dyspeptic magnate was as sour-faced as usual. He nodded curtly when he saw Releston; glowered as he looked at Crozan. Then he advanced and spoke directly to Coyd.

"Sorry to annoy you with this visit," declared Rydel, gruffly. "It is paternal duty, not friendship that brought me here. I came to ask about my daughter."

"Ah, yes," nodded Coyd. "Your daughter Beatrice is still in Virginia, with Evelyn. I saw both of them this morning, before I left."

"I suppose that Beatrice was all broken up when she received that letter yesterday?"

"What letter? She did not speak of it to me."

"I wrote her from New York, telling her about that fiancé of hers. I saw a report that the bounder had eloped with some French actress in London. At least that was the rumor."

"Yes, yes!" exclaimed Coyd, chuckling as he rose to his feet. "I remember it now, Mr. Rydel. It was Evelyn who told me about the matter; not Beatrice. Your daughter, it appears, was indignant, rather than broken-hearted. But I did not know that she had learned the news through a letter from you."

"Allow me, Mr. Rydel." Coyd paused, chuckling, and extended his hand, which the magnate received half hesitating. "Allow me, sir, to extend my full congratulations. You have been freed from the menace of a most undesirable son-in-law."

"Thank you, Mr. Coyd," acknowledged Rydel, ending the handshake. He was smiling in spite of himself. "Of all the conceited dolts I ever encountered, that actor was the worst. Montgomery Hadwil! Bah! I would sooner have my daughter marry one of my chauffeurs!"

Turning about, Rydel looked at Releston. His smile faded as he addressed the senator.

"Well, sir," said the magnate, "I have finished my brief business with Mr. Coyd. Since you are present, Senator, I take this opportunity to inform you that I have just arrived back in Washington. Should you wish to see me at any time, I shall be at my home."

"You have been in New York all this while, Mr. Rydel?"

Rydel swung about. The question had come from Foster Crozan. This interference in Rydel's affairs apparently enraged the magnate.

"I said," he repeated, "that I arrived back in Washington this morning. Where I have been during the interim is my business. Not yours, Crozan."

Abruptly, Rydel turned on his heel and strode stormily from the room. Coyd, head tilted to one side, watched the magnate's departure rather curiously; then signaled to Tabbert to descend and usher Rydel from the house. Jurrick went over to the medicine chest and began to take out bottles. Doctor Borneau spoke to the secretary.

"Mr. Coyd has taken his prescription," stated the physician. "Tabbert prepared it. He will need no more medicine until tomorrow."

Coyd had seated himself heavily. He looked weary as he beckoned to Jurrick. Doctor Borneau showed an expression of sudden anxiety.

"Prepare those reports, Jurrick," ordered Coyd. Then, to his visitors: "Gentlemen, I am weary. My mind is befogged again; probably through over effort. Bah! Rydel coming in here like a wild beast! I tried to humor the man; to show him some consideration. He is impossible!"

DOCTOR BORNEAU motioned to Senator Releston. The gray-haired solon nodded and spoke to Crozan and Harry. The two followed him downstairs; they encountered Tabbert on the way, and the secretary conducted them to the front door. They entered Releston's sedan; this time there was no coupé parked opposite.

"What do you think of Rydel?" Releston asked Crozan as Harry drove them back toward the Barlingham. "Do you think he had some purpose in visiting Coyd? Do you believe that he saw my car outside? That he made a pretext for entering?"

"It would not surprise me," answered Crozan. "That was why I challenged him. Did you notice how abruptly he treated me?"

"Of course, Crozan, your question was rather pointed."

"I meant it to be. Here was my reason, Senator. Rydel went to New York the morning after Coyd's statement to the press. That was significant. It meant, logically, that Rydel wanted to be on hand for the rise in the stock market."

"Good reasoning, Crozan."

"But the rise was spiked. Accordingly, Rydel had no further purpose in New York. Logically, he would have come back to Washington."

"Quite logically."

"So I intimated as much, Senator, to see what his reaction would be. Rydel guessed what I was driving at; he had to parry my thrust. He took the tack of pretending that he had really stayed in New York."

"He did not say so, outright."

"I take it he was afraid to do so. Afraid that one of us might have seen him here in Washington."

"Have you seen him here, Crozan?"

"No. I seldom leave my rooms at the Barlingham; but Rydel does not know that fact. That is why he hedged—as I expected he would."

REACHING the Barlingham, Harry parked the car and went up to Releston's apartment. The senator instructed him to keep in close touch with

Congressman Coyd, in reference to the speech which Coyd intended to deliver. Harry found other duties; it was almost evening before he managed an opportunity to leave the senator's apartment.

Dusk had obscured the Hotel Halcyon. In Suite 808, a figure was seated in front of the writing table. It was The Shadow, in his guise as Arnaud; Burbank was off duty, asleep in the other room. The telephone buzzed; The Shadow answered it. He spoke in a quiet, methodical tone, a perfect imitation of Burbank's voice. Harry Vincent reported.

Five minutes later came a report from Clyde Burke; the reporter was keeping tabs on the police investigation of Weed's murder. Twenty minutes later, Cliff Marsland called in, reporting for himself and Hawkeye. They had picked up no facts concerning Walbert and Quidler, except that the dicks had checked out of their respective hotels.

It was obvious that the sleuths had decided to decamp after hearing of the raid at Stew's gambling joint; and the news of Weed's death had doubtless spurred them to an immediate departure.

The Shadow was no longer concerned with Walbert and Quidler. They were harmless; it had been Jake's idea, not theirs, to torture Cliff. The Shadow had assigned Cliff and Hawkeye to more important duty. Cliff was watching Dunwood Rydel's home; Hawkeye was covering the F Street garage, where Mullard frequently took the big limousine.

Tyson Weed's death was a mystery to the police. The Shadow was content that it should remain so. With Weed eliminated, the plans of crooks would proceed. That suited The Shadow; for he knew that their chief purpose was the gaining of wealth, not the taking of human life.

Men of crime would work as they had before; through Congressman Layton Coyd. The Shadow had gained an insight into their procedure; fitted facts showed him the answer that he had sought. When crooks chose to move, The Shadow would do likewise. Already he had guessed when their new stroke would come.

For in the facts that Harry Vincent had reported in detail were clues that The Shadow needed. He saw the approach of opportunity for men of evil to thrust in quest of wealth. One failure had not balked them; another chance was due.

A chance for greater wealth; a cleanup that would surpass the attempt to build up munitions stocks. That chance which crooks were prepared to seize would be a chance for The Shadow to counteract their superstroke.

CHAPTER XVI
TWO DAYS LATER

TWO nights had passed. It was noon in Washington, the sidewalks an inferno from the heat of the sun. Mild weather had been followed by an unexpected heat wave—if such an occurrence could ever be called unexpected in Washington.

Coming from the Hotel Barlingham, Harry Vincent entered a drugstore and put in a telephone call. The voice that answered him was Burbank's. Harry reported tersely.

"Coyd's this morning," he stated. "Doctor's order final... Coyd to speak from his home... Radio electricians have completed installation... Coyd's speech denouncing utility profits approved by Releston... Returning to Coyd's with copy. Will remain there..."

His report ended, Harry entered the parked sedan and drove to Coyd's. Mose admitted him, and Jurrick met him on the stairs. The secretary shook his head solemnly; the indication was that Coyd had felt the heat severely.

When Harry arrived in the second-story living room, he found the congressman slumped in his chair. Looking up, Coyd smiled weakly as he saw the copy of his speech in Harry's hand.

"Releston likes it?" he inquired.

"The senator is highly pleased," responded Harry. "In fact, he feels that you have gone further than essential. Those utilities that you mention—"

"I understand," interrupted Coyd. "My speech almost condemns them. Why not? Their rates have been excessive, Vincent. To state that they will be placed under permanent regulation is a wise step."

"Senator Releston knows that," assured Harry. "But he told me to remind you that the committees intend to fix the rates definitely. Once regulation is made, the government's part will be done."

"Do you know what that means, Vincent?" demanded Coyd, sitting upright, despite the protest of Tabbert, who was present. "Once the rates are settled, they will make economies that will enable them to build new profits.

"They will grasp!" Coyd extended his hands and clutched the air. "They will grasp, like octopuses—or octopi—drat it! Hand me that copy of my speech so I can see which is correct: octopuses or octopi.

"No—never mind! I'll read it correctly when I come to it. Anyway, those utilities will grasp. They always grasp, the lot of them. I shall defy them—"

Coyd slumped back, gasping. His eyes closed wearily. Harry spoke quietly.

"ACCORDING to Senator Releston," declared Harry, "the danger does not lie in the future. Once the utilities are properly regulated, their profits cannot be too great. At least those of certain utilities, the ones which the committees have specifically named.

"The danger, sir, is in the present. Should a false statement be made by either you or Senator Releston, the prices of stocks would leap. Huge profits would be made by present holders; and there is every reason to suppose that a hidden group has invested heavily in those securities."

"I know it," said Coyd, with a weak chuckle. "I know it, Vincent, and that is why I have worded my speech accordingly. I want to make those stocks go down; I want my revenge upon the scalawags who tried to clean up on munitions.

"I was nearly the goat for that game. Even yet, I cannot understand how or why I made such strange statements. My worried brain must have tricked me to do the very thing that I would not normally have done.

"That is why I have gone to the other extreme. I have made my speech so strong, so full of adverse inference, that small stockholders will unload at the present price, which is a fair one, and leave the swindlers holding the bag, unable to sell except at a great loss. Why does Releston object?"

"He does not object," replied Harry, tactfully. "At the same time, he showed reluctance in finally approving statements which tended to exaggeration. He told me to mention that fact, Mr. Coyd. However, he said that he would have disapproved any statements that might have aided speculation."

"I have placed none in my speech," remarked Coyd. "So the matter is settled, Vincent. Sit down, if you intend to remain here. Let me rest a while. I expect to rehearse my speech after Doctor Borneau arrives."

HALF an hour passed while Harry lolled in a chair. Tabbert and Jurrick stole in and out at intervals. It was Tabbert, finally, who approached and spoke quietly to Coyd, napping in his chair by the window.

"A radio technician is here, Mr. Coyd," said the red-haired secretary. "He wants to install some apparatus. Some sort of device to increase the intensity of the sound."

"Tell him to proceed, Tabbert."

The secretary went out. He came back, lugging one end of a large box, the size of a typewriter desk. Jurrick was at the other end; with them was a stooped man in overalls, whose back was toward Harry. The box was shoved into a corner. The man in overalls squatted in front of it and began to make connections.

Both secretaries had gone out when the man arose to survey his job. Even then, Harry had not seen the fellow's face. He saw the man pull an order book from his hip pocket. Coyd, his eyes open, spoke to Harry.

"You sign it, Vincent," ordered the congressman, wearily. "Neither of my secretaries are here."

Harry met the man in overalls; he scrawled his name on a line which a finger indicated. The radio man tore off a sheet of paper from beneath and thrust it into Harry's hand with the quiet statement:

"The receipt slip. Read it carefully."

The man in overalls had walked through the doorway before the meaning of his words struck Harry. Looking after him, The Shadow's agent saw only his back disappearing at the head of the stairs. That quiet tone, however, had impressed itself. Harry knew the identity of the man whose face he had failed to see. It was Burbank!

Glancing quickly at the receipt slip, Harry saw coded lines inscribed in bluish ink. He read them rapidly; the import of their message impressed itself upon him. Then the writing faded, word by word—a trick of messages that came in The Shadow's disappearing ink.

SOME thirty minutes after Burbank's departure, Doctor Borneau arrived. He examined his patient solemnly; then called for the prescription and gave Coyd a double dose. The weary congressman perked up a bit; he decided to rehearse his speech at once. This was a procedure which Coyd never varied.

Jurrick and Tabbert joined the audience. Harry took his place in the corner, leaning against the big box that Burbank had installed. He watched Coyd prepare; then, when the speaker had taken his stand in the center of the room, Harry quietly shifted the top of the big contrivance.

A click sounded; Harry was the only person who heard it. Coyd was loudly clearing his throat; after that preliminary, he adjusted his tortoise-shell spectacles and proceeded to read aloud from the copy that he gripped in his hands.

Coyd's manner was mild at first. His introductory words were addressed to the members of the National Progress Society. Gradually, Coyd worked into his theme, the future of the nation. He spoke wisely of utilities, their value to the public; his words showed good will and appreciation of those who had served the people.

Suddenly, his tone became bombastic. His papers in his left hand, Coyd gestured with his right. He denounced graspers, grafters and their ilk. Head tilted sidewise while he read from his typewritten notes, he continued his gestures, wagging his right forefinger as he named certain companies, one by one.

The "rogues roll call," Coyd termed it. He denounced these special companies; he declared that they had deceived the public by deliberately refusing to make possible economies that would produce lower rates. He added that their game was known; that its doom was near.

Congressional measures, Coyd prophesied, would force the creation of a control board that would base rates upon those of sincere utilities that had already found ways of giving maximum service at minimum cost.

Harry had read Coyd's speech; it had struck him as chaffy; but when Coyd delivered it, The Shadow's agent became lost in admiration. With all his bombastic force, Coyd could be both eloquent and effective.

When the congressman slumped to his chair, exhausted, the room still seemed to hold the ring of his powerful speech. It was a quarter of a minute before Harry remembered a duty; with a quick pull of his hand, he shifted the top of the cabinet back to its original place.

COYD'S face was flushed. Somehow, despite his exhaustion, he had retained his high pitch. Doctor Borneau felt the patient's pulse and ordered an immediate rest. Tabbert and Jurrick came up to aid Coyd; the congressman pushed them aside. Rising from his chair, he walked to the door of the bedroom. Standing there, he turned and spoke to Harry.

"You heard it, Vincent," chuckled the congressman. "Go back and tell Releston about it. Invite him here tonight, to hear it for himself."

"Sorry, Mr. Coyd," said Harry. "Senator Releston has a previous engagement. Of course, he will hear your speech over the air, at the dinner which he is attending in Baltimore. But—"

"Too bad," interposed Coyd, gloomily. Then: "Bring his friend, Crozan, if you wish. He can see my delivery and tell the senator about it afterward."

Suddenly wearied, Coyd went into the bedroom. Harry strolled out with Tabbert, while Doctor Borneau was making notes and Jurrick was replacing the medicine bottles in the cabinet. At the bottom of the stairs, Harry paused to light a cigarette; as he tarried, Borneau and Jurrick came down the steps.

Tabbert had gone. Harry started up the steps, remarking, in passing, that he had left his hat in the living room. Reaching there alone, Harry went to the big box; he shifted the lid; it came up several inches. Reaching inside, Harry made adjustments: when he closed the lid and slid it, he heard locks click tight.

Harry had followed instructions received through Burbank. His work was done for the time; what the aftermath would be, Harry could not guess. He knew only that he had done The Shadow's bidding; that some strange climax would later be staged to close a baffling drama.

Something must be threatening, despite the fact that Coyd's speech was written, approved and rehearsed. The outcome was a mystery to Harry. What the finish would be, only The Shadow knew!

CHAPTER XVII
FIGURES IN THE DARK

SEVEN o'clock. A torrential rain had broken the day's heat wave. It was dripping still; the lights of Washington were hazy through the steamy atmosphere. An hour yet remained before Congressman Coyd's speech would go out over the air, as the finale of the scheduled banquet.

Across from Dunwood Rydel's mansion, two men were seated in a parked coupé. Cliff at the wheel; Hawkeye beside him. Both were watching the rain-soaked driveway with the garage beyond. A light glimmered suddenly to attract their attention. It was under the porte-cochère. The front door opened and Dunwood Rydel stepped into view.

A limousine rolled from the garage. It was the big car that Hawkeye had seen that night on Q Street. The car skirted the mansion; Rydel boarded it and the big machine rolled from the drive. After it had passed, Cliff started in pursuit. The course led to the Lotus Club.

When Rydel alighted, he gave brief instructions to Mullard, who was the chauffeur at the wheel. The man nodded and drove away. Cliff followed him in the coupé; but Hawkeye was no longer aboard. The little spotter had dropped from Cliff's car to put in a call to The Shadow.

Mullard picked a twisting course through slippery streets. Cliff kept the trail; he followed the limousine northward along Seventh Street. Then Mullard changed his tactics; he began to zigzag over the same territory. Apparently he was deliberately trying to shake off any followers. Cliff let him take a turn; then waited.

Soon Mullard's car appeared, crossing the street a block ahead. The glare of a bright electric light was the giveaway. Cliff followed and made the corner. As he turned, he saw the limousine parked by the curb, a block and a half ahead. Then the big machine started suddenly; it zipped for the nearest corner and shot out of view as Cliff was coming up.

The chase was ended; but Cliff was sure that he had found a goal. The building before which Mullard had stopped was an old, three-story house; Cliff knew it by the proximity of a street lamp that had partially revealed the standing limousine.

Like the house that Hawkeye had visited on Q Street, this building was a residence converted into an apartment.

It bore the name plate: "Northern Arms."

CLIFF parked his coupé. He went into the lobby, pushed a bell beside a name and listened in hope of luck. The door clicked; Cliff entered. Instead of going upstairs, he sneaked to the rear of the hall and waited.

A door opened above; a voice shouted; then the door slammed. Some annoyed apartment dweller had decided that the ring was a hoax.

While outside, Cliff had noted one point in a preliminary survey. Windows, first and second floors front, had been lighted. The slammed door had apparently come from the second story back; a likely guess, for Cliff had pressed a button marked 2B. The third floor, therefore, seemed like a good bet. Cliff sneaked up the stairs and reached it.

This building, like the one that Hawkeye had visited, was equipped with a rear fire escape. This was required by law in both cases; for none of these old houses were fireproof. Cliff took the rear apartment as the easiest mode of entry. He reached the fire escape and leaned over to a locked window.

Using a thin prying tool, Cliff tried The Shadow's system. His efforts were comparatively clumsy; for he required several minutes before he could catch the lock, and he chipped the woodwork into the bargain.

When he finally opened the window, Cliff slid into a small kitchen; from there, he reached a darkened hall, with a bedroom on the side.

Using a flashlight, Cliff spotted a suitcase. He opened it; the first objects that he saw were papers and letters. Cliff examined them and chuckled; he opened an envelope and produced a handful of newspaper clippings. These were all he needed.

Continuing through to a living room, Cliff calmly turned on the light and picked up a telephone. He dialed the Hotel Halcyon. He asked for 808. Burbank's voice responded. Cliff reported. That done, he stretched out in a comfortable chair and laid his revolver on the table beside him. Cliff was prepared to wait as long as necessary.

MEANWHILE, Dunwood Rydel had met two persons in the Lotus Club. One was Coyd's daughter; the other was another girl, a blonde whose attractiveness was quite as marked as Evelyn's. This was Beatrice Rydel.

The girls had come in from Virginia. Delayed by the storm, Beatrice had called her father; he had told her to meet him at the Lotus Club.

The trio went into the upstairs dining room. As they were ordering dinner, a man strolled in and took a table close by. It was The Shadow, guised as Henry Arnaud. Quietly, he ordered a prompt dinner, stating that his time was short.

"Father," remarked Beatrice, "we are in a great hurry. Evelyn wants me to go with her to hear her father's speech. He is delivering it from his home, you know."

"Humph," growled Rydel. "So that's why he was so testy this morning. I had forgotten about that plagued speech of his."

"Father!" reproved Beatrice. "You are forgetting Evelyn—"

"That's all right, Beatrice," laughed the brunette. "Daddy has said many mean things about your father."

"He has?" queried Rydel.

"Yes," acknowledged Evelyn. "Many times."

"Humph." Rydel's tone was a chuckle. "Maybe the old codger is a good fellow after all. I like people to be frank. Come to think of it, he is frank."

"Why don't you come with us?" queried Evelyn.

Rydel shook his head.

"Not for the speech," he decided. "I have a conference with some friends, here at the club. Mullard is to take the limousine back and come for me in the coupé. I believe, though, that I can get away by nine-thirty. I shall have Mullard keep the limousine in town; then I can come along for Beatrice."

"And meet Daddy," added Evelyn.

"Perhaps," said Rydel. "Anyway, you girls can call Mullard and have him take you to Coyd's in the limousine. I sent him to the F Street garage. I told him to wait there in case you needed him."

"We have my coupé, father," reminded Beatrice. "We can drive to Evelyn's in it. Then I can call one of the chauffeurs and have him take it home from there, since you will be coming in the limousine."

An attendant entered and spoke to the headwaiter, who indicated The Shadow. The attendant approached and delivered a message. The Shadow read the statement that Mr. Burbank was calling. He left the table, went to the lobby and answered the telephone. He received news of Cliff.

Telling the attendant to cancel his dinner order, The Shadow left the club. Hailing a taxi, he gave a destination. When the driver reached an empty house, he paused, puzzled; then the fare was thrust into his hand. The door of the cab opened; the passenger was gone.

The driver blinked. He had remembered a man with a briefcase. Yet no such passenger had alighted; in fact the driver had no recollection of anything but a gloved hand, tendering him his fare and tip. Shrugging his shoulders, the cabby drove away along the puddly street. The Shadow, turning the nearest corner, saw him travel by.

NEARLY a block ahead, a limousine was halted by the curb. As The Shadow *swished* forward through the darkness, he caught a glimpse of a figure by the machine. An instant later, the big car shot away. Continuing, The Shadow reached the back of a huge brownstone house. He had arrived at Congressman Coyd's.

Moving through the passage beside the house, The Shadow reached the front. He seemed unconcerned by that brief sight that he had gained upon arrival. Outside, he discovered a parked sedan; it was Senator Releston's car. Harry Vincent was already at Coyd's.

Long minutes passed; a phantom shape had glided out of sight. Elsewhere, however, a watcher had found something to observe. Hawkeye, stationed outside the F Street garage, saw a limousine swing into the entrance, a dozen minutes after The Shadow had spotted the same car at Coyd's.

Inside the garage, Mullard alighted and hailed an attendant. The fellow came over; the chauffeur put a query:

"Did the boss call?"

The attendant shook his head.

"Listen, Stevie." Mullard drew the fellow aside. "I got a hunch that old Rydel is checking up on me. I've been riding around in this bus of his, and the gas bill's kind of heavy. See?"

Steve grinned and nodded.

"Got a date with a gal," confided Mullard. "Want to slide out of here along about nine; and I won't be back for an hour. Maybe some snooper is watching. Give me a break, will you?"

"How?"

"You know that old entrance over on the other side?"

"Sure. A couple of old junkers are blocking it."

"Shove them out so I can use the door. Worth a couple of bucks for your trouble?"

"You bet."

The attendant went away. Mullard remained by the limousine, away from Hawkeye's range of vision. Though he had not spied the spotter,

EVELYN COYD—daughter of the congressman, vacations in the country with the daughter of her father's enemy.

Mullard still figured that a car had trailed him. If so, it might have come back to the front of the F Street garage, after being shaken in the chase. By using the forgotten side door, Mullard was making a sure thing of a getaway.

EIGHT o'clock was nearing; it was the scheduled time for Coyd's speech. The Shadow, watching from the passage beside the brownstone house, saw a taxicab jolt to a stop in front. A man alighted; he was the radio technician sent to make the hookup. He had evidently come from the banquet, allowing ample time for the final arrangements.

Hardly had the cab moved away before an imported coupé stopped before the house. Two girls alighted; Evelyn Coyd and Beatrice Rydel had hurried through their dinner in order to be in time for the speech. They, too, were admitted to the house.

Softly, The Shadow laughed as he merged beneath the darkness of the walls. His suppressed mirth faded, lost amid the patter of raindrops on the eaves above. A phantom shape, obscured in blackness, his time for action had come.

Every occurrence of this early evening had fitted The Shadow's analysis. A superscheme was ready for its payoff. Men of evil purpose had grasped their opportunity. They had planned and labored, prepared to offset counterthrusts; but they had not reckoned with the master who was due.

The Shadow.

CHAPTER XVIII
DECISIONS CHANGE

WHILE The Shadow still lingered outside the darkened brownstone house, a group of persons had assembled in Congressman Coyd's upstairs living room. Foster Crozan was seated there, in a comfortable easy chair. He was talking quietly with Evelyn Coyd, who was seated opposite; while Beatrice Rydel was chatting with Hugh Tabbert.

Doctor Pierre Borneau was also present. Smoking a cigarette, the physician was slowly pacing back and forth across the room. In the corner stood Harry Vincent, his elbow resting on the big box that Burbank had delivered. Harry was watching the radio technician complete the hookup.

The radio man had ignored the big box. Harry had expected that. Burbank had faked its hook-up; the only real connection that the box possessed was a wire to an isolated floor plug. The technician, in fact, had wondered what the cabinet was doing here and had decided that it was some mechanical device which did not concern him.

His work completed, the technician was using the telephone to call the downtown banquet room. Harry Vincent used this opportunity to note the other persons in the room. Tabbert interested him most; Harry noted that the red-haired secretary was scarcely listening to Beatrice Rydel's chatter. Tabbert was looking at Evelyn Coyd, who, in turn, was deliberately ignoring him.

Harry could see the clenching of Tabbert's fists; he knew that the fellow was thinking of Don Jurrick, whom Tabbert considered as a rival. For it was obvious that the hometown boy was in love with the congressman's daughter.

"Where is Mr. Coyd?"

The question was asked by the radio technician, a weary-faced, businesslike individual. Tabbert suddenly realized that he was being addressed. He turned about and spoke.

"Mr. Coyd is downstairs in his study," he stated. "He went down there with you, didn't he, Doctor Borneau?"

"When I awakened him," replied the physician, "he asked if he might go downstairs. He seemed in good spirits, so I permitted him to do so. Mr. Coyd is quite alert this evening."

"I heard Jurrick's typewriter going," stated Tabbert, "so I suppose that Mr. Coyd is dictating some additional notes. Shall I go down and tell him that we are ready?"

"You'd better," informed the radioman, moving to a square box where a switch was located. "The announcement is due inside of ten minutes."

TABBERT started for the door. He stopped as he heard footsteps. Two persons were coming up the stairs; Tabbert recognized Coyd's voice and came back into the room. Half a minute later, Coyd entered the room with Jurrick at his elbow. The sleek secretary was speaking in a low, half-pleading tone.

"Enough, Jurrick," said Coyd, sharply. "You are in my employ to take orders; not to criticize my decisions. Go take a chair and say no more."

A scowl showed on the congressman's dry features. Then Harry saw a blink of eyelids, a sudden twitch of lips as the shock-haired man spied Beatrice Rydel. For a moment, fingers clutched nervously at open air; then Evelyn Coyd sprang up from her chair.

"Daddy!" she exclaimed. "You don't mind our surprising you? I thought you would like to have Beatrice and myself here tonight."

The girl had placed her hands on Coyd's shoulders. Mechanically, he kissed her on the forehead; then spoke, nervously, as Evelyn stepped away.

"No, no, daughter," came Coyd's response. "I do not mind. It was rather startling, though, to know that you had arrived so unexpectedly."

Though he spoke to Evelyn, his eyes were still toward Beatrice. The blond girl looked half puzzled; Harry saw her start to speak, then hesitate. Evelyn, too, was wondering; and Harry was not surprised. The Shadow's agent had noted many of Coyd's moods; the present one was different from any that he had previously observed.

Fingers moved through the shock of black hair. The action changed the man's mood. Coyd's face became firm; his voice sounded brusque. Doctor Borneau motioned to the girls; they sat down at the physician's order.

"Only a few minutes, Mr. Coyd."

"Good." Coyd's tone was firm. With this response to the radio technician, the speaker of the evening swung about and faced the group. "Good. But I still have time to say something that will interest all of you."

A tense pause; then came the congressman's tone tinged with a sneer:

"I have altered the contents of my speech. I have done so because I am weary of interference in my affairs. In order to declare my independence, I shall deliver statements that will end all meddling on the part of others. From such persons, for instance, as Senator Ross Releston."

Coyd's tone was sarcastic and biting. Harry saw a gleam in the congressman's eyes as they were focused first upon him; then on Foster Crozan. Harry watched Crozan rise from his chair, only to he waved down.

"Tonight, I shall speak of utilities." Coyd's voice was intoning the words. "But I shall not condemn them. Nor will I state what Senator Releston has said—that rates will be fixed once and for all.

"Instead, I shall declare that these specific utilities will not be regulated at all." A gesturing hand flourished a sheaf of papers that Jurrick had typed. "I shall assert that their affairs do not come under congressional jurisdiction; that the committees will have no report concerning them."

CROZAN was on his feet. Violently, his fist was shaking in Coyd's face. Harry had never seen the senatorial candidate so indignant.

"Outrageous!" stormed Crozan. "Do you mean, Mr. Coyd, that you intend to state a deliberate untruth? To create a totally erroneous belief on the part of the public—"

"My original remarks were not entirely correct."

"They recognized definite possibilities. There was a chance that the committees would go further than already decided. This new statement, however, is a bald lie. If Senator Releston were here—"

"He is not here, however," came the sneering interruption. "As for you, Crozan, you are nothing but a private citizen. Your interference in my affairs is unwarranted."

"I am acting for the public good. Do you realize, Coyd, what you will do? No denial—by Releston or anyone—will be capable of stopping disaster. The truth can never overtake a lie. The munitions scandal will be nothing compared with this. Tomorrow, stocks will soar sky high. Speculators will unload—"

"Let them. Their business is their own."

"But afterward, Coyd! The dupes who will buy those securities at your instigation! Think of them! When Congress resumes session, when the committee reports are given, the fixing of utility rates will cause a drop to normal or below. Honest persons will be bereft of long-saved earnings—"

"That is their lookout, Crozan. My interests are my own. Independence is a virtue that I value, Crozan."

"Independence!" Crozan's tone was irony. "You are showing no independence, Coyd! At last you are flaunting your true colors—the skull and crossbones of piracy. I believed in you, Coyd. I thought—like Releston—that your statement regarding munitions had been an unaccountable error.

"Both Releston and I were deceived on that occasion. Deceived by your glibness and your whining. It is plain, now, that you were working for the very graspers whom you pretended to denounce. A hidden syndicate, operated by one man whose lust for wealth knows no bounds.

"You were forced to back down that time, Coyd. However, you have found another opportunity to serve your evil master. This time the speculation lies in those rotten utilities that you said you would denounce. You will get your pay from that big money grabber who is behind the whole scheme.

"I shall name him, Coyd. I was right from the start. I should have known it today. That crook came here in person, to see if you were still in line. Tonight, he has sent his daughter as a reminder of your crooked duty.

"You are working for Dunwood Rydel! He stands to win fifty million dollars through your vile efforts! You will receive your portion. That is, you would receive it, were I not here to stop this outrage. Your speech, Coyd, will not go over the air!"

Both of Crozan's fists were against Coyd's jaw. Suddenly, a defending arm shot forward; the drive of Coyd's fist sent Crozan sprawling back into his chair. Spluttering, Crozan came to his feet again.

"Stop him, Tabbert! And you, Jurrick!"

BOTH secretaries hesitated as they heard Coyd's command. Then Tabbert saw Evelyn; Coyd's daughter was stopping Beatrice Rydel, who was coming toward Crozan, shouting her indignation at his statements concerning her father.

Tabbert waited no longer; with a contemptuous glance at Jurrick, the red-haired secretary pounced upon Crozan and pinned the square-jawed protester in his chair.

Crozan fought back. He had the strength of an athlete and was a match for Tabbert. But Jurrick, forced to follow Tabbert's action, had come into the fray. Together, the secretaries ended Crozan's resistance. Overpowered, Crozan glared at Coyd; then heard the congressman's sarcastic words.

"Sit quiet, Crozan. One move from you will lead to your ejection. One word from you will mean the end of your political career. You have no authority; it is not for you to interfere with my activities."

Crozan quieted; his face was bitter. Beatrice had subsided under Evelyn's coaxing. Doctor Borneau had stepped forward to protest against his patient's fury. Harry saw Coyd's shaggy head shake. Borneau stepped back.

"Nearly ready, Mr. Coyd."

It was the radioman at the switch. The fellow had taken no part in the altercation; his worry concerned the broadcasting of Coyd's speech. Nimbly, Coyd's hands unfolded the new notes; Harry saw sneering lips above the congressman's pugnacious jaw. A sudden hush filled the room. Crozan, head bowed, was silent.

Then came words from a loudspeaker. It was an announcer at the banquet hall, stating that the guests would hear from Congressman Layton Coyd, the speaker of the evening. The announcement ended; the radio man swung the switch and nodded. Coyd stepped to a microphone that was standing on the table. The air was ready for his speech.

AT that instant, a whispered sound crept

through the room. Low, sinister, almost spectral, it came as a baffling tone of suppressed mirth. A symbol of the unexpected, it died as suddenly as it had begun; but not too soon. Involuntarily, every person in the room had guessed the spot from which the whispered mockery had come. All swung toward the doorway to the hall.

The door had opened. Standing within the portal was a being cloaked in black. Firelike eyes were glowing from below a hat brim; beneath those sparkling optics bulked a brace of automatics, clenched in thin-gloved hands. One .45 was aimed directly for the figure of Congressman Layton Coyd, covering Doctor Borneau also, for the physician was close by the table.

The other weapon was pointed to the chair where Jurrick and Tabbert still guarded Crozan. Neither of the secretaries could make a move. Wagging slowly, the automatic moved from one to the other, while Crozan sat gasping, in between.

Evelyn and Beatrice stared from the wall by the door to the bedroom. The radio technician slumped; his shaking hands came upward. Though no gun aimed in his direction, this bystander was chilled with fright.

A decision had been made; its upshot, a total change in the speech originally prepared by Congressman Layton Coyd. Damaging words were ready for the air; to be uttered by those fuming lips that now twitched upon Coyd's blanched face. Those new words, however, were destined never to be uttered.

The Shadow had countermanded crime. He had reversed the decision. He was here to see that justice would prevail!

CHAPTER XIX
THE SHADOW SPEAKS

OF all the persons in that hushed room, only one responded with swift action. Not The Shadow; his part required no motion other than the tantalizing manipulation of the automatics. Like steady pendulums, the guns were moving to and fro. One .45 wagged its muzzle between the figures of Coyd and Borneau; the other gun shifted back and forth along the trio at the chair, where Foster Crozan was still flanked by Tabbert and Jurrick.

The man who strode about was Harry Vincent. Stepping to the table, The Shadow's agent clutched the microphone with his left hand while he drew an automatic from his pocket with his right.

Setting the mike on a chair in front of the big corner cabinet, Harry promptly opened the box by pressing a hidden spring. A disk record began a slow revolution; Harry applied a phonographic needle; then stooped and dropped the front of the box. That done, he stood alert, his own gun ready.

From the cabinet came the loud tone of a throat-clearing cough. A pause; then a friendly voice began to speak. Listeners stared as they recognized the words of Congressman Layton Coyd. The speaker was going over the air; but not in person. This was a recorded program, a word-for-word reproduction of the original speech that Coyd had rehearsed that afternoon.

Harry had followed Burbank's instructions to the letter. Harry's own report had given The Shadow ample time to arrange this setup. In this very room, Harry had managed to record Coyd's words during the afternoon rehearsal. Afterward, he had found opportunity to make the required mechanical changes in the recording device.

Coyd's voice was eloquent as it continued. Harry had caught the congressman's attention that afternoon; Coyd's gestures and his oratory had been delivered directly toward the vital corner. The tones from the record drove home their message. Brief, but pointed and emphatic, Coyd's denunciation of manipulated utilities rang out for all the world to hear.

No listener made a move. The lazy motion of The Shadow's automatics continued unrelenting. At last the speech was done. Still, those in the room sat silent. From hidden lips came a chilling tone, an eerie laugh of whispered triumph. As The Shadow's quivered mirth subsided, Harry Vincent stepped over and pulled the switch. The room was no longer a broadcasting chamber.

THE SHADOW'S gloved hands ceased their motion. Harry had become an added threat with his single gun; those whom The Shadow had covered were too cowed to make a move in face of the three weapons held ready by the cloaked master and his agent. Rigid listeners expected some pronouncement. It came.

"Open the door to the bedroom."

The Shadow's words were a command. Evelyn Coyd, near the door, could see the gleam of those dominating eyes. Nodding, the girl stepped over and tried the knob. The door was locked.

"Give her the key."

These stern words were addressed toward the table. A twitching showed on the face of Coyd as the man's hand started for his pocket. Then came a glare of defiance—an expression entirely different from any that Coyd had ever shown.

"No!" cried the man by the table. "No. I do not have the key. You cannot enter there—"

Hands clutched the lapels of the smoking jacket as the shock-headed man raised his head and delivered his dramatic utterance. The Shadow's eyes were upon Doctor Borneau; Harry, springing forward, jabbed his automatic against the physician's ribs and plucked the key from Borneau's pocket.

Coyd's unfamiliar tone had ended abruptly. It was Evelyn who gave the next cry. She was staring at that transformed face. Her eyes were noting the glisten of the shocky hair above. Wildly, the girl blurted the truth.

"You are not my father!" she shrieked. "You are an impostor! I should have known it when I first arrived here! You were different—"

Beatrice Rydel had joined her friend. She, too, was staring at that wild-eyed man whose face resembled Layton Coyd's. Evelyn knew only that the visage, the pose, could not be her father's; but Beatrice had suddenly recognized who the man must be.

"Montgomery!" she exclaimed. "Montgomery Hadwil! You—your face is changed—your hair dyed—"

THE false Coyd swung back against the table; his faked lips gave a venomous snarl. Recognition complete, he resorted to frenzy. His dramatic egotism came to the fore, in spite of a sharp warning from Doctor Borneau.

"What of it?" demanded Hadwil, viciously. "What if I did choose to deceive the world? Bah! How else could I have gained the wealth I wanted? Your father refused—"

"Enough, rogue!" interrupted Crozan, coming to his feet. "You can make your confession later. We know you for an adventurer, seeking a marriage that would bring you wealth. Dunwood Rydel refused it; he told you his daughter would receive no dowery. He knew that money came first with you."

Hadwil was spluttering; the glare of Crozan's eyes made him end his fuming. Still accusing, Crozan drove home another statement.

"Rydel offered you money," he scoffed. "He gave you an opportunity. One that allowed you to continue your profession as an actor. It meant an alteration of your features; but what of that? It was no more than a minor operation, designed to bring you wealth. Come, man, confess. I can promise that you will be dealt with leniently."

"Very well." Hadwil had calmed. "I did as Rydel told me. I went daily to the Hall of Representatives; I watched Layton Coyd and learned all his mannerisms and gestures. I rehearsed them to perfection.

"I went to a small private hospital outside of Washington. There the operation was performed. After that, I lived in an apartment on Q Street. Rydel placed a car at my disposal. A limousine with a chauffeur named Mullard.

"He brought me here one day to make a trial of my new identity. The next day I came again and issued the statement on munitions. Tonight, I made another visit; I came here to deliver a speech as Rydel wanted it."

"We have your confession," remarked Crozan. He was in the center of the room, confident that he was backed by The Shadow's guns. "Next, we should hear from you, Doctor Borneau. Hadwil is guilty merely of an imposture. Perhaps, Doctor, your deeds were more serious."

"Slightly," asserted Borneau, with a grimace. "I, too, was hired by Rydel. Some time ago, a sculptor named Lucian took a cast—a mask—of Congressman Coyd. Someone—Rydel or his chauffeur—entered Lucian's studio and stole the cast, leaving a batch of broken plaster on the floor.

"A second mask was taken—for that statue on the mantelpiece—but I had the first. I used it as a mold for a facial operation which I performed on Hadwil. You understand, of course, that I was deceived at first. I thought that Rydel was friendly to Coyd; that the purpose was to have Hadwil serve as Coyd's substitute when the latter was indisposed—"

"That is irrelevant, Doctor," interposed Crozan, sternly. "Let us know what you actually did to Congressman Coyd."

"I gave him two prescriptions," admitted the physician. "Neither was really harmful; but one stimulated him and afterward, when its effects wore off, he felt melancholy. That accounted for his troubled mental condition. He needed more stimulus, either through medicine or outdoor exercise."

"And the other prescription?"

"Contained an opiate. So Coyd would sleep on the days that Rydel wished to substitute Hadwil in his stead. I learned the real game, too late—"

"What about your past, Doctor Borneau? How did you come to be in Washington?"

"I was concerned in some trouble at Saigon, Mr. Crozan. Fortunately, charges against me were dropped. Never made, in fact, since I promised to leave Indochina. Even the French Embassy did not know about the matter. It was a personal concern."

"What about these men?"

Crozan was indicating Coyd's secretaries. Borneau shook his head.

"Neither was implicated," the man replied.

TABBERT'S face was pale; for a moment, he was about to blurt out something, then desisted as he saw Evelyn stare accusingly in his direction. Before the girl could speak, Harry caught a signal from The Shadow. He handed the key to Evelyn. The girl hurried and unlocked the door.

Harry gently urged Beatrice Rydel to follow her. The blonde obeyed mechanically; she seemed dulled by the confession that she had heard involving her father.

As Evelyn opened the door, she uttered a cry. Beyond, stretched on the bed, was Congressman Coyd, clad in his dressing gown. Evelyn showed fright at first, thinking that her father was dead.

Then her tone was one of gladness, as she discovered that he was breathing, deep in slumber. Beatrice joined Evelyn in an effort to awake the sleeping congressman.

"That is fortunate," decided Crozan, staring through the open door. "After all, Rydel could not have afforded to murder Coyd. That would have meant you taking his place permanently, Hadwil. Yet Rydel would have been capable of murder—"

Crozan paused suddenly. Harry, near the door of the bedroom, saw a motion from The Shadow. Calmly, Harry closed the door. As Crozan turned about, The Shadow's agent twisted the key and pocketed it. Evelyn and Beatrice were locked inside the room.

"Murder!" boomed Crozan, turning to The Shadow, who stood as a silent judge. "Dunwood Rydel committed murder! He had reason to do so; for there was one man in Washington clever enough to have penetrated his scheme. I refer to Tyson Weed. He was murdered by Dunwood Rydel!"

A SARDONIC laugh came from The Shadow's lips. It was a burst of chilling mockery, a gibe that carried stern accusation. No longer repressed, those eerie tones rose to fierce crescendo. Ending abruptly, they left echoes crying from the walls, like chilled responses from a myriad of quivering, unseen tongues. Foster Crozan trembled; his confidence was gone.

"Your game is ended," pronounced The Shadow. "Your efforts, Crozan, to pin suspicion on Rydel were overdone. If he were the schemer that you wish to make him, he would have avoided the very steps that you have named.

"Rydel's contempt for Hadwil was known. It was returned by Hadwil. Collusion between the two was unlikely. Had Rydel chosen to use Hadwil, he would not have employed his own car for transportation of the impostor.

"Nor would he have permitted his daughter to make friends with Evelyn Coyd. No schemer would have called upon a girl like Beatrice to aid him in his fell plans. Nor would Rydel have come here as he did this morning, making himself conspicuous just prior to the climax.

"Moreover, when you challenged him, Crozan, Rydel—had he been a villain—would have had a perfect alibi for his recent whereabouts. He would not have evaded your question.

"You, Crozan, with all your bravado; you are the man of crime. You placed aides at every spot; you bribed Borneau, Hadwil, even Mullard. To make all safe, you chose an agent in this very house."

The Shadow paused. His eyes were upon the two secretaries. Tabbert cried out spontaneously:

"Jurrick! He was working with Borneau! I wondered why he used to shift those medicine bottles. Why he always informed me that Mr. Coyd was in the downstairs study; that I was to go there and not come up here. I never saw Mr. Coyd actually go in there. Jurrick must have met Hadwil at the side door—covered his departure when the man left—"

Tabbert stopped, quivering. Jurrick was shrinking away; backed against the wall, he showed his guilt by manner and expression.

Again, The Shadow spoke.

"Tyson Weed visited Montgomery Hadwil," he pronounced. "The lobbyist guessed the impersonation; his detectives had reported Layton Coyd in two places at the same time. Weed offered terms to Hadwil. You saw their danger, Crozan.

"Only you were available at the time of Weed's murder. Mullard was taking Hadwil to a new hideout. Borneau was at the embassy with Senator Releston. Jurrick was here with Tabbert. It was your task, Crozan, the elimination of Weed. You could not entrust it to some underling as you had that theft at Releston's.

"You wanted those papers as a prelude to the game; to make it look as though Rydel were guilty. Tonight, with your schemes balked, you prompted your tools—Hadwil and Borneau—to make confessions. They did so, knowing that they would be convicted of minor crimes alone. In their confessions—to gain your favor further—they named Rydel as the master crook. Rydel, instead of you—"

Crozan had cowered; yet his face was venomous. The Shadow's automatics were moving from man to man, covering the master crook and his trio of helpers. A murderer was trapped, his accomplices trembled, helpless. They, too, dreaded The Shadow's wrath, now that justice faced them.

THEN came the unexpected. Harry Vincent was the one to see the danger; for The Shadow, concentrated upon Crozan, had deliberately left Harry on guard. Standing by the door to the bedroom, Harry could see past The Shadow, who had advanced into the living room. He could observe that far doorway to the hall, the only spot that offered possible complications.

Gun in hand, Harry uttered a sudden shout of warning as he saw a figure leap into view. The Shadow heard it, twisting inward, he performed a fading motion just as an evil rescuer came springing past the threshold.

It was Mullard. The chauffeur had slipped Hawkeye. He had come here with Rydel's limousine, to pick up Hadwil. Alarmed by the delay, Mullard had entered Coyd's home. From the stairs, he had heard The Shadow's tones. Revolver leveled, this underling of crime was driving in to aid his evil master, Foster Crozan.

CHAPTER XX
CRIME'S END

TWO guns cracked simultaneously. One was Mullard's revolver; the other, Harry Vincent's automatic. Mullard was aiming hastily for The Shadow; Harry was shooting for the spot which he had been covering—the space inside the door.

Mullard's bullet whistled by The Shadow's whirling form. The cloaked avenger knew that the first shot would be wide; he was wheeling about to aim with deliberate purpose. His automatics covered Mullard simultaneously. Ordinarily, The Shadow would have mowed down the intruder before he could take new aim.

But Mullard was already sprawling. Harry's timely shot had clipped the in-rushing chauffeur. Mullard's revolver went bouncing across the floor to bash against Burbank's cabinet. Its owner writhed helpless, moaning in agony. Harry's shot had found his left shoulder.

As The Shadow wheeled to cover Mullard, a fiendish shout resounded. Foster Crozan had lost no precious moments. From his pocket the archfiend was snatching a .38; he bounded forward, aiming to shoot The Shadow in the back. Hard after him came another, drawing a revolver also. Montgomery Hadwil was seeking to aid his chief.

The Shadow's spin had not ended. It was a complete twist, off at an angle at the end of the room. Whirling with his first fade, The Shadow had planned to clip Mullard; to keep on in his revolution and deal with the foes whom he knew would make a break.

Shots at Mullard had been unnecessary. The Shadow was almost full about before Crozan could fire. The crook's gun spoke; a whistling bullet clipped the brim of The Shadow's hat. Then, as Crozan fell upon the cloaked fighter, an automatic spoke. Its burst came just as Crozan jabbed his revolver against The Shadow's body.

A finger faltered; The Shadow's automatic gave a second spurt as Crozan wavered. The master crook sprawled heavily upon his adversary, losing his gun as he fell.

Shifting, The Shadow swung Crozan's form as a shield, just as Hadwil, pumping shots from a .32, came plunging upon his dead chief and the living foe.

HALF sprawled by Crozan's death plunge, The Shadow saw Hadwil above him. The face that resembled Coyd's was flushed with fury as the hand beside it thrust the .32 between The Shadow's eyes.

Hadwil's previous shots had buried themselves in Crozan's sagged body; this bullet—so the transformed actor believed—would finish The Shadow.

The slug never issued from Hadwil's gun. The Shadow's arm had already swung inward, under Crozan's arm. A muffled roar from The Shadow's automatic. Hadwil's lifted face showed agony. He tried to fire; The Shadow smashed the revolver with a stroke of the automatic.

The gun went skidding across the floor as Hadwil slumped backward. He was the man who had doomed Tyson Weed; at heart a murderer like Crozan, Hadwil had gone to a deserved death.

Twisting away from the sprawled bodies, The Shadow was ready with his automatics. His enemies had shielded him in the fray; if remaining foemen were prepared for battle, they, too, could have it. But as The Shadow cleared for further action, he saw that the cause was won.

Harry Vincent had sprung forward to down Crozan and Hadwil. Doctor Borneau had sprung in to stop Harry's surge. The physician was unarmed—Harry had learned that when frisking him for the key to the locked bedroom. Hence, Harry had driven blows with his automatic, to clear the physician from the way.

Borneau had resisted the flaying strokes, long enough to hold back Harry. But at last, the physician had succumbed; he had dropped to the floor, holding up his hands in surrender. Turning to aid The Shadow, Harry saw his chief triumphant.

Another struggle was ending. Don Jurrick had started forward, later than the others, reaching to pull a gun from his pocket. Hugh Tabbert had taken care of that adversary.

Fiercely, the red-haired secretary had snatched the revolver from Jurrick. He had followed that by slugging the sleek underling with merciless punches. Jurrick was lying huddled by the big chair, Tabbert, fists clenched, towered above him.

The radio technician had picked up Mullard's gun and was holding it gingerly. That precaution had been unnecessary. No fight remained in Mullard. Harry's shot had clipped him properly.

The rogue was still moaning on the floor.

Hearty pounds came from beyond the bedroom door. The Shadow hissed an order. Harry, still covering Borneau, moved back and produced the key with his left hand. The Shadow was backing toward the hall, both automatics ready. With no need to watch Borneau, Harry unlocked the bedroom door.

As The Shadow wheeled to cover Mullard, a fiendish shout resounded.

CONGRESSMAN COYD was on the threshold. Fully awake, he stared with startled eyes at the havoc which filled the living room. Harry spoke; Coyd nodded. Turning, he ordered Evelyn and Beatrice to remain where they were. Stalking out into the living room, Coyd took imperious charge of the scene.

Harry, gun in hand, backed Borneau to the chair beside which Jurrick lay. Tabbert collected the revolvers that were on the floor; then Coyd ordered Borneau to attend to Mullard's wound. Disarmed, these minions were helpless.

Borneau, as he obeyed, glanced toward the doorway to the hall. That was the spot to which The Shadow had retreated. There was no sign of the cloaked form in the blackness; but the cowed physician suspected that The Shadow was still there.

Someone was hammering at the front door. The pounding ceased; footsteps clattered on the stairs. Mose had admitted a visitor. From the hall came Dunwood Rydel; the magnate had arrived at the finish of the shooting; and had been hammering for admittance ever since.

Consternation showed on Rydel's face as he gazed about, anxiously seeking his daughter. Harry explained briefly what had happened, adding that Beatrice was safe with Evelyn.

Coyd understood for the first time. He thrust out a firm hand; Rydel received it. Together, these men who had stood apart congratulated each other above the dead body of Foster Crozan, the arch-plotter who had tried to work evil to them both.

New sounds from below; the doorbell was ringing the arrival of a new visitor. Seeing victory secure, Harry Vincent went out through the hall and down the stairs, to find Mose faltering to answer the call. Harry sent the servant away and opened the door himself. It was Senator Ross Releston.

"I left Baltimore early," explained Releston. "We heard Congressman Coyd's speech through the radio in the automobile. I was in a friend's car, you know. I told them to bring me here at once."

The senator paused; then gripped Harry's arm.

"I heard the weird laugh," he added. "The others merely wondered about it—they thought that somehow a mystery program had worked in with the banquet broadcast. But I understood. I knew that something—"

HARRY nodded. Accompanying the senator to the stairs, he explained the vital points as they went upward. Senator Releston gasped when he heard of Foster Crozan's traitorous dealings.

"Crozan was the murderer," asserted Releston, decisively. "No doubt about it, Vincent. We have witnesses to his statements; to those of his hirelings. The three whom we now hold—Borneau, Jurrick and Mullard—will be forced to declare the full truth."

"They have already done so," returned Harry, as they ascended to the second floor. "Borneau told facts; up to the point where he named Dunwood Rydel as the villain, instead of Foster Crozan."

"He will retract that lie," assured Releston. "Crozan is dead; his threat will no longer influence Borneau. Now that the crisis has passed, Vincent, the game is plain. I should have realized that Crozan's virtues were a pretense. Secretly, his desire was for worldly pelf.

"I felt sure that speculators had been buying those utility securities, Vincent. That was why I dropped my original objection to Coyd's genuine speech. The prices will drop—as they should—and the losers will be those rogues who connived with Foster Crozan."

"What of those associates, Senator?"

"They will gain what they have deserved. Financial ruin. We shall press them no further; for they are not of Crozan's criminal type. Murder was his own choice, Vincent. We will learn—I am confident—that Crozan's entire fortune is tied up in those utility stocks. He, himself, must have been the chief speculator. He probably salvaged his original investments in munitions and threw millions into this bigger game."

HARRY VINCENT could detect a note of finality in the gray-haired senator's tone. Justice had triumphed; The Shadow's work was done. There would be finishing details, Harry guessed; and in that assumption he was right. But The Shadow's remaining tasks were trifling.

Word to Cliff Marsland, to call the police; then depart from the apartment where he had been waiting in case Montgomery Hadwil had slipped loose and fled thither. The law would discover that hideout, where Hadwil's cherished press clippings, his letters, articles of makeup and disguise would be disclosed as proof of his part in Crozan's game.

A message to Hawkeye, to forget the F Street garage, where he was no longer needed as a watcher. To Clyde Burke, also, telling the reporter to visit Crozan's rooms at the Hotel Barlingham.

Evidence would be uncovered there as well. Records of stock purchases; perhaps a duplicate of a planted cable from Europe, that had told of Hadwil's supposed elopement with a foreign actress.

After that, Burbank. Like The Shadow, the contact man would leave the Hotel Halcyon and make his departure from Washington. Other missions awaited The Shadow and his agents. Soon Harry Vincent would join them.

Glimmers of such thoughts flashed through Harry's mind as he and Releston reached the threshold of the living room, where Layton Coyd and Dunwood Rydel held mutual charge of cowering prisoners. Suddenly the senator stopped; his face was solemn as he harkened to a strange, uncanny sound from below.

It was a weird burst of departing laughter; from the depths of the first floor hall, near the side door that led from this old house. Chilling, solemn mirth; more a knell than a token of elation. Eerily it shivered to a shuddering climax. A host of echoes faded into nothingness.

The author of that mirth was gone. The parting laugh had sounded the final triumph of The Shadow.

THE END

THE MAN WHO CAST THE SHADOW

Walter B. Gibson (1897-1985) was born in Germantown, Pennsylvania. His first published feature, a puzzle titled "Enigma," appeared in *St. Nicholas Magazine* when Walter was only eight years old. In 1912, Gibson's second published piece won a literary prize, presented by former President Howard Taft who expressed the hope that this would be the beginning of a great literary career. Building upon a lifelong fascination with magic and sleight of hand, Gibson later became a frequent contributor to magic magazines and worked briefly as a carnival magician. He joined the reporting staff of the *Philadelphia North American* after graduating from Colgate University in 1920, moved over to the *Philadelphia Public Ledger* the following year and was soon producing a huge volume of syndicated features for NEA and the Ledger Syndicate, while also ghosting books for magicians Houdini, Thurston, Blackstone and Dunninger.

A 1930 visit to Street & Smith's offices led to his being hired to write novels featuring The Shadow, the mysterious host of CBS' *Detective Story Program*. Originally intended as a quarterly, *The Shadow Magazine* was promoted to monthly publication when the first two issues sold out and, a year later, began the amazing twice-a-month frequency it would enjoy for the next decade. "This was during the Depression, so this was a good thing to be doing. I just dropped everything else and did *The Shadow* for 15 years. I was pretty much Depression-proof."

Working on a battery of three typewriters, Gibson often wrote his Shadow novels in four or five days, averaging a million and a half words a year. He pounded out 24 Shadow novels during the final ten months of 1932; he eventually wrote 283 Shadow novels totaling some 15 million words.

Gibson scripted the lead features for *Shadow Comics* and *Super-Magician Comics,* along with a

Walter B. Gibson in 1941, celebrating ten years of *The Shadow Magazine* and more than 200 novels.

Walter Gibson in 1966 with pet rooster China Boy and three recent books

Photo by William Radner

1942 *Bill Barnes* comic story that foresaw the United States dropping a U-235 bomb to defeat Japan and end World War II. He also organized Penn-Art, a Philadelphia comic art shop utilizing former *Evening Ledger* artists.

Walter also found time for radio, plotting and co-scripting *Nick Carter—Master Detective, Chick Carter, The Avenger*, *Frank Merriwell* and *Blackstone, the Magic Detective*. He wrote hundreds of true crime magazine articles and scripted numerous commercial, industrial and political comic books, pioneering the use of comics as an educational tool. In his book *Man of Magic and Mystery: A Guide to the Work of Walter B. Gibson,* bibliographer J. Randolph Cox documents more than 30 million words published in 150 books, some 500 magazine stories and articles, more than 3000 syndicated newspaper features and hundreds of radio and comic scripts.

Walter also hosted ABC's *Strange* and wrote scores of books on magic and psychic phenomena, many co-authored with his wife, Litzka Raymond Gibson. He also wrote five *Biff Brewster* juvenile adventure novels for Grosset and Dunlap (as "Andy Adams"), a *Vicki Barr, Air Stewardess* book and a *Cherry Ames, Nurse* story (as "Helen Wells"), *The Twilight Zone* and such publishing staples as *Hoyle's Simplified Guide to the Popular Card Games* and *Fell's Official Guide to Knots and How to Tie Them.*

No one was happier than Gibson when The Shadow staged a revival in the sixties and seventies. Walter wrote *Return of The Shadow* in 1963 and three years later selected three vintage stories to appear in a hardcover anthology entitled *The Weird Adventures of The Shadow.* Several series of paperback and hardcover reprints followed and Walter wrote two new Shadow short stories, "The Riddle of the Rangoon Ruby" and "Blackmail Bay." A frequent guest at nostalgia, mystery, and comic conventions, Gibson attended the annual Pulpcon and Friends of Old-Time Radio conventions on a regular basis, always delighted to perform a few magic tricks and sign autographs as both Gibson and Grant, using his distinctive double-X signature. His last completed work of fiction, "The Batman Encounters—Gray Face," appeared as a text feature in the 500th issue of *Detective Comics.*

Walter Gibson died on December 6, 1985, a recently begun Shadow novel sitting unfinished in his typewriter. "I always enjoyed writing the Shadow stories," he remarked to me a few years earlier. "There was never a time when I wasn't enjoying the story I was writing or looking forward to beginning the next one." Walter paused and then added, a touch of sadness in his voice, "I wish I was still writing the Shadow stories."

So do I, old friend. So do I. —Anthony Tollin

Walter Gibson and Anthony Tollin